ISBN-13: 978-1494986834

ISBN-10: 1494986833

Names, characters, and incidents depicted in this book are products of the author's imagination or are used fictitiously. Any resemblance to actual locales, or persons, living or dead, is entirely coincidental and beyond the intent of the author.

Cover by Candace Bowser http://www.candacelbowser.com/

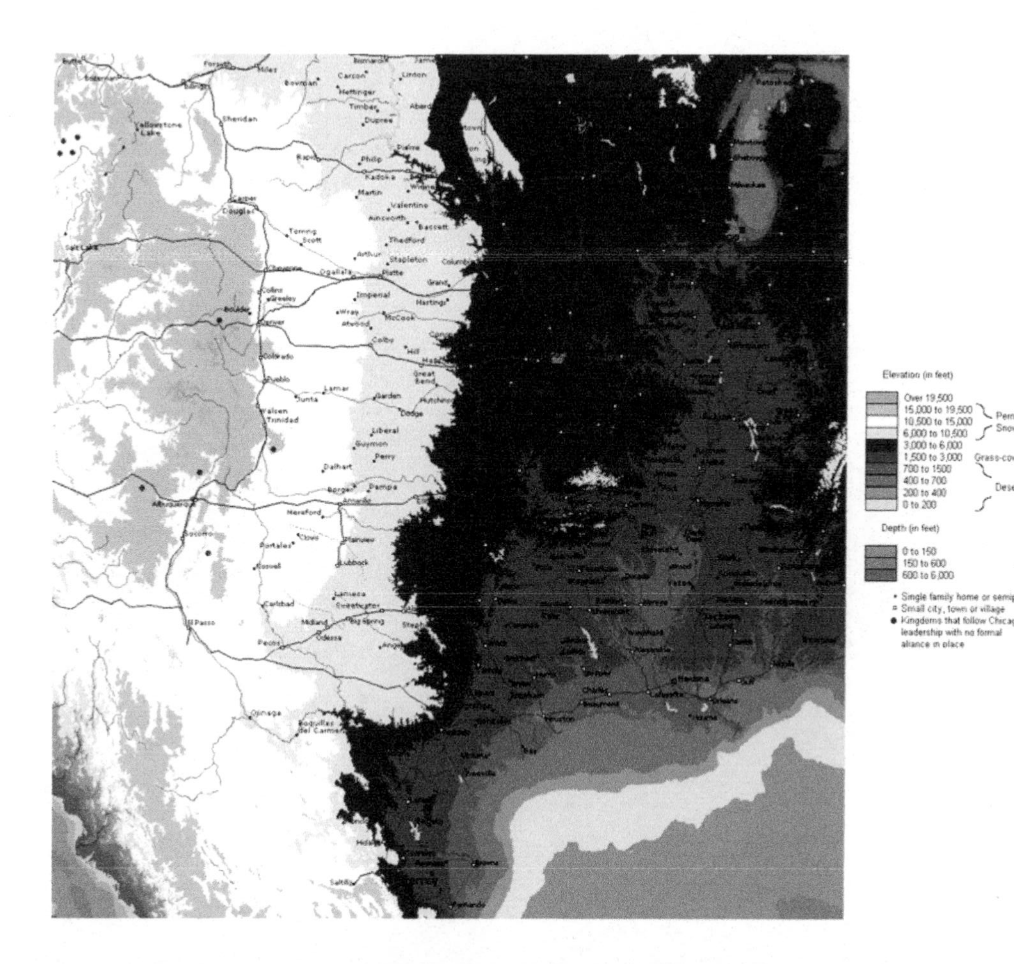
Elevation (in feet)
Over 19,500
15,000 to 19,500
10,500 to 15,000
6,000 to 10,500
3,000 to 6,000
1,500 to 3,000
700 to 1500
400 to 700
200 to 400
0 to 200
Permanent Snowcap
Grass-covered Sand Dunes
Desert
Depth (in feet)
0 to 150
150 to 600
600 to 6,000
Single family home or semipermanent camp
Small city, town or village
Kingdoms that follow Chicago's leadership with no formal aliance in place
Yellowstone Lake
Sheridan
Bowman
Carson
Linton
Hettinger
Timber
Dupree
Philip
Kadoka
Martin
Valentine
Ainsworth
Bassett
Thedford
Douglas
Torring
Scott
Arthur
Stapleton
Ogallala
Platte
Imperial
Hastings
Wray
Atwood
McCook
Colby
Hill
Colorado
Pueblo
Lamar
Junta
Garden
Dodge
Walsen
Trinidad
Liberal
Guymon
Perry
Dalhart
Borger
Pampa
Amarillo
Hereford
Clovis
Plainview
Portales
Roswell
Lubbock
Lamesa
Sweetwater
Carlsbad
Midland
Big Spring
Odessa
Pecos
El Paso
Socorro
Albuquerque
Ojinaga
Boquillas del Carmen
Saltillo

Contents

Half-Breed

by

Anna L. Walls

The world was coming apart. An asteroid had collided with the moon and both bodies had been shattered by the impact. Unable to continue their experiments, the scientists ordered them destroyed and then fled.

Brian was supposed to destroy them and burn all the records, but he couldn't bring himself to kill them. They were good kids, and so fascinating. They were innocent and far more intelligent than anyone cared to know.

A meteor crashed into the ground somewhere close. Half the complex had already been smashed by another such impact. A beam supporting the ceiling came crashing down, knocking Brian to the ground, pinning him to the floor. The pain robbed him of breath. He couldn't leave them in those cells. They deserved better. He threw the keys toward them, hoping they made it close enough for them to reach.

Another impact shook the place and more of the ceiling came crashing down. He didn't hear the jangling of the keys. He didn't feel the hand brush his eyes closed.

She sat on a rock, holding her knees close to her chest, feeling cold in the night air. Tears ran down her cheeks. Her daddy wasn't coming home. In her heart, she knew this was true. The rain of burning destruction told her she would never see him again. Behind her was the crater that used to be her house. Her mom and her baby brother had been in there. She had been playing in the barn. It was the best playhouse in the world. It had been shoved all sideways when the meteor hit the house and a flying piece of wood had cut her cheek.

Movement on the road caught her attention. It was almost completely dark, and thousands of fires glittered everywhere she looked. Something white caught her eye down on what was left of the road, the road that should have brought her father home. Those white spots almost glowed in the shadows. They just kept moving; they didn't seem to notice the fire falling from the sky. Once she spotted the movement, she could pick out quite a few of them. But something else was there too; she couldn't make out what from this distance. They were all moving up the road toward her.

They gathered around her, the noses of the…well, she'd seen pictures of wolves, but these were way too big, though they seemed nice enough. Person or giant wolf, they mingled together like they were all one group, all the same family. None of the people looked older than twelve or so. Some of the older ones leaned heavily on others, some carried infants and toddlers, and others carried puppies.

The boy with the white hair – she was sure he was the one she had spotted first – he knelt directly in front of her. He had a brown blotch of hair at his right temple and pale blue eyes just like his 'wolf' had. His 'wolf' was probably the prettiest one in the bunch – all silver and bluish.

The boy pushed a lock of copper-red hair out of her cut. The blood had dried in the cool breeze and it pulled a bit. "She is his," he said, in a calm rumble of a voice that didn't fit his age.

"Leave her. She is one of them. She will slow us down," said someone behind him in a similar deep voice.

"She is Brian's. He was always kind to us. He set us free. We owe him our lives, our freedom. The least we can do for him is try to protect his young." With his thumb, he brushed at the smudge between her eyebrows, but it did not come away, and then he brushed her tears away with a dry palm.

There was some grumbling at his words, but no real dissension, so the boy with the white hair picked up the little girl, and they were off again, heading deeper into the mountains. Massive rocks fell all around them, spraying fire everywhere. They ran on. They had no choice.

The girl with the copper-red hair could not run with them, so she was passed among the strongest of them, as were the youngest of their own. Some seemed to be ill, and some were injured, but they struggled on between others. All they could do was keep moving and hope to avoid the falling sky…some didn't.

The clan never knew the years were counted and they never thought to start. Their concern was preparing for the next hunt, or the next birth. Only by preparing, could they survive the winter that never went away.

Young as she was, Brian's daughter provided them with the foundation that carried them through.

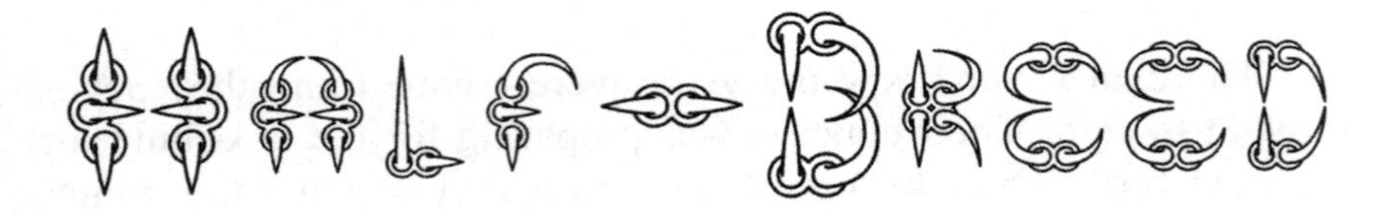
HALF-BREED

Half-Breed

by

Anna L. Walls

Canis curled tightly in his old blanket and listened as his mother entertained another man. He was loud and stomping around. His mother would have red marks on her face again when he left. He could never ask her about them and when he touched them, she merely smiled sadly and held his hand away from them.

His mother had entertained men ever since he could remember, and ever since he could remember, Canis was hidden away whenever someone came to the door. Sometimes, one of her men, or the house owner would find him anyway, then they would travel for a while before his mother found them a new place, and then it would start all over again.

She didn't bring a man to their tiny room every night. On those free nights, Canis's mother would bring out some much-abused paper, and with a coal from the fireplace. They would curl up on the warm hearth together and she would help him trace his letters.

Canis had no problem tracing the letters, but when it came to grouping them into words, it was as if he stumbled into a giant dark chasm. His mother was very patient with him, but she couldn't understand how wide and dark that chasm was. It was as if a vast empty hole was inside his head right where writing words and speaking sentences were supposed to be.

Canis could read though. His mother read to him from their one tattered book over and over again. He had the words of the story memorized, but his mother didn't suspect, not even when she caught him reading it; she merely assumed he was looking at the pictures. There was no way he could tell her otherwise.

Canis was working on a surprise for her though. Whenever she was away, he struggled to say a single word…Canis…his name. If he could say his name, maybe he wouldn't have to hide anymore. His mother told him it was the name of a star – that it had something to do with his father and his father's family, but he didn't understand and he couldn't ask.

The first time he succeeded in uttering the whole word in one halting piece, it felt like a rope had been tossed across that vast emptiness in his head. It was like a single strand of spider's web strung across a canyon so wide the other side could not be seen. That strand was so small and fragile compared to the vastness, but Canis could feel it and he treasured its hold.

When he finally showed his mother his achievement, she cried. "Wonderful, Canis. Wonderful," she said with tears streaming down her face. She pulled him into a long hug. "I'm so happy you can talk now."

It wasn't the response he expected, but then, perhaps something had happened while she was away. It had happened before.

The man his mother was entertaining this time was stomping around, banging on the table, and shouting about his plans. Canis could scarcely hear his mother's quiet voice as she tried to calm him. The man ranted of riding and cutting, but Canis didn't understand it all. He hoped he didn't cut her hair; he liked her shiny copper braid, it was long and silky. He would stroke it while she read to him. Suddenly the man fell into the closet where Canis hid, breaking the door with his weight.

Startled, Canis snarled a yelp and the man reached for him. Cornered in the closet, he couldn't dodge away so he was forced to fight back the only way he could. His sharp teeth left four slices in the man's hand, but the man didn't pull away from the pain.

His blunt nails scored painful welts across Canis's chest as he grabbed for him. He cried out when Canis's teeth drew blood, but the pain only seemed to increase his rage. He pulled Canis out into the light and gave him a shake, roaring, "You hid a beast in your closet, woman? A Changeling, I say; only animals have eyes that glow in the dark. It was an animal that bit me, I say. What is this witchcraft? It's bad enough you have hair of the devil's fire. This spawn with an animal's teeth and glowing eyes is proof of your witchery." He shoved the woman from his path.

He headed for the door with a snarling bundle of fury in his meaty hand.

Canis's mother wailed her denials. "No, that's my baby. Look at him. See, he's just a child. Give me my baby. You can't take my baby."

The man wasn't listening. By the time he reached the inn's common room, Canis was struggling in earnest. Every time he came close to finding more flesh with his teeth, the man would give him another violent shake.

Brandishing his prize and shouting "changeling" and "witchery," and with blood staining his arm, the man whipped the patrons of the inn into a superstitious frenzy. He grabbed Canis's mother by her hair and threw her out among the crowd, yelling, "Witch" and "Demon child." In minutes, everyone was shouting, and there was a surge for the door.

From his vantage point at the end of this arm belonging to such a mountain of man-flesh, Canis could see his mother's red hair over in the middle of the crowd. Someone grabbed her long braid, and he heard her scream.

Hearing the sound, Canis put new effort to freeing himself. He curled around the hand holding his tunic and tore a gash in the arm, winning his freedom this time as blood spurted rather than dripped.

Outside, people on their way to early morning market joined the mob. With sticks, fists, and clods of ice to dodge, Canis couldn't keep track of his mother who was being pushed away somewhere else.

One man swung a stick; perhaps he intended to throw it, perhaps not, who can say, but the blow knocked Canis into a man near the edge of the crowd. The man hadn't heard the cry of 'changeling', nor did he suspect anything but a pickpocket when Canis careened into him. He snagged hold of the boy's shoulder and flung him out into the frozen slush of the street. No sooner had he turned him loose then the man who started it all spotted Canis. His shout was incoherent, but his bloody-handed point was unmistakable and Canis became the new target.

Instinctively, Canis tucked and rolled where the man threw him, but to his dismay, he looked up to see massive creatures with very large hooves plunging and kicking directly above him. Before he could roll completely free of the danger, someone else had his hand on him, and others were pushing the mob back.

No matter how hard he tried, Canis couldn't break this new man's hold. The man's powerful fist held his tunic in back this time. The material drawn tight in his fist prevented Canis from turning enough to find skin and draw blood.

For perhaps a whole second, Canis thought he was going to be thrown aside once again, but his hopes were dashed when the man looked him in the eyes. With a wave of his hand and a curt "collar," Canis found himself wearing a metal ring around his throat. Attached to it was a metal chain. Both items were alien to him; both frightened him more than ever before.

As soon as his chain was hooked to the big-ringed chain running among others who wore the metal around their necks, Canis clawed at the ring and threw himself against the chain with a panicked frenzy. The others on the line gasped in surprise and clutched at their ends of their chains in an effort to protect themselves from his struggles.

Moments later, men descended on him again, and his hands were bound behind his back. Though they could prevent him from clawing at the metal ring around his neck, they couldn't stop him struggling, despite one man's hiss of, "I'll cut your legs off if you don't settle down." But Canis didn't settle down, not until he was exhausted from his struggles, and the man never carried out his threat.

When his panic mellowed, Canis started to think. *These people will not be able to hold me forever. There will be an opening sometime. I will wait and watch for an opportunity, then I will escape, I* will.

As they traveled, two men paced the length of the line at all times. Every time they came close to Canis, he snarled a warning, but it only won a snicker, and the next time around they would walk a little closer or make an abortive reach for him, anything to win the next snarl.

Sixteen other people shared the chain attached to the back of a large wagon. Another wagon followed behind them. The whole train moved slow enough for those on the line to walk, though it was a brisk pace. It served to keep them warm.

Canis could only follow where the metal led. He watched all those around him; there were more people than he'd ever been around in all his life, and all of them were watching him. Those attached to the chain, walked in silence, having long since accepted the immobility of the metal. He watched the others too – especially *them.* Two of them paced up and down the line. Two others rode horses and still others drove the wagons. They too watched him; he didn't like being watched.

The sun was high in the sky and the frost was melting from the tips of the grass when the free men handed out breadsticks and then passed around a flask of water. There was no stopping though. Canis didn't get anything. With his hands tied behind his back, he couldn't feed himself, and when a guard reached to feed him, Canis went for the hand instead.

"I told you, you shouldn't have teased him," said his cohort.

Canis did the same when the other man offered water. "See, I can't even give him any water. It'll be your fault if he doesn't make it to camp on his feet."

"I don't give a shit. That brat almost took my hand off when I put the collar on him. Let him drag a few miles. Teach him a lesson."

"You'll regret it if he gets hurt. Patro don't like his property damaged."

Regardless of their words, no more food or water was offered to Canis, though the water flask was kept available to the others most of the afternoon.

The sun was touching the horizon when they finally came to a complete stop. While an old woman who appeared out of nowhere made a fire, a man handed out rolled blankets to those on the chain. Two of the free men took some of the leashes and went off in search of firewood. Those left behind settled down where they were. When the man with the blankets reached Canis's place in line, he merely tossed a roll at Canis's feet, giving him no excuse to snarl his warning, though he got one anyway.

When the blankets were all handed out and the one big tent was set up, the man who issued all the orders, the man who had caught him from under the horses' hooves, pointed at Canis and the two men not on firewood duty. "You two; give it a bath. I've been smelling it all day and I can't stand the reek any longer."

When one of the men unhooked Canis's leash, he was thrilled. *Here is my chance.* He wasn't sure what their plan was, but *his* plan was escape. He'd gotten away from one man, he could get away from this one too; he wasn't as big as the other man had been.

What he didn't expect was, as soon as they were out of sight of the camp, the man who held his leash laid a crushing grip on his shoulder and ripped away his clothes. His cry of pain only won laughter, this time from both men.

With a snarl, Canis leapt as high as he could and tried to twist free at the same time. His effort almost broke the hold on his shoulder, but the man tightened his grip, and then the other man caught an ankle. Suspended between the two of them, he still fought, kicking and thrashing and snarling.

Despite his struggles, they managed to dunk Canis in the cold gray water. He kicked and thrashed even harder, but he couldn't break their grip – not entirely. The one man lost his grip on his shoulder once, but the other man used the opportunity to dunk him

hastily swiveled to watch, and then he forgot all about his pants and the need to be prepared to fend off an attack.

Patro and two of his guards were beating down the other two guards. Quickly and brutally, the two men were subdued, stripped, and collared with heavy collars that bore little resemblance to what Canis wore. "You dare to damage my property," Patro shouted at them as their brutal collars were held under the control of those they'd worked alongside only moments ago. "I know how much money you don't have. You couldn't afford the fine for damaging my property if your life depended on it." He leaned closer to them. "And believe me, it does." Patro pointed behind him at Canis without turning to find him. This, as nothing else the man did, raised the hairs on Canis's neck and he pulled his pants up, hastily tying them in place. "If he sickens and dies because of what you've done, I'll see to it you are up for sale on the next available auction block," Patro promised.

"But we didn't do nothin'," wailed one of the men. Patro's heavy fist silenced him. When the man picked himself up from the ground again, there was blood at the corner of his mouth and under his collar.

Patro waved the men away. "Chain 'em to the sides of the wagon," he said. "I won't have them disrupting the others on the line." Then he stormed off to finish harnessing his horses.

As they were about ready to move, Patro came to Canis's place on the line and unhooked his leash. Without a word, he led Canis to the side of his wagon. Canis was starting to think he would be attached to the same ring as the man who stood there glaring at him, but Patro swept him up and planted him on the seat. The rough handling forced a yelp of surprise and pain from Canis, but then Patro was climbing up on the seat beside him, so Canis gulped back any further sounds. The sudden move made his head spin, though, and the spinning wouldn't go away. The wagons were no sooner in full motion than Canis's world took a spin into blackness.

When Canis opened his eyes again, he figured the blackness

had lasted only a moment or two; the horses were only just stopping, and once again his tunic was in the grip of a very large fist and Patro was staring at him. He hurt so much. Just as he grabbed Patro's wrist in an effort to be free of his grip, his stomach lurched violently and he was helplessly heaving bile onto the road. When no more would come, Canis sat back shaking and wiped his mouth with the back of his hand.

"Are you finished?" asked Patro. When Canis remained quiet, Patro climbed down off the wagon again and then he lifted Canis down beside him, somewhat gentler this time. He led him up to the back of the lead wagon – the wagon that carried the tent and all their bedding. He unrolled a heavy blanket and laid it aside, then he lifted Canis up into its place. "You lie down." He hooked Canis's leash to something on the outside of the wagon and then spread the blanket over him. "There'll be no walking for you for a day or two." He wedged a jar down between the bedrolls so it wouldn't tip over. He lifted the lid and dipped a small cup in, bringing out water, which he handed to Canis. "Drink that, now." He stood there and watched Canis drink. "You drink one of those every time you throw up." He started to head back to his wagon, but turned back after only a single step. "And even if you don't throw up, you drink at least four cups before midday." He held up four fingers to show how many four was. Some people couldn't count.

That evening, Patro had one of the remaining guards take Canis to the river for another bath. "You did see what happens around here when someone damages my property, didn't you?" he called after the man before he disappeared down the path.

"You don't need to worry about me, sir," he said.

Canis didn't have it in him to struggle. He could scarcely walk. *I will wait. I will wait as long as I can stand it. A real chance will come.*

This man was quite gentle, almost as gentle as Gem. He took great care of Canis's bruises. He helped Canis take his clothes off and laid them aside.

"Well, look at you; you can't be more than five. How old are you?" When Canis didn't answer, he went ahead with the bath. He quickly dipped water from the river and soaped him down. The late day was still warm and the man found a spot of sunlight, but being wet was still really cold.

When Canis's body was washed, the man wrapped Canis's tunic around his shoulders and had him bend over so he could wash his hair. When he was satisfied, he helped Canis dress again and then they went back to the camp. This whole ordeal left Canis baffled. His experience with baths was now two, and they couldn't possibly have been more different, one from the other. As he thought on it, he figured he didn't really like water much; it was fine for drinking – and maybe washing some, but so much as was in the river – it made him uneasy, almost as if it might reach out and smother him.

When they returned to camp, they found it already set up and organized. As soon as he was within reach, Gem went to work on his matted hair again. She'd only just started when Patro came up to them.

If Canis had been less cold and more agile, he'd have moved out of his easy reach. As it was, Patro merely rested his big hand on his forehead. "Fevered," was all he said. He shook his head and handed Gem a can of cream. "Work this into his hair, it should loosen the matting some. We might have to cut some of that out, though." Then he lifted Canis's chin so he was forced to look him in the face. "Those are the most remarkable eyes I've ever seen. Drink a lot of water, boy. I want you to finish that jar before you sleep." He brushed Canis's cheek. "You'll make someone a fine collector's item when you grow up."

Canis ran a fever for two more days, though he was never ill again, and he rode in the wagon for an entire week; it took that long before his gait was better than a step with one foot and drag the other one up to it. He ate his meals too, though he refused to take his bowl from the hand of the guard who offered it to him.

The man would offer it and then set it on the ground – Patro's orders – but Canis wouldn't touch it until the man had left the area.

Gem worked on his hair every available moment and used up four of the cans of cream Patro produced. It was a full eight days before she was able to run a comb through it all the way to the scalp. His hair had been kinked and matted for so long, now that it was combed out, it looked like a rusty haystack stacked in a high wind by a one-handed farmer. Some of it was long and other sections were quite short.

When signs of settlement began to encroach on their travels, Patro came up to Gem and Canis. "You look like a shag dog looking through that mop of yours. Comb it all to the front, Gem. He needs a hair cut." He showed Gem what he wanted by holding a fist at the top of his forehead as if he were holding a ponytail there.

"Yes, master," said Gem. When Gem had his hair gathered in her small fist, Patro tipped Canis's chin up so he could see clearly what he was about to do. He drew Canis's attention to his hand and slowly drew his belt knife.

It had been days since Canis had seen reason for alarm, but he knew a knife when he saw one. Canis stiffened, ready to break away, but Gem remained quiet so he held his ground.

Patro pulled out a lock of his own hair and cut it with the knife. Then he reached out and tugged at a bit of the hair extending beyond Gem's hand then made a cutting motion. "All I'm going to do is cut your hair. You have to hold still; understand?" He watched for some kind of response or reaction.

Canis looked from the knife to Patro's face, but he could detect no malice there and Gem remained quiet. Patro slowly reached out and took the hair protruding beyond Gem's hand, then he moved the knife closer. Canis was hissing his stress long before the knife touched his hair, but he held his ground until the task was done. When he was released, he moved to the end of his leash and curled up in a tight ball.

Gem looked after him sadly then cleaned up the hair that had been cut away. After she handed the cuttings to one of the guards to be thrown in the fire, she came as close to him as she could. Because of the way their leashes were attached to the line, she couldn't reach him, but she tugged gently on his leash and called to him. After some cajoling, he gave in to her desires and moved close enough for her to fuss over him some more; it served to quiet his shaking nerves.

Slave Business

The next day, they came into a huddled collection of brown shacks and shops and Canis overheard the word 'Mankato' said to one of the men chained to the wagon. Patro stopped them in the center, near one of the larger buildings. People materialized from all around to look at them, and all but Canis stood to meet them. Some of the visitors touched one or another of those on the line, pinching an arm or a belly or telling them to turn around, which they did docilely. Some spoke to Patro, but Canis couldn't hear what they said very well. Patro took one man along the line, pointing out one or another of the men and talking numbers. Then there was a nod; the man pointed to two of those on the line and counted several chips of metal into Patro's hand and led the two away.

Canis watched their departure with some interest. The exchange of metal for a person was another new thing in a whole world of new and frightening things. Both must have some value else such an exchange would not happen. What that value was, he could not understand.

Canis had given up trying to defend his space. He'd learned that there was no fighting the metal around his neck or the leash that led to the heavy chain attached to the back of the lead wagon, and he had seen what Patro had done to those two men. Perhaps he could be trusted, he'd watch and see – it was sure he was nothing like the men who frequented his mother's room.

The metal antagonized him though, far more than the weight

would account for. Though he was accustomed to his mother keeping him hidden, this kind of containment chafed. He longed for the hiding – he could be very quiet in his small dark corner. There were no dark corners here.

This vast outside – he'd been outside before – his mother had moved them a few times that he could remember, but it was mostly at night. He never understood why. He never considered it before. It was the way it was. He had time to think about it now, though. After what had happened back in Paul City, he wondered if that was why his mother had traveled at night. He wondered if there was something about him that was the cause of it all.

Now more than ever, he wished she were here. He had questions. *What had happened? What was a changeling? What was a witch?* But then, so many things would be different if she were here. If she were here, she would wear metal around her neck like Gem. If she were here, maybe she would have been traded for chips of metal like those men. He wondered what happened to her. Somewhere down deep inside, he knew she was dead, but if he didn't allow himself to think on it, he could continue to believe that he would find her again someday.

The tent wasn't set up since Patro stayed in the building for the night. The old woman who cooked their food, Mia was her name, did so from in there too. Otherwise, little changed for the rest of them.

They left at full light the next morning leaving behind the river they had been following. As they were about to pull out, Patro went to the two men chained to the side of his wagon all this time and turned them loose. "The boy didn't die so you get to remain free of the collar." He shoved them away from the wagon. "Get out of here."

"Our clothes…" started one of the men.

"Consider the loss of your property the fine you paid for damaging my property," said Patro as he climbed up onto his wagon and whipped his horses into motion, leaving them behind in the street without a stitch.

They traveled into the afternoon sun for days, on a well-worn track across plains covered with tall grass and dotted with the occasional small ranch or farm. Sometimes the people who lived in these isolated places would come out and watch them pass, but none of them called for Patro to stop.

On the tenth day they reached a tall embankment of earth. The unnatural ridge was way above their heads, but the track they followed led to the top. Once on top, Canis was surprised. The top was very wide and very flat. Though some short, scraggly grass grew here, most of the surface was bald.

"I feel better now we've reached the high road," commented one of the guards to the other. "Now, at least we have a chance of spotting someone coming at us."

The other man merely nodded his agreement and scanned the horizon.

Canis's wonder at this new vantage kept him distracted from the sameness of life on the trail, but it caused his confinement to weigh even heavier on him. The overabundance of telltale scents drew his curiosity – he so wanted to follow those scents and see where they led – to meet whatever generated them – to taste what he found. Their morning and evening gruel filled his belly, but didn't touch this new hunger.

After six days on the high road heading directly into the setting sun, they reached a city that was obviously a trading center for all the farms in the area. The buildings were low, and the streets were very wide leaving plenty of room for parked wagons along the sides and for the passing of two in the middle. They spent a week on display in the square, sleeping under the wagons at night, though Canis was allowed to keep his blanket and stay under the wagon all the time.

Once again, he watched as Patro exchanged a burly young man for some bright metal and later he handed out some different, darker metal for two older men; they looked tired, but Patro handed over the dark chips for them and seemed pleased.

The stay out in the open of the road had been a pleasure for Canis, but staying out in the city square was hard. The days wore on Canis badly enough, but the nights were worse. Always someone was walking somewhere, or he heard raised voices somewhere else. Sleep was impossible. Even after several days of nothing more than a few moments of shut-eye, Canis wasn't exhausted enough to ignore the sounds, and he would startle awake at every one. Patro gave Gem something to wipe on his face under his eyes on the third day.

"There. You look so much better now," she said when she was finished. He couldn't imagine what it was she had done or why it would make him look better.

It was a relief when their journey continued, the road they chose took a different direction putting the rising sun on their left. The high mound of the road sliced across the grasslands like a knife-cut turned inside out. Canis was so tired he tripped twice though the route wasn't at all bad. When he tripped the third time, Patro put him on the back of the wagon on the blanket rolls again. Canis slept all day long, waking only when they came to a halt that night.

On the fifth night, they camped down in a wide river valley not far from another big river. The next morning, the road curved into the morning sun, and two days later, they reached another small city. Misery City resembled Paul City in many ways. Most of the buildings had more than one floor and a few even had three, if counting the layers of windows was any indication.

This city was a launch point for a considerable amount of river traffic. Such things as harvest goods, cattle and lumber could be seen heading downriver, but though the place fairly swarmed with people, Patro only kept them there for two nights, and none of those on the line were traded for any of the metal chips.

When they left, they stayed with the river valley, keeping the morning sun on their left as the river allowed. The grass was turning yellow, the far away trees, when any were in sight, were generous with golds and reds, but the sky remained blue and the sun warm. Canis's face took on a nut-brown color making his pale eyes appear to glow.

Ten days later, they reached the royal seat of Omaha. This city was vastly different from any Canis had seen so far. The attachment of 'royal seat' to the name of the city must have something to do with the buildings being stone rather than wood. They were not as tall as those in Misery City, but many of them were covered with shingled red stone instead of the yellow grass so common everywhere else. Or maybe it was that the streets were covered with smooth rocks laid carefully together to cover the dirt. There would be little mud on these streets. Otherwise, Canis could see no reason for the extra long name.

Patro took them to the market square and to one of those massive stone buildings, then he went inside while the rest of them waited. He came back out with a ring of four keys. Moving a couple at a time, those on the leashes were taken to great stone cages with bars on their front wall. When they were all behind bars and without their leashes for the first time, Canis found a dark corner and curled up with his arms around his knees. When the heavy metal door clanged shut, Canis winced as if he'd been struck. If only he'd known how bad this cage would feel, he would have made a break for freedom. Maybe he was growing used to his captivity.

"Gem," said Patro. Even his voice made Canis flinch. "Try to get him to come out of that corner. He's not for sale yet, but he's got to start sometime." Canis didn't look up to see who Patro was talking about.

"Yes, master," replied Gem.

While the metal collar had antagonized his nerves, the bars were positively suffocating, though the cell was plenty big enough to stretch out or walk around. Sitting in a dark corner was no comfort. Even Gem's gentle touch sent him cringing inside.

"Move around," she said. "Let the people see you." He tried, but all he could do was pace along the bars like a caged animal.

Patro saw this and gave Gem permission to desist her encouragement. His prowling was affecting the other five slaves in the pen.

Gem pulled him back to his corner, but it was no use; once set in motion, Canis couldn't seem to stop. In an effort to make Gem happy, he sat in his corner, but now that he'd moved once, he had to go again. He went and tested the bars, but they were just as sturdy as before, and still too close together even for his spare frame.

The first time he reached through the bars, he tried to follow his hand, but the others pulled him away from his effort to slip through. Gem's explanation of "we'll all be beaten if you get away" was enough to halt that try, but he couldn't seem to stop pacing as long as freedom was just on the other side of those bars. It was so close. He could touch it, almost. If he reached, but he didn't really dare, not very hard. He couldn't resist slipping his hand through though, just a little, just to feel the wide-open air, even though it was city air, at least it wasn't caged air.

Canis's days in the cage became a grueling cycle. He'd pace to the bars and test their strength. He'd reach through, sometimes here, sometimes there, as far as he could reach without alarming his companions. He'd allow Gem to pull him away and head him back to his corner. In frustration, he'd curl up on his agony unable to cry, unable to explain the pain. Then the cycle would start again; he couldn't stop, just as he couldn't lie down and sleep.

The nights were no better. Though they were farther from such common noises as a couple having an argument in the night, the city sounds were still there. Armed men walked through three or four times every night, and one night they chased another. Sometimes there was a cat yowling a mournful call or fighting another cat and sometimes it was a dog barking in the distance, even the slamming of a door far away served to startle him awake.

There was no rest. Not here. Freedom was just there, just over there, so close yet so far away.

During their stay, Patro exchanged over half of those Canis had become familiar with. Numbers were discussed about Gem too. Despite his inexplicable restlessness, Canis listened closely to the numbers discussed whenever Gem's name was mentioned. Apparently, Patro wanted many chips of the metal he called gold in exchange for her flesh. It was confusing, but he was relieved that she didn't go.

Writing in the Sand

Their departure from the city of Omaha came as a relief for Canis. His desire to put as much distance between him and those bars made the pace of the wagons seem slow though he knew they traveled no slower than before. He was so anxious to be away, he ignored his exhaustion, and the desire to pace within the range of his leash was nearly irresistible.

Still heading mostly in the same direction, following the big river that twisted close to the road from time to time, they reached a small town called St. Joseph. It was almost two weeks since they left the stone city so Patro stopped here to take advantage of the sheltered location and the close proximity of the river. They made camp among the trees lining the river. The entire next day was bath day as the guards – they had left Omaha with two new men – took them one at a time to the river. After their baths, some got their hair cut. The men scraped the hair off their faces while the women combed and braided each others hair.

Though the bathing was in what Gem called 'comfort', Canis still refused to wash on his own, though his struggles were only to resist going into the water. Those who handled him had been fair enough. He just couldn't bring himself to get into all that water, though he had grown to like being clean. He wished they would figure out some other way of getting clean that didn't involve so much water.

They traveled across rolling grasslands now, and the incessant wind forced Patro to break out cloaks for the slaves in order to protect their skin from windburn.

During this leg of the journey, Canis was initiated to camp chores and he did the best he could. Under the supervision of the guards, he collected firewood and helped to set up Patro's tent. He still tried to keep as much distance between himself and those same guards as he could, but he worked hard.

On the evening of the fifth day, they reached another city with 'royal seat' attached to the name. Canis's earlier supposition about the name having something to do with stone must be wrong. Though larger than other towns built of wood, there was no other outward difference. Maybe a certain size was the thing. At any rate, the city was called Kansas.

Regular meals and washing over the last two and a half months were making a marked difference in Canis's appearance. He was heavier and his skin was now a porcelain texture emphasizing his stony expression. Even his hair was showing improvement, though it wouldn't look much like hair until all of the damaged straw had grown out enough to be cut away.

During their week's stay at Kansas, Patro sold four slaves and bought two more. After weathering time in a stone and barred cage, sleeping in the market square under their wagons was a not an issue. He didn't really sleep, not really. He only dozed; opening his eyes enough to spot and identify whatever sound or scent had alerted him and then drifting off again. Here, where the wind never really stopped, he found the scents to be very informative if he took the time to decipher them.

Here also, Patro took on another wagon to carry more water. When the new wagon, heavily loaded with water, pulled up to their hitching post, Canis wondered what the road ahead would be like. They already carried four big barrels with them and Patro saw to it they were filled at every stop. *Why would they need eight more?*

They headed directly into the morning sun this time and out into the wind-driven grasslands again. The road might have been another high road, but it offered little protection from the cold winds. They had left the trees far behind leaving only scrub brush to break the wind; even the tall grass had been left behind in less windy climes. The grass here was short, tough grass, but as they traveled, even that became scarce.

After eleven days, they reached a dusty little barge town called Overton late in the evening. Patro only spent one day here – time for them all to take a break from the incessant wind and to hire them a barge to cross the river. Early the next morning, they were on the road again, reaching another dusty town called Columbia late the next night.

The next thirteen days, on a road that scarcely qualified as a road, brought them to their next stop, Louis City. After being barged across yet another massive river that did little to wet the surrounding landscape, their routine changed somewhat. There was no more high road, merely a dirt track across the sandy hills. When the wagon got stuck, everyone learned quickly to pull along with the horses.

They camped at Vernon Wells, eight days into this leg of their journey. Why the place was named after a well, Canis couldn't figure out. It was a collection of buildings and nothing more – one day, the wind would claim them too. They were camped among the buildings and Gem was fussing over him again.

Canis liked her a lot so he decided to show her what he could do. He carefully traced the letters C a n i s in the sand.

When Gem saw what he was doing, she said, "What's this?"

Canis pointed to himself and laboriously pronounced, "Canis." Then he saw a look of concern in her eyes. He thought she was going to cry like his mother had. He tried to say not to, but the words wouldn't come. His struggle was brief, though, as just then Patro came up behind them.

"So, you *can* talk. I was beginning to wonder. How about telling me your name?"

Alarmed and dismayed at being caught with his guard down, allowing a potential enemy to come so close undetected, Canis jumped and pulled away, staring at Patro with his unblinking stare.

He hated surprises.

"His name is Canis," said Gem.

"Canis is it," said Patro. "Well, I suppose it's a fitting name; it goes with the eyes. I think I'll even let him keep it, at least until I sell him." He looked at Canis a little longer then he knelt down directly in front of him. "Listen, boy. You're a slave now. It's time you learned how to act like one. I've let you go because I think you're going to be special someday and you haven't been too healthy, but I think your lessons can start, now that I know you can talk. Do you understand?"

When Canis stared at him, showing no inclination to respond, Gem interrupted again. "I don't think he *can* talk, master. I think his name may be the only thing he can say and that's not easy for him. He can write it too." She pointed to something on the ground. "At least, I think that's his name; I can't read. But that's all. I honestly believe he can't talk."

Patro looked at the writing in the dust. It did indeed spell out the boy's name in clear and perfect letters. He looked back up into the boy's eyes. "Can you understand me?"

Canis was near panic once again. Never before had someone asked him a direct question – not one where they expected an answer anyway. His mother would ask all manner of little questions, but she never expected him to answer, it was just her way of talking to him.

Patro was waiting for his answer. Did he understand? No, he didn't, but he couldn't tell him that either – the words just wouldn't come out, no matter how hard he tried. He did the only thing he could do. Slowly, he moved his head from side to side once; it was nearly a twitch, but it was the best he could manage.

"It's simple," said Patro with a frown. "Do as you are told and I'll be fair with you. Disobey me and you'll get a whipping. Understand?"

Well that was clear enough. He dropped his chin in a nod, but he still didn't understand, not really.

"You better learn to do better than that, but it's a start. Gem, I know you've been working with him. Teach him some of the rules tonight."

"Yes, master," she said and curtsied low. This was a tremendous responsibility for her. Until now, she had worked with the boy simply because she liked and pitied him, but now she was responsible for what he learned. She had yet to convince him to bow to the masters. If he didn't do that, now it was entirely possible she would be punished along with him for his transgressions.

Patro attempted to take up some of Canis's education too. Surely, if the boy could speak and write his name, he could say other words. Much to his disappointment, it seemed that what Gem said was true, Canis just couldn't make words come out of his mouth, and writing seemed to be just as difficult, though his tracing of letters were perfectly clear.

Gem wasn't having much luck either. Canis learned how to do many chores around their camp. He did what he was told readily and to the best of his ability, even to the point of watching when someone showed him a better way, then using what he'd been shown. The biggest problem they constantly ran up against was the way he associated with the people around him. Though he was willing to do the work he was asked to do, he couldn't be persuaded to take his eyes off of whoever was issuing the order long enough to bow an acknowledgment. In fact, he couldn't be made to bow at all, not to anyone.

They were half way to Louisville when one of the new guards took it upon himself to show Canis, and by association, Gem, that free men did get bowed to by the slaves in their presence. He had watched these two ever since Kansas and he couldn't believe the slave master permitted such behavior from slaves, regardless of how young they were.

He approached the two of them where they were clearing the ground for the camp. "You two," he called. "We're to collect firewood. Come with me."

"Yes, master," said Gem with a graceful curtsy, but Canis's

tiny nod went unnoticed and unlooked for.

With a blow that dropped Canis to the ground like a stone, he said, "Bow to your master, slave. I will not tolerate your insolent stare."

Canis was stunned both by the blow and by the ferocity behind it. He'd been struck before, but that had been by the men who had discovered him.

Gem was a well-trained slave, and though she hated to see the boy struck, she made no sound or move against a free man – she had no right – and when the guard turned on her, because, obviously, Canis's transgression was her responsibility, she made no move to avoid the heavy strap laid across her bowed back.

Canis was not so well trained, though. When he saw the strap come down on Gem who had done nothing to deserve such a thing – not that he would have allowed it in any case – he sprang to her defense. He didn't know what the mob had done with his mother. He hadn't been able to protect her, but this was only one man, one man was no problem. With a snarl, he was off the ground and in the middle of the guard with a fury that had only been seen from him on the first day of his capture. The difference was, after more than two months of regular food and exercise he was strong and healthy.

Surprise, as well as the very effective attack of a boy who was far stronger than he appeared, knocked the man to the ground where Canis continued his attack until the other guards finally got a hold on him and pulled him off. Then, except for breathing a little hard, he stood quietly and glowered at the man as he pulled himself to his feet.

When the man was standing, his damage was visible for all to see. He had deep scratches on his face and neck, plus there was more than one wound that could only be bites. One took part of his ear, and some of the skin on his neck was obviously missing, a chunk of his chin was gone too. "You filthy little animal. I'll kill you for this," he said as he dabbed at some of the blood running down his front.

Patro joined the volatile gathering seconds after the fight was broken up. "You will *not* kill one of my slaves," he said as he pushed his way into the middle of the gathering. "What happened here?"

"Your pet attacked me," said the guard bitterly.

"My pet?" said Patro. "I do not have pets." He looked at Canis who was covered with just as much blood as the guard was. "You men were all informed of the potential consequences of damage to my property at your hands. How much of that blood is his?"

"I don't know; not much I'm sure. He was the one doing all the scratching and biting," replied the guard sullenly.

"From your pay will come the cost of the water I have to use to wash away the blood to find out the answer to that question, and if we run short, you will be the one going thirsty. You will also pay for his tunic and pants that are now blood stained and useless, and if he has been damaged, you'll be added to my chain; maybe your price will make up for what I lose from his sale, but I doubt it. Now, someone, explain to me how this came about."

When no one was readily forthcoming with an explanation, Patro turned to Gem. "Tell me what happened, slave."

"Yes, master," said Gem from where she knelt. "The master," she indicated the bloodied guard with a wave of her slender hand, "ordered us to accompany him to collect fire wood, then he struck Canis to the ground and started to whip me. That is when Canis attacked him."

Patro turned to the guard. "Why did you strike my slaves?"

"The little brat didn't bow. He just stared at me like…like I was beneath him or something, and she's with him all the time. She should have taught him how to behave by now."

"You may have been justified to strike young Canis, but not Gem. Gem is worth at least five thousand gold pieces to me on the block in Chicago, *if* she is undamaged. Can you afford to compensate me for that kind of a loss?"

The guard blanched. "No sir," he replied.

"Well then, when you own your own slave, you may

discipline her any way you please. Until then, I suggest you refrain from damaging my property. You…" he pointed to the guard who held Canis, "get him washed up then bring him to me." He turned back to the bloody guard. "You, go see Mia, and get those wounds patched up."

An hour later, the guard brought Canis to Patro's tent. "He has no open wounds, sir," said the guard.

Patro looked at the growing bruise that was threatening to dominate the entire side of Canis's head. "Whatever possessed you to attack a free man? I won't even mention the fact that the man was more than four times your size."

Canis couldn't explain and didn't try. *It was the right thing to do.* He stood there quietly.

"I'm going to have to beat you. Go and wait by the wagon wheel."

Canis was confused. *Why wait by the wagon wheel?* He'd wait and see. All his short life, he'd had to wait to find the answers to his questions. He was used to waiting.

As Canis turned to follow the guard back outside, Patro stopped him. "Canis, you are going to have to learn to bow to whatever free man speaks to you." He paused for a moment as Canis turned to look at him. "I just gave you a command. I am your master. I am a free man. Bow to me."

Gem had many times pointed out how he was to act, but bowing destroyed his view and made him vulnerable. He would never lower his eyes to a potential enemy, and he had yet to find anyone who was not such an enemy. This man came the closest though; he deserved an explanation – he tried. He looked around the tent without seeing its contents, trying to find some means of explaining. His mouth opened. He raised a hand. It was no good – no use. The only way to explain was to use words and there were no words. He closed his mouth and dropped the hand. He was out of the tent a moment later. Even the guard who controlled his leash was surprised by this development. It was more communicative animation than either of them had ever seen out of him.

When Patro went out to the wagon a few minutes later, Canis was standing there waiting for him. “Take off your tunic.” When the tunic was on the ground, Patro signaled to the guard to tie the boy’s hands to the top of the wheel. With his hands tied to the top of the wheel, they were level with the top of his head. He looked so small tied like that. As soon as they were secure, Patro began to whip him. He used a whip that was about three inches wide and about four feet long with a stiff core. It raised a long wide welt, but it didn’t break the skin or bruise. Patro laid ten stripes across Canis’s small back, “for the attack on a free man,” he said.

Canis stood stoically letting only a small gasp escape his lips at the first stroke, a reaction to the pain to be sure, but more to surprise. Only a moment ago he was trying to explain. *No more. Never again. He was an enemy after all.*

After the last stroke, Patro reached around and gripped the boy’s chin. Canis didn’t flinch. He scarcely felt the touch over the pain that was coursing through his body from the whip. As soon as he met Patro’s eyes he said, “Ten strips for attacking a free man, and now I’m going to give you three more for not bowing to me. From now on, you will get three stripes for every time you do not bow; do you understand me?”

Canis didn’t answer. He didn’t even try. *Never again, I will never trust him again.*

After the last three stripes, the spectators dispersed. Canis sagged. The wheel was too big to allow for his knees to reach the ground, but he collapsed just the same allowing his chest to take his full weight on the hub.

Setback

Canis curled up on his blanket when he was taken back to his place in the line that evening. Assuming he was sleeping, Gem didn't bother him except to drape his tunic over his shoulders. Supper was long over, but he wasn't hungry anyway.

The next morning, when the guard approached to give him his bowl of gruel, Canis growled at him and crab-walked away to the farthest reach of his leash. He wouldn't even let Gem approach him. He warned her off with an unmistakable snarl. In fact, anyone who approached to within the reach of his leash got the same warning. The calm level stare everyone had become accustomed to was replaced with a hateful menacing glare. It was impossible to tell if he even recognized the people around him.

When this was reported to Patro, he immediately came to investigate. Patro saw that Canis had yet to touch his food and that he was curled up in a tight ball on his blanket, his tunic lay where it had dropped when he had been roused by the guard who brought his food, and the signs of his whipping, still red but no longer raised, were plainly visible. "Canis, what seems to be the problem?" he asked.

Though Canis had been watching his every move, he bristled at the sound of his voice.

"Canis, pick up your tunic," said Patro, more to see what he would do, if anything.

Canis's wariness increased and his eyes narrowed further than they already were. Patro could see that his eyes were dilated more than the dim light of the dawn warranted. "Gem, have you talked to him?" asked Patro without looking away.

"No, master, he won't allow me close," she replied.

He considered the situation. "We'll stay here a day. Maybe the wind won't be blowing so hard tomorrow." He didn't believe so for a moment, but he'd give the boy that much time to recuperate. Canis was apparently shocky from the whipping and what had been 'tame' in him before was buried under the pain. He unhooked the end of Canis's leash and made to lead the kid to his tent. If it weren't for the guards following, it was likely the leading would have been more like dragging, provided Canis didn't decide to attack his back.

Canis went, hunched and dodging and snarling every inch of the way. Once the leash was again secured to a slave ring inside Patro's tent, Canis slunk to a dark corner.

Patro watched him all day to see when he fell asleep or returned to himself.

Canis didn't sleep or even close his eyes for a doze. Every time Patro moved, he would growl a warning at him. It was a very long day for both of them, and the night was no better.

During the night, Canis came to a decision. *I cannot keep this up. Not like this. I will go back to waiting. I am good at waiting.*

When Patro came to check on him, he did nothing. Patro handed him his tunic and Canis accepted it from his hand and put it on.

"Canis, will you listen to me now?" asked Patro.

Canis looked from him to the tent flap where he could hear the guards moving around as they got the morning moving, then after a short hesitation, he sat down again.

"Do you understand why you had to be whipped?" asked Patro.

Canis looked at him.

"Damn it kid, I wish you could talk. Why can't you talk? How did your mother talk to you? Did you even have a mother? How about a father? Why did those people throw you out into the street in front of my horses? I have a lot of questions and you can't answer them, can you?" He studied Canis's face carefully. "Canis, you need to bend that stiff neck of yours and bow to the free men who speak to you. Like I said last night, from now on, if you don't bow, you will earn three stripes with the whip. Do you understand?"

Canis refused to respond. There was not the slightest crack in the ice that were his eyes or the stone that was his face. It was unsettling that so much stone and ice should belong to so small a child.

Patro closed his eyes and sighed. If last night was long, today may well be longer. He rose and returned Canis to his place on the line.

That day was indeed a long one. Canis did not bow so much as an eyelash to any order he was given, and in response, he received three lashes for every offense. He stood without the need for restraints each time, then went about whatever task he had been given to do. By the time the sun went down, he no longer wore his tunic and kept it tied around his leash. His small back was so raw that it hurt to have the material rub it. By the end of the next day, the guards were all reluctant to talk to him. They had learned that, rather than bow, he would take his three stripes, and only a sadist would continue to dish out such damage to one small boy.

One evening, six days after the attack, the guards rounded up three of the slaves to gather firewood. For this and other such chores, the guards were usually in control of the leash while the slaves did the gathering and carrying. It was also common for Canis to be on the wood gathering crew, so this evening was no different. At least it was no different until they were out of sight of camp.

Only a handful of minutes after the camp was no longer in sight, Canis picked up a fist-sized rock and threw it at his guard, knocking him senseless. He then gathered up his chain and sprinted off into the brush.

He had to act quickly; the alarm was already being called. He needed to find a place to hide. He wasn't big enough to out run any of the guards in an open chase. With a snarl at himself, it occurred to him that he might have picked a bad time to make his escape. Though he'd succeeded in getting away, keeping his freedom might not be so easy. This was not a very good country for hiding. The brush was rather large, but it was sparse and none of the few things that could be called trees were near big enough to climb, let alone hide in.

He managed to find a small gulch where he buried himself in the sandy dirt and loose brush. He waited. He was prepared to wait all night and well into the next day. He suspected Patro wouldn't let him go easily, but he hoped he wouldn't want to delay his travels for one small slave who had to be beaten several times every day.

Patro and his men searched throughout the night and all during the next day. They found Canis when he came out of his hiding place shortly after it became dark again. He wasn't easy to catch and Patro knew that if the boy managed to escape again, there would be a slim chance of capturing him a second time. It was an unfortunate development.

By the time Canis was returned to the line with his hands and arms securely bound behind his back and a gag in his mouth, all four of the guards bore some mark dealt out during his capture. One sported a black eye that matched the one Canis still had, another had several scratches, another almost lost an eye, and the guard who already bore several wounds dealt out by Canis, was bleeding again from more than one of them and sported a few more as well as a new limp.

From that point on, Canis stopped trying to be good. All his efforts had only drawn whippings and the occasional beating. *No one will ever touch me again. No one will get close enough without me tasting some blood.*

For three days, Canis was kept bound. One of the guards did manage to remove the gag without injury, though it was a close thing. For three days, no one could get close enough to feed him; he didn't even allow Gem to get close and she was forbidden to try after he almost succeeded in biting her hand. For three days, he walked along with the rest of the line, though he maintained as much distance from the others as his chain would allow.

On the evening of the day before they were to reach Louisville, it was Mia who brought him his food. Mia held a unique position in the camp. She had been a slave all her life and had done just about everything there is for a female slave to do somewhere along the line. Now, she was rather old. Her resale value was next to nothing on the block, but Patro had found her to be valuable despite her age. She was the camp cook and occasionally the camp healer and it wasn't uncommon for Patro to take her advice about the slaves when she offered it.

She knelt down on the edge of the perimeter Canis guarded and watched him closely. His eyes were wary and resentful and his hands were still tied behind his back. "Canis, I know you're hungry. I've never hurt you. Will you allow me to feed you?" she said with a soft voice.

She had never seen the like before in all of her years, but she persisted. With a bowl in one hand and a jug of water in the other, she moved forward on her knees and she was rewarded with a snarl. "No, Canis. You have to eat. You can't continue to starve yourself. Please let me feed you." She moved forward again.

Canis was so hungry, and though he hadn't noticed it before, Mia sounded just like his mother. She had the same soft voice, and for a moment, it was his mother who knelt there. He tried to warn her away with a snarl as he curled up into a tighter ball, but a tear escaped to trail down his dirty face.

"Oh, Canis," she murmured. She set aside the things in her hand and drew the small bundle of boy into her ample lap. His snarls and struggles rapidly turned into sobs.

Mia held and rocked the boy for a long time. Word reached Patro about this newest development and he went to see.

As Patro stood over them, Mia looked up at him. "You're not

going to be able to turn him into a slave, master. He can't do it; it's more than just being able to say the words or bow."

Patro stood there and considered them for a long time. As a slave, by the time he was about sixteen, Canis would have been every bit as valuable as Gem was now, even if he couldn't make him bow. He could be such a collector's item with those glowing blue-gray eyes in that porcelain face and that shock of red hair that was starting to become such a rich copper color.

He sighed. "All right, all right." He reached down and unlocked all of the chains. "Try to convince him to stay. He's not old enough to take care of himself yet." He left, taking the collection of chains with him.

During their stay in Louisville, Canis never left Mia's side; she had worked a miracle as far as he was concerned. The chains were gone. The kiss of freedom – something he'd always wanted and had never tasted – was his to feel and explore, but he wasn't about to leave Mia unprotected; he'd guard her with his life if need be.

Along the road to Indianapolis, he ventured out of her sight more often. She was well protected in the caravan and those far away, oh so enticing scents simply had to be explored.

By the time they reached Chicago, the marks of the turmoil that had ended Canis's enslavement was gone as if it never happened. Also by then, Canis was beginning to hunt at night. He went to great lengths to make such movements unseen though he was less careful returning. He preferred to keep them guessing about his movements and whereabouts, and allowing the guards to see him returning without knowing he'd left, accomplished that nicely. He was rather proud of the fact that he usually brought back something to add to the cook-pot.

Half-Breed

by

Anna L. Walls

Chicago School of the Sword

It took quite a while before Canis stopped snarling at anyone who came too close to him or Mia, but with her chiding him every time she heard, he eventually desisted, though he never lowered his guard. By the time they reached the desert again a year later, Canis seemed to be back to what had been normal for him before the unfortunate incident at the wagon wheel. He did the work he was asked to do and did it to the best of his ability and without the supervision the slaves on their leashes required.

The boy who strode through camp now, bore little resemblance to the child who had come into their lives a little over a year ago. The matted straw that had been his hair in the beginning had long since been trimmed away and the heavy copper strands that were left behind were long enough to tie back with a strip of leather. His porcelain skin glowed with sun-kissed health and his frame had stacked at least a foot to his height. Aside from these remarkable features, he looked like most any other skinny kid. His wiry strength was only apparent when he shed his tunic. That's when the corded muscles, so incongruous to his young age, were visible.

Canis hunted most every night, especially when towns and cities were no longer in sight, and it wasn't uncommon for him to bring back a couple rabbits or grouse, which Mia added to the morning gruel; this addition of meat to the slaves' diet improved their energy as well – even Patro could see the difference.

When they traveled across the desert between Kansas and Louisville, he would bring in such things as snakes, big lizards and long legged rabbits the size of a small dog.

Patro couldn't figure out how he was being so successful at these hunts when he didn't have any weapons. He had seen the guards teaching the kid to shoot a bow, but when he hunted at night, he didn't use a bow. The guards hunted along their path every day, but their luck paled compared to the boy's nighttime forays, though they generally brought back larger animals.

Whenever they were around strangers, Canis stayed close to Mia. When she went into the town market, he was her shadow and carried all of her purchases. She even got permission to buy him some new clothes. He was growing so fast, and if he wasn't a slave, there was no point in dressing him like one. She wouldn't let him have the black shirt and pants he picked out, but he flat refused to look at the lighter colors she wanted. In the end, he got dark blue pants, a white linen shirt, and a sleeveless tunic that matched the pants. She would have bought him a pair of boots but Patro wouldn't allow it; he didn't want to invest the money into boots he'd outgrow in a few months. She did buy him a heavy, wool cloak with a hood that happened to be brown; winter was never far away in the north. Since it brushed the ground, he would be able to use it for two or three years before it was too short.

These shopping trips allowed Mia to keep Canis away from the auction blocks and slave displays. Therefore, he wasn't around when Gem was sold. Her sale brought Patro more than seven thousand gold pieces from a very prestigious house of pleasure in the city of Chicago. Patro was able to sell four more slaves to the same house, though they didn't bring as much all together.

That night, Canis was restlessly prowling the halls of the slave house when he saw some people who didn't belong. They were leaving Patro's quarters late at night and they were acting in a very unusual manner, they even left Patro's door open when they left.

None of the three men saw Canis where he lurked a few yards away in a dark hall; he was only another shadow among shadows.

When they were out of sight, Canis approached the door to investigate. Inside, Patro was sprawled on the floor, though he was starting to move.

"Canis, did you see them? They got everything," he said hoarsely, as he brought a hand to his bleeding head.

Canis was off. He owed no allegiance to Patro, but he was good to Mia and that was enough for him. A few seconds later, he found the men who had taken Patro's gold and followed them to two more waiting in the alley. When he was finished with them, they lay very still and he was on his way back to Patro, leaving them where they fell in the melting slush and new falling snow.

When he reentered Patro's apartment, he found the man sitting at his small table. He deposited the gold in the middle of the table then soaked a towel in a washbasin on the counter. Then he pulled Patro's hand away from his blood-drenched head and placed the towel there.

"Go get Mia," said Patro, but Canis no longer took orders from Patro – common sense chores were one thing, but Mia could do nothing here. He put the gold away in its locker then paced the floor; he wouldn't leave Patro alone so debilitated. Near dawn, he heard a noise out in the hall and opened the door. Passing by was one of the slave house clerks. Canis showed the man his bloody hand and beckoned him into the room.

"What happened here, Master Patro?" asked the man.

"Someone robbed me," replied Patro as he held his splitting head.

"I'll get the housemaster. He'll be very upset to hear about this. Oh my. Oh my." He was out the door, running all the way, and Canis could still hear his cries of "oh my" several turnings away.

A few minutes later, the man returned with three others, the housemaster, his best healer, and the man who was in charge of house security. To have one of the slave masters attacked within house was a tremendous blotch on the house's reputation. If word got around, it could drive him out of business, and Patro was one of his biggest clients, being one of the few slave traders who traveled around the entire valley. His commission from this one slaver's sales lined his pocket with comfort for an entire year. To lose him would be a real pinch.

Half an hour later, Patro was tucked into his bed with his head neatly wrapped. Mia sat by his side and still Canis paced the floor.

"Canis, sit down," said Mia. "You did very good tonight. Master Patro is very pleased with you."

That was not why Canis paced. He had never killed before, though he'd wanted to at times. A dead body was…still, *too* still; it bothered him. It bothered him that it had been so easy. It bothered him that they had been so vulnerable. *Were people really so weak?* He expected people to be harder to kill than the animals he hunted, but there was surprisingly little difference other than size. Without their weapons, they died just as quickly as a rabbit.

Because of his injuries, Patro was forced to remain in the city for five days longer than he had intended. The housemaster, in an effort to keep Patro happy, didn't charge him for the additional days of his enforced stay, and house clerks brought all potential transactions to his apartment. On the fourth day, Patro ventured out for the first time since the foiled robbery.

When he returned, he sent for Canis. "Canis, you have saved me from a grievous loss and for that I owe you a debt. Would you come with me?"

If Mia hadn't brought him, Canis wouldn't have come to the summons, but now that he was here, he looked at Patro with his ever-present blank stare; it was all he could do to hide his curiosity. A gentle nudge from Mia prompted him to take a step toward the door – the closest signal of assent he would give.

Patro led the way up the Grand Market Street. It was an amazing street at least two hundred yards wide, paved with stone and sporting constables at almost every corner. People crowded the stalls, making way slowly for passing carriages and even slower for the occasional cart drawn behind a slave, unless a stick-wielding personal guardsman was clearing the way.

Eventually Patro led them to a large building. It might not have been the biggest building in the city, but it was certainly the biggest building Canis had ever seen, excepting perhaps the slave house complex where they usually stayed. It was stacked four stories high with the uppermost windows up under sharp eves. It loomed over most of the other buildings in the area, though Canis could see other buildings as high or higher farther on. Over the door hung a massive sword carved out of wood, and painted on the blade was the words *Chicago School of the Sword*.

Canis had learned several new words during his travels with the slave master. He knew what a slave was now and what a beating was, but this was a new word. He wondered what 'school' meant and he wondered what other new words waited for him in this building. He would have to be on his guard – he was always on his guard, but this was new. He didn't like new things.

Inside, a wiry man with gray hair met them, though that looked to be the only sign of his age. Patro wasn't an overly tall man, but this man scarcely cleared his shoulder. He was little more than five trim feet of compact muscle.

"Canis, this is Master Dagon, and he is not called master for the same reason I am," said Patro. "Master Dagon is a master of the sword as well as many other skills. Because of what you did for me, I would like to further your education in this way. You're quick and you're smart, and you've already shown me that you're a good fighter. Because of that, I have hopes of seeing you in the arena under my banner." He turned to Master Dagon. "Master, this is the boy I spoke to you about. I believe he has a lot of promise. As we agreed, I will pay for his room and board as well as his lessons for one year."

"He's very young," said Dagon. "It'll take him a year to develop some skill with a small sword. It will take him two or even three to become skilled enough to enter my classes, and longer still before he's big enough to be allowed to compete in the arena, no matter how skilled with the sword he becomes in the time he spends here."

Patro nodded then turned to Canis. "Do you want to try this?"

This was indeed a surprise and doubly so because it was a pleasing surprise this time. He studied Patro's face for a long moment, looking for any sign of deception. When he didn't see any, he turned to explore farther into the building.

Patro and Dagon followed. "He doesn't say much," commented Dagon.

"I've never been able to get him to talk. It can be frustrating, but he's smart enough," replied Patro.

Canis went to the first door of many that lined the entry hall on both sides. Inside, he saw three people. The older man, young though he looked, was showing a lunging motion to two half-grown boys. He watched for a few minutes then he turned back to Dagon. The question was obvious as was the signs he used to ask it. He pointed at Dagon and at the three in the room.

Dagon smiled. "I'm glad to see that you can make yourself understood. I'm not teaching this class because these are beginners. I won't be teaching these young men until they are much further along in their training. However, the young man who is teaching here *is* one of my students." He called out to the young instructor. "Leonard, could I bother you for a moment?"

The man named Leonard nodded to them, then he waved his two students to rest, and came over.

"Leonard, this is Canis. He may be one of your students if he decides to stay. Would you like to show him some of what he will learn here?"

"Certainly, Canis is it? Have you ever handled a sword before?" asked Leonard.

Canis looked at him for a moment, then for the first time in over a year, he responded to a question put to him by another person; he twitched his chin sideways in denial.

Leonard was surprised in the inhibited response but he took it in stride and led Canis over to a sword rack where he selected a lightweight slender blade that was not too long and handed it to Canis. Standing beside him, he brought up his own much heavier sword and showed him, by example, how to hold it, then he showed him a few basic swings and thrusts with a brief explanation for both.

Canis imitated everything Leonard did. He knew what swords were used for. He'd been around Patro's guards for close to two years, and though they hadn't used them very often in actual fighting, it happened, and they frequently practiced with them, either with each other or alone. Canis knew that swinging a sword was different from swinging a stick. He also knew that he was supposed to hang onto the sword, though he was very good at throwing a stick.

Leonard continued the abridged lesson. "Would you like to try your hand against me now? I'd like to see how much you remember." He faced Canis and saluted. He held the salute until Canis imitated the move, then he said, "The salute is a show of sport. It means that you mean your opponent no harm. Now, to add to the fun, would you like to make a wager?"

Dagon watched Canis's every move and he smiled at this. "I'll wager. For every successful block he makes, I'll knock off one gold piece from the price of his tuition, and if he draws blood on you, Leonard, you get to make up my losses, if there are any."

"Master Dagon, that's a little stiff don't you think," protested Leonard.

"No, I don't think so. Surely, you're better than a kid who has never held a sword before, if not, I may start you back at the beginning again.

Patro was smiling too. The price for these lessons was going to be expensive. If Canis could knock off at least one gold piece from that price, he'd be thrilled, and he knew how crafty Canis could be. Neither Leonard nor Dagon knew how much damage this small boy could do to four big guards *without* using a sword.

Canis was excited; he couldn't believe Patro actually wanted to improve his fighting skills; he listened to every word Leonard said and imitated all his moves. He noted things like weight-shift and shoulder-slant. He planned to use it all in this challenge. He would need it if his enemies persisted in being men. He had one small thing in his favor though; he was far more deadly than any of them suspected. No one knew how five thieves had died in the alley behind the slave house.

Dagon moved the two of them into the middle of the floor, waving the other two students aside to make room. Then acting the part of referee, he marked the beginning of their match.

Canis stepped into the attack boldly. Never before had he matched against another person in a contest that wasn't a desperate struggle for life or freedom. Until most recently, he had always fought to escape. There was no way he would survive an all-out battle – he wasn't big enough, so he needed to survive in order to be able to fight another day. This fight bore none of those risks; in fact, he was *supposed* to learn this skill. With this, he could stand against any man, even if they too held a sword.

He blocked the first and the second of Leonard's swings with his sword braced by his naked off hand. He saw nothing wrong with doing that because the sword he held, though clearly a sword, it was no sharper than a stick. With each block, he forced himself closer to his opponent. Then he spun completely inside of Leonard's reach and elbowed him in the stomach, causing him to double over in surprise. The unfamiliar weight and length of the sword, now supported by only one hand, dropped, and the only stretch of the blade that had any edge left on it laid a tiny cut on Leonard's arm, but Canis had control of that arm.

He threw his whole weight against the arm in his grip as he spun out and around his opponent. Overbalanced, Leonard toppled to the floor on his face in an ungraceful sprawl. Canis's momentum carried him around to sit on Leonard's back. Leonard's sword hand was bent across his back in Canis's lap. Not only did Canis have full control of Leonard's sword arm, but his left heel was over Leonard's shoulder and his right one was over Leonard's neck.

Dagon barked a loud guffaw. He had never seen such a

combination of dirty street fighting and clumsy swordplay, not to mention the fact that small children normally didn't dive into a fight, even if they knew it was staged for fun. As soon as he had recovered enough to talk and make himself understood, he said, "He did it. I didn't think he'd get more than one block in if he tried, but he blocked you twice *and* drew blood, though I think *that* was pure accident. What went wrong, Leonard?"

Leonard was still picking himself up off the ground. "I don't know, sir," he said. He hadn't had much of a chance to analyze the encounter. All he knew was that he screwed up. A kid half his size shouldn't be able to take him so easily, and he took him all the way to the floor – how humiliating.

"You underestimated your opponent," said Dagon still chuckling. "And you've spent too much time in the classroom. You need to get out more."

Canis had never been around much laughter and it took him a moment to determine that the laughter was not directed at him, though he was sure he had been the cause of it. He was starting to like these two men, even though he didn't quite understand the banter that passed between them. He had never been around people who chided each other, then laughed about it. All interaction around the slave caravan was very careful and proper, and before he came to the caravan, all he remembered was hiding from people. He didn't remember much laughter anywhere. He liked the laughter.

"Well Canis, are you staying?" asked Patro.

In response, Canis picked up his and Leonard's dropped swords and handed Leonard's back to him. He made no move to put the other sword away or even hand it over. This was his 'yes' answer, but it was also his desire to remain armed among armed enemies, an advantage he'd never had before and wouldn't relinquish easily now.

"I think he's staying," said Patro and he handed over a pouch of gold.

Dagon opened the pouch, drew out two pieces of gold, and

handed them back. “As per our wager, young Canis made two successful, though unorthodox blocks. And you, Mr. Kansas will bring me two gold pieces at your earliest convenience.”

“Of course,” said Leonard with a wry smile.

Canis looked at the young man. *Kansas? Why would he be named after a city? Was he? Or was it just a coincidence?* He might never know, and he certainly couldn’t ask.

Patro stepped up to Canis and handed him another money pouch to which he added the two gold coins Canis had won. “This is spending money for you. Make it last. You don’t know much about the real world so be careful, and be safe. You know my route; I’ll be back here next year at this time. We’ll discuss continued lessons then.” He extended his hand to shake on it, but Canis wasn’t about to surrender his hand into another’s grip, least of all Patro’s. He accepted the money pouch then stood back to gaze at Patro with eyes long since schooled to neutrality. When Patro and Dagon left the classroom, he followed them back to the main entrance where Patro shook hands with Dagon before leaving.

Would Mia come? He didn’t think so. He would miss her. He would see her again next time Patro was in town.

Lessons

Dagon showed Canis to the room he would be using during his stay and then left him there with, “You start in the morning, but I want you to understand, here we teach the use of the sword; I don’t ever want to see another display like that. There is a time and place for dirty fighting, and it’s not here. Here we fight clean. Do you understand?”

Canis thought he did, but he wasn’t sure and he couldn’t ask, but then the sword master was gone. He’d learn this clean fighting and see what it was all about.

He looked around his room. He’d never really had a place of his own. With his mother, his place was her closet. With the slave caravan, there was no place, merely a blanket roll, and seldom the same one. In his opinion, it had been infinitely better than sleeping in the closet. After the chains were taken away, he slept next to Mia wherever she slept, and if that was under a roof, it was usually in the corner of the kitchen.

It had always been difficult for him to sleep in an unfamiliar place, so he pulled the blankets off the narrow bed and made a nest in a dark corner behind his small wardrobe. The room was many times larger than his mother’s closet, almost the size of her room, but he couldn’t bring himself to sleep out in the middle even though the door was closed.

The only other furnishing in his room was a small table under his one glass window and two chairs. He found the window fascinating. He’d never seen a window with glass in it before. His mother's window had been covered with a sheet of oiled parchment. It let some light in, but there was no view unless the window was open, and she almost never opened it.

The view through the glass was slightly distorted and sounds from the street were uncomfortably muffled, but the weather would be held out. He never really liked sleeping in the wind, and he'd rather hear the comings and goings of people so close to where he slept, but perhaps, if the glass held out the wind and rain, it also held out people. At least he wasn't on the ground floor. He looked down on the alley, if he craned his neck, he could see people walking by on the street, but no one walked by below his window. That suited him just fine.

It was difficult for him to be around so many strangers and he missed Mia greatly. From her he could gauge how he should react to new people. Sleep refused to come at more than a doze, even though those strangers remained on the other side of his closed door. Every creak and sigh of the big building brought him fully awake, though he heard no nighttime people sounds.

Early the next morning, those strangers began to troop past his door in chattering numbers, so Canis opened it a crack to watch them pass. Most of them were young like the students he'd seen in Leonard's class, but there were a few older people, and unless they walked alone, they were all laughing and boisterous.

Canis waited until he figured the bulk of them were passed before he crept down the hall to see where they all went. About half way down the stairs, he saw Leonard heading up.

"There you are. I was just coming to find you. Master Dagon wanted to make sure you were familiar with the ropes. Come on, let's go get some breakfast."

He led Canis into a crowded, noisy room smelling of all sorts of food. Canis froze at the door, but Leonard turned back to retrieve him. "Come on. There's nothing to be afraid of here. You're hungry, aren't you?" He pulled Canis forward to a counter where he handed him a plate, then led him to another counter where he loaded his own plate with eggs, bacon and toast, then he poured himself a large glass of juice.

Canis couldn't remember having ever eaten food like this, so he selected a healthy helping of bacon and ham. That much he recognized for sure. He'd try other things another day. He didn't pour himself anything to drink because he didn't see any water. Drinks of white, yellow, and purple were too strange and too sweet.

Tentatively, he sat down in a chair next to Leonard who proceeded to introduce him to the others sitting at the table. Canis didn't try to remember the names or who they belonged to, he couldn't say any of them anyway; instead their faces fell into a group of 'maybe not an enemy'. As Canis looked over the other occupants of their table and then at those in the rest of the room, he saw that he was by far the youngest there.

After breakfast, Leonard led him to his class. Leonard wasn't going to be the one teaching him after all. Before he left him to his class, he said, "Listen, Canis; regardless of what we did yesterday, you're not here to fight, not yet anyway. You're here to learn how to use a sword, so listen to Kendall; he's a good teacher. He'll get you started right."

Kendall may have been a good teacher, but the three other boys who were his classmates didn't seem to be here to learn how to use the sword. They were more interested in laughing and playing. At first, he liked the sound of laughter, but he was rapidly finding it irritating.

After two hours of disjointed instruction, even Kendall was starting to lose his temper. Canis had long since drawn away from the others in an effort to be able to differentiate between the instruction and discipline needed with the other students. Finally, as another round of laughter started, Canis reached out and smacked the ringleader in the face with the cane they had been given to use instead of a real blade.

The boy started to howl in pain, holding his bleeding nose, and the other two started to holler in protest at the action, so Canis rounded on each of them in turn with a vicious snarl, brandishing his cane in an unmistakable promise of more. As soon as he saw in their eyes that they understood his message, he returned to his place and took up the last pose Kendall had been trying to teach them.

The other three looked from him to Kendall who took up the lesson again as if nothing untoward had happened. Not brave enough to return the challenge in front of an instructor, the bloody-nosed ringleader, and one other stormed out of the room, but the third one elected to remain.

After lunch, the younger students went out into the city. Their lessons were over. Canis didn't know or care where they went or what they did. Almost all of them left the building and didn't start trickling back until suppertime or later. He didn't bother to follow their example. Hunting would be very poor this far into the city.

It didn't take the students long to find out that Canis wasn't much fun. He never spoke to anyone, and when they tried to make fun of him or pick on him for not talking, or for being too young or too small, he showed no reaction. At least he showed no reaction if they refrained from touching him. They all found out quickly that Canis wasn't at all afraid of a fight. Within a couple weeks, most of the students took to ignoring him. It was easier than trying to talk to him and a lot easier than trying to fight with him. That didn't mean there were no confrontations. Every so often, some new or otherwise clueless student could be enticed to have a go at Canis for one reason or another, and the student who had received a bloody nose at Canis's hand on his first day could almost always be counted on for a scene, all he needed was a new idea whispered in his ear.

The first such incident happened outside the cafeteria right after breakfast on his second day. In an effort to give Canis a bloody nose payback, he swung the cane at Canis's face as soon as he stepped into the hall. Canis ducked and the blow hit another student who had the misfortune of being directly behind Canis. He caught the cane in his throat and was rushed to the infirmary.

These fights were a bother for Canis so he ended them as quickly as he could, trying not to cause too much damage, but he learned from them too. They served to keep him alert and they taught him how fighters thought.

Canis used the quiet afternoons at the school to explore the building and some of the surrounding neighborhood. It didn't take him long to discover why the younger students only had classes for morning hours. Those young teachers who taught the beginning classes in the morning had their own class in the afternoon. This was the class that Dagon taught. Other classes were held in the building, but it was the classes Master Dagon taught that Canis was interested in.

Canis slipped into the room without being noticed and curled up in a dim corner to watch. *This* was a *class*. Twenty students were paired off with each other. Unlike in the beginner's classes, the moves taught here were complicated multiple attacks and blocks; each set might take up to a minute to complete if they were going slow. Dagon was moving among them correcting a move here or a stance there. Every so often, a new set would be introduced then another stretch of time would pass where it was practiced and corrected until Dagon felt they understood it well enough.

The next step was to have them try it at speed. It was obvious to Canis why, though they were using real steel swords, they were quite dull. Their sharp blades remained at their hip.

He liked watching these classes. He came every afternoon and he was quiet enough that it was over a week before Dagon noticed the extra shadow in the corner.

One day, just after leaving the room, Canis overheard Dagon calling Leonard and Kendall to hang back, and he stopped to listen. "Does that kid have a change of clothes?"

"I don't know, sir," said Kendall. "I haven't been in his room."

"He looks like he's been sleeping in that outfit. You two are excused from class tomorrow. Take him shopping. Get him something to wear. Whatever he doesn't have."

"Yes sir," said Leonard.

Since the summer was well under way, the city was warm and dry. The citizens were out in droves crowding the streets with their bodies and their sound. Going into the city with Leonard and Kendall was nothing like going with Mia. They stopped at several venders and bought an assortment of confections, which they munched on while pointing out the sights to Canis.

Canis quietly shadowed them and listened to their banter while he allowed himself to be fascinated by the variety of people passing by.

Eventually they wound their way through the throngs to a shop where Canis could buy new clothes. When they were finished, they were carrying several new packages and Canis was wearing all new clothes, this time the black he'd wanted last time, and he was wearing a new pair of boots. All his old clothes, aside from his cloak, had been left behind for the shopkeeper to dispose of.

They were wending their way back to the school by way of the other side of the market street when Canis came face to face with a most magnificent beauty. Her hair was piled high and glittered with jewels and her face was skillfully painted. She was dressed in fine silk that hid and yet hinted at every graceful curve, and fine satin slippers protected her delicate feet. At her shoulder stood a mountain of a man who was obviously there for the beauty's protection, and because of him, there was a gap in the press of human bodies. Canis would never have done more than stare at her if she hadn't called his name. "Canis, I didn't know you were here. How are you?"

"Wo, Canis; do you know her?" asked Kendall.

He did know her. Gem stood elegantly before him holding her hands out toward him.

Canis touched her slender manicured fingers then went on to explore the silky gown with a tentative finger, then her hair. He was careful to touch without disturbing anything and yet needed the touch to confirm the reality of the apparition before him. She, in her turn, ran her manicured fingers through his copper-red hair.

"What do you think?" she said. "I spend two hours in front of a mirror every morning. My master wants me to be perfect before he will allow any of his clients to see me."

Canis looked at her. She had a new master now. She was no longer a part of Patro's line. He knew that, but seeing her here like this, his view of Patro and his line seemed diminished. He gently reached out and touched her painted face, then looked away. He had treated her badly there at the last, and he didn't know how to make up for that.

She reached out a manicured hand and caressed his cheek. "I'll miss you, Canis. Take care of yourself."

Kendall and Leonard walked backward until Gem and her bodyguard was no longer in sight. "I don't think I have ever seen someone like that," said Kendall.

"I think I'm going to have to save up my gold. I think I know which house she might belong to. There's certainly not many who could afford to buy a girl like that," said Leonard.

"What gold?" said Kendall. "You're as broke as I am. You'll never have enough money to knock on the door let alone get another peek at that."

Canis didn't want to consider what his two new friends were talking about. He figured he knew, but knowing that Gem belonged to someone else bothered him more than he could readily understand. He felt a protective flair, but he knew he had no right to it, not anymore.

The Carnival

Three months later, talk of the arrival of a new type of caravan called a carnival, spread through the school like a wildfire spreading across the prairie. Apparently, this carnival also made the rounds every year, but since their home was here in Chicago, they spent the winter here.

Everyone at the school talked about the things they had seen displayed last time it had been in town, and they speculated about what might be new this year.

It was difficult for Canis to understand what they were talking about. *What kind of caravan had wares for display and not for sale? How could such a caravan afford to continue every year?* He had come to understand the exchange of gold or silver for flesh or supplies and now the exchange for services such as his sword lessons, but he couldn't understand the exchange of coins for merely looking at something.

He found out when Kendall and Leonard took him to see the attractions at the carnival. For one or two coppers there was a variety of games in throwing rings for small prizes or shooting arrows for larger prizes. Kendall and Leonard participated in many of these games, but they walked away with relatively few prizes. Canis watched avidly, but since no one offered for him to try, he tried none of them. They looked far too simple to hold his interest for long and he could see no practical purpose to the prizes.

They then paid to walk through a complex lined with many mirrors designed to confuse the eye and get the person lost or turned around. Leonard and Kendall laughed uproariously at the different warped reflections, but Canis found them quite unsettling. He couldn't get out of there soon enough.

Many booths had as many different kinds of foods for sale, and other booths sold sweets of all kinds and colors. Leonard and Kendall bought samples of most everything offered, but Canis bought only one thick sandwich. The sweets smelled far too sweet, though he tasted some of what his companions bought.

In another area, there was a man who was supposed to be the strongest man in the world and people could pay their copper and go into the tent to see for themselves. In another tent was a woman who supposedly sported a full man's beard, and like before, people could pay to enter her tent and see for sure. Canis was beginning to understand how this strange caravan could afford to continue its operation; he was also learning about curiosity.

In the center of the camp was a very large tent, and for a silver coin people could go in and see the show. The picture posted outside showed men doing acrobatics high in the air while on the ground there was something involving a huge creature with its tail hanging from its face. A pretty girl, who wore little more than ruffles, rode on its neck. In other places in the picture, the girl was guiding the strange creature to do things like sit up and stand on its head. Then there were fancy ponies that trotted around while a young man stood on his head on the back of one, or did the splits between two others. It looked fascinating, but only Canis had any silver and neither Leonard nor Kendall thought to ask for it so they moved on to cheaper attractions.

In another section of the grounds was an assortment of cages holding such things as a striped pony, a great maned cat, and a creature that could have been human if it weren't about twice the proper size, covered with course black hair and sporting teeth large enough to rip off a man's arm.

In a nearby tent, was a collection of smaller cages and boxes that held smaller animals such as large snakes, strange looking rodent-like creatures and smaller varieties of the big, black-haired, human-like thing.

Then Kendall and Leonard led him into the one tent they were most anxious to see. This tent had a two-headed calf and a two-headed snake. These were stuffed, but the glass case was small enough to allow a close look. Over in one corner was a man who had an extra arm growing out of his shoulder and a third eye on the side of his head; he wasn't stuffed. He stood up and reached for anyone who came close.

Other small ugly creatures were displayed here, some of them were alive, but Canis lost interest in the deformed displays when he saw a man in a cage at the back of the tent. The cage was too small for him. It was scarcely big enough for him to sit down with his knees drawn up tight, but this wasn't what attracted Canis's attention. The man had eyes like his, though his hair was short and white, tipped with gray, with a black swath three fingers wide at his temples.

Canis walked up to the cage for a closer look. As he approached, the man bared his teeth in a snarl. His teeth in front were small, sharp pebbles; larger, longer, teeth framed them.

"The wolf-man," said Leonard and he tried to growl back at him, but ended up laughing at his own pitiful attempt. "He was new a couple years ago," he told Canis.

"Look at his teeth," said Kendall. "They're just like a wolf's teeth."

"Why do you think they call him the wolf-man?" said Leonard as he jabbed Kendall in the ribs.

Canis scarcely heard them. He ran his tongue over his own teeth behind his closed lips. He had the sharp side teeth, but not the small front teeth, though his were smaller than average. No one ever glanced at his teeth. Even when he attacked the guard, no one questioned why it had been so easy for him to draw blood and tear flesh.

Ignoring his friend's antics, Canis stood there and looked at the man, studying everything about him. As the wolf-man watched his friends warily, Canis noticed his profile was rather long.

Straight on, his face didn't look any different from anyone else, but from the side, the lower half of his face was pushed out about an inch farther than his forehead.

He wore what looked like the tattered remnants of some hide with gray and black hair. It looked as though someone had skinned out the wolf for which the man had been named, then they tied two of the paws together and draped it around him with the knot at one shoulder. They had offered him no other clothing.

The man stopped snarling as soon as Leonard and Kendall moved away to scrutinize something in a small glass case. Then he reached a hand out through the bars toward Canis and spoke. With words that were uttered around too many teeth and sounds that seemed too deep to be coming from a human chest, he spoke softly. "You have your mother's hair."

He did have his mother's hair. But how would this man know what his mother's hair had looked like?

"Come on, Canis," said Leonard. "It's getting dark. We should be getting back to the school."

Canis drew away reluctantly, but before he left the tent, he thought he saw a tear trail down the man's face. *Why would he know what my mother's hair looked like?* That question bothered him; it bothered him a lot.

That night, he couldn't sleep. The wolf-man's face was constantly before his mind's eye. *What had been wrong? Something was odd and it wasn't just his face.*

He got up and dressed. He thought of the man's words as he ran a comb through his hair. He would have tied it back, but he couldn't find the cord and he didn't want to light a lamp to look for it. He slipped out of the school and down the street. In his dark cloak, he moved like a ghost, slipping past the patrols and street people without being noticed.

When he reached the circus compound, he found the place dark and quiet, though apparently men guarded its streets too. Carefully, he moved through the encampment until he found the tent that had held the strange man.

He slipped under the back flap, which was no easy task; apparently the people who set up these tents had such actions in mind. They wanted people to pay to see their attractions, not sneak in through the back.

Inside it was very dark, but he found the bars of the cage that had held the man. The cage was empty. He struck his thigh with a closed fist and allowed a small hiss of frustration to escape his lips.

He regretted the small sound when a powerful hand darted through the bars and grabbed his shirt. The move to crush him into the bars was abruptly switched to a gentle brush through his hair accompanied by an unmistakable sniff and a soft moan.

"You came back." The powerful fingers traced Canis's face, causing him to shiver with pleasure. "When you left, I didn't expect you to return." The fingers ran through his hair again. "You're alone, aren't you," said the man in a soft rumble. "That must have been hard on you. Our children usually pair off with pups by the time they can walk and are never alone. You can't talk can you? It's sometimes hard for me to talk too. I'm alone now and it's so painfully lonely. I don't want to die in here like this." He gripped Canis's shoulder and rocked him while he rested his face against the bars of the cage.

"Listen, son, there's a million things you should know, and I doubt I have time to tell you everything, but I'll try. I am your father, and I have been looking for your mother ever since she ran away from us more than eight years ago now. She was pregnant and she must have been irrational." He paused. "That's a long and twisted story that'll have to wait for some other time. When I found her, I was too late. She was already dead. I was little more than irrational then too. My companion…" He stroked the pelt he wore. "My companion and I weren't able to fight our way free of the mob, and when Rrewarr died, a part of me died too. That is how they captured me.

"When I woke in this cage, I thought there was no hope of finding you, I wasn't even sure if there was a 'you', but here you are, dressed in fine clothes. I'm so pleased and proud of you to be able to do so much among the humans. But I must warn you; if you are at all like us, soon you will need to join, and to do so you must go into the mountains. Your cries will not be heard if you stay here." The thought of such cries seemed to awaken an urge of his own. He drew away and curled up stifling a moan that threatened to emerge into a full-fledged howl.

Canis listened to the man, his face, and the strange coloring of his hair pictured only in his head. His words had been carefully formed as if each one had to be carved out of the air before it could be understood. *He said he was my father.* Canis had little reason to disbelieve him. His words about being alone hit a cord he was very familiar with, though he never understood why.

Whether this strange man was his father or not – whatever his relationship with his mother, if indeed it was *his* mother he'd known – nothing he could think of, warranted this man to be behind bars like this. He did not deserve to die, not like this. Nothing did, and he was dying little by little, he could smell it. Canis felt around the cage until he found the lock. It was a simple hasp, but it defied any leverage from inside the cage. Canis opened the lock and the cage door.

The man sat there in stunned silence until Canis reached in and pulled him out by the pelt he wore. He then propelled him toward the back of the tent where he had entered. As the man was on his way under the edge of the tent, Canis locked the cage again. At least the ruse would buy them a few more minutes; no one would know he was missing until they tried to make him come out of his sleeping box in the morning.

Outside, Canis led off through the dark streets of the city, taking care to avoid even the lowest beggar, and into the piles of rubble just beyond the edge of the city. The stones were dusted with frost that melted during the day, but at least from here the man could circle the city and find his way back to his mountains without being seen.

In a small cleft between mounds of rock, he pulled the man

around to face him; he pointed north then flattened his hand to his chest and said, “Canis,” his one and only word.

The man smiled. “My name is Orion. My name is well known in the mountains. Come to us. Come home.”

Canis nodded his understanding, but he pointed to the north yet again. When the man, Orion, still hesitated, he gave him a gentle push in that direction and watched his loping stride until he was out of sight. The desire to run with him had to be about the strongest desire he had ever felt. To know this wholeness pulled at him with a pain he scarcely understood, but he had an obligation. Patro had paid gold coins for him to learn the sword. He was obliged to learn it or pay Patro back his coins and he had none.

The sky was beginning to lighten behind him by the time the school came into sight. He slipped into his room only long enough to find the cord that bound his hair back and hang up his cloak, then he went down to the cafeteria for an early breakfast.

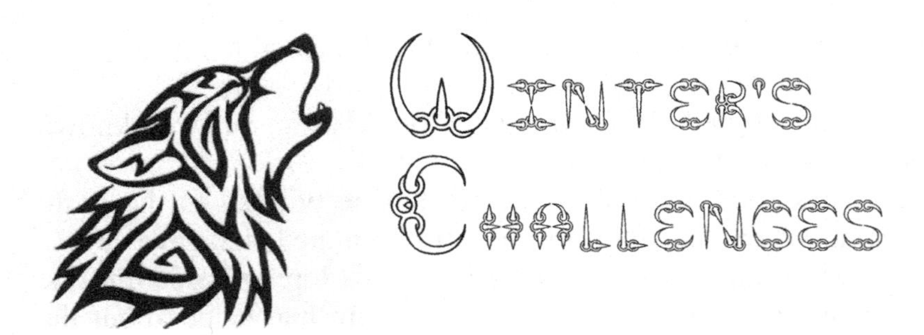

Winter's Challenges

As winter gripped the city, new students began to arrive and Canis and his one classmate found themselves lumped together with other students under Leonard's tutelage. Even with the new students, Canis was still the youngest in the school, though he now knew that he was nearly nine years old, more than two years older than what Patro had thought.

With ten students in the class, Leonard ran it more like Master Dagon's class, with the students paired off with each other to practice the things he taught. Canis liked doing this. He liked pitting himself against this unknown knowledge. He only regretted not being able to do it all day long. He was forced to satisfy his desire by being a spectator in the afternoons.

As the winter wore on, Canis's attendance in Dagon's classroom became somewhat sporadic. It didn't take long to discover what he was doing with his afternoons. It was Kendall who noticed him coming out of an empty classroom shortly before supper one evening. When he mentioned it to the master, Dagon came to see what he was doing in that empty classroom. He was practicing what he had been taught in his own classes and trying some of the things he had seen while watching the advanced classes.

"All right, I get the message. I think you're too young, but I'll okay your advancement to the next level."

Canis watched the sword master closely with his icy eyes. *What was this test Dagon was talking about?*

"I'll have Leonard test you tomorrow. You'll have to pass all three tests before you can participate in my class. I also want you to stop these unsupervised practice sessions; I don't want you practicing something I haven't taught you yet. Bad habits are hard to unlearn."

The testing was an interruption to the regular order of the class instruction. When Leonard announced to the class, "Today is Canis's testing day," the students drew around in a circle to watch.

Canis and most of his classmates hadn't been at the school long enough to watch a testing so they had no idea what to expect.

Leonard took a few minutes to explain the testing to the entire class. "Master Dagon insists his students pass three tests before they can enter his class. The first is to climb that rope." He pointed to a knotty rope hanging among others, knotted and smooth, in the corner of the room. "You are to touch the ceiling, then win a sparring match against one of your classmates. The second test is, of course, more difficult, and the third is still *more* difficult. I can't tell you what they are because Master Dagon doesn't want you to study only in preparation for the test. Do you understand?" He asked the last question to Canis personally. He still considered Canis's inability to speak to be a handicap involving all of his brain.

Canis nodded. *It sounds simple enough.*

"All right then, up the rope you go," said Leonard.

The ropes had always hung there and Canis had seen students climbing them, but after finding the task simpler than it looked, he had not looked at them again. It was obvious that doing that exercise was not an issue with him; his slight frame and wiry muscles made the task look like a stroll down the boulevard.

When Canis reached the floor again, Leonard had his opponent picked out. This first test was supposed to be fought against a peer, but Canis had no peers in this school. His opponent was the one student he had entered this class with. Leonard handed him the cane they used in class and the two of them squared off.

"Lets make this a clean fight now, boys," said Leonard. "Defeat will be counted when one of you can no longer fight a clean fight or had clearly lost the encounter."

The fight was a short one. Canis was quick and crafty. In a dozen moves, he had his classmate disarmed and pinned against a wall with the tip of his cane.

"That was almost too easy, Canis. You passed," said Leonard. "Master Dagon was right to have you tested. You be sure to let me know when you think you are ready for the next test." He turned back to the rest of the class to call them to order.

Canis remained where he was standing, and when Leonard turned back to him; he was surprised to see the questioning look in his eyes. Those eyes might be ice cubes in that porcelain face, but they could be very expressive if one took the time to look. "You think you're ready for the second test *now*? Well, perhaps you are, but I refuse to give a student two tests in the same day. If you still insist on it, you can take the second test tomorrow."

Canis dipped his chin and took his place in the line while the rest of the class muttered in astonishment.

The next day, before class could do more than line up, Canis tugged at Leonard's sleeve and tapped the hilt of his cane.

"So, you're still determined, are you? Listen, Canis, students don't usually ask for this test until sometime after they start using real metal and you haven't advanced that far. Are you still sure?"

Canis's jaw muscles jumped several times, but he gave him his nod.

Leonard studied his small frame with a frown, but the boy's determination was written in every inch of him. "All right then, go to the armory and pick out your weapon, then come back here. We'll start your test as soon as you return."

Canis turned and ran from the room heading for the armory, pausing only a moment to glance at the rack standing by the door. The weapon he would choose would be the one that would replace the cane in his hand for the rest of his lessons, or in his case, until he outgrew it. He wanted to choose carefully.

He returned to the class half an hour later with a battered and scratched sword, but it fit his smaller hand and swung easily for him. It was shorter than many of the swords used by the students, but it was slim and straight. Sharpened, it would have an edge on both sides. Canis saw that as twice the danger, thus making up for its lack of size. The equally battered sheath hung from his belt. It was an unfamiliar weight that he was very conscious of.

Leonard looked at his choice and frowned again, but only for a moment. Most students picking out their first metal sword chose the flashiest or largest they could hang on to, and there were several such swords specifically displayed in order for the student to learn that lesson, only to ask if they could pick another after a few days. Canis obviously had not done this. "Up you go," said Leonard as he indicated the rope he had chosen for this test. It was a bulky rope without any knots.

This was very different from the knotted rope he had climbed the day before. It was bulky enough that Canis, though his fingers were long, he could scarcely get a grip on it and his arms were sore from the day before.

"Your opponent will be waiting for you when you get back down. Be ready for him. Few fights are fair, but I still expect a clean fight in this classroom."

Canis took Leonard's words to mean that his opponent might start the fight before offering a proper salute, if not sooner. *I will be ready.*

The climb was slower; Canis had an inordinate amount of trouble gripping the thick rope depending as much on his fingers clawing the heavy cords as he did the strength of his hands and arms to hold them there. After touching the ceiling, he came to the conclusion that he would have been better off without his boots; he could grip the rope better with his feet.

Then he slipped and fell.

With a wrenching twist that pulled something in his back, he managed to land like a cat, but it was still a hard landing. He now had a shooting pain in his right foot and his left hand was numb. Ignoring his pain, he drew his sword and leapt to battle the single opponent in the center of the room.

Leonard was as stunned by the fall as he was by the attack that followed it. He scarcely had the time to abandon the thought of carrying the boy's broken body to the infirmary, and bring his mind back to the fight, before the Canis was on him and pushing him back.

They fought several turns around the room with Leonard advancing just as much as Canis did. That was the point of the test. All Canis had to do was hold his own against a more advanced student for a short time, but Leonard's instructions were to go one step farther and test the boy's endurance, and especially his determination.

Leonard was just opening his mouth to announce the test over and passed when his sword was knocked from his hand by a move he had never seen before.

Canis rapped the back of Leonard's hand hard with the flat of his sword tip, stunning his grip with the force, then with a quick reversal, he brought his sword up under his wrist with another powerful, flat-sided hit, knocking his wrist up, leaving his hand behind to open helplessly and drop his sword from his numbed grip. A blink later, the point of Canis's blade was tucked neatly under his chin.

"You have passed," said Leonard, his voice echoed in the overly silent room. "With flying colors, I might add."

Canis sheathed his sword then turned with a limp to pick up Leonard's sword.

The limp drew Leonard's attention to the rest of Canis's posture, now that the fight was over. Canis held his left arm cradled across his middle, and he walked with a stiff hunch that hadn't been there during the fight. When Canis brought him his sword, he said, "You hurt yourself when you fell, didn't you? Report to the infirmary."

For once Canis didn't question the order or even nod his

diminutive nod, nor was there the gleam of glee at his victory that might have been in any other student's eyes regardless of the pain; he simply limped slowly out of the room.

The healer was surprised to see the youngest student in the school come hobbling into his ward. In the boy's short stay here, several students had come here after having tried to pick a fight with him. Witnesses had always proven him the attacked, but it was the attacker who always had to be sent to the infirmary. "Took on more than you could bite off this time, did you?" he said. "Climb up here on the table. Let's have a look at you."

The healer gently took Canis's arm and slid his sleeve up above his elbow. "Looks like you managed to break your wrist. What else did you do?" He helped Canis out of his shirt and caressed a hand down his back leaving a trail of goose bumps in its wake. "You pulled several muscles in your back. How did you manage that? This isn't good. I'll have to inform the Master. A fight shouldn't be carried to this extreme. You were limping too. Let's have a look at your leg." He folded Canis's pant leg up as far as it would go, but it wasn't until he eased the boot off that Canis hissed with pain. "And to top it all off, you've torn some tendons in the bottom of your foot. It's a wonder you didn't dislocate something. I can fix that, but I think we'll have to put a cast on, just to make sure it heals completely."

Canis watched the healer closely; he couldn't see how he could tell what was wrong beneath his skin before bruises had begun to show.

The healer fixed a metal shaft to the right side of the table. "Wrap your hand around that and don't let go. I'm going to have to set the bones in your wrist and it's going to hurt. You hold on to that bar and hold as still as you can. If you can't hold still enough, I'll call in some help to hold you down. There's not much I can do for the pain."

Canis's eyes widened with fear, but he gripped the bar. He was no stranger to pain, but he had never seen a bone being set before.

Despite his best efforts, Canis couldn't hold still enough, so the healer went to Master Dagon for help. With Master Dagon pinning Canis to the table and the healer wrapped around his arm, they succeeded in setting the bones in his wrist to the healer's satisfaction.

Canis was shaking when it was over, so he didn't protest when the healer told him to remain lying where he was. He would be tending his foot next anyway.

Master Dagon stayed through it all, and after the healer gave him instructions to report to the infirmary every morning, he walked with Canis to the foot of the stairs and watched him hobble up to his room.

Canis limped into the classroom the next day directly after his first 'fix-it' at the infirmary. Leonard pulled him aside at once and escorted him to a different classroom. "You passed your test. You don't belong with the beginners any more."

His new instructor was a middle-aged man with streaks of gray beginning to show in the black hair at his temples. He also had an angry scar running from the outer corner of his right eye to the corner of his mouth, pulling both into a twisted expression that made reading his face difficult. Canis had never seen the man before, and he was surprised that he was an instructor here. He wondered what he did when he wasn't teaching.

The man presented him with a formal salute, and as soon as Canis returned it, he waved him to the side to wait and Leonard left.

Canis stood by the wall and watched until the instructor brought that particular lesson to a halt. He then waved Canis forward. "I have been informed about your injury during your test. Since you will miss some of the first hour of this class, you will make up the time after class." He then waved Canis to pair off with a student who had been matched with the instructor before.

The next hour was spent learning a complicated offensive

form.

In the last two hours of the class, the students were supposed to use what they had learned in the first half of the class, but Canis had missed the first hour, the defensive half of the lesson, so the instructor was right at his shoulder, showing him the moves and making corrections as they went. Having been present for the offensive lesson, Canis did better during the last hour of class.

After the class was over and the other students had left, Canis waited to get his instructions from the teacher.

The teacher waited for a healthy count of ten after the door was closed before he said anything to his newest, and by far youngest, student. He had seen few people wait with such stillness, but he refused to be impressed by the Master's pet.

"My name is Master Stanton and that is how I expect you to address me whenever you wish to speak to me. Apparently, you consider yourself skilled enough to take my class so don't expect any coddling. No boy this far short of shaving should be allowed past the first test, but you have been allowed to take both the first *and* the second in as many days, and after only a few months of instruction. Nothing but favoritism could have allowed you to actually pass either test. The standards of this school must be sadly slacking. Maybe Dagon is getting old. He has informed me, though, that you will be allowed to take the third test as well. I think both you and he are fools even to consider it. You are too small." He sighed and narrowed his eyes then with a tightening of his mouth, he continued. "Since you are being considered for the next test, it is my obligation to inform you that it will bear little resemblance to the last two. At some time of Master Dagon's choosing, you will receive a message. That message will contain the instructions for your test. For your information, the test will take place within this building and you will have a limited time to complete the task. This test is designed for a man to complete, not to mention a student with more years of training under his belt than you have. I promise you that I will not let the standards lapse for a child."

Canis took in all the information Master Stanton laid out, disregarding the obvious slur that fairly dripped from the last word. He had never had things handed to him easily and didn't expect it now. His injury concerned him most. Not since his first night with the slave caravan had he ever had an injury like this, one that slowed him down or interfered with his movements so much that favoring them or not was a conscious decision.

Stanton spoke again. "We have already covered the defensive part of the lesson you missed; there's no point in going over it again, so to replace that we will spar for the rest of this hour and for every makeup hour until the healer clears you as sound." He drew his sword and saluted.

Canis watched the tall man as he spoke. It was obvious to him that Stanton didn't like him very much. That information came through in more ways than just what he said. His entire body language spoke of detest, and his scent spoke of anger. Then again, the likes and dislikes of other people was only information to be aware of and filed away.

The blades in the school were all alike in one respect, they were all little better than blanks of varying lengths and styles with a variety of hilts and guards attached, and Stanton's was no different. Long and straight with only a slight curve near the tip, it sported only a cursory cross-guard; apparently, Sword Master Stanton preferred to rely on his skill to protect his hand.

Canis returned the salute and their match began. By the time their hour was over, Canis's back was screaming and his foot was throbbing.

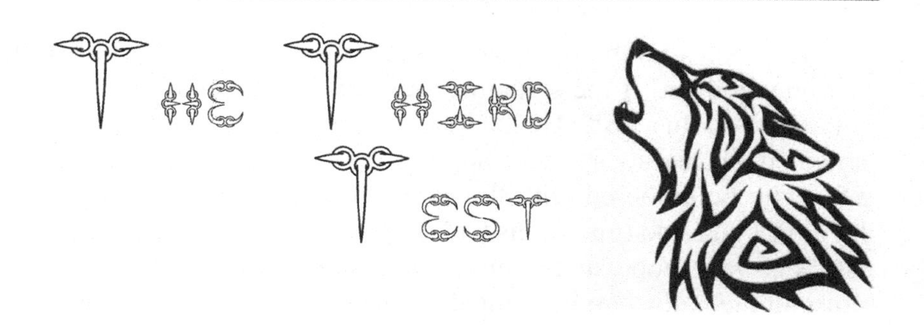

The Third Test

Canis was out of his casts and his bruises were gone in less than three weeks, but he didn't get his message until yet another two weeks had passed. Slipped under his door sometime during the night, was a folded and sealed parchment. He thanked his mother for teaching him how to read, though it was possible she had no idea. He read:

> *Agent Canis;*
>
> *Master Dagon has been kidnapped and is being held hostage somewhere within the school. You have six hours to find him and extricate him from the school to a carriage that will be waiting to remove you from the area. You must consider every hand within the school to be set against you.*
>
> *Lord Santos, King of Chicago.*

He knew that the message was simply the initiation of his test, but he wondered if the signature was real. Why would the king be interested in his test? He tucked the parchment inside his shirt, strapped on his sword, and donned his cloak. He wasn't exactly sure why he bothered with the cloak, but he liked the impulse, so he didn't take the time to discard it again. He left his boots behind. He was very good at hunting, and boots would make far more noise in the halls than he wanted to make.

Making use of a skill no one knew about, Canis ghosted through the halls of the school quickly. The students and their teachers all would expect him to search every room in order to find his quarry, but Canis had a much more efficient method.

Less than an hour after stepping out of his room, Canis was on the fourth and topmost floor of the school near the back. He expected Dagon would be difficult to find, but he didn't expect to follow his scent to such an odd location.

He peeked around every corner he came to, and here he discovered two students from his class standing outside a door at the far end of the hall. They stood at leisure on either side of the door talking with each other in low voices.

Dagon and Stanton were here too; to a degree it was all to be expected, but then he smelled *blood*. The smell of blood took away the limits of the contest and made the hunt real and very dangerous. Then there was the muffled sound of something hitting flesh and a stifled cry of pain from the direction where the two students stood guard. They only glanced at the closed door before continuing their quiet conversation.

Canis took no chances, he darted the length of the hall on silent feet, and launched himself at the feet of the closest student. The man went down loosely, rapping his head hard on the floor and lying still afterward. His momentum carried him into the feet of the second student, but the man had a moment to recover from his surprise. The moment wasn't good enough. Canis succeeded in pulling his feet out from under him anyway, and then Canis was on him in a heartbeat and had his fingers in his hair. With a sharp jerk that left several strands of the man's hair in his hands, Canis rapped his head against the floor and left him senseless beside his cohort.

Without rising, Canis tested the door. It was not locked; few of the doors in the school had locks. Taking care to make no further noise, he drew his sword for the first time and took a breath. This had to be a trap, and the noise of his skirmish couldn't have been avoided. His opponents within the room would be prepared for him to be short so he hugged the floor and flowed into the room like a snake.

The smell of blood and fear spoke of the inordinate danger in this room. The legs looming over him told him that his low entry had the desired effect. Like a snake, he struck, imbedding his single fang into the closest thigh. Dull though his sword was, it still had a point. His strike was rewarded with a roar.

Having never stopped moving, Canis flowed away from the downward cut that came after him, and the light from the window showed him a bright and sharp blade. If this was a test, it was deadly, and he was at an even greater disadvantage. He couldn't afford to duel even for a moment against a sharp blade, so with a very quick exchange, the sword was sent flying, accented by another roar when he buried the point of his blade deeply into the man's shoulder.

He pulled his blade out with a jumping backspin that carried his hand all the way around to drive the pommel of his sword into the man's temple, dropping him in a heap on the floor.

He landed and allowed himself to go the rest of the way down to crouch on the floor with one hand resting on the chest of…Stanton. One hand was ready to use his sword in whatever way might present itself, the other told him that Stanton was still alive, while his eyes took in the rest of the room before he moved. He scooped up Stanton's sword and used it to cut the ropes holding Dagon to a ladder-backed chair. He had struggled against the ropes and there was blood on his wrists and ankles, there was also blood on his face and dripping from a cut in his hair staining the gray and running down the side of his face to drip off his nose and chin. All the players were here, but this much blood and damage said that something much bigger than his test was going on here.

Canis lifted Dagon's chin to look in his face. He needed to know if he was well enough to walk. Though Dagon opened his eyes, he didn't seem able to hold his head up, so Canis silently thanked the man's mother for making him small and sheathed his sword. He looked at Stanton's sword and decided to launch it out the window. He wouldn't have a free hand to carry it and he couldn't leave it behind him. He stepped out into the hall to retrieve the weapons of the men out there and did the same with them. It wouldn't take them long to find their swords again. A glance would reveal the broken window and the swords would be easy to spot lying in the alley, but those same weapons would not be coming up behind him soon. He'd reach the carriage that was supposed to be waiting out front long before anyone else could make it down to the alley, and if it wasn't there, he'd be out of the building, and he could find a safe place to hide until Dagon was more alert.

He pulled Dagon over his shoulders, grunting – the man was heavier than he looked – then he made his way down the back stairs that led to the kitchens and the alley. He hurried through the slush of melting snow – regretting the tracks he was leaving behind – and around to the front of the school where he saw the carriage behind a matched team of white horses in shiny black trappings just pulling to a halt. Something was painted on the door too, but Canis didn't pay any attention to it.

He pulled the door open and eased Dagon onto the floor of the carriage. Hands from inside pulled him farther in and propped him up on a seat, while a voice from the carriage's depths said, "Get in."

Canis hesitated, but did as he was told. He was alarmed when the man who sat across from him knocked on the roof and the carriage began to move again. He would have jumped out, but because he could, he didn't. Then the man turned to Dagon who slumped beside him, tipping his chin up and getting a look at the blood-smeared face for the first time. He turned on Canis, furious. "What's the meaning of this? What did you do to him?"

The only answer Canis could give was to hand over the message he had received that morning. It was still morning. Little more than an hour had passed since he first read that message.

"This isn't the message I sent. That's not even my handwriting." He handed the message to the man sitting next to Canis who was keeping a cautious eye on Dagon in order to keep him in his seat.

Canis eyed the man across from him carefully. He was too thin in Canis's opinion. He looked to be worried about Dagon, but other than that, there was no way to determine what kind of connection there might have been between any of the three men in the carriage.

The man continued to study Dagon slumped beside him, then he turned back to Canis. "Answer me, what did you do to him?"

Canis couldn't answer, he wanted to, but he couldn't. He rested a hand on his throat and shook his head.

"Dagon told you about that, my lord," said the man who sat beside Canis.

"Oh yes, I remember now." He sat back with a sigh. "You will see to the investigation of this, Corbin," he said softly.

Canis reached forward and lifted one of Dagon's limp hands and pushed the sleeve up to show the two men the bloody rope burns. The lord who still had no name grimaced and growled. "Someone will pay for this."

Canis then drew a line from his right eye to his mouth.

"What are you trying to say?" said the man addressed as Lord.

Canis pointed at the different wounds on Dagon and then drew the line down his face again.

"I don't understand. Do you know what he's trying to say, Corbin?"

"Maybe Dagon will understand when he wakes up," said Corbin.

The carriage ride lasted a good fifteen minutes. Then they turned into a vast walled compound, and drove through the center of what would be a carefully manicured garden in a few months and up to the front of the largest building Canis had ever seen. This building dwarfed the school and the slave house combined.

Slaves in red enameled collars and dressed in red hose and white tunics, rushed out through the slush to meet the carriage and were sent scurrying again at the lord's command, to retrieve the healer with all possible speed. While they waited, Corbin spoke at length to a man who was also dressed in red and white, though it was a uniform with loose pants instead of hose. He had a long sword at his hip and a pike in his hand. Canis couldn't hear what was said, but when he was finished, that man also ran off.

They stood for a moment and watched Dagon on his way in the care of the healer who, in contrast to everyone else Canis had seen here so far, wore a plain brown dress and tied her long blond hair back with a white ribbon. Then Corbin rested a hand on Canis's shoulder and guided him in the wake of the lord. They strode through a door large enough to accept a carriage, and it ushered them into a stone monstrosity of a house.

Inside, the lord strode through a torrent of curtsying ladies and bowing gentlemen all dressed in fine and colorful clothes full of lace, shimmers and rustles. Scattered among those people were dozens of slaves all wearing red and white with shiny red collars. Another slave, this one had the added decoration of a red sash around his waist, glided up to the lord and presented him with a tray that held something in a cup. He took it without thought, then took a seat in an overlarge, ornately carved chair on a raised platform. As soon as he was settled with his cup, the crowd in the room resumed their swarm. The confusion was further magnified by more than one troop of entertainers.

Corbin had retained Canis at the door to the chamber and as the lord took his seat, he bent down and whispered in Canis's ear. "Do not touch your sword in that room or I may have to kill you."

Canis looked at the man in surprise, but his expression spoke only of seriousness, not malice. He turned back to the odd display in the room full of people.

The lord sat in the massive chair with his chin propped on a fist and his eyes to the side. He was ignoring the swarm of humanity in all their glittery clothing. He radiated fury and the people gave him a wide buffer of open space. At least most of them gave him space. Canis watched as one woman curtsied deeply in front of him. She was dressed in many folds of gem-encrusted red material that hugged her form to the waist and flowed out wide over her hips to eventually brush the floor like an upside-down rose.

She must have said something because the lord lifted his chin from his fist and looked at her. Her presence must have reminded him of the rest of the men and women in the room. Slaves were not to be noticed, they were to be there when needed and gone when they weren't, and the entertainment was little better.

The lord stood and looked over the heads of the crowd until he found Corbin and Canis standing outside of the room. The woman was still in her deep curtsy. Her legs had to be shaking by now. He waved his hand in a shooing motion. "Leave me. All of you; go," he said and resumed his seat.

The people all left by routes that apparently led deeper into the massive complex. The woman who had curtsied to him was the last to go and reluctant to do so even yet. It took another wave of the lord's hand to send her out of the room.

When everyone was gone, he nodded to Corbin who then guided Canis into the room. When they were two thirds of the way across the polished floor, Corbin halted them, bowed deeply, and then straightened again.

Canis watched this display without copying it. Slaves bowed to free men but he had never been able to bow to anyone. *Who was this man that even free men bowed to him?* He didn't look like the other slaves he had seen here. Canis turned his eyes back to the lord and steeled himself. *What will this man, who it seemed free men bowed to, do to me?*

The lord's expression was still dark, but he seemed not to notice Canis's lapse. Corbin *did* notice, and his hand on Canis's shoulder tried to press him into a bow.

Canis couldn't control his response to this any more than he could bow in the first place. He snarled softly, pulled out of Corbin's grip, and stepped out of his reach. He struggled to erase the action before it was too late, but what was done was done.

"What was that all about?" asked the lord as he rose and approached them. Corbin was glowering and his hand rested on the hilt of his sword. The lord walked right up to Canis and lifted his chin. Canis kept his hands carefully away from his sword and looked up into the face of the lord.

"Amazing eyes," said the lord. "I don't believe I have ever seen such a color in my life. And no fear, did you notice, Corbin. Will you not bow to your king?"

Canis's eyes widened with surprise. This man was the king. He had never seen a king before. He didn't understand what there was about him that made him a king. He wasn't entirely sure what a king was in the first place.

"You actually didn't know; I'm astonished." He released Canis's chin. "I'm your king, Lord Santos Chicago."

Canis rested a hand on his own chest and struggled with the only word he could say. "Canis." He did not bow; he didn't try.

"Do you still not bow? Even after…"

"Don't bother, Santos. As I understand it, his back is as stiff as a pike and he's far more dangerous than he looks."

Everyone turned to see who had spoken. Canis was pleased to see Dagon walking into the room. He had a bandage around his head and he carried himself tenderly, but he seemed well enough.

King Santos turned to Dagon. "What's the meaning of all this, Dagon. This wasn't supposed to be part of the plan." He waved his hand toward the bandage on Dagon's head.

"No, it wasn't." He swayed and a slave was there with a chair for him to sink into. Other chairs appeared as well and when Canis lagged in sitting, Dagon said, "Just sit, boy. I've no patience left."

Canis perched on the edge of one of the chairs and listened to what Dagon had to say.

"I told you of the plan, Santos. To see if this kid was skilled enough to enter my class, he was supposed to capture me and bring me out to you unharmed. Because of his size, I was prepared to allow him to succeed, if he showed sufficient skill. Instead, someone…" He gingerly touched the side of his head and winced at the memory of the blow. "Someone knocked me out. I woke in a small storeroom at the top of the school. Stanton ties a mean knot." He flexed his bandaged wrists and Santos glowered. "After my struggles were silenced again, the next thing I knew was waking up here. I remember some vague scenes, but nothing I can grab hold of."

"The boy carried you out across his shoulders," said Corbin. "He came from the alley. He must have brought you out of the building from the back door."

"I was almost ready to have him flogged until he gave me the message," said Santos. They missed that Canis suddenly went ridged and wary. Corbin produced the message and gave it to Dagon who read it and scowled.

"Well," said Dagon. "I need to return to the school and sort this all out. Stanton has much to answer for, I think." He rose from his chair and swayed slightly.

Corbin rose too and caught his elbow. "I'll come with you. An investigation is already underway. There should be something to report by the time we get there."

Dagon groaned and looked at the king. "You didn't."

"Brother, you were beaten and bound in your own school. I couldn't ignore that," said Santos.

Canis started in surprise. *They are brothers.* No wonder they were so familiar. *If the king and Dagon were brothers, what did that make Dagon?*

As they headed back to the school, Dagon said to Canis, "Since there were no witnesses, I must rely on your word; did you fight a clean fight?"

Dagon wasn't looking at him, but Canis knew who he was speaking to. He fingered the bloodstain on one of his cuffs and shook his head.

"The boy doesn't go overboard with his expressions, does he?" commented Corbin.

"No, he's very contained. It's the tinder for many small skirmishes outside of the classroom, and every one of them had to be sent to the infirmary. He even disarmed Leonard during the last test and I had to send him to the infirmary as well."

Canis didn't know Leonard had been hurt. He looked sharply at Dagon, but the man didn't seem to be angry about it.

"Leonard insisted that the fight was as clean as he could have wanted from one of his students, and to top it off, the boy had been injured by a fall before the actual fight."

"Why did you let him take the test if he was injured?" asked Corbin.

"He fell from the rope. Leonard saw that he had hurt his hand, but the boy pressed the attack anyway so Leonard went ahead with the test. It was only after his visit to the healer that we learned he had torn up a foot and wrenched his back on top of his wrist being broken."

"That's impressive," said Corbin as he looked down on Canis from his lofty height. "Are you going to pass him with this test, even though it turned out to be something other than a test?"

"I haven't decided yet. There were no witnesses, at least none whose word I'll listen to, and he said he didn't fight clean. I'll have to think on it."

"I don't quite understand this fixation you have taken in regard to a clean fight. There are many dirty tricks that can make fighting with a sword highly dangerous."

"There is, and I do my best to teach them all, but young Canis has two very different forms of fighting. He seems to be very good with what we are trying to teach him at the school. He's flexible and imaginative, but he has another method of fighting too, one I think he must have been born with. Until he is much older, I intend that he keep the two separate. He can combine them after he has learned whatever I can pour into him."

Corbin gazed at Canis again. "I find that hard to believe. He doesn't look old enough to be that feisty."

"Well that settles it then," said Dagon. "We'll let Corbin decide if you're good enough to pass your test. Mind you, he's the best swordsman I have ever seen besides myself, which is why he stands in my brother's shadow."

Canis looked up at the tall man while he fingered the bloody cuff of his shirt again.

Dagon chuckled softly. "I'll be sure and warn the healer to expect you both. I doubt either of you will be able to avoid drawing a little blood."

The school was swarming with soldiers by the time they arrived. All of the students were confined to their rooms while the rest of the school was searched. The scene of the crime was easily found by the amount of blood in the area and the broken window. A slight blood trail lead out the back door to disappear down the alley, but there was no telling who the blood belonged to and it was quickly lost in the street. None of the men Canis had fought could be found in the school, but their absence told their names. The rest of the instructors and upperclassmen were all questioned. They had all been aware of the testing that was to take place today, but none of them had known the plan. All of the students were released to go about their business, though their liberties were curtailed until Stanton could be found, or it was proven that he had left the city.

After peace had been restored to the halls of the school, Dagon took Canis and Corbin to an empty classroom. "Now then, Canis, make it a clean fight this time. Corbin, you might want to select a sword from the rack to preserve the edge on your own."

Corbin did as Dagon recommended, he wasn't willing to chip his blade if he didn't have to.

When they were ready, Dagon called, “Salute,” and when they had both done so, he said, “Begin.”

Corbin was obviously the better swordsman, but Canis stood toe to toe without fear and was learning Corbin’s forms as fast as he used them. He gave way only by sidestepping or fainting rather than by blatantly retreating. It took twenty minutes for Corbin to disarm him – much longer than he expected.

“Pass, pass I say,” declared Corbin. “This boy has more skill than I’ve seen in years. Did you see what he was doing? He was using my own forms against me and he only missed a few small details.”

“Yes, I saw,” said Dagon.

Canis retrieved his sword and returned to the center of the floor.

“Now Corbin, would you like a taste of the boy’s other style of fighting?” asked Dagon.

Corbin looked at Canis, who stood there at his ease. He could see that the boy wasn’t as ‘at ease’ as he looked. Another man might have missed that detail. “Sure, you call it.”

“Call it; how do you call a fight like this? Very well, get ready.”

Assuming that the other style of fighting Dagon spoke of was some form of wrestling, Corbin tossed the sword he had been using to slide over by the weapon’s rack and hunched over in a wrestler’s stance. Canis hadn’t moved a muscle. He hadn’t even sheathed his sword. After all, if he wasn’t fighting with his sword, what else was he doing?

“Begin,” said Dagon. He had no idea what to expect. Other than the very first exchange with Leonard, he had never seen Canis fight outside of the classroom. He had only seen the results. He was every bit as surprised as Corbin was.

Canis exploded into action. He flung his sword at Corbin forcing him to straighten from his crouch and dodge aside or be hit by it. Canis followed the sword just as quickly as it had flown. He flowed up Corbin’s frame and over his shoulder before the man could lay a hand on him, but Canis did not jump down his back. Canis snagged a hand under Corbin's chin in passing and planted his feet firmly in the small of Corbin's back using his weight to drag the taller man further off balance in an astonishing continuation of his original dodge. Long before the big man hit the floor, Canis swung his weight further around. By the time their bodies came to a stop, Corbin was sprawled on his face and Canis could either tear out Corbin's throat or break his neck before Corbin could do anything about it, and he knew it.

Unable to speak, Corbin slapped the floor with the flat of his hand and Dagon called, "Break," ending the fight. Canis released him and took several steps away to watch him warily.

Corbin picked himself up off the floor and looked at Canis rubbing his throat. "I never would have thought… I seem to recall you saying he was more dangerous than he looks. I believe you. If you don't pass him this test, you should go visit your healer and have your head examined. Then again, perhaps you should put him in a cage. I'm not sure I feel too comfortable knowing a child who is this dangerous is growing up in this city." As he spoke, he watched Canis go from merely wary to just short of hostile.

No one is going to put me in a cage again. Not ever.

Dagon called him. "Canis, run to my office and find me a parchment, quill and ink. Go on."

Canis sidled from the room, keeping Corbin in sight until he could put a solid door between them.

As he was returning with the writing things, Canis saw the tall man leaving the school, and then Dagon took Canis and the writing materials back to his office before sitting down to write on the paper. When he was finished, he offered the paper to Canis. "Take this to Master Devon, the armorer. Do you know him?" Canis nodded. "He'll measure you for a proper sword. You'll report to my class as a full student as soon as it's finished, until then your time is your own. Congratulations." But before he completely released the paper into Canis's grip, he said, "If I ever catch you throwing your sword away again, I'll thump you up side the head until you see stars. *Never* disarm yourself. I don't care how well you can fight with your hands; *never* throw away your sword."

Canis could only nod his tiny nod. *Corbin threw his sword away. He thought the fight was going to be without swords, but I needed him to stand up, I needed him to lift one foot off the floor. Taking him down would have been so much harder if he had kept his stance.*

Stanton stood in the center of the room. The only thing he wore was his silk small clothes and the bandages at his shoulder and around his thigh. Guards stood in every corner and he knew that, while the woman was in the room, if he so much as swayed, he would likely be meeting death.

The woman was small, she scarcely came up to his shoulder and her gem encrusted red dress clung in a manner that made him want to touch her. "You told me you would be able to ensure that this…this boy, did you say? would be blamed for my brother's death. Instead, this boy succeeded in getting Dagon away from you and out of the school *alive*. What went wrong?" She walked around and around him, slowly trailing a hand along his skin as she spoke, as if exploring the contours of his muscles. At her question, she allowed her hand to trail down and she punctuated her question with a sharp pinch on his thigh wound.

Stanton gasped and almost lost his balance. He was already unsteady from loss of blood and dizzy from the blow that swelled one eye nearly closed. "The boy showed up far sooner than we anticipated. He's surprisingly strong for someone his size, and apparently, he has a rather unorthodox form. I wasn't informed…"

The woman continued her slow orbit, trailing her hand over his body. She felt him trembling and wondered if it was all from weakness. "You told me that before, so what you're really telling me is that he took you by surprise. A *child* caught *you* by surprise. I caused you to be placed there because you were among the best in the arena. Are you growing lazy? Do you miss your collar? I remember a time when nothing caught you by surprise." She trailed her fingers down his face. "Well, almost nothing." She allowed her hand to drop to his shoulder and she squeezed it hard.

He gasped and dropped to his knees with the pain. The abrupt movement of his thigh muscles won an inarticulate cry, but he managed to remain straight under her hand. It took three full gasps before he could reply. "I am at your mercy, Mistress," he whispered. He didn't trust his voice any louder. Her hand still rested on his shoulder.

"I am glad you remember, slave, but you have failed me, and now Dagon knows you. At the very least, he and Santos will have the entire city searched in an attempt to find you and your two incompetent helpers. What am I going to do with you?"

Stanton hung his head. He still shook in the aftermath of the pain her fingers had caused. "Your wish is my command," he said to her slippered feet. He liked her feet.

"I suppose I could put all three of you into the arena. Dagon occasionally trains a slave to that end, but he doesn't like to watch his training spent there so he never attends. It's not likely he'll see you. Santos loves the arena, but he doesn't know your faces so he's not likely to recognize you." She combed her fingers through his hair, then gripped it hard and tipped his head back in order to look him in the eyes. "I could still find some use for you in the arena."

"As you wish, Mistress," said Stanton. The alternative could well be death and he so very much preferred to live.

She spoke to the room at large while still studying his eyes. "All possible connections between this slave and me must be erased. Take him to the dungeon and return him to his collar. Collar the other two as well. The others were free men. They will need to be educated to their new status and they may need to be silenced, but I don't want them to be scarred." She released Stanton's hair and trailed her fingernails up under his chin. "This one might need reminding too." She planted a firm and penetrating kiss on his mouth sending long missed charges through his body. He was moaning with inflamed desire long before she was finished. He was sobbing from denied desires by the time the guards had propelled him through the door.

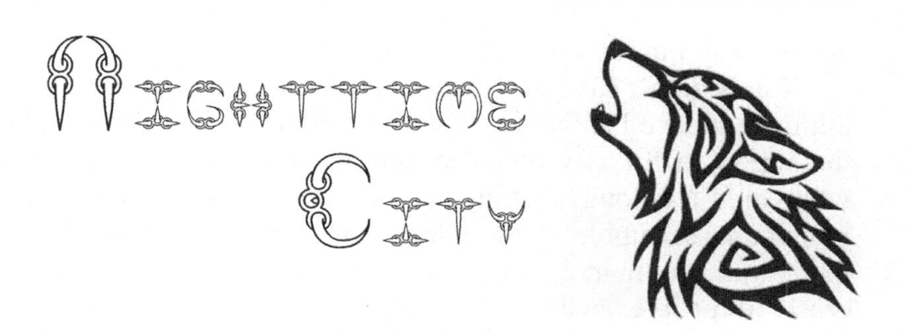

Nighttime City

By the time Patro returned in early spring, Canis could hold his own against his classmates with genuine skill with his sword, not crafty tricks and unpredictable moves, though a drawn out duel was still out of the question – there was no way he could match blunt muscle strength or endurance against an adult yet. There were still some gaps in his education, but they remained gaps for only moments. To fill in those gaps as fast as possible, Master Dagon insisted he still participate in the intermediate classes. He was only nine years old now (though Patro counted him somewhere around seven), and his classmates averaged twenty.

Patro was there and gone again so quickly, Canis didn't even learn of his visit until he was informed that he was paid up for another year, and another pouch of coins was handed to him. Canis wouldn't have allowed Patro to spend the money on him again, but he didn't have enough himself. What Patro gave him for spending money wouldn't even make a dent in the bill, and it was still Patro's money. A trip through the slave market that evening showed him that Patro had already left the city. *I will have to find another way.*

Eager to find a way to make some money, not only to pay Patro back but to continue his lessons, Canis took to roaming the city in the evenings. He knew Patro expected him to come back to the slave caravan where he would likely act as a guard while the caravan was in motion and to fight in the arena when they were in a city, but he now knew that he didn't want to travel with the slave wagons any longer.

Canis didn't have much luck in his quest, though. He was only a kid, and since he couldn't talk, he couldn't ask for work. Pacing the streets of the city revealed nothing that didn't involve taking what didn't belong to him, so he took to wandering into the mountains of rubble at the edge of the city. The quiet he found there was soothing; it was a relief to be away from the constant crush of people, even if for only an hour or two. Few people ventured very far into these ruins and fewer still came there at night. He took to hunting here too and sometimes he would take the time to roast his kill over a small fire.

He was turning a fat rabbit over his fire one night when a group of men stepped into the light. "What gives you the right to come into our territory and eat our game?" said one of the six rough-looking men who closed in on him out of the darkness.

Canis stood, and when the men saw that he was only a kid, they began to laugh. When Canis didn't react with a proper amount of fear, they moved in to teach him a lesson.

Canis carried his own sword. He had earned the right as soon as he passed the third test. The sword had been his reward, though dull blanks were what they still used in class. Like the sword Canis had used so far, the one he picked out from the smith was double-edged and slim, and per the recommendation of the smith, only a couple inches longer than his old one – still short when compared to other swords, but on him, it measured like a long sword.

The men weren't about to give him the opportunity to use it, but that didn't matter; by the time Canis was finished with them, he had a cut that scraped across his ribs and an arm that he couldn't lift above his shoulder, but all six of the men were incapacitated.

He looked at them. He was, after all just a kid. He picked up his rabbit and ate it as he headed back to the school where he woke up the healer to get his side mended.

The next evening, he was strolling down the Grand Market Street on his way to the ruins when a patrol approached him. "Hey, kid," said one of the constables.

Canis stopped at were he would have turned off the Grand Street and waited to see what they wanted.

"A couple guys were picked up this morning and they were pretty beat up. When we asked them who had done it, they said it was a kid with red hair and white eyes. There aren't too many people who match that description. Did you beat up those guys?" The question was asked with some amusement in their tone, but an answer was expected just the same.

Canis merely stood there and studied the three men for a moment, then with a slight nod, he turned to continue toward his destination.

The guards watched him pace down the lamplit street. "No way that kid beat anyone up," said one of the constables to his partners.

"Considering who they were, all I want to do is thank the guy, whoever he was," said another.

The summer's heat was at its peak when Canis started to run a low fever. He had only had one fever before, but that was from ill health, physical abuse, and a long dunking in a very cold river. Thinking it was just a product of the hot days, he refused to let it slow him down. As the fever climbed, Canis sought the cool night streets for relief. He took to roaming the dark city streets all night long, then driving himself during both the morning and afternoon classes.

One such night, Canis came across the same three constables he had met before. Five thugs had them badly cornered. When Canis came upon the fight, one of the constables was already on the ground and another had just been disarmed. When Canis came up behind the thugs, he caught their scent and knew them as the same men he had fought before.

Canis flowed into motion; he hamstrung the closest man, dropping him wailing in an ungainly heap to curl up on a leg that would no longer function. Then he raked his fingernails across the face of the next man he reached, causing him to reel backward screaming and clutching at his face. He reached for a new grip and hooked the man's throat, pulling him over backward and down with enough force to lay him out, senseless or dead, he didn't care. Without missing a beat, he stepped and spun; his blade reached out, slicing the tendons on the side of the next man's elbow before he could deal out a killing blow to the disarmed constable. Then, still spinning, he took two steps to the side and sliced upward, relieving the next man of his entire hand. The fifth man would have run from the swirling black ghost with glowing white eyes, but he tripped over one of his compatriots and fell head long, stunning himself in the process.

With all of the thugs down, screaming or silent, but out of the fight, Canis allowed himself a moment of weakness and sank to one knee for a breath or two, then he stood to face the constables.

One was bending over their injured friend. He looked up at the other one and said, "Go back to the station and bring a wagon. I'll tie these…things up so they can be hauled away when you get back." Then he turned to their benefactor. "Hey kid. Glad to see you. You don't look too good. Are you okay? Did you get hurt?"

Canis wiped his blade off on the shirt of the man lying closest, then started to shred that shirt to tie up its owner. Then he suddenly had to get away from the whole scene.

Several dark turns away, Canis was depositing his supper in the gutter. He knew it wasn't the fight or the blood, though he had heard of such reactions to killing. It was the fever, he was sure of it, it had happened before – once.

Shortly before dawn, when hunting produced nothing he was looking for, when frustration at not knowing *what* he was looking for grew too great to contain, he let out a howl, and then cringed as he heard the sound echo across the city. But as if now started, it filled a cavernous need, he howled again. It wasn't long before his throat, totally unaccustomed to making sounds, was painfully raw from the effort so he choked down more and headed back to the

The furry black Wulfen face was the first thing Canis saw when he opened his eyes, but he had been aware of her presence long before that. His fever-fed dreams evolved into a canine presence of his new companion. Visions of puppy play merged into hunting trips shared by both Wulfen and man. Then one day, a long absent man returned to the clan.

This Wulfen, Rrusharr, was too young to recognize the man, but she understood his belonging to the clan. His words had prompted her journey, a journey across grassy miles and wet rivers avoiding the sight of men.

Canis recognized the man in those thoughts. He was the man named Orion, the man who said he was his father and his words told of the existence of a son, and the fact that he had grown up…*alone*.

Canis didn't realize how *alone* he had been until now. He felt filled to bursting from it. He was afraid to open his eyes for fear that the glorious fullness would use the opening to drain away, leaving him empty again, emptier than before, so much emptier having felt this fullness.

Rrusharr felt Canis's fear and her soft humor rumbled through his mind.

Canis opened his eyes then and met the steady gaze of the dark gray eyes in the black face resting on his chest. He let out a sigh of relief when the fullness did not drain away.

Kendall heard the sigh and leaned closer. He wasn't willing to lean too close to the great black beast. “You’re awake. Are you feeling better?”

“Yes,” said Canis. Both he and Kendall were surprised by that single word. It was almost the first word Canis had ever uttered and it came so easily. Surprised too because it came out in a deep thrum, though it was lighter and younger-sounding than his father’s, but only Canis knew that.

Rrusharr rose and stepped down from the bed allowing Canis to sit up. He couldn’t remember the last time he had eaten. “I…am…hungry,” he said, speaking deliberately as if testing the sound of each word. “And my throat is…raw.”

“That’s not surprising,” said Kendall. “You shoulda heard yourself, and no one can remember the last time you were in the cafeteria for more than two or three glasses of water.” He brushed a hand across the sheets. “It looks like you sweated it all out. I’ll tell Master Dagon. I’m sure he’ll want to have this replaced.” He helped Canis dress under the critical gaze of the wolf, much to her amusement. “Come on; let’s go get you something to eat,” he said when they were finished. “The cooks are going to have a fit over your…pet, though.”

Dressing was exhausting, but he was too hungry to go back to bed. “She is not my pet. Her name is Rrusharr.” The name came out of the back of his throat as more of a growl, but it was almost a word. “She is my…my other half,” said Canis.

“You really don’t think the cooks are going to care about that, do you? That voice, coming out of you, is going to take some getting used to,” said Kendall.

“The alternative would be for her to roam the halls hungry,” said Canis, though Rrusharr had generated the comment; she enjoyed the reaction. She found these lowland humans rather amusing, sometimes.

When they reached the top of the stairs, Canis leaned against the wall. Just the short walk from his room to the head of the stairs drained him of what little energy he had.

Kendall took most of Canis’s weight as they headed down the

stairs.

Leonard met them at the door. "What are you doing? We could have brought something up. I see it's still here."

"I think it…she…is here to stay," said Kendall.

"Really, the cooks are going to love this," said Leonard. "I gotta see this." He accompanied them back into the cafeteria.

The four of them created quite a scene. Fortunately, there were few students left in the cafeteria to see it.

When the cooks were informed of the hungry wolf, they didn't react quite like Leonard and Kendall expected. As it turned out, there were always leftovers or bones to dispose of and they were tired of the number of rats the discarded food attracted out back along with the rest of the trash generated by the school. Their biggest concern was that Master Dagon wouldn't allow the wolf to stay.

Mention of that concerned Canis too. He wanted to stay. He wanted to learn what Dagon had to teach, but if Rrusharr wasn't to be allowed to remain, then he would leave too. There was no question of that – not any more.

As he worked his way through his breakfast, Canis thought about drumming up the energy to make his way to Dagon's apartment and bring the issue directly to him first, but he was saved the trip when the man came looking for him. Obviously, someone had already informed him that Canis had come down to eat and he'd come to see for himself.

"I can't allow pets in here," said Dagon as soon as he entered the room and saw the wolf gnawing on a meaty ham bone next to Canis's chair.

Both Canis and Rrusharr looked up at him when he said that, then Canis stood to face him. "I will pack my things right away," he said.

"What? Where are you going?" he said, then… "What did you say?"

"Master Dagon," said Canis in the soft rumble that was his new voice, "please allow me to introduce Rrusharr, she is my other half. Where she goes, I go. If she is not welcome here, we will leave."

"You can talk. I thought you couldn't talk," said Dagon.

"Until Rrusharr came to me, I could not," said Canis. He reached up, almost touching his temple and closed his eyes for a moment as if the memory was still painful – it was. "There was an…emptiness in my head that made it impossible."

"Really," said Dagon. He looked down at the black wolf still lying on the floor with a bone propped up between her front legs, staring at him with unblinking eyes. He looked back at Canis, then around at Kendall and Leonard, then back at the wolf. "That's a wolf."

"Yes," said Canis. Rrusharr's amusement was tickling at the back of his mind again, though she was less than happy with the reference to being called a wolf.

"Wolves are dangerous."

"Yes," repeated Canis. "Rrusharr has no intention of hunting in your territory."

That wasn't exactly how Dagon would have worded his concern, but it was close enough. "Well…" He looked around again. "We'll try it and see how it works out. I don't want you to leave." He glanced down at the wolf before looking at Canis again. "Sit down before you fall, better yet, go back to bed. I expect to see you in class again as soon as you're able." Frowning, he turned and left the room.

Canis sank back into his chair gratefully and Rrusharr returned her attention to the bone she had been working on. People were strange.

"Oh, Master Dagon…" called Kendall and he sprinted after him.

"Do you want me to help you back to your room?" asked Leonard.

"No, go to your class. I will be fine," said Canis.

"Are you sure?"

"Yes. Go," replied Canis.

After he had gone, Canis sat at the table until Rrusharr was satisfied that nothing more could be worked off of her bone, then he made his way back to his room. Before he was half way up the stairs, he wished he had taken Leonard up on his offer, but he made it.

When he entered his room, he found two of the house slaves inside. He leaned against the wall until they were finished making his bed. As he watched them work, he was reminded of Gem. He wondered how she was doing. Perhaps he would try to find her someday.

When they left, carrying his old mattress with them, he threw himself onto the new mattress without bothering with the covers. It was too warm and he was too tired to drag the blankets over to his corner.

He slept most of the next two days, during which time he and Rrusharr seemed to meld even tighter into a single entity. It felt as though their bones and muscles were meshing into a single body. Canis quickly discovered that he would not only know Rrusharr's thoughts, but he would also feel what she felt, even something as simple as her movements. He found that out when he felt her step down from the bed then he woke again when he felt her gleefully hunting fat rats among the trash in the back alley.

He made his way to class four days later and Rrusharr of course came with him. It was an interesting development, but it worked out well enough, and it didn't take long for every one to get used to the dark shadow that waited patiently, watching from an equally dark corner.

After a few more days to catch up more on spent energy, Canis and Rrusharr took to leaving shortly after the afternoon class. First, they went for an exciting hunt among the piles of rubble. Then they spent the rest of the evening roaming the streets. He still wanted to make enough money to pay Patro back for all he had done.

One thing he did was look up the three constables. With Rrusharr's help, he found them quickly on his fourth evening.

"Hey, kid, we haven't seen you for a while," said one of them. "Is that a wolf? I don't think I've ever seen a black one."

"I am glad to see you are well," said Canis, trying to make his low voice less of a rumble, ignoring the reference to Rrusharr.

"If it weren't for you, none of us would be well," said another one of the constables. He too eyed the black shadow at Canis's side.

"I wish to earn some money. Could you tell me how I might be able to do this?" asked Canis.

"Make some money?" said one of the men. "You're just a kid. That could be difficult. I know first hand how good you are, but you're just not very big. All the jobs I can think of involve heavy lifting or a long term commitment."

"I am accustomed to hard work, but I wish to finish taking lessons at Master Dagon's school and I have a debt to repay," said Canis.

"You go to *that* school," said another one of them. "I should have known. How else could you be so good? You must have been born with a sword in your hand. I didn't think he let kids into his class without passing some tests."

"I did not have a sword in my hand until I came here," said Canis. "And I have passed his tests."

"I have an idea," offered one of the men. "It's risky, though. There's the fight club on the north end of the city almost every night."

"The fight club? The kid could get killed there," said another man.

"I can see that. I was meaning for him to do some betting is all," said the first man.

"What is this place?" asked Canis.

"It's like a cock fight only it's men who fight, and they fight dirty. Stay away from that place, kid," said another of the men. "Dead bodies are always being found around there and they're not always fighters. The king doesn't sanction it anyway."

"What is this betting you speak of?" asked Canis.

"You pick the man you think will win the fight and you bet some money on him. If he wins, you get the money bet on the other guy," said the constable who came up with the idea.

"*I do not think you should try that,*" said Rrusharr. "*We are still too young to match against elders even in this.*"

"What about the arena?" asked Canis.

"Yeah," said one of the men. "You could probably do better there. The fights are more fair, the slaves who fight in the arena are more carefully matched, and it's harder to bet."

"Slaves fight in the arena?"

"Yeah, only slaves. It's for the king's entertainment. He doesn't like free men to kill each other for sport."

That was not pleasing news to Canis. *Patro had plans for me to fight in the arena, but if only slaves fight there, then Patro still thinks of me as his slave. Was all of this a trick?* "I need to make four hundred gold pieces by next summer."

"Four hundred gold pieces; that's a lot of money," said one of the men in disbelief. He eyed the wolf that had seemed to go very still, though she hadn't been very mobile before.

"Yes," said Canis. He wanted to pay Patro back for the last two years he had already paid for. He also wanted to pay for his lessons coming up and the next year's lessons himself. Only when he had no debt to Slave Master Patro would he feel truly free. Then again, he wondered about Dagon. *Surely, he was aware that only slaves fight in the arena. Why then was he training me to that end?*

"Listen kid, I'm sure we'll find something you can do to earn some money, but four hundred gold is a lot. We'll do what we can to drum something up for you, though. We all probably owe you our lives. We owe it to you to do what we can."

"Sure thing, kid, we'll find something for you," said another.

Canis nodded and turned away. He could ask no more from these men, but he had learned something here tonight. He would need to be on his guard now. No one would put chains on him again. Never again would someone lay a slave whip across his back. Never again would he look out at the world from behind bars.

Rrusharr's soft agreement hummed through his mind as they disappeared into the dark alley.

The Blessing

The constables came through for Canis about a month later. There was an influential merchant in the city. There were many actually, but influential people have enemies and this merchant had a daughter. Apparently, someone had kidnapped his daughter and the constables couldn't find her or her kidnappers. They thought of Canis, or more accurately, they thought of Rrusharr, though they didn't know her name.

The three of them came to the school and asked for Canis. When he came out of the class to meet them, one of them said, "We might have a job for you. Master Hale's daughter has been kidnapped and we are having some trouble finding her. We thought you might be able to help. Would you come with us to speak with him?"

"Yes," said Canis and he left with them without even a glance over his shoulder at Leonard who watched him from the classroom. He didn't tell anyone where he was going. He was responsible for himself. He was a free man.

The merchant's house might have been smaller than the school, but it was grander by a long stretch. The inside was polished and gleamed with both silver and gold gilding. The many tall windows let in the sunlight through their sheer silk curtains.

One of the constables introduced him. "Master Hale, this is Canis, he's...pretty talented. We think it might be worth your money to hire him to find your daughter."

"Why would I want to hire a *boy*? Are you telling me you are giving up on my daughter?" said Hale incredulously.

"Sir, we don't have any leads," said another of the men.

Canis stepped forward. "Sir, I do not ask for pay if I am not successful. You will pay me only if I can bring her back to you."

"Is that so? And just how much money do you expect me to pay you, boy?" asked Hale insolently.

"What is your daughter worth to you?" asked Canis.

Rrusharr moved closer. She didn't like this man.

Neither did Canis, but if he paid, he would find the man's daughter for him.

"What? What is *that* doing in my house?" cried Hale in alarm.

"This is Rrusharr. She will help me find your daughter, but if you are not interested, then we will be on our way." Canis turned and started to leave, but one of the constables snagged his arm.

"Master Hale, reconsider. There has been no ransom demand," he said. "We don't even know if she's still alive."

Canis cast a sharp glance at the man holding his arm.

Hale gave way. "Very well. I will pay you one piece of gold if you can find my daughter and return her to me."

Canis turned his eyes of ice back to the merchant. "I would think your daughter is worth more to you than one gold coin, but since I am young, I will accept your offer. May I see her room?" said Canis.

From the contents of her room and her clothes Canis could tell that the girl was only a small child. Smelling her pillow gave him a scent, but the room as a whole struck him as rather odd. As he wandered through the house in search of how she had been removed, he could find no other sign of her presence. He did, however, locate the window where she had been taken from the house and he followed.

The trail vanished soon after reaching the street, but that didn't deter Canis. He was on the hunt and he was good at hunting.

Canis methodically combed the city and found the girl on the evening of the fourth day of his search. He also found that she was not a prisoner here. The fact that her scent and her mother's scent spoke of mother and daughter told him that she had every right to be here.

What was he to do? Both the girl and her mother were better off where they were, but if he didn't return the girl to her father, he wouldn't get paid and if he gave up his first hunt, it wasn't likely he would get another. He knocked at the door.

When the woman opened the door, Canis said, "Ma'am, I was hired by Master Hale to find and retrieve his daughter. I have found her, but now I have a problem. Your daughter belongs here, but if I do not take her back I will not get paid, and I need to make some money to pay back a debt."

The woman was surprised to see such a young boy at her door, especially with the announcement he gave her, but she could tell that he'd not lied. The fact that he laid his entire dilemma at her feet was another surprise. "Hale hired you? I wonder why. I'm surprised he didn't have the guards combing the streets for us."

"He did. How many I am not sure. They could not find you, so friends of mine thought of me, or perhaps they thought my companion might be able to do what they could not."

Rrusharr stepped into the light from the door and the woman took a step back in alarm.

"We are not a danger to your family, and I will not force your daughter to go with me, but perhaps you should consider, that if I could find you, Master Hale might be able to find someone else who can find you too."

"It is my greatest fear." She stood aside, clearing the door. "Come in, it's late. Supper is nearly ready and we can talk about this."

As she set about finishing supper and setting it on the table, she did some thinking. In the end, she came up with a workable solution to his dilemma. "Here is what you can do; return Dora to her father, get his gold, then take her again when you leave. If you can do that, I would give you four gold pieces. It's all I have of my own gold. I simply couldn't dip into my new husband's gold for something like this. It wouldn't be right."

Canis gazed at the anxious woman while the girl, Dora, caressed Rrusharr's silky whiskers, which sent shivers across Canis's shoulders causing Rrusharr to chuckle softly in his mind at his discomfiture. He heaved a big sigh. "We will try it," said Canis.

Dora looked at him with wide, very blue eyes. "I don't want to go back there," she said.

"I do not want to take you back there, but I was hired to find you and I have," said Canis. "I have also accepted the contract to return you back here, so I will do that too, if you will trust me to do so."

"Oh…well…okay," said Dora in a small voice.

Before she would allow them to leave, Dora's mother invited him to pray to the Mother with her and her daughter for his success. He followed them to a small room and gazed at the little white statue in its center. "What is this?" he asked.

The woman stepped up beside him. "This is our shrine to the Mother. Have you never seen one?"

"No." He had never heard of a shrine and she had said *the* mother, not *a* mother, or even *her* mother. "Who is this Mother?"

The woman gestured a graceful hand toward the small statue. "She is the Mother. She is the Mother of everything, every plant, every animal; She brings the heat in the summer and the cold in the winter. Everything around us is woven into Her tapestry."

Canis looked at the woman beside him and felt a shiver run down his spine. "Why is she here in your house?"

The woman smiled, she saw fear flash briefly across his eyes. "She is here to remind us that She watches over us all the time. We keep a shrine here so we can worship Her whenever we feel the need. Many houses have a shrine much like this one in it."

Canis looked back at the small statue. "You use words I have never heard before. I find it difficult to understand what you are saying." He studied the statue a little longer. "This is not the only…?" He waved his hand at the statue and included the tiny room in the motion.

The woman touched his elbow and led the way into the room. Worshiping the Mother is a very private thing and it comes from the heart. If you have never done so before, perhaps you would simply like to get to know Her first. Make yourself comfortable." She indicated the small rug spread on the floor in front of the statue. There was no other furniture in the small room. "Take as long as you want."

"What do I do?" asked Canis.

"Whatever is in your heart," said the woman. "By the way, my name is Loren. Find me when you are satisfied and I will get Dora ready for you." She left him and Rrusharr in the room and quietly closed the door.

Canis looked at the now closed door; there was no latch on it. He had never seen a door without a latch. This one had only a simple knob in the center of the panel. He turned back to the statue. Its detail fascinated him. He knelt down on the rug and felt Rrusharr settle down by the door.

As he studied the quiet face, he felt a soothing calm come over him and he bowed his head. He thought he might have slept. He hadn't done much of that since he started his search for the girl. He thought he might be dreaming when he saw Dagon and several of his students searching the city and knew they were searching for him. He saw Dagon meet up with the three constables who had led him to this job. *What were they saying?*

His view swooped in on them as if he were a bird.

One of the constables was speaking. "Yes, he came to us looking for work. He wanted to earn some money. We thought he could help us in locating a kidnapped girl since he has that wolf with him. We haven't seen him since he took the job."

"What girl was kidnapped?" asked Dagon.

"Master Hale's daughter. We had already exhausted everything we could think of. Canis was our last hope, he had that…wolf."

"I didn't know Hale had a daughter. I've been to his house

many times. He sells good quality weapons and I've never seen a child of any age around there. I don't even remember him having a wife."

"We saw her room, sir."

"Listen, you got the boy into this, you find him and bring him back; do you hear me. If you don't, I may have to take this to the king."

"Yes sir," said the constable.

When Dagon and his companions left to continue their search, one of the constables turned to another and said, "Have you ever heard of Dagon taking such an interest in one of his students?"

"Never, he always turns them loose for us to try and control. We've locked up plenty of his students and he never came looking for them. I wonder what makes this one so special?"

Canis didn't hear the response. He opened his eyes to look up at the statue again. "I owe Master Patro my life, but not all of it. Does he think to keep me as his slave and fight me in the arena? If you are the Mother of us all, help me to find my path. Help me to do right, but I will not return to the collar." He glanced toward the darkening window so he took up the flint and lit the candle that rested on the pedestal of the statue.

In the flickering light of the candle, he thought he could detect movement in the statue. Then again, perhaps it was just another dream. The tiny hand reached out and she touched her thumb between his eyebrows. "Your stand is solid and your arm is strong. I give you my blessing," she whispered in a voice that was clear like a crystal. "You will find your people. You will take them what they need. You are the bridge."

When Canis reached a hand up to feel where she had touched his face, he felt something hard between his eyebrows. When he prodded it with his fingernail, he found it to be quite solid. Not like a scab on his skin, more like a piece of bone protruding through it, though there was no pain when he touched it, nor was there any blood.

He stood and looked at his reflection in the dark glass of the window made into a rude mirror by the light of the candle and the darkness outside. When he pushed his hair out of the way, he saw, between his eyebrows, a white stone. At least it looked like a stone. Though it was white, he'd seen bone before and it definitely wasn't bone. It was about the size of a fingerprint, and he touched the glass in the dew of his breath to compare. It didn't protrude very far, and it looked have some glitter in the center, though this light was too poor for detail. Looking at his reflection, reminded him of his father and he turned his head to the side. Maybe his nose was a little long, but then maybe it was only his age. His profile didn't look any different from anyone else's.

He went and faced the candlelit statue again. "What have you given me?"

The candlelit face only held a soft smile that spoke of tenderness and love. A thing he had seen before, from time to time, long ago, when his mother had the time.

He sank back down to the rug and bowed his head low, a move he hadn't been capable of until this moment. The next thing he knew was a gentle hand on his shoulder scarcely a second after Rrusharr's soft thought told him that the hand belonged to Loren.

"I didn't expect that you would be here so long. You must have been tired." She gasped. "Oh my. What is that?"

For a moment, Canis forgot what he had seen in the dark window, and then he noticed that the window wasn't dark anymore; it was morning. He stood quickly. "We should go." Then he saw where her eyes were looking and reached up to touch the stone again. *In hadn't been a dream. Not that part anyway.* He wondered if any of the rest of it had been. "She said She gave me Her blessing. She called me a bridge. What does that mean?"

"It means you are blessed by the Mother. I have never seen such a gift, it's beautiful."

"But I do not understand."

"It means she watches over you."

With a flair of anger, Canis said, "Men have sought to be my master. Does She do so too? If so, then I do not want this blessing."

The Mother is not a master," said Loren. "She is simply the Mother, and She has directed Her attention toward you." She studied the dark expression on Canis's face. "It's a good thing. Trust me, it is."

Canis wasn't too good at trust. Trust had always come back to bite him, but he didn't see much choice, the stone was there, imbedded solidly into his skull. He would see where it led him. "We should go."

"Would you consider breakfasting with us before you go?" asked Loren. "My husband has returned. He would like to meet you."

Canis was about to decline, but a less than gentle reminder from his middle betrayed the fact that they had spent the last four days hunting something they wouldn't be eating, and last night's supper hadn't been enough to make up for it.

Loren smiled. "I think you better join us."

Canis followed her out of the shrine and into the kitchen where the rest of her family was gathered.

Loren's husband looked at him critically. "You're a bit young to be doing this kind of work, aren't you?"

"So many people have told me," replied Canis. "I need to raise a good deal of money and work is scarce for me."

"Why do you need to raise so much money?" asked the man.

"I wish to return the money Master Patro paid to Master Dagon for my lessons in the sword. Then I thought to continue the lessons with Master Dagon by paying for them myself, but I have learned something that may cause me to reconsider that plan."

"Master Patro – isn't he a slave trader?" asked Loren.

"He is." Canis dug into the food on his plate while leftovers were found for Rrusharr just as she was beginning to picture the rats in the alley behind the school.

The man ran his hand down his face as if by doing so he could wipe away the troubles before him. "I run a caravan around to the closer settlements and farmers. I make three different trips during the summer that take about two months each. I can't pay you much, but you can come work for me."

Canis studied the man for a while. He wondered if he could actually afford an employee, or if he even needed one. "I may consider your offer one day, but I feel I must repay my debts before I leave the city. Otherwise, Master Patro may think I am running away from him. I do not wish to bring my troubles down on you."

The man merely raised an eyebrow and finished his meal. When he rose from the table, he kissed Dora on the top of her curly head then gave his wife a peck on the cheek before leaving to go to work.

Canis and Dora left shortly after, leaving Loren to wait at home alone.

No Good Deed

Canis hired a carriage to take them across town and the driver wanted extra for Rrusharr to ride along. Canis merely shrugged. “She can run along side.” Rrusharr even perked up at the idea.

“No, no. Can’t have no wolf spookin’ my team. Just get it in, but you pay extra if it claws up the seats.”

“Fair enough,” said Canis, and he lifted Dora in.

When they reached Hale’s house, he told the man to wait for them, then left Rrusharr there to make sure he actually did.

“Stay close to me,” he said to Dora just before he knocked on the door.

When they were ushered into Hale’s presence, he said, “Well, it took you long enough. Go to your room, girl.”

Dora reached out and took a hold of Canis’s tunic.

“I have brought you your daughter. You owe me for the job,” said Canis.

“I spoke to Dagon. I don’t owe you anything. In fact, I think I’ll turn you in and collect the reward he put on your head.”

All the alarms went off in Canis’s mind and he felt Rrusharr go on the alert as well. “If you will not pay me, then I am under no obligation to return your daughter to you,” he said, his voice coming out in a low growl. He turned to leave and found his way blocked by three of Hale’s personal guards. Dora let out tiny whimper of fear. “You are making a mistake,” he growled at them, but they didn’t heed him. He hadn’t really expected them to.

He drew his sword and faced the guards. "Stay *very* close to me, Dora," he whispered and he gripped the material at her shoulder to hold her well within his reach.

Two of the men opened their mouths to laugh at such a small boy standing up against them, but that was the only opening Canis needed. He knew he didn't have the strength to stand toe to toe against them, not all three of them at once, so he used their distraction and overconfidence to dart between them, creating further confusion by sliding his blade along the thigh of one of the men as he ran past. Since the cut went to the bone, the man would likely be lame for life unless Hale had a very good healer. The confusion and screams of the wounded man bought him enough time to get Dora and himself back into the carriage.

The driver wasn't happy about driving a getaway vehicle, but he had all he could do to maintain control of his team as Rrusharr ensured they moved out at a good clip.

A few blocks from Hale's house, Canis had Rrusharr bring the horses to a stop, then he paid the driver for his time and risk, and sent him on his way.

When the carriage was out of sight, Canis headed off through the alleys. The circuitous route he chose took them all day, and allowed Canis to keep a close eye on their back trail, he eventually brought them back to the house of Dora's mother well after dark.

At the door, Dora was engulfed in the arms of her mother. His job totally botched but finished, Canis left to return to the school and possibly another conflict.

"Wait," called Loren. She ran after him. "You forgot your payment."

"No," said Canis without stopping his stride. "I did not forget. Keep your money."

"But you really should take something."

"No. I did very little except place your daughter in danger. I will not take payment for that."

"We all knew it could be risky, but you protected her and you brought her home. You did what you agreed to do. You should get paid for that. Besides, if you never take pay, how will you ever be able to pay off your debts?"

Canis stopped and faced her. "I may not be able to do that now."

"Yes you will. You have the blessing of the Mother. You will accomplish great deeds." She pressed a pouch into his hand. "You are welcome in our house any time and for any reason." She gave him a brief hug then went back into the house.

Canis wasn't prepared for the hug and wasn't given the opportunity to return it. All he could do was look after her retreating back until she was back inside of the house.

He spent the rest of the night roaming the ruins trying to decide how to approach Dagon.

It was afternoon when Canis returned to the school. First, he went into the cafeteria to see if there were any leftovers from lunch, then after putting away two large sandwiches, he went in search of Master Dagon and found him in his classroom. He slipped into the class without attracting much attention; at least not until Dagon reached his position in the line.

"You will remain after class," said Dagon, the only thing he said to him, then he continued the class as if there had been no interruption.

After class, Kendall and Leonard hung around. "Hey kid, where have you been?" said Kendall.

"Save it for later," said Dagon and waved them out of the room.

With a look that said, 'You're in trouble now,' they left.

As soon as the door was closed, Dagon started in on Canis. "How dare you disappear like that? Where were you?"

"I took a job. I was doing what I was hired to do."

"And what was that? You're not old enough to take a job."

"You already know what I was doing, but I will tell you why. I am trying to make enough money to pay Patro back."

"Pay him back, for what?" said Dagon as he paced back and

forth in front of Canis.

"Pay him back for these classes. When do you think I will be ready for the arena? Perhaps I could pay him back with winnings from there."

"You're good, boy, but not good enough for the arena. The…the fighters in there would chew you up and spit you out in the first fight."

So, he really did *know what he had been doing. What he had seen was true, not a dream.* "Why did you hesitate in calling them fighters? Why did you not go ahead and call them slaves. If only slaves are allowed to fight in the arena, how is it I am being trained for that?"

Dagon looked at him hard. "Where did you learn that?"

"It does not matter. So, it is true. Patro still considers me a slave, and you do too. A slave can have no money and therefore could not possibly owe a debt or get paid for a job. Tell Patro for me that I am *not* a slave and that I *will* repay him his two hundred gold pieces, but I will no longer remain here. You will never see me again, because if you do, then I must believe you are hunting me; it would be a mistake to hunt me." He turned to leave the room. When he reached the door, he turned back. "Thank you for what you have taught me."

He went to his room and assembled his belongings. Watching the door, Rrusharr informed him of the approach of Leonard and Kendall.

"Are you going somewhere?" said Kendall.

"I must leave," said Canis.

"Why? You're paid up until next spring, aren't you?" said Leonard.

Canis turned to face them. "What did you pay for your lessons here?"

Kendall and Leonard looked at each other. "Ten gold pieces," said Kendall, and Leonard nodded.

"Why would someone pay Dagon a hundred gold pieces for those same lessons?" asked Canis.

Both of them gasped then their mouths settled into a silent 'O' before they looked away.

"That is why I must leave."

"But...if...it's true...you *can't* leave," said Leonard, and Kendall looked at him, frowning.

"Put it into words. If *what* is true?" said Canis.

"Everyone knows that Dagon sometimes trains slaves to fight with a sword," said Leonard. "I suppose it's to improve their chances in the arena. The extra money would probably be for security reasons. If you're a slave, then you have to stay for as long as your master wants."

"I do not *have* a master because I am *not* a slave. Slave Master Patro picked me up off the streets when I was...I do not know how old I was...little. He had me in chains until I nearly went crazy. He removed them and I eventually recovered...mostly." The memory brought back the feeling he'd had no outlet for at the time and he shuddered. "He will never put me in chains again."

He finished tying his clothes into a bundle with his money pouch securely in the middle. "He was robbed once. They got away with thousands of gold pieces. I recovered it, then he brought me here. At first, I thought he wanted me to become good enough to be one of his guards on the caravan. Then he mentioned the arena so I figured I would fight when we were here in order to bring glory to his name. I would have done all of that, gladly. He was good to me, mostly. He was fair. But if he considers me his slave, then I will do none of it for him. I will find work and I will repay his losses, but I will *not* be his slave. I will not be *anyone's* slave." He slung his bundle across his shoulder and headed for the door. A twinge between his eyebrows caused him to look up at Leonard quickly and he saw the expression on his face. "Do not try to stop me, Leonard. We are friends. I do not want to mar that."

"I can't let you go," said Leonard.

Canis scarcely let him finish his sentence. With only a bit of a leap, he gripped Leonard's throat and carried him to the floor where he stayed quite still, then he faced Kendall.

Kendall shook his head. "We were hired to guard you, to keep track of you, but I wasn't sure why, until now. I thought you must be some rich man's son or something, maybe even some relation to the king, the way Dagon acted. I've never believed in slavery and no one in my family owns one. I'm not going to turn a friend of mine into one. Be careful. Perhaps you should leave the city for a while. You might be able to find work on a farm."

Canis nodded and went on past him leaving him to see to Leonard.

He turned to go down the stairs, but he knew that Dagon wouldn't allow him to just stroll out the front door.

"*Follow me,*" said Rrusharr and she showed him the way to the back alley that didn't involve complicated doors.

Several blocks away, Canis stopped. "What do I do now? Where do I go?" He felt so lost and adrift.

"*You should go to the mountains. You belong with the clan,*" said Rrusharr.

I do not know the way. I have never been there. I know that my mother was north of here when I last saw her, but Orion, said he had found her dead. I belong nowhere."

"*Let me take you to the clan. You belong there.*"

"How can you say that? I have never been there."

"*The clan is in your blood. I know this is true. I could not have found you otherwise. We need a place to hide for a while. We need time to grow up. We need time for slavers to forget about you. Only then can we do what you need to do. Only then can we work for the yellow metal and pay back man-Patro.*"

Canis saw the sense in Rrusharr's words, but he zeroed in on one thing. "*We* need to grow up? I thought you were already grown up. How old are you?"

"*I was born on the same day as you were. I too am only a half grown pup.*"

"Really, well I guess that shows you what I know about wolves," said Canis, but as soon as the word was uttered he felt the insult and hurt it caused.

"*I am no common wolf. I am Wulfen. You have much to learn.*"

"I am sorry; I guess I do. Lead the way."

Rrusharr did just that. She soon found a place where they could hide until dark. Moving only at night, it took them two days to clear the city without being seen by anyone, not an easy task, since people wandered the streets at all hours and those who wandered the streets at night were the more unsavory kind.

Running Away

Canis knew that the high roads were the most heavily traveled, so once they had cleared the city, they stuck to the back roads and game trails. They ate better with more room to hunt, but Canis needed more than game meat so they searched out small farms along their route where, for a few hours work, he could earn a meal and a night under a roof. Most of the time it was the barn roof, but there was usually plenty of hay and Rrusharr was there to keep him warm.

Canis knew nothing about farm life. Of course he didn't; his life had either been in hiding, with the slave caravan or in the school. With the slave caravan, he had gathered wood for their fire, but on these farms, he learned how to split much larger sections of trees with an ax.

After his first stint at the splitting block, he figured Dagon should incorporate the task into his training session. If his students could lift their arms after an hour swinging an ax, then they were ready to swing a sword.

He also learned how to harvest. He dug potatoes and picked beans or peas. He learned how to swing a scythe and bind stocks of grain to stand and dry. He also learned how to pick corn and berries of all sorts. He worked hard and counted himself lucky to learn it all.

And just as Loren had said, almost every house had some kind of small shrine to the Mother. They were all different; some were little more than a tiny niche in the wall or a marked off corner in the house, others were in a room all to themselves. Some houses were too small and didn't have room inside for a shrine. Those farmers built a small stall outside the door. The one thing that was the same in all of them was the small statue. It might vary in size or pose, even the sculptor's skills varied, but it was obvious that it was the same 'person'.

Canis took advantage of these shrines; he liked the feeling he had after sitting for a few minutes at Her feet. There was never another event remotely like at Loren's house, but it didn't matter.

He traveled for eight days in this manner before he encountered his first major obstacle. He knew there were rivers out here, but he hadn't thought on how he might cross them. It was Rrusharr who found the harbor town where he could buy passage across. When he was on the other side, he stood to watch the bargeman make his way back across. "How did you get across before? I cannot see you giving that man any money for a ride," he asked Rrusharr.

"*I swam*," said Rrusharr matter-of-factly. "*There are other rivers to cross*."

At that news, Canis figured he'd have to stick closer to the high roads.

Three days later, he approached a farm that looked strangely quiet, though it was obvious that the place had been lived in. The fields were recently harvested and groomed in preparation for the next planting and the kitchen garden was carefully tended, there were even late flowers blooming in a small patch by the front door. Rrusharr allowed a soft growl to mark her position while she voiced her worries in a more familiar way. "*Something is very wrong here.*"

Canis felt it too. "Look around. We may have to leave, but I would like to understand this, if possible."

"*I remind you, we are pups.*"

"I remember," said Canis. "I will be careful." He looked into the barn first where he found two empty stalls, though it was obvious they had been used recently. In the house, he found things in scattered disorder quite out of character from the rest of the place. Rrusharr also reported finding no one in or around the outbuildings, though scents were only a day or so old.

In the corner of the small house was another shrine so Canis knelt down. "What happened here?" he asked, wondering if he would find an answer in this manner.

A vision rocked him back on his heels. Four men came to the house. The man was beaten senseless and dragged out into the yard. The woman was raped here on the hearth, and then she was taken out to lie beside her husband where she was raped again and yet again by each of the men until she stopped screaming. The children weren't exempt from their attention, but Canis couldn't stand any more. He pulled himself away from the shrine, and its vision of horror, to go back outside.

"We have to find them…if only to bury them," said Canis as he sucked at the crisp fall air.

"*I thought you might say something like that,*" said Rrusharr. "*Follow me; I found a trail.*"

Canis stashed his belongings under the roots of a tree not far from the house, and then with his sword in his hand, followed Rrusharr down a trail anyone could have followed. They had made no attempt to hide their passage. Obviously, they didn't expect anyone to come looking for them.

It was near dawn before he found their camp. A careful circle around the edge confirmed that this was the party he had been following. The camp was a dump. The oxen were still hitched to the wagon and it didn't look like they had even been watered let alone fed. Gear was unloaded only enough to make camp and things in the way were dumped aside haphazardly.

Canis ghosted into the camp taking advantage of every shadow with Rrusharr only a darker shadow among shadows. He circled each of the three things that passed for tents. The scent of unwashed bodies was strongest in the first one he passed and he would have to save the one in the middle for last. Inside the third tent, he found the two children. Both of them were so traumatized that they didn't even move when he untied them.

The boy looked to be about the same age as he had been when Patro captured him. The girl looked to be about a little older, but she was small. She was such a little girl; her age didn't matter. He took the children out of the tent and led them off into the brush.

"*There is movement,*" said Rrusharr.

"Come," whispered Canis.

When Rrusharr showed up, Canis had her watch the children while he went back for their parents. He hoped he would be getting both of them.

He watched the camp from the shadows as it woke up. The fact that the children were missing wouldn't be discovered for a while yet. The four men set about starting their day.

While the men were out front, Canis slipped in through the back of first tent. Inside he found the much-abused woman, but she was still alive. When he untied her, he asked, "Where is your husband?"

"I don't know," she whimpered. She was too abused to grieve yet. She opened her mouth to say more, but could only gasp for air as tears flooded.

"Can you walk?"

"I…I'll try." She shook so bad she could scarcely stand.

Canis hurriedly pulled her out of the tent and hastened her away from the camp as fast as she could move. When they were comfortably out of earshot from the camp, Canis stopped and sat the woman down at the root of a tree. "Remain here. Do not stray from this place no matter what. I will return for you."

The woman snagged Canis's arm. "My children," her eyes echoed her dread.

"They are safe. Stay here. Do you understand?"

"*The cubs wander,*" said Rrusharr.

"Can you bring them here?" said Canis.

The woman looked at him oddly. "Bring what here?"

Canis held up his hand for her silence while he listened for Rrusharr's reply. "*Rrrr, perhaps.*" There was a distinct growl in her voice.

"If you cannot get them to come here then keep them together, I will find you."

The woman stood up and brushed Canis's hair back from his forehead. "I thought so. She watches over you."

Canis shook his hair out of her grip. "Stay here. Rrusharr may be able to guide your children here. She will not be able to find you if you move." That wasn't true, but he didn't want her to wander back into the camp.

"*Tell her not to fear me.*"

Using the only word he knew that she would understand, he said, "Rrusharr is a wolf. Do not fear her. She will watch over all of you. Stay here."

The woman sat down again as she looked around for the creature her savior was speaking of. The remains of her clothes were in shreds and she was still shaking so Canis shed his cloak and handed it to her. It was too small, but it was far better than what she had.

He went back to the camp in search of her husband. He slipped into the tent he had taken the woman from; he hoped to be able to reach the center-most tent from here. The children's absence had just been discovered and one of the men was yelling for the others to look for them.

One man burst into the tent where Canis hid. In his haste, he didn't notice the extra shadow in the dark. Canis snatched him by the neck and propelled him into the floor where he lay senseless. When the man didn't reemerge, another man, the loudmouth, came in to see what was holding him up.

Canis was about to treat him the same way as the first man, but his throwing aside the tent flap revealed his cohort sprawled on the floor and put him on the alert, and he was a step out of reach. Though Canis only gave him a second, it was enough for the man to draw his knife. Moving faster than most men taken by surprise, the man succeeded in burying his knife in unseen flesh, but it didn't save his life.

Wounded, Canis couldn't afford to be lenient. He pulled the knife from his thigh and used it to slice the throat of the man who planted it there, and then he made short work of the other man as well, then he slipped out of the tent again and moved to the back of the last tent.

This tent had an occupant, but he wasn't moving. The smell of blood and fear was strong, but it didn't tell if he still lived. Canis didn't have the time to look any closer, not until he took care of the last two men in the camp.

He sidled around toward the front of the tent in time to see one of the remaining men go into the tent he had just vacated in search of his comrades. He was too far away to silence his alarm and waiting was draining his energy.

In the back of his mind he felt Rrusharr guide the children to their mother; she was lending them her body heat. Canis was wishing for some of that heat as a chill shook him.

The man came out of the tent screaming about the dead men and the missing woman. Canis met him less than three steps from the tent with a leap and a cut that lifted his head clean away from his shoulders. The last man saw him and took off running. Canis tried to follow, but his wounded leg was leaden and he couldn't match the pace.

Rrusharr knew this; she also knew that three of the four men who threatened them all were dead and her charges were safe, so she ran around the camp and met the last of the bandits from the side. His throat was torn out before either of them hit the ground.

Canis went back into the last tent. The man bound to the ridgepole didn't move; he looked dead, or very close to it. As he cut his bonds, he asked, "Mister, can you move?"

At the different touch and very different voice, the man stirred. "Who are you?"

"I have come to find you. If you can get into the wagon, I will go get your family and you can head for home."

The man struggled to rise, muttering, “My family? Home?”

Canis used the ridgepole to pull himself to his feet, and then he pulled at the man to get him moving as well.

Half way across the camp, the man was moving on his own so Canis went to locate the others and bring them in too. He carried the little girl who gripped his neck with all the strength in her small arms. Her tiny voice came from a point close to his neck. “You smell different,” she said.

Canis was having trouble now that the adrenaline was washing out of his bloodstream, but he had to chuckle when both he and Rrusharr voiced almost the same thing at almost the same time in response to the little girl’s words. “Only because I need a bath.”

“*You need a bath.*”

Bleary eyed, Canis made it less than half way across the camp toward the wagon when his leg failed him. He dropped to his knees and one hand hard in an attempt to protect the little girl from harm.

Her cries to her mother went through him with little understanding. Even Rrusharr’s concern was only a buzz. He felt someone bind something around his leg before blackness took him completely.

The woman and her husband lifted him into the wagon and took him back to the farm with them. After they got him into the house, the farmer went out to tend his oxen. They were anxious to be back in their comfortable stalls where there was food and water. He pulled the harness off and left it where it dropped; his battered body refused to let him do more.

The woman made Canis as comfortable as she could, then she turned to her children. She didn't know what to do for any of them, but when she saw the children curled up on the cold hearth with the big black wolf, she let them be. She couldn't think of anything better than home and security and right now, that great big black wolf was security for them, for all of them.

After building a fire in the fireplace, she turned back to the young man who had brought them out of that hell and horror. It took some doing, but she managed to pull his sword belt free and get his pants off him so she could get a clear look at his wound. It was in the back of his leg and he had lost a lot of blood from it. She bound it up with a clean rag and covered him warmly.

When her husband came in, she started to do much the same for him, but he gently gripped her by the shoulders and looked her directly in the eyes. "Kellee, you know you can do better. I've seen it. Do it now. Heal yourself first, and then help the children. That should be the easiest. Then you deal with the boy and me. I'll heat up some soup for us."

"But Davis, I don't know how…"

"You know well enough, and we can't send for anyone. It's too far and none of us are in any shape to try," said Davis.

She nodded; she was terrified that this terrible burden was resting on her shoulders. Sure, she had fixed one of the oxen when it had been snake-bit and couldn't walk, but her own family; how could she do that? She went to the shrine for a moment to ask for strength then she did as her husband said. She healed the deep bruising ache in her body then went to the sleeping children. She rested her hands on their curly heads and tried her best to erase the damage and its pain in their small bodies.

Kellee's efforts were rewarded when they shifted in their sleep and loosened from their coil. She then accepted the bowl of soup from her husband and drank it thankfully, then she helped him out of his grimy, blood stained clothes. With gentle fingers, she brushed away many of the bruises and bound his broken ribs, then she helped him into the big bed beside the sleeping boy so he too could sleep.

With her family sleeping, she rested a hand on Canis's forehead only to find, to her dismay, that he had developed a fever. She rolled him onto his side again and unwound the bandage she had placed there not so long ago. The wound had swollen since she had wrapped it and the bandage was now far too tight. When the bindings were off, the wound seeped a sickly fluid laced with blood. The blade might have been poisoned or perhaps just dirty. "Oh, Mother, how do I do this? This is not bruises or aches."

Canis rolled over onto his back and searched for the voice.

She reached up and brushed the heavy copper strands from his eyes and in the process, brushed across the stone she had noticed before. When she touched it, he opened his eyes a slit. She caught up his reaching hand and held it to her cheek. "I don't know what to do," she said more to herself than to the boy in front of her.

"Trust…trust yourself," whispered Canis and he closed his eyes again.

She could see no choice. This boy had risked his life to save them for no reason. If he were to die because of it…well, it would be just wrong, very wrong. Not for the first time she regretted that her parents hadn't been able to send her to the healer's school. "The midwife would be so much better at this kind of thing," she said to herself.

"The question you need to ask yourself, Kellee, is, did Sara become good because she went to the healer's school or because she kept trying?" said the comforting voice of her husband.

With a sigh, she laid her hand on Canis's leg and concentrated. He moaned and pulled away, but her husband's strong hand held him still. She worked until she was exhausted, then she wrapped a thick cloth around the leg and covered him again.

She turned and put a few more logs on the fire, then found a nest in her husband's favorite chair to curl up in. When she woke again, she saw her son sitting alone on the hearth next to the massive wolf, devouring a bowl of cold soup. She didn't have far to look to find her daughter, though. She had crawled into bed next to the boy who had saved them. The top of her curly blond head was all that was visible on his shoulder, though he hadn't moved.

Kellee helped her husband out of bed, over the boy; he was too stiff and sore to climb out himself, then she set the last of the soup in front of him while she started breakfast. When it was almost ready, she lifted her daughter out of bed and set her at the table to eat.

After breakfast, she shooed the children outside with their father to help him with the chores, then she turned to their guest. While he moaned and struggled weakly, she worked to pull more of the infection from the wound, and then she turned to the chaos that was her house and began to put it back in order.

The battle went like that. Every morning she found her daughter curled up with him. On the third night she woke when he let out a soft grunt. Her daughter had crawled into bed with him again and apparently, she had bumped his leg.

"What are you doing here?" he whispered to her.

"I have bad dreams," said the tiny girl. It came near to breaking her mother's heart to hear those words knowing there was nothing she could do about it.

Canis let the girl pull the blanket over them and his fingers combed through her pale curls. "No more bad dreams," he whispered. "No more bad dreams." He drifted back to sleep again.

The next morning, his fever gone, he succeeded in sitting up and eating a meal. He recovered quickly and was soon limping around after the farmer, helping him do some of the things his son wasn't strong enough to do. He also went and dug up his belongings so the clothes he had on could be washed and mended; there were none in the house that would fit him. They even hitched up the wagon again and made several trips back to the bandits' camp to retrieve belongings left behind.

A week later, Canis announced, "It is time for me to move on. Winter is as good as here. Soon it will lock up the mountains completely and I will not be able to penetrate them."

"You should wait," said Davis. He pointed out the window at the first few flakes of snow.

"I have waited too long. I wanted to be in the mountains *before* winter," said Canis as he rose from the table.

"Can't you at least wait until the storm stops?" asked Kellee.

Canis looked out the window while dismay gripped his heart. "No, I cannot."

"We thought you might say something of the sort," said Davis. He nodded to his wife and she retrieved a bundle and handed it to him.

When he unfolded it, he discovered a heavy coat and some tall boots lined with wool.

"They're old things of mine," said Davis. "I'm afraid they'll be big for you, but you need more than what you have this time of year. I don't know if you're going to make it all the way into the mountains, it's a long way, but we wish you good luck, and be careful."

Canis was sad to be leaving this family, but he had to go. He couldn't stay here; he was hunted, and those who hunted him would come down on this kind family very hard if he was found here. "Thank you for these gifts and for your generosity. I will remember it."

"No, it is we who must thank you," said Kellee. "If it weren't for you, it's quite likely we would be dead and the children sold into slavery, if they would be so lucky." She folded Canis into a warm hug. "And thank you for giving me strength."

Canis was surprised at those words. "I did nothing."

"You told me to trust myself. Because of that, I was able to help you heal."

"I do not remember saying anything," said Canis. "But you are a skilled healer."

Kellee blushed at the compliment, but had to protest. "I have taken no lessons; I am not so skilled."

Canis looked at her puzzled. "You do not need to take lessons to learn something that is in your soul." Then he turned to assemble his belongings. He was confused. *Where did those words come from? What did I know about what was in her soul? Who am I to speak of trust, me, who can afford to trust no one?*

Davis came up then, with another gift. "Here, wrap your things in this. It's oiled and it will keep everything dry. It's big enough for you to wrap yourself up in at night so you can sleep dry even when it snows."

"My thanks, truly," said Canis. "I never would have thought of such a thing."

"You don't strike me as a city boy," commented Davis.

"I have led a sheltered life," said Canis and left it at that. These people did not need to understand his life.

Just before he was to walk out the door, the little girl, Lisa, tugged on his coat. "What do I do when I have bad dreams again?"

Canis knelt down in front of her. "You tell the bad dream to go away or you will tell me." He ruffled her feather soft curls then touched the stone on his forehead. "I will know."

Lisa's face lit up. "Okay," she said and threw her arms around his neck. "I will never forget you," she said into his neck.

Canis set her in her mother's arms and left the Freeport house for the snowfall outside. It felt like an abrupt departure, but there was no helping it. If he stayed there any longer, he might be convinced to stay for the rest of the winter. He wiped the wetness from his face and trudged off down the road. Long before he elected to stay at another farm, he was thankful for the gifts the Freeports had given him.

Canis ran into another big river six days after leaving the Freeport family and it was another entire day before he found a town where he could buy passage across. His stash of money was growing thin.

Four days after the crossing, he stopped at another farm. All of the last five days had been in a wet, wind-driven snowstorm that was just short of rain. He had bypassed three other places, but they had looked little better than deserted and he hadn't wanted to impose himself upon them.

The farm where he finally did stop was also poor, and the man who owned it was reluctant to take in a boy this late in the year, not to mention his overgrown dog that looked far more threatening than it seemed. Canis was about to move on when the man, who never named himself, offered him a night or two if he would clean out the barn. In the end, Canis remained for another two days while he repaired the barn's roof. He'd had a difficult time finding a dry place to sleep at night and he knew that the rest of the animals inside were having the same problem.

By the time he left, his things were dry again. It was a full six days before he saw another sign of human life. He had reached another wide river and he was forced to buy another crossing. So far, no one had questioned that he traveled alone at such a young age and no one had done more than glance twice at Rrusharr, to assess her weight and the fare to charge accordingly.

Into Winter's Teeth

The road west vanished completely before the end of the second day after leaving the last crossing town, but that didn't stop Canis. The foothills were in sight on the far horizon.

Six days later, he came across a north-south high road. Its elevation allowed it to be scrubbed free of snow. If he were where he thought he was, this road could lead directly to where his mother had lived – where he had first crossed paths with Master Patro. He was not prepared to cross paths with him again in the near future, but with snow sticking on the ground even during the warmest part of the day, he wasn't too concerned. Master Patro would be far south this time of year.

At the point where he crossed the high road, there was another high road heading directly west. Without a matching route coming from the east, and having never been repaired, it was impossible for wheeled traffic to use, so no fresh trails went that way, but Canis took it anyway as a welcome alternative to trekking through more of the tall snow-packed grass. Four days later, it vanished completely, but Canis relished the opportunity to have three dry camps along its path.

Twelve days of traveling through untracked grassland and two blizzards later, Canis found his way to another reminder of Master Patro. Misery City was blanketed under a foot of snow and nothing was moving on the river except the water and the occasional chunk of ice.

After being completely unsuccessful at buying passage across the river at any price, Canis took the plunge and swam across. He was carried far downriver before he was able to pull himself out on the opposite bank, and if it weren't for Rrusharr, he would have drowned in the river or frozen to death on the other side.

He took two days to warm up and dry out again, and then Canis headed northwest up the big river and into the long-looked-for foothills, but ten days later, his enthusiasm was running out. Traveling across the plains had its problems – mostly finding a way across the massive rivers that crossed his chosen path – but now that he was in the foothills, he was running into canyons, and they and the weather were presenting a different problem.

The snow was rapidly becoming too deep, but Canis kept plowing on. He left the big river to follow a smaller one leading farther into the mountains, but it disappeared under the snow after seven days so he forged on with only a distant peak to lead him.

Two and a half weeks later, he crossed another riverbed, but the season was late enough that it was very shallow. Thanks to the tall boots his long-ago benefactor had given him, he didn't get his feet wet in crossing it, but afterward the terrain and the now thigh-deep snow started to give him trouble again and he found his path pushed farther north than he intended, but perhaps it was for the best. He considered himself lucky to find an abandoned cabin to shelter in so far from any other sign of habitation. From this point, he tried every day to penetrate deeper into the foothills, but as if winter had held off as long as it could, it descended on him like it was making up for lost time. Just when he thought he might be able to make real progress, more snow would fall and he would be back to struggling for his next meal.

As the winter wore on, hunting became even more difficult. Game either burrowed under the snow and seldom came to the surface or migrated out of the hills entirely in search of graze under less snow. Even collecting dry firewood was becoming almost impossible as the level of snow crept over the lower dead branches of the bigger trees.

If he allowed himself to think about it, he regretted coming this far this late in the year, but what did he know, so he didn't allow himself to think about it much. He would have made no different decisions and he couldn't turn back now. He kept fighting, one day at a time.

As the weather grew colder, there was somewhat less snowfall. By now, Canis had discovered that walking on cut branches kept him on top of the snow, so he brought some green branches back to the house and figured out a way to weave them into large pads that he could tie to his feet with strips of leather.

After many trials and failures, he developed something that worked well enough. With that, he and Rrusharr agreed to move on. If they stayed much longer, hunger or cold would take them, it was only a matter of which they would succumb to first.

With the large pads on his feet, their pace was only limited by how far Rrusharr could go, so she set the pace and picked the route. She had come out of these mountains, so she was the one to lead them back.

As they crawled their way into the mountains, winding around the higher peaks, Canis and Rrusharr hunted rabbits, squirrels, and lemmings for food. Both of them lost all of the little fat that remained on their bodies, becoming lean and tough.

Canis had always hated doing much with his hair other than combing it. He had learned to like that feeling and he took the time to comb his hair every day, morning and night; it served to remind him of Gem, he treasured his memory of her. His hair had grown well past his shoulders by now and the hair she had kept cut away from his eyes now reached past his chin and he kept it shoved behind his ears.

As the weather grew colder and dryer, he had stopped binding his hair back since it was thick enough to act as a hat fairly well most of the time, but when the temperature started to stay far below freezing, he wanted something more.

Canis started to keep the pelts from their small kills and made rudimentary mittens and a hat that covered his ears. He had no idea how to make them soft, but they worked well enough and he managed to accumulate enough new ones to be able to replace what gave out.

Every day he would stuff snow into his water jug until it wouldn't hold any more and sling it on his back under his coat. It was heavy and bulky, but he carried little else. He wore all of his clothes all the time these days so the only thing he worried about carrying was his oilcloth and his blanket wrapped around his money pouch. The sword at his hip was almost a forgotten item, except when he needed to chop branches from trees for firewood.

The next thing he experimented with was making a bow with a few arrows. He had a hard time finding a straight piece of wood that would bend, but he eventually settled on a sapling, or at least the top of one, which was almost six feet long. Then he pealed and sharpened a few straight sticks to serve as arrows. With a bow, even a crude one, hunting became a little easier, making it possible for them to cover more distance during a day.

As he penetrated deeper into the mountains, the snow under his feet seemed to be not so deep or perhaps it was more compacted since it was still plenty deep enough. The trees grew farther apart and much bigger than anything he had ever seen on the plains. He found one once that was hollow, though it was still green. The hollow core was large enough to crawl into and when he found his way down to the roots, he had a chamber large enough for both him and Rrusharr. Hunting was good in the area so they stayed there for three days while his things dried out and they caught up on sleep.

Canis lost all track of time and distance, in fact, he almost forgot what his goal was in the constant battle for food and warmth, so he was unprepared when they encountered a hunting party of three men and six Wulfen. He stared at them from hiding for several minutes while they gutted and quartered a moose, loading the sections into one of the sleds they had with them.

They were dressed in some kind of bleached leather with a bulky coat with a furry hood. If they chose to do so, they could lie still on the snow and they would be difficult to pick out until they moved. And the Wulfen with them were positively huge. They all stood waist high to the man who watched over the others while they worked. For the first time, Canis understood why Rrusharr kept telling him that *they* were still pups. She was little better than half their size, huge in her own right, but compared to these adults, she was very obviously young.

It was Rrusharr who recognized these men. Canis and Rrusharr had been lying behind a snow-covered log watching them. Suddenly with a glow of happiness, Rrusharr sat up as bold as can be and howled a greeting, at the same time informing Canis of family.

At the sound, the men went on the alert instantly and looked prepared to defend their kill with all their might, which was considerable.

Canis could understand the feeling. Having spent months living on the edge of starvation, he too would have defended that kill with his life. In fact, he might have considered taking that kill if there had been less of them. He envied the hunting party's strength and skill in being able to bring down one of the massive monsters he had only been able to watch. He couldn't bring himself to try for one. If he could find and catch it after he wounded it, he would be forced to waste most of the kill. He wouldn't have been able to take the meat with him nor stay by the kill. The meat would have frozen too hard to eat within a few hours anyway.

With their hiding place compromised, Canis took his stand beside Rrusharr and watched while one of the men, accompanied by three of the Wulfen, cautiously approached them. As soon as he was within shouting distance he called out, "Who are you?" The voice was a deep thrum and carried far over the cold snow.

"I am Canis and this is Rrusharr. I am looking for Orion,"

replied Canis in a voice that was raw from long silence.

"Rrusharr? Orion said she must have left to go find you. I am Ursa. Come. You must be hungry."

The last thing Orion had said to him was that his name was known in these mountains. Well, if it got him a meal, Canis would be very happy with that right now.

He accompanied Ursa back to the rest of the hunting party, noticing as they walked, that his profile was like Orion's. He stood for the round of introductions. Aside from Ursa, there was Aries and Cetus. With them was a whole series of throaty names that sounded all too much alike to keep separate on the first try. He did, however catch that one of them was an older sibling of Rrusharr's, but he didn't catch which one it was and none of them looked much like her.

When the men started to load the meat and hide onto their sleds, Canis bent to lend a hand, then, as soon as they were ready, he took up a rope and leaned into the load. It wasn't long before he was relieved of his burden, though the man named Aries chuckled when he did it. "Keep that up and you'll get strong soon enough. For now, let's us just get this home before the next storm sets in."

Canis felt bad about not being able to help in some way, but in contrast, he was relieved not to have to pull the heavy sled. He was having enough trouble walking in the men's large footprints. Their stride was much longer than his and their snowshoes were narrower, so the trail was narrower than one his snowshoes would have made. He kept tripping over his own feet.

After tripping for the third time, Canis stepped out of the trail and walked with the Wulfen. Some of them walked in front and others followed behind, but most of them ranged to one side or the other and kept watch in case the hunting party was followed. The smell of a fresh kill was a strong attractant to scavengers, not to mention larger hunters.

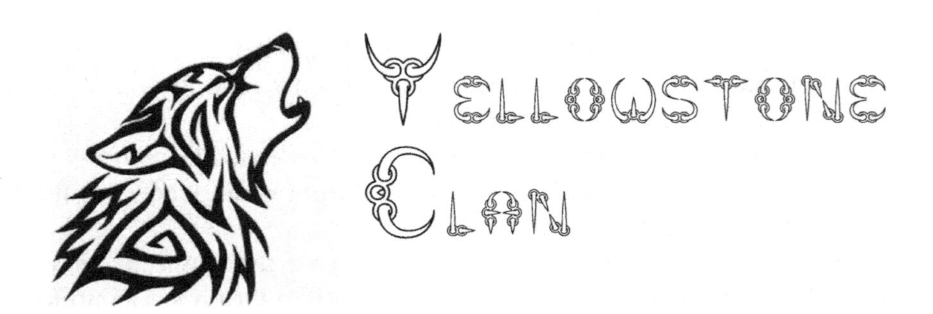

Yellowstone Clan

When they reached the village two days later, Canis was amazed at the sight. It was a large stockade, built of heavy poles set upright side by side, leaving only small slits between where irregularities in the log didn't allow for them to sit closer. The layout was roughly circular and around the inside were the homes of the people who lived here. Those too were made of logs, though these were laid out horizontally and stacked, their corners interlocking. These logs were chinked thickly with a combination of fur, clay, and moss. The roofs of the two story homes provided a sentry walk around the wall and Canis could see a long-faced youth up there doing just that. The central yard had been left in the grip of a huge amount of snow and ice that had accumulated there, but the flat roofs that extended far out over the doors, and likely a good deal of labor, ensured there was ample room to walk around in front of the homes.

News that a stranger was with an incoming hunting party, spread through the village quickly, so several women and children were there to greet them at the gate, with them was the rest of the pack of giant Wulfen and pups. Canis had no trouble picking out those showing gray with age and some of the youngest were barely able to hold their fat tummies off the ground. All of them eyed the newcomer with open curiosity.

Aries turned to a half grown boy among the crowd. "Go bring Orion."

"He is not well today," said a woman who carried an infant

wrapped in a soft pelt. Canis noticed that the woman had a far less prominent face. Apparently, the protruding profile was obvious only in the men.

"Well then, we'll just have to bring his surprise to him," said Aries.

"And what surprise is that?" asked the woman as she eyed the stranger in their midst.

"This," replied Aries as he rested a hand on Canis's shoulder, "is his son, come all the way from the plains. He's only about a year late."

The woman looked at him critically. "Hmm, might be her son, but he doesn't look like one of us. Where is Rrusharr?"

At the mention of her name, Rrusharr shouldered her way through the crowd of people and wolves to stand at Canis's side.

Only marginally satisfied, the woman waved him away with a curt "Take him" and turned to another man who took up the lead on one of the sleds and they headed off in the other direction.

Aries watched her go with obvious admiration in his eyes as he handed his snowshoes and weapons to the half-grown boy he had spoken to before. "She's my wife, Andromeda."

Canis looked up at the big man and watched him watch her retreating back. "She lives with another man."

"Yes, but she will warm my furs tonight."

Canis was surprised by this small revelation, though he knew little of man and woman relations. Most of the women in his life had been pleasure slaves. Otherwise, he had always assumed that it was a pairing of one man and one woman. That's all that he had ever found in any of the homes he had entered. Then again, he had to admit that he had entered few homes. Perhaps that other man was a brother. Perhaps they didn't 'pair' the way he was thinking.

When she disappeared around the curve of the mound of snow dominating the center of the stockade, Aries turned in the other direction. "Come on, I'll show you where your father lives. He still stays in the house of your mother." He began to lead the way around the stockade.

"I thought my mother ran away," said Canis.

"She did. She didn't like clan life. I suppose she tried; she took your father as her mate, but she still left, and after she was pregnant too. It was a foolish thing for her to do. I don't understand it. We found her as a half-grown child wandering the mountains alone. She grew up here, but still, she left one day when Orion was out hunting. He immediately left to search for her. He was gone for eight years before he found her, but it was too late, she was dead and you were gone. He was gone from here for so long; we thought he was surely dead. Since Rrewarr's death, he has not been strong. It is hard to be alone."

"Is there no chance another companion will come to him?" asked Canis.

"There is still a slim chance, but he has been here for more than a year and he doesn't call. I suppose it's hard; he has been alone for more than three years. The chances grow slimmer as time passes. Perhaps you can bring him back to life enough to attract the attention of another companion."

As Aries talked, they passed four houses and another gate before coming to a stop before the first door after the gate. When there was no response to his scratches, he pounded on it with his fist.

This noise won a wordless growl from a point over their heads, so Aries led the way into the house and up a set of wide steps located against the back wall. Canis propped his snowshoes and bow in the corner, and hung his quiver of arrows on a hook by the door and followed him.

The second floor was a collection of half walls and curtains, but Aries found his way through the maze to where an old man lay amongst a mound of dirty furs.

If it weren't for the ratty pelt the man still wore, Canis wouldn't have recognized him as the same man he released from the carnival over a year ago. He looked to have aged twenty years since then.

Orion pulled himself up to sit in the middle of his nest and looked closer at who was intruding into his space. He stared for a long time at the shock of red hair before he made his eyes move down to take in the face beneath it. There was no mistaking who was standing beside Aries. The coat he wore was too big and he still had his bedroll slung over his shoulder, but it was… "Canis?" he said in a raspy voice, firing up a rough bout of coughing.

"Yes. I came." Canis didn't mention that he was here to hide out from the slaver, Patro. He didn't think his sordid history would matter to the man much. He doubted that the institution of slavery penetrated very far into these mountains. In fact, he had seen very little of it outside of the city.

"Ah, you can talk now. Rrusharr found you. I hoped she would." Another fit of rasping coughs shook him and he wilted back to the furs.

Canis was appalled at what he saw, but Aries led him away. Down on the main floor, Aries stopped him. "As Stephanie's son, you have a right to stay here. Take care of your father. He was a great hunter…once. I'll send my daughter over with some food. She will also show you how we do things here."

That suited Canis just fine. Things were obviously different here. In the mean time, he explored his surroundings. After dropping his bedroll and his coat in a nearby chair, he found a back door leading to a space between the stockade wall and the back wall of the house. It was about half-full of wood so he split some and built up the fire in the hearth that dominated the center of the room. Then he explored the contents of the shelves he found in what might pass for a kitchen. He found the makings for tea near the back of one shelf and started to look around for some water.

He was just trying to figure out a likely water barrel not too far from the fireplace when a soft scratching came at the door. When he opened it, he saw a girl about his same age. She had pale gray hair streaked with black. In one of her hands, she carried a large covered dish, and hanging from the other was a covered bucket.

"Hello, my name is Nike. Father asked me to bring this for you and show you around." She handed the things she carried to

Canis. The first thing she did was go directly to the barrel by the fireplace and pull the lid off the top. With hardly a glance inside, she replaced the lid and made a face. "That is where you should melt your snow, but it needs to be cleaned out first. I'll bring you some sand to use. Scrub it good, it's bad."

"Where do I get the snow to melt?" asked Canis hoping he wouldn't have to haul it far.

"Out there in the center of the yard. We let the snow build up in the winter for that purpose. In the summer, there's a spring there. After you get that thing cleaned out, you bring in snow every day. I like to do it in the evening so it has all night to melt. Keep this full and you'll never want for water especially since it's only the two of you. How's he doing? Father said he had a bad cough."

"Yes he does. This whole place is very dirty. It would help him if it were cleaner."

"I know. He won't let anyone come and clean for him. He's very proud. When his woman left him… It was very bad for him. He's been like this, more or less, ever since he returned." She looked at him with a critical eye that resembled her mother's very much. "Maybe I'll take you as a mate when I'm older."

"No, I do not plan to stay here for the rest of my life. It would not be right to take a mate and then leave."

"Why did you come if you don't plan to stay?" she asked.

Canis wondered how much he should let the clan know about his past, but he figured an answer had to be given. "I needed a safe place where I can grow up, then I must go; I have a debt to repay. Beyond that, I have made no plans."

She studied at him for a while then returned to the reason for her being here in the first place. "Well, there's stew in the pot and water in the bucket. If you need anything else, just come and scratch on our door. We're almost directly across the yard, ninth door around." She then took him around the house and pointed out were things were kept, commenting occasionally on the lack of one thing or another. "You will probably have to borrow some things from the others in camp, but if you do, be sure to replace it next summer. I'm sure someone will show you how to collect what you need, just ask. You're new; you're expected to ask. If you don't, everyone will think you're being stuck up, and that's just foolish. I have to go; mother expects me to help. I'll see you tomorrow." With that, she swept out of the room and was gone.

Canis took a bowl of stew up to his father and made him eat it. Signs were evident that he had done little of that when left to his own resources. After eating his own bowl of stew, he filled and lit a lamp since the day was fading rapidly. With the lamp in hand, he went upstairs and found another mound of furs. He shook them out and promised himself that he would give this place a thorough scrubbing tomorrow. He was tired, but he was still hungry, so he went back down to split the rest of the cold stew with Rrusharr who daintily licked the dish clean.

He woke in the middle of the night to the sound of his father coughing again, so he went down and poured him a mug of water into which he sprinkled a pinch of salt. The man was dehydrated and the salt would help.

Once again, he needed to make the man drink all the water. His depression was taking its toll on him.

Canis was just drifting off to sleep again when a wail went up around the stockade sending a chill down his spine. It was an eerie sound as the Wulfen population broke into a howl that traveled around the stockade in a wave that began and ended at one of the houses to the right of where Canis was staying. He could see nothing from his window; it wasn't glass, it was covered with a thin membrane to let in light, not to see out of, so he went outside to investigate. Three doors over was another break in the wall with another well-used trail leading out into the surrounding mountains. Coming in through that gate was a blood trail, and a few yards farther around the way, at the end of the blood trail, was the body of a Wulfi. It had been able to drag itself this far, but it was alone and it could go no farther.

Canis could hear the lookout on the roof spreading the alarm as he knelt down by the Wulfi. It raised its head to look at him.

When those eyes locked on his, a tremendous wash of despair came over him, then the pain-filled story flooded into his mind. It was a story of a hunt gone bad and a man lost. A giant bear cornered the rest of the hunting party, and this member was doubly sad that he had not the life left to lead anyone back to save them.

"Show me where to go," whispered Canis as he gripped the bloody pelt. "Show me."

A flood of trail markings and scents filled his mind. It was all topped off by a life and death fight with a mountain of brown flesh and foot-long claws swung by paws big enough to knock down most any tree Canis had ever seen before coming here to the mountains. Rramerr fed him his last memories in reverse and ended his touch with his hopes before he sighed out his last breath.

For one of the few times in his life, Canis was overcome with emotions and he tipped his head back to voice another wail. As it too was carried around the stockade, he opened his eyes to find several people standing around him. He couldn't distinguish any familiar faces through the tears that caused his view to be sparkled in the lantern lights many of them carried.

Canis was infused with Rramerr's desperation. "They are in trouble. We have to help them," he said as he struggled to blink the tears from his eyes.

Ursa rested a hand on his shoulder. "We can't do anything. We don't know where to go."

"Yes we do, we have a blood trail, and we have what Rramerr told me. We have to go now. Capricorn was wounded before Rramerr left and Gemini is dead, that leaves only Corvus to get them home; that is if the bear does not kill them all if they try."

A murmur went around the gathering. "How do you know the names of the hunting party? You have only been here half a day," said Ursa.

"I told you, Rramerr told me. He told me everything he could before he died."

"Wulfen can't speak to anyone but their joined companions," said Ursa with a gentle tone that came very close to saying 'you must be mistaken'.

"Fine, I will go alone," said Canis and he strode back to his father's house to get his things.

As soon as he was alone along the path, Rrusharr spoke to him, "*He is right. It is not possible for us to speak to anyone but our joined companion and each other.*" After Canis gathered his coat and sword, Rrusharr spoke again. "*Do I need to remind you that we are pups? We do not stand a chance against grown men. It will take many men to bring down the bear you have seen.*"

Canis headed upstairs to tell his father where he was going. "You do not need to remind me. It is my hope that the others will follow, if only to protect an idiot like me."

"*This could anger them.*"

"I am willing to risk it."

"What are you risking so soon after coming here?" asked Orion from his nest just as Canis pushed aside the curtain to his room. He sounded sleepy, but Canis was glad he wouldn't have to wake him.

"I am risking my welcome. I am going to hunt bear." He tested the memory of the trail he would be following. "I will be gone for at least a couple days."

"That is risky for a boy your age," said Orion, speaking calmer than Canis would have expected. "Take my bow. You do know how to use a bow, don't you?" He waved a hand to a rack on the wall and yawned hugely. The rack held an elegant composite bow made of hard wood and shaved horn and polished to a fine sheen. Hanging with it was a quiver full of long, black-fletched arrows. When Canis had taken them down and strung the bow, Orion continued. "The red ones have poison on the tips; be careful with them. Make sure of your aim." He rolled over with a sigh.

"I have learned," said Canis. "Thank you. And you, I expect you to eat everything you are given while I am gone. I will know if you do not. I will be back soon." Orion just mumbled and rolled over again. He was snoring by the time Canis had his blanket rolled up.

At the bottom of the stairs, he tried the draw of the bow. He was thankful for all the farmers and their wood-splitting chores. He could barely draw the heavy bow. He would have to aim quickly; there would be no holding and picking the perfect target. He added wood to the fire and headed for the door.

As he was leaving, he saw his father's snowshoes hanging by the door near his own. They were better. He grabbed those too.

Hunting Bear

Though the trail was freshly burned into his mind and the blood was sharp in his nose, the path he followed left him feeling incredibly small and foolish, coming out here all by himself, at night, and especially on this mission. What did he know about hunting bear? He'd never laid eyes on a bear before.

He was forced to move slowly, belying the tragedy still ringing in his mind. Only the bright stars that glittered overhead lit the trail; a misstep could halt his hunt before it could even begin. Knowing what may still wait at the end of this blood trail, he couldn't risk it.

When the sun began to lighten his surroundings, he was able to move faster and took up a trot, a move made ungainly by the unfamiliar snowshoes and yet he knew he would not have done as well using his own.

By noon, he was forced to slow again as the blood trail dimmed to the occasional bloody footprint. Five men and what looked like the entire pack of Wulfen caught up with him soon after and pulled him to a halt for a much-needed break that included food and water, which he had neglected to bring. Their much longer legs once again made him feel small, but he was so glad they had come. They brought with them three long sleds with furs laced inside of them.

The original three men Canis had met were here, and with them was another man by the name of Gemini who was the twin of one of the men they were looking for. The fifth man was a man named Herculis. He was a somber man who looked wide enough to be two men.

Gemini came up to him; he was uneasy about something and seemed reluctant to speak, and yet bursting to say it. Finally, it came out. “Did Rramerr really speak to you?” asked Gemini.

“Yes, he did,” said Canis. He was very much like the man in Rramerr’s memories.

Gemini turned and went to look at the bloody footprint at the edge of their resting place.

“He was very close to his brother,” said Aries who brought him a water skin.

“I would think so since they share the same name. I think I would find that confusing,” said Canis.

“When twins are born who are alike, it is common for them to share a name. It is thought that since the ancestors caused them to share a soul, it would be presumptuous of us to separate them by a name.”

Rested, fed and impatient to be off, Canis headed down the path again, this time he didn’t feel so alone. Two Wulfen preceded him with their noses following the bright red drops in the snow. Rrusharr trotted at his side and the rest fanned out all around them. Everyone was on the alert; a bear that attacked humans was serious trouble, and a wounded one was worse.

They pushed their pace as hard as they dared, but it was still near sundown before they reached the area where the hunt had taken place. When the blood trail gave out, they were forced to rely on Rramerr’s memories. Canis led them unerringly to the place where Gemini had been cornered when the bear had first come upon them during the hunt. With bear sign everywhere, the hunters spread out.

They saw, in the growing darkness, the bulk of the moose at the base of a tree almost on top of the body of a man. Before the moose had succumbed to the many arrows that protruded from its side and neck, he had managed to crush Gemini against the massive tree.

On the other side of the tree were clear bear prints in the snow. Each one could hold six men's footprints side-by-side within its width. Wide claw marks ripped at the bark of the massive tree as the bear had reached for the man on the other side. The hunter had been forced to choose which death he faced. An enraged and wounded moose or a hungry bear big enough to carry away the moose. The bow still in his hand showed that he had been given only a few seconds in which to choose, and the empty quiver said that he had gone down fighting.

Broken arrow shafts littered the trampled snow around the tree showing the number of arrows the other hunters had fired into the bear only to draw the infuriated beast after them after it swatted away the shafts. This is where the blood bath began. The snow was trampled and churned by the bear and the Wulfen that had harried him in an effort to give their hunters time to launch more arrows or find safety if they could.

Canis barely had time to take in the thousands of tracks, splatters of blood, and wads of torn hair scattered around the scene before he heard a rumbling whoomph followed by an echoing popping sound, and then the snow was crunching and squeaking under something moving quickly. He spun and readied an arrow, pulling the string tight against his cheek.

Despite the darkness, he spotted the charging mountain of blackness instantly as it contrasted starkly with the white snow. He knew that its enraged speed would never be stopped, just as he knew that the arrow in his hand was a pitiful weapon against such a mountain of charging rage.

If he were going to die here, at least he too would go down fighting. In the seconds that he knew were all that remained of his life, he loosed the arrow at a glint a fraction to the right of center of the charging blackness, then he drew his sword; it felt like a toothpick in his hand. The other hunters had fanned out around him and were firing arrows as well. In a replay of a scene that had already failed once, the Wulfen were closing in, ready to pull the bear's attention away from its charge to give the hunters vital time to continue the attack. Rrusharr was at his side, ready to throw herself at the bear's face at the last moment.

All of their efforts were unnecessary; without a sound, the massive beast was dead long before it ceased to move. It careened to a sliding halt less than a foot from where Canis stood transfixed.

As soon as his numb mind could comprehend the fact that the mountain of bear laying in front of him was never going to move again, he saw the red-painted arrow; the glint he had targeted had been the bear's left eye. The poison hadn't even had time to act; the arrow had penetrated the brain bringing its agony and rage to an abrupt end.

As soon as this realization sank in, Canis wilted to the mangled snow, his extremities quite numb. The sword dropped from his hand. It looked so small lying there only a few inches from the massive nose of the bear. He found the arrow once again, it was nearly level with his eyes, the crown of the head loomed higher, and the mound of its shoulders would have been taller than Aries standing. He reached out and pulled the arrow from the bear's eye. It slid out as if it hadn't had a point on it at all, and yet the flinthead was almost as wide as his palm.

The other hunters were not so indisposed. With the bear no longer a threat, the Wulfen quickly located the hunting party where they had managed to hole up. The fallen bow broken by a bloody paw print told of at least one stand before the entrance of the cave had been seen.

The mouth of the cave was low and small enough for a man to crawl in. The cave then opened up into a fair sized chamber, though the ceiling was too low for a man to stand up.

The bear hadn't been able to break away the stone, but the numerous gouges all around the entrance told of his unceasing drive to get at those inside. Capricorn lay in the center of the chamber. His chest and arm had been sliced to ribbons when the bear knocked the bow from his grasp. It was his fall that had revealed the mouth of the cave. Rramerr had attacked the bear from the back, thereby buying the others time enough to get into the small cave. Then when the bear's attention turned back on the men in the cave, Rramerr had been able to make his way back to the stockade hoping to be able to return with help.

The hunters bundled Capricorn and the body of Gemini in two of the sleds. In the third sled, they put two of the Wulfen that had been injured during the fight. Aries, Gemini, and Ursa pulled the sleds while the other two men set about dealing with the now frozen moose.

Aries ordered Corvus and Canis to return to the stockade as well. Though neither of them was injured, both of them were young and quite shaken by the experience. With them went those Wulfen who had accompanied the hunting party; they were exhausted and had earned a respite as well as a large dish of meat. Also with them were the companions of the men who pulled the sleds. The rest would guard the battlefield until help could return to retrieve the meat. With such a high price paid for meat, nothing would be wasted.

They traveled throughout the rest of the night and all the next day, but since their burden was more delicate this trip, they didn't reach the stockade until it was nearly dawn again.

The sled bearers dispersed to take their burdens to their homes. Ursa made sure Canis found his way to his father's house before he took Corvus home. Word of the hunt passed through the camp like wildfire and every able-bodied man in camp packed up a sled and went to help retrieve the kill.

When Canis entered his new home, he was pleased to see his father was up. He was also relieved that he didn't have to try to find something to eat on his own. Orion pulled a covered dish from the hearth stove. In it was a heavy slab of meat and a heap of greens. It was delicious, but Canis was so hungry it could have been gruel and he would have eaten it with relish.

As his stomach filled with food, his eyes became heavy, and it was all he could do to climb the stairs to the pile of furs that had been his nest for half a night a lifetime ago. As he slogged toward his destination, Orion pulled at his coat and shirt dropping each article as it came loose. Canis was sound asleep before the man could pull the first boot free.

Canis slept the next day and the following night to wake with the dawning of the next day. When he went downstairs, he found his father by the hearth oiling his bow.

"They tell me you were able to draw this. Few boys your age can draw their father's bows," said Orion.

"Then why did you tell me to take it?" asked Canis.

Orion dropped the bow to his lap. "I don't remember saying such a thing. I woke to find you gone with my bow and my snowshoes. When Nike came with food, she told me about the arrival of the Wulfi and your insistence that he spoke to you. This has never been, not in all of our existence; how is it you can hear another's companion?"

"So I have been told as well. Perhaps it was merely the desperation, the need to tell someone of the disaster and I was the only one there willing to listen. No other Wulfen has spoken to me."

Orion resumed polishing his bow. "Perhaps, but if it wasn't for you, more than one hunter would have been lost in that debacle."

"I must see Capricorn. Do you know if he is well?" asked Canis, though he didn't know why he wanted to see him.

"Nike informed me that, as of last night, he burns with a fever, but his soul still clings to his bones. Lyra's house is four doors to the left from here."

"Father," said Canis "something puzzles me. Do the women rule here?"

Orion put the bow down again. "Rule is not the correct word. We don't live like the humans on the plains. We hold our women in very high esteem; without them, we would cease to exist very quickly. Therefore, women are the mistresses of the home. They choose their mates and decide the details of our lives. It is a man's obligation to protect her and see that she has a house to be mistress of, as well as plenty of food and children."

"That explains a few things," said Canis. "I will go see Capricorn now. When I return, you are going to get a bath," said Canis as he rose.

"What?" said Orion with indignation.

"You stink," said Canis with a grin, as he stepped through the door.

Remembering to scratch rather than knock, Canis called on the home of Lyra and Capricorn. A small girl opened the door and Canis was reminded of another little girl, though there was no resemblance other than size. "I have come to see Capricorn. May I come in?"

The girl turned and hollered into the house. "Mom! The new guy is here to see daddy."

There was movement from deep inside the house and a moment later a very pregnant woman appeared at the door. Her eyes were red and her face was pale, but she spoke boldly enough. "Capricorn is very ill."

"I know. May I see him?" said Canis.

With a shrug, she stepped aside and led the way up the stairs to her husband.

The man lay among the furs like the dead. The only sign of life was the shallow movement of his chest and the fact that he was drenched with sweat.

Canis knelt on the furs beside Capricorn and pealed back the pelt that covered him. Underneath he saw that the claw marks hadn't been touched and they now smelled and seeped badly with infection.

Canis looked at Lyra with indignation. "Why haven't you done anything for these?" he asked.

New tears leaked down her face. "They're from a bear. There's little that can be done for them."

"There must be something. Get me some water." Canis knew

he wasn't a healer, but surely, he could do something.

When Lyra left the room, Canis suddenly felt detached from himself almost as if he had been set aside while his body acted on its own. He thought he ought to struggle, but he felt no alarm.

He came back to his senses and his body when Lyra came back into the room. He pulled his hand back from Capricorn's bloody chest, and noticed him looking at him, though his face was slack and his eyes didn't have much focus to them.

"He's awake," said Lyra. She set the bowl of hot water hastily aside, grabbed a rag from another bowl, and dabbed at his forehead. As she leaned over him to do so, she noticed another thing. "The infection is gone. This will barely scar. What did you do?"

Canis looked at his bloody hand and then down at Capricorn's chest; it was still cruelly sliced, but the wounds were clean, and no longer angry and swollen with infection. He shook his head. "I do not know. I…I do not know."

Lyra took up the bowl of hot water and started to dab at the ugly wounds while Capricorn flinched, then faded again with a sighing groan.

As she worked over her husband, Canis slipped out of the house and back to his own. He was utterly bewildered about what had happened.

To the Stars

Two days later, the men returned with the meat from the hunt. It had been impossible to skin the frozen moose, but they were able to hack it apart with axes in order to divide the load up among the sleds. They brought the skull back too, it would be skinned out and mounted over Libra's house, and the choicest pieces of meat would belong to her and her family. The hunters brought the hide of the giant bear back with them too, but it vanished in another direction.

Gemini's body, now thawed, was straightened, washed, and dressed in his best. The clan all stopped by to pay their respects while Eridanus comforted his wife.

Everyone was concerned for Libra because of her pregnancy. Few enough women were born to the clan in the first place and death during childbirth happened all too often. A strain like this might have undesirable effects.

Only the oldest of Libra's three children was old enough to understand what had happened. He knew his father was going to be leaving never to return. He took a certain amount of pleasure in starting in on the head of the moose, even though it was only just beginning to thaw. He laid the strips of hide he was able to cut from it on his father's chest. His father would take them with him to the stars.

Canis paid his respects too, though he hung back. He had not known the man or his family. Finally emboldened, he knelt before Libra with the arrow that had killed the bear held in both of his hands. "The beast responsible for your husband's death has paid."

He hoped she might take at least some comfort from the knowledge.

Libra took the arrow with trembling fingers, and then Canis slipped away and back to his home. He was restless and confused. He found his way to the roof of the house and found that the roofs of all the houses joined. A narrow bridge extended across the stockade gateways so a sentry could walk the entire circle of the camp.

Canis paced the circle restlessly. *Why have I been thrust into this chaos so soon? Why couldn't I have just slipped into this life quietly to just grow up in safety until I could leave again, but, instead, everything goes all strange as soon as I get here? A joined Wulfi speaks to me – something never done before. I draw my father's bow and kill a monster bear when kids my age can't normally draw their father's bows. And to top it all off, I heal a man everyone had given up on just because his wounds were from a bear. What did I do to deserve this? What will they expect from me now?*

He came to a halt facing east and studied the contours of the landscape lit by the lowering sun behind him. Though he could see for miles, he could see no sign of the plains. He was standing there when Eridanus found him a few minutes later.

"Your gift was very generous, if…a little odd. The bear didn't touch Gemini. How is it that you say the bear was responsible for his death?"

"You did not see where he lay," said Canis speaking softly as he still regarded the horizon. "The bear had him trapped. He was only safe from the bear if he stayed where he was against the tree…to keep the tree between him and the bear. He couldn't even climb it because it had no lower branches. He wouldn't have stood a chance if he had tried to run to the side." He paused for a moment, remembering the trampled ground. "No, it was the moose that killed him, but it was the bear that kept him there."

"I see. Thank you for bringing him back before he was ravaged." He studied the back of the strange boy before him. His red hair, unheard of in the clan, though it was so like his mother's, reached past his shoulders and he still wore the strange clothes he had arrived in. "Thank you for bringing them all back." There was another pause then Eridanus turned to leave.

"Wait," said Canis. He turned to face the man. "May I ask you a question? It is of a personal nature."

Eridanus looked at the boy that now faced him. It was difficult to tell what was behind his icy eyes. He shrugged. "I'm sure you have many questions and I'm also sure that no few of those questions will be of a personal nature. Ask."

Now that he had permission to ask, he didn't know how to put it into words. He started with a simpler question. "May I know your name?"

"That's not a very personal question. My name is Eridanus, but I thought you knew our names already."

Canis shook his head. "I only know what Rramerr told me; you were not mentioned, but that was not the question I wished to ask. The woman in there…" He waved a hand vaguely toward where she lived.

"Libra, her name is Libra," supplied Eridanus.

"Libra," Canis nodded. "I thought she was Gemini's wife and yet she leans on you. Are you her brother? Forgive me…"

Eridanus smiled. "I see. Let me see if I can explain. There are almost twice as many men here as there are women. It has always been that way, more or less. That is why it is common for a woman to have two husbands. Sometimes she chooses them at the same time; Libra chose Gemini and me at the same time. Sometimes a woman stays with only one mate for a year or two before choosing another. Only seldom does a woman *stay* with only one man."

"Does that mean she, Libra, will choose another husband…someday?" Canis winced at the question. He wished another man was standing here. He felt utterly insensitive asking these questions of this man at this time.

Eridanus covered the last of the distance between them and rested his hands on Canis's shoulders. "Do not cringe when you ask your questions. I understand your curiosity and it is all something you should know. Find me any time when you have these hard questions. I promise to try my best to answer all of them. Now, to answer this last question." A fleeting look of pain flashed across his eyes. "She might choose to bring another into our house, but I think it won't be for a while. We both need to adjust to this loss first."

Canis nodded and accompanied Eridanus as he headed back to his wife, but when he went down into his house, Canis remained on the roof. Every house had an access to the roofs and there was a narrow ladder up to the roofs at each of the gates. Canis took the ladder at the north gate and strode out along the still visible blood trail. He felt Rrusharr close by, but she didn't disturb him. This restlessness was something he needed to sort out on his own and he didn't plan to go far.

A few yards from the walls, he knelt directly on the path. He reached down and touched a finger to one of the red marks still visible in the snow. "You had a plan for me, didn't you," he said to the air around him. "Why would you leave me to figure it out for myself?" The next thing he knew, he was sitting fully on the frozen snow and Orion was resting a hand on his shoulder.

"Did you hear me? What are you doing out here in the dark?" asked Orion.

Canis looked around; the sun had gone down. He must have been sitting here for hours and yet he didn't remember actually sitting down. He pulled himself to his feet. "I was…just thinking," he said; only he hadn't been. He had been blank – utterly devoid of thought or sense. He had been outside of the walls and yet he had felt safe, and not just because he knew Rrusharr watched over him.

As they turned to head toward their house, Canis asked, "Father, what will happen to Gemini…to his body? Does the ground ever thaw out enough to bury the dead?"

"We are not like the bear who buries his kill to ripen for another day. We will give his mortal remains to the stars." He could see that this answer didn't mean anything, but he didn't have a better one. "You will see tomorrow night."

The next day, Orion took Canis out to show him how their firewood was gathered. Several of the men and boys of the clan were already working on a massive tree, and they had been working on it for some time already. The stump was at least a hundred yards from what was left of the tree and still the men with the big saws were forced to work over their heads to cut the next section free. "If they're lucky, they'll make two such cuts today. Those men over there…" he pointed to another two men who were beating at one of the rounds already cut free, "…will break up those rounds. At the end of the day, everyone will take a sled load home. The boys work along the trunk." He called out to an older youth. "Leo, come show Canis what to do. I'll go back and get our sled."

Both Canis and Leo looked after Orion as he picked up an ax to help with breaking up another of the big rounds. "He's not well," said Leo.

"I worry that this will make him cough again."

"If it does, just load up your sled with whatever is available and take him home. He probably won't like it, but you might be able to make him go."

"Is that how it works?" asked Canis.

"Pretty much. Everyone who comes out here and works on a tree takes home a sled load of wood. This is the best time of year to fill your wood slot."

"Why is that?" asked Canis.

"Because the days are longer and warmer, but not too warm. Many days will go by without a storm so we take down a tree, then the clan works on it until it's all hauled in. This one tree will come very close to filling everyone's needs."

Canis looked again at the size of the tree. Just this portion that was left made the logs used in building the stockade look like saplings and yet those logs were every bit as big as, or bigger than, the firewood Canis had split during his travels west.

Canis worked along side Leo all day, though Orion went home after only an hour or so. They, and other boys of the clan, cut the branches from the tree then cut them up into sections. They took turns working the saw and stacking the rounds or piling up the parts of the branches that would not be used.

That night Orion and Canis followed the rest of the clan out of camp. All but the youngest carried a torch. Gemini's closest family and friends carried his body as well as that of his companion, Rramerr, on woven pallets.

About an hour from camp, they came upon a large hole in the snow. Men had been working here all day with shovels made of bone, scooping away at a mound of snow. As soon as the mourners arrived, the bodies of the dead were laid on the exposed branches from some previous firewood tree, and then with an air of ceremony, everyone tossed their torch onto the revealed branches.

Canis watched the fire grow hot, driving the spectators back. He also saw thousands of sparks fly up into the night sky. He knew what he was seeing, and he knew that everyone around him *knew* what they were seeing, but it *looked* like the sparks were going up and joining the stars. The smoke, that was very hard to see in the dark, looked like the souls of the dead leaving the body to be carried to the stars along with the sparks of ash from the fire. It was a very beautiful thought, but it was a very sad thought as well. Of the little he understood about the Mother, he couldn't imagine anyone wanting to leave Her gentle embrace. For him, these two had gone back into Her arms. For the others, they had joined their ancestors among the stars.

His thoughts were interrupted by a disturbance farther around the circle. Moments later a small child was tugging on his coat. "You helped my daddy; you can help her too," piped the small voice and Canis recognized her as the daughter of Capricorn.

"What happened?" asked Canis as he allowed himself to be pulled along.

"Libra fainted," said the girl.

Canis groaned. He was not a healer. He was relieved to see Libra already being helped to her feet by Eridanus before he reached them.

The next day, Canis was on his way back to the woodpile when he met Lyra at the door.

"Hello," he said. "How is Capricorn?"

"He is recovering, thank you. He wishes to see you."

"Me, why?"

"I'm not sure," she replied. "Will you come?"

Canis shrugged and followed her to her home. Upstairs again, Canis sat down on a short wooden stool.

Capricorn was much better than the last time he had been here and he was appraising Canis with a critical eye. "I have heard several stories about you," he started out hesitantly, then he plunged directly into the reason he had wanted to speak to him. "I would like you to hunt for my family until I am strong again."

Canis didn't know what he expected, but it certainly wasn't this. "I have only been here a few days and there is much I do not know about how things are done around here. Surely, a boy like me is never asked to shoulder the responsibility of a man's family, not when there are other men around, anyway."

Capricorn smiled. "True. You are a stranger, and under other circumstances, you would never be approached, not this soon, but I think you will get a lot of practice hunting. Because of those stories, many of the clan will want you to be a member of their hunting parties, and despite what or how much is taken, every member of the party earns an equal portion. What I am asking of you is that you share your portion with my family. Believe me, it is not something I ask lightly. I am taking advantage of the stories circulating the camp and I am taking advantage of a boy. I don't like taking advantage."

Canis considered what Capricorn said. If he did go on several hunting trips and earned an equal share of each hunt, he would likely accumulate more than he and his father would need. "If what you say happens, I would have little time to preserve the food I brought in. Nor would I have time for other duties of the house. If I brought my entire take here, would your wife preserve the meat for me?"

Lyra, who had been listening from the curtain that was their door answered. "Preserving meat is tedious, but not difficult. Surely that is not all I could do for you in return for this favor."

"I do not know; what would be fair?" asked Canis.

"You will bring in many furs with your hunts. I'll tan all the hides you bring in as well as make sure that your father gets fed while you're gone."

"This seems very generous of you. Could I ask you to teach me these skills as well?"

"I would be happy to teach you," replied Lyra with a smile.

Capricorn looked greatly relieved, but he still felt guilty about the whole deal. "Take my father's bow and string it. If you can draw it, I'll give it to you," he said.

Lyra, lifted down the bow that hung on the wall near where she stood and handed it to Canis.

He strung it and took a stance to draw the string. Like with his father's bow, he could pull the string back to his chin, but he couldn't hold it there without starting to shake.

"Get my old bow," said Capricorn and Lyra disappeared from the room to return a few moments later with another bow. This one was simpler, made only of wood and a few inches shorter.

Canis strung it and drew it to his cheek. It had a smooth pull and rested comfortably in his hand.

Capricorn nodded. "Take it. It's yours."

Canis smiled one of his few open smiles. "My thanks," he said as he unstrung both bows and handed the heavier one back to Lyra who then handed him the quiver of arrows that went with the bow he was keeping.

Canis stood out in front of Capricorn's house, His original destination forgotten.

Seeing him with a bow in his hand, Eridanus asked, "When

are you planning to go hunting?"
Canis looked again at his new possession. "Soon."

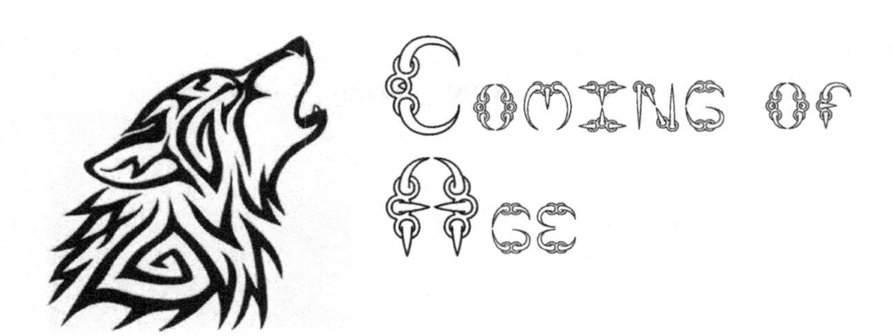

Coming of Age

Just as Capricorn predicted, all the men wanted Canis to accompany them on their hunting trips; they considered him very lucky, but few of them tried to become close. His red hair marked him different and there was no forgetting that.

When he wasn't hunting, he was out working on that monster tree in order to fill up their supply of firewood. If he found a free moment, he went up onto the roof to practice with his sword –he didn't want to forget this skill.

Nike took it upon herself to move into the house with Canis and Orion. She was almost of age so no one objected. Everyone assumed she would take Canis as her mate when she did come of age. Until then, it was commonly agreed that Canis could use the help. It was not easy for a man to run a home alone.

By the time Capricorn recovered, Canis had managed to prove himself a skilled hunter rather than just a good luck charm and both their stores were chocked full of a wide assortment of meat, and both of their wood slots were stuffed to the brim.

Spring was well underway and the snow underfoot was starting to grow annoyingly soft. With the two major chores accomplished, both Nike and Lyra started to take Canis out to teach him how to collect the wild herbs and other plants that filled their diet. They wore the snowshoes of their men for this and carried large baskets slung on their backs to fill with the leaves and vines that found their way up through the snow. They also watched for several varieties of mushrooms showing up on rotted deadfall warmed by the sun.

Orion's health went in waves. There were times when he was healthy and spry as a youngster, and then there were times when he couldn't get out of his nest. These waves seemed accented by the warming of the weather, though they were bad enough during the cold of winter. Canis was thankful for Nike's presence during Orion's bad spells because she was able to keep him from wallowing in his despair too deeply.

During his better days, he taught Canis how to make a bow out of simple wood as well as composite, and how to select the best wood for the arrows. He also taught him how to bend the wood for their snowshoes and how to cure the gut used for the webbing. He was a wealth of information and Canis tried to drink it all in, along with the flood of other information forthcoming from the rest of the clan.

Even during midsummer, much of the ground was covered with snow, but there were some places where the summer sun melted the snow to the ground. The stockade and its surrounding clearing was one such place, and the spring that provided them with water during the summer flowed clear, though it was warm enough to steam most of the time.

When the snow was melted as much as it would, several of the men took Canis on an expedition into the rockier part of the mountains they lived in. As a new male member of the clan, he was taken to where they collected the rocks they made into their arrowheads. They make other tools out of the sharp stone too. The white stone was brittle and slightly porous, which made it perfect for poisoned arrows, but it was fragile and new rock was collected each year. Aries and Capricorn made sure he understood how to select the best stones and Orion showed him how to shape them. After many trials and failures, Canis build up his own store of potential arrowheads and tools.

Though the sun was warm and the snow in their valley was mostly gone, the temperature was still very near freezing even during the heat of the day, but the chill didn't stop the clan from welcoming their newest member into the ranks of manhood. By Orion's count, Canis was twelve years old now, and he was a bit young for such a ritual, but he had proved himself a skilled hunter and a hard worker, willing to shoulder the responsibility of caring for his father and the house of his mother as well as the house of Capricorn so soon after coming here.

One day, Draco, the oldest man in the clan, came and scratched on Canis's door. When Nike opened it, he pushed into the room and attempted to corral Canis, but even though it had been a while, and he had let down some of his guard, Canis wasn't going to be corralled easily ever again.

Ultimately, it took five grown men to contain and subdue Canis while their companions cornered and subdued Rrusharr. All of three men were required to carry him bodily out of the door, bound hand and foot, with Rrusharr a similar bundle close behind.

Canis was confused and enraged, and his captors bore the marks of his and Rrusharr's fight. They were lucky – and they knew it – that he had taken to leaving his belt, and its knife, hanging by the door. That didn't stop him from drawing blood. All of them bore plenty bite and scratch marks.

There must have been every adult male in the stockade gathered outside Canis's door when they brought him out.

"It took five of you?" said Algol, who lived with Ursa under Cassiopeia's roof. The innuendo raised several chuckles around the crowd.

"I see you all did a good job of letting him draw blood," said Scorpius, winning another round of humor.

Draco growled and tossed a bloody strand of hair out of his eye. "His knife was hanging by the door." There was no round of laughter after that. Draco's grim expression was enough for them to understand how things might have been different if that small detail had been otherwise.

As they made their way, Canis struggled to free himself while those not immediately concerned with containing him, ranged ahead. It was near dark before they put him down, and a simple camp and fire was waiting for them. When they began to cut away Canis's clothes, he renewed his struggles. He was exhausted, but he couldn't let himself take this peacefully. This all bore too close a resemblance to his initiation to being a slave.

Because of his struggles, it took quite a bit of care and effort to cut his clothes away without drawing blood, but they managed it. When each portion of his clothing came free, they threw it on the fire.

When all of his clothing had been reduced to ash, they forced him, still struggling, into the creek that ran next to their camp. The water was cold enough to turn his pale skin blue within seconds and his muscles, heated by his struggles, cramped painfully.

Subdued by cold and exhaustion, Canis had no choice but to submit to the men's attention as they brought out bars of soap and began to wash him from head to foot – even his hair – and in the process, his bonds came away. Even Rrusharr was not exempt from this part of the proceedings. By the time they were satisfied, Canis was shaking uncontrollably and he couldn't have fought them if he had tried.

They brought him and Rrusharr out of the water to stand by the fire and then they toweled him off with soft furs as Rrusharr made a point to shower them all as she shook loose water from her pelt. Too cold to do anything, Canis glowered at them where they gathered across the fire from him.

Speaking for the first time since this started, Draco spoke somberly. "The waters from the deep that grants our clan life washes the boy away, leaving only the man behind. Is there anyone here who still sees a boy?"

No one replied. Canis wondered what would have happened if they had – perhaps another dip in the creek. By now, Canis knew that these men meant him no real harm so he stood shivering and waited to see what would happen next.

Draco's rumbling voice broke the silence. "Then we must clothe and feed a man of the clan."

With those words, each man of the clan brought forth an

article of clothing and they each placed their article on him with dignity and reverence. Canis wondered if this was what it must be like to be an infant. A brief picture of Gem dressed in all her finery came to his mind and he wondered if someone helped her dress, but he pushed that memory away; it didn't fit with this.

When he was dressed in warm boots, fur-lined pants and shirt with a heavy coat and hood over it all, they each gave him and Rrusharr something to eat or drink. When he had consumed all of their gifts, the ceremonial air vanished and they all sat down around the fire pulling Canis with them.

The rest of the night was filled with storytelling and much drinking. It wasn't surprising that, after several passes of the jug, jabs about how difficult it had been to take Canis in the first place, came out again. No one questioned that he did it. Apparently, he had been right to struggle, it was expected, but they hadn't figured on the desperation behind the struggles.

It took some prodding and cajoling, but eventually they were able to entice an abridged story explaining the reason behind his desperate struggles. He also promised them that his knife would never be over by the door again, but then, apparently, keeping his knife close was another lesson he was supposed to learn, since they all laughed uproariously when he said it.

With the coming of the dawn, the men wended their wobbly way back to the camp, escorting Canis back to his house before filtering off to their own homes. Though he had consumed enough of their fermented drink to be unsteady on his feet, he was not so drunk that he didn't notice the changes in the house left in a riot of destruction the day before. Paramount was the huge mound of fur now taking the place of the leather chairs that had been broken during the fight.

The women of the clan had apparently been waiting for him and stood when he entered. They too each had a gift for him. Five of them stood by the giant pelt. It finally occurred to him what they were presenting him with. He had almost forgotten that the hide from that huge bear had been brought back along with the moose.

Numbly he went over to it. It did a very good job of filling one entire corner of the floor in a pile that would make a plush and ample couch. It would be very comfortable to curl up on near the hearth. When he examined a portion of the underside, he saw many arrow holes, all carefully mended with tiny stitches. He wondered how many such holes there were in the whole hide. None of those wounds had killed the beast.

A soft touch on his shoulder drew his attention away from the bear hide. Lyra was standing in front of him. She draped around his neck a necklace made of the bear's claws and teeth. Each claw was set in an intricately carved wooden set that looked like a toe of the bear. The claws were separated from the teeth by red colored beads. All of it was on a thong that was braided from finely stripped leather. It was quite a work of art.

Libra claimed his attention next. She set in his hands a wide belt woven from fine strips of tanned and dyed leather. The end result was very colorful, very flexible, and sturdy as well.

Cassiopeia gave him a tooled white-flint knife and a sheath to go with it and she helped him put it on the belt Libra had given him.

Andromeda gave him a leather pouch containing an assortment of smaller blades. There was a gutting blade with a hook on one end, a stout blade for cutting tendons and boning a kill and there was a wide two-handed blade for scraping the hide. There was also a small awl and several coils of greased tendon for mending on the trail if necessary.

Canis was overwhelmed with the gifts the women had given him. No one had ever really given him a gift before. When he looked up from his last gift to try and express his thanks, he saw the door closing behind Andromeda; the other women had already left.

When Nike came up to him and took his coat, he said, "They all left before I could tell them my thanks."

She looked up at him. "You do not thank the clan for becoming a man." She led him to the table and set his breakfast before him.

"Where is father, I have not seen him since we returned."

"Your father went to sleep. He grows very tired easily these days. He is very proud of you, though. A boy doesn't usually become a man for another two or three years."

Rescue Mission

Winter came again after the brief warm season that barely qualified as a summer. Canis's hair now reached half way down his back and Nike had taken a liking to braiding it every morning before he went up on the roof to practice with his sword.

The winter was heralded by snowstorm after snowstorm. It was what defined their existence and there was nothing they could do but wait for the season to catch up with itself again. It was a time for tending to their gear and making new and keeping the snow shoveled off the roofs.

As soon as the winter storms had made it a certainty that winter was in full swing, it became hunting season once again. Canis was growing to like this life, but the debt he owed still nagged at his sense of honor, and he wished he would grow up quicker. At twelve, he had earned the right to be considered a man here, but Patro would not be the only man to see only a ten-year-old boy if he were to return now.

One day, after practicing with his sword on the roof while the sun cleared the horizon, a scratch came at the door. Leo and Eridanus were there, waiting for him to go on a hunting trip. As he tied his belt around his waist, Nike held his coat for him then he was out the door. They hadn't quite made it to the west gate when a boy caught up to them. "Capricorn says for you to come," said the boy out of breath.

The three of them followed the boy around to the south gate, where a group of three Wulfen stood hackles up as if ready to attack each other.

"What is going on?" asked Canis as he came up on Capricorn overlooking the conflict.

"I don't know. I can't get anything out of them. I thought perhaps you might…"

Canis groaned inside. "That only happened once."

"I know, but it's worth a try. My companion refuses to explain, Lyra's too. It has something to do with the pack leader and Draco's not here."

Though the Wulfen population of the clan was nearly double the human population, Canis knew most of the Wulfen by sight; he also knew who they belonged to, so he could tell at a glance which of the three seemed to be at odds. He stepped forward and faced the strange Wulfi squarely. "Explain yourself. You intrude here."

The Wulfi looked up at him; in fact all three of the Wulfen looked at him, and the two that belonged to Capricorn and Lyra backed away to stand by their family. The third, a big gray Wulfi with heavy shoulders, stared at him cocking his head back and forth as if surveying him first with one eye, then with the other. When Canis stared back just as boldly waiting for an answer, he got it.

"You will do," he said.

Canis was relieved to hear the voice, but he was puzzled at the words. "Why me?"

"*You can hear,*" replied the massive gray Wulfi. "*You will follow me.*"

"Will I?" said Canis surprised. "Why would I do such a thing?"

"*Because the companion of my mate will die if you do not.*"

"You are from a different clan then?" said Canis. He could hear the stir behind him caused by his words. A visitor from another clan was almost unheard of.

The Wulfi started to pace and grumble with impatience, but he answered with a slightly different tone, "*Yes, will you come?*"

"Yes," said Canis. He turned to Lyra. "I will need a pelt large enough to wrap around a person and some extra food. His companion is in trouble, and apparently they were closer to us than to home. We will go find him and bring him here. There's plenty of room at my place. Please inform Nike."

His demands were hastily met and they were off at a trot out of the southern gate. They brought their three sleds because it was still a hunting trip and there was no sense in passing up a shot if it presented itself just because they didn't have a way to move the kill afterward. Since this was a rescue mission, they would hasten to that end, but quick game wouldn't hold them up and meat was vital.

Since the Wulfen numbered many more than people to join with, it was common for several of them to choose to accompany hunters. They took the provision and protection of the clan very seriously, regardless of having joined or not. It benefited everyone if the hunts were profitable. Since a strange Wulfi was accompanying this hunt, nine of their own Wulfen accompanied Canis's hunting party, partly out of curiosity and partly out of a show of clan strength.

Traveling at a trot most of the time, it took them two full days to reach the gray Wulfi's destination, only to find no sign of a camp. The man lying on the ground looked no bigger than Canis, and curled close beside him to lend him warmth was the second Wulfi, the mate of the great gray Wulfi striding on Canis's right side mirroring the smaller Rrusharr's position on his left.

With only a brief thought to who would be so foolish as to travel alone in the company of only two Wulfen, Canis brushed the hood back to find, not a man, or even a boy, but instead a young woman. Recovering from the surprise, he continued the examination and found the broken leg at the same time the woman told him of it through clenched teeth.

The three of them lifted her carefully into the sled and wrapped her warmly in the extra furs.

"Larrarr said her mate had gone for help," said the woman. "I didn't expect him to succeed."

"You need to be much warmer than you are before we can do anything for your leg. We will make camp here tonight," said Canis. He might be only twelve, but he issued orders easily and the men he hunted with found no objection to them. With a vaguely formal gesture, Canis introduced the three of them. "My name is Canis and this is Leo and Eridanus."

The woman looked at each of them as their name was spoken, but gave no further acknowledgment to the gesture, then she looked at the speaker. "Do you have anything to eat? I'm starved."

Canis looked at the woman with some surprise. "We do, but would you not rather eat something hot?"

"Yes, that would be good too," she said.

Canis frowned; her imperial manner was grating. *Perhaps it is just the pain.* He handed her a water skin and moved off to collect wood for a fire with the others.

She accepted the water skin with a look of surprise, but Canis gave her no opportunity to say anything else.

Until meat was brought down during a hunt, hunters ate boiled grains. While it cooked, he handed the woman a cup of hot tea.

"Tea, didn't you bring any food? I haven't eaten for days," said the woman who had yet to give them her name.

"Your water skin is empty. You have had no water for a while either," said Canis. "We will set that leg before you eat."

"But I'm hungry now," pouted the woman.

"You will waste it if you eat now, drink your tea," said Canis calmly.

"*Good luck taming this one, boy-man,*" said the gray Wulfi from where he lay on the edge of the firelight. Only the glitter of the fire in his eyes could be distinguished in the darkness.

Canis looked at him, but made no comment. He took up a stick and began to carve it smooth. When he had accumulated three such sticks, he nodded to his friends who stood to help. Looking directly at the woman's companion, he said, "Setting a broken leg is painful. You must not interfere."

The Wulfi, a fine boned creature with strong brown accents in her silver fur, looked him in the eyes then sauntered over to lie down by her mate. Her wide belly spoke of new pups one day soon.

The woman gasped with indignation. "How dare you order my companion?"

"It is best and she knows it," said Canis as he knelt and pulled the furs away. The swelling made it very hard to pull the bone straight, and her screams echoed through the night air. By the time they were finished, the woman was near fainting and tears streamed down her face.

Sickness and injury was a constant threat, but members of the clan were solidly healthy creatures so Canis's 'skills' had only been called on once since the events of his arrival. At that time, he discovered that he would go…then he would wake afterward with no memory of what he had done. This time was no different. He remembered speaking to the woman's companion and he remembered pulling the furs away from her legs, but there was nothing after that until he was tucking the blankets around her again.

He handed her another cup of tea. Her stomach needed to settle down some before she tried to eat.

She accepted the tea silently while wiping the tears from her face with shaking fingers.

When her hands stopped shaking some, he asked, "Do you need to relieve yourself?

She looked up at him as if she was having trouble comprehending the question, then she laughed a shaky laugh. "What will you do about it?"

"Nothing if you do not want me to. Eridanus is married. If you wish, he can help you to the edge of camp and help…with your leg."

She looked at the other two men as if assessing their size and age, or perhaps weighing their worthiness then she just shrugged and looked away, folding her arms across her chest. "Not now."

Canis silently dished her up a bowl of the meat-laced gruel, and then dished one up for himself. They ate in silence. When the gruel was cool enough, they dished out a portion for each of the Wulfen too. The pot was polished out by several of the different Wulfen; each of them hoping to find a crumb or flavor missed by another. Using the last of the tea to wash out the pot, Canis and the others began to prepare for the night. Peace wasn't to be had just yet, as the woman couldn't hold her bladder any longer.

The morning was a mild confusion of packing up, eating a chunk of dried meat and filling their water skins with snow to melt during the day. Eridanus again helped the woman to the edge of camp before they packed her warmly in the sled, then they headed back toward the stockade.

They traveled much slower this time. The woman's life was not in danger and meat was necessary, so the Wulfen fanned out in search of game. A young bull moose was flushed early in the afternoon, but the shot was spoiled when the woman chose to fling aside the pelt that covered her, picking a crucial moment to do so.

After watching her fidget for several minutes, Leo said, "If you're finished, we'll continue the hunt."

She just glared at him.

Thanks to the larger than usual number of Wulfen, they still had control of the beast, and they were slowly bringing it back around, so the hunters set up for another shot. The direction they were coming from had a small rise just beyond where their sleds waited, so Canis had the others boost him up into a tree. Just as the moose was starting up the other side of the rise, the woman reached for the pelt. She was fidgeting again.

Canis launched one arrow at her, pinning the pelt to the snow, effectively freezing the woman. A second later, he shot again successfully driving a long arrow deep in front of the moose's shoulder.

Two steps later, the moose was in range of the others and it fell soon after.

They spent the rest of the afternoon skinning and quartering it. The load would be heavy for two sleds, but not impossible.

That night their gruel was liberally laced with liver and healthy sections of the toughest meat was portioned out to the Wulfen who chewed on it with relish. The woman huffed and glowered through it all, but she was refusing to speak to Canis.

When Canis handed her, her bowl of gruel, she said, “I don’t like liver.”

Canis merely shrugged, sat down with her bowl, and picked up the spoon. Before he could get the first mouthful to his mouth, she snapped, “What am I going to eat?”

Canis handed her the bowl again; this time she took it. She tried to pick through it at first, but the liver was already cut into small pieces and most of that had essentially dissolved with the cooking. When she set it aside again, less than half finished, Canis said, “We will not be heating that up in the morning, but I guess you can eat it cold.”

That set her off. “Who do you think you are? You’re just a kid. How old are you anyway. And what possessed you to shoot at me?”

Canis looked at her with a steady, unblinking gaze few could hold; she was no different. When she glanced away, he answered. “I am a hunter. I have hunted in a direction I had not intended, simply because I was asked to come find you. I am old enough to hunt, old enough to set your leg, and I did not shoot at you, I shot at the pelt to keep you from flopping it around again and spoiling the hunt entirely. Because of you, we will have to take turns pulling the meat sleds since they are overloaded. You will eat what you are given. It will make you strong and heal your bones quicker. When we reach the stockade, you will be my guest until other accommodations can be arranged.”

“Your guest, what makes you think I would want to be your guest?”

Canis shrugged. “I guess you could go home,” he said and finished his meal.

The woman ate a couple more bites in silence, made a face, and then set her bowl down on the other side of the sled. If she thought any of the Wulfen would clean the bowl for her, she was sadly mistaken. The great gray Wulfi made sure none of the others went near her bowl.

In the morning, she munched on the frozen gruel. Having not eaten much the night before, she was very hungry, and though the men all pulled dried meat from their provisions, none was offered to her.

They traveled slowly that day; the route was mostly uphill and the sleds were heavy. Their travel was punctuated by a wide assortment of complaints, most of which dealt with the fact that her head was lower than her feet, giving her a headache, or so she said. During a rest brake, they turned her around in the sled. Then her complaints were that there was too much pressure on her leg.

When they turned her around yet again at the next level opportunity, she didn't complain quite so much about the angle, but she did manage to complain about something all the way until they made camp. By then they were all silently thankful that they would reach the stockade the next day.

At the stockade, Eridanus and Leo silently carried the woman into Canis's house and laid her on the bear hide near the hearth, then they left to take care of the meat. It would have to be thawed out before Canis's portion could be brought to him.

Family Problems

After hanging up his snowshoes and coat, and leaning his bow in the corner, Canis kicked off his boots and looked around, not seeing his father. Nike was there at the fire fixing a warm soup for lunch. She poured him a cup of tea and handed it to him. Her eyes were all red from crying and her face was pale.

"What is it?"

"Oh how wonderful, a house run by children. Why did you bring me here?" said the woman, but no one seemed to hear her.

"Your father…" was all Nike got out. Canis shoved the cup back into her hands and ran up the stairs.

He wasn't prepared for what he saw when he pushed aside the curtains to his father's room. "Father?" he said bewildered.

When there was no response, he moved closer to his father's nest. Orion lay there peacefully, but it was obvious he was no longer there. Canis sat down. His mind seemed to stop. He heard a strange sound and realized it was his own voice as he moaned. An agony had opened up in his chest and he didn't know how to fill it.

Soon after, several women of the clan moved in and took over. Canis was guided back downstairs and was carefully watched and entertained. Orion too was brought down where he was bathed and dressed in his finest clothes. A never-ending parade of people and Wulfen traveled through the house to pay their respects.

Through it all, Canis was in a fog. Occasionally he heard the sharp voice of the new woman as she spoke to different members of the clan, but he didn't register what she was saying. He couldn't think. The man who claimed to be his father was dead, and he had hardly taken the time to get to know him, to hear his story, to ask about his mother. Now he was gone and the story was lost.

Someone handed him a cup and pressed him to drink it. He did vaguely, noticing that it was bitter, then he knew no more.

Gentle hands woke him and he was aware that it was dark, but he couldn't have said whether it was that night or another. The hands that woke him guided him to follow the procession out of camp. A torch was placed in his hand. Dimly, he was aware of coming upon a hole in the snow and the pile of branches that had been revealed. He watched as men placed the body of Orion out in the center; with him was the carefully folded pelt of his long dead companion.

Canis knelt on the mound of snow around the edge of the pyre. "I am sorry, father," he said softly.

Belatedly he let the torch fall onto the branches. The rest of the clan's torches followed and as the dry branches caught and the fire heated up, someone else's hands pulled him away from the heat before the snow melted out from under him. He stood swaying, watching the sparks fly up into the sky, watching the smoke writhe against the stars. "May the Mother hold you gently in Her arms," he whispered. "May your ancestors welcome you to their hearth," he said only a little louder.

It was Nike who led him back home. Inside, she helped him out of his coat and she was hanging it up when his guest spoke.

"Now what's to become of me, there isn't even a man in the house any more," she said petulantly.

Canis no longer functioned in a fog, but his pain was still very tender. He rounded on his uninvited guest and spoke with a snarl in every syllable. Several days of misery traveling with her, topped by the shock of his father's death, had removed all restraints. "I will warn you once; I was not raised among the clan. I grew up on the other side of the mountains where women are not nearly so rare or treasured, where even women were known to be beaten. You have done nothing but behave badly since the first time you opened your mouth. Mend your ways or you will find yourself out in the snow alone again."

Both the woman and Nike were stunned by the vehement words. Nike had never heard Canis lose his temper before.

Canis stalked up the stairs. He was furious, furious at himself for loosing his temper with the woman, furious at spoiled opportunities, furious at the world for making him what he was and handing him the life he had been dealt. He shed his shirt and picked up his sword before heading up onto the roof. Using the stars as targets and the dark shadows of the surrounding towering trees as enemies, he fought, letting the ferocity in his heart burn itself out against the shadows.

The next day, in an effort to make up for his uncharacteristic loss of control, Canis took it upon himself to help Nike make a place for their guest.

Frustrated with their guest's imperial nature and rude stubbornness, Nike finally asked. "What *is* your name anyway? Or is it a secret?"

"It's Halley of course," she said, as if everyone should know her name just by being in her presence.

Nike overlooked the manner, and at first, it appeared Canis did too. He merely strode to the wood slot out back and brought in a pair of already shaped pieces of wood and started to soak them in preparation for bending.

Halley was obnoxious, but not stupid; she recognized those pieces of wood. "What are you making snowshoes for?"

Canis looked her directly in the eyes. "I am making them for you. Yours were broken when you fell. I have a feeling that as soon as your leg is healed, you will need new ones. I am sorry that I cannot direct you to the next clan holding."

The woman was speechless. When she did find her voice, she said with disbelieving incredulity, "You can't kick me out."

Canis smiled, but it was a smile that narrowed his eyes dangerously. "Yes I can," he said with a soft growl under his words. Then with a sigh, he sat down on the bearskin near her.

Involuntarily, she shrank away from him. She had to force herself to remember that he was not a full-grown man, not yet, but she remembered him saying something about beating women.

Canis sat looking at his hands for several minutes before he spoke. "I was not taught how to mix with people and have always chosen to watch the people around me very carefully and reserve reaction for those who came close. I have learned, with this watching, that a soft voice and a carefully considered word will win much more respect than an angry voice that can only criticize and hurt. While you stay here, I will not wish you on any other member of this clan. I will make every effort to *show* you how you appear to others. You were rude not to introduce yourself when I told you my name. You should remember that you are not in control of your surroundings. This house was my mother's house and since I am the last remaining member of my family, it has become mine. When I leave here, I will give it to Nike for all the help she has seen fit to give me. You are at my mercy here, and like I told you before, I was not brought up in the clan." Canis sat there for a few minutes longer, but when Halley didn't seem inclined to any response, he rose and donned his coat. Picking up his snowshoes and ax, he headed outside.

Nike was very logical in the things she did for Halley. The woman had a broken leg. She couldn't do much of anything for herself if it was out of reach or if it required that she stand or walk, so she brought Halley her food or drink and cleared away her dishes when they were empty. She also lent a patient ear when the woman chose to talk, which was quite a lot.

After Canis's little speech, the woman was quiet, far quieter than she had ever been since her arrival. Nike stared at the closed door for a long time. She had never heard him say so much all at once since she met him almost a year ago.

The strange silence stretched for nearly an hour, both women completely immersed in their separate thoughts, before being interrupted by his return, and then his actions held their curiosity, as they watched him like a pair of owls.

He brought with him several different sticks that he proceeded to peel and smooth. When he had most of them rudely peeled, he stood up before Halley. “Stand up,” he said as he held his hand out to pull her to her feet.

Tentatively she took his help and he pulled her to stand, one legged, beside him. He handed her the stick he had peeled. It was every bit as tall as Halley was.

She took it with a puzzled expression on her face. “What’s this for?”

“It is to help you get around; try it.”

Hesitantly, she tried it. Gripping it with both hands, she took a few hops across the floor. The stick helped, but it was obviously awkward, and she threatened to kick the stick out from under her with every step.

Canis frowned and shook his head. “That will not work.” He handed her another stick. This one was about waist high with a large knob on one end. “Try it.” It was better, but wobbly. He looked at her. “Will that do or do you have a better idea?”

“Are you asking me?” she said.

“Yes,” said Canis simply.

“There was a man in our clan who broke his knee very badly. He never walked right on it again. He made himself a stick that rested under the shoulder. It seemed to work well for him.”

Canis took the longer stick, measured it to her shoulder, then he went to the wood slot to cut it with his hatchet. When he was finished with it, he put it under his own arm and hopped around with it. The woman was about the same height as he was and it seemed to work well enough. The end of the stick would bruise the underarm in the first few steps so he sat down to make further modifications.

Using something his father had shown him, he pegged the two pieces together solidly, then he found a scrap of hide that still had the hair on it and stitched it over the cross piece. Finished, he went back into the house and handed it to Halley.

She hopped across the floor once again. "This seems to work just fine," she said with gratitude, "Thanks."

Canis smiled. "You are welcome." He then went over to the furs that were in the process of tanning while Halley went back to her position on the bear hide.

"If you'll give me a small one, I can work it here," said Halley.

Canis brought her a rabbit hide. "Thank you."

She nodded. She really didn't know how to act this way, but she did like his smile much more than the glare that chilled his icy eyes. Blue, gray, and brown eyes were common, but she had never seen eyes that compared so closely to the snow that surrounded them.

A few days later, Canis went out on another hunt. They still had their year's stores to fill and it was almost wood hauling season. With him went the great gray Wulfi that had come with Halley. Watching he and Rrusharr trotting side by side, Canis had to ask, "You like him, don't you?"

"*He is very strong,*" replied Rrusharr.

"Does he have a name?" asked Canis.

"*Ggrrawrr,*" replied Rrusharr.

"*You are different, boy-man,*" said Ggrrawrr.

"When is your family due?" asked Canis.

"*Soon,*" replied Ggrrawrr.

"You're talking to both of them aren't you," said Leo.

Canis smiled. "Yes I am. You should try it sometime. They are all members of the clan."

"But they won't answer."

"Perhaps you have not said anything worth responding too," said Canis.

When they returned from the hunt, Canis was greeted by a tearful household. "What is wrong now? If some tragedy happens every time I go hunting, I may stop."

"It's Larrarr, she has labored for nearly two days now and nothing," said Nike.

Canis looked at Halley and saw the pain and horror in her eyes and pale face.

Larrarr had claimed a warm dark corner almost as soon as she had entered the door. She was very wide in the belly. Canis feared that perhaps one of the pups was sideways and she was too small for it to turn.

Like every other time, this time was no different, even though it was a Wulfi he touched. Canis's awareness stepped aside and the healer took over. When he woke to himself, a third pup was being rolled around by its mother's diligent tongue. His arm ached and he looked down to see it bleeding freely.

He went to the counter to fill a bowl with water so he could wash and Nike came to help. She bit you hard. I tried to help, but it was as if you didn't even feel it. I didn't know what to do."

Canis spoke very softly. "I felt nothing. I remember nothing. I never do."

Nike looked up at him in stunned wonder. "But Capricorn and…and her," she whispered.

"I do not remember them either," he said.

"How can that be?"

Canis only shook his head and sought out the bottle of astringent they kept around for just such an event.

Nike opened it and pulled his arm over the bowl. Canis hissed and let out a stifled curse as she poured it over the wound, then he let her wrap it in soft strips of leather.

When Nike was finished with his arm, Canis went back over to the corner and stood looking at the new little family. "Are you all right, Larrarr?" he asked.

He was rewarded with a low and tired hum of contentment with an underlying note of regret.

"It's all right, I will recover."

He went in to see Halley; Nike was giving her a drink. He

vaguely remembered the smell and knew that Halley would be sleeping the rest of the day at least.

"Will I go through that if Rrusharr has trouble?" asked Canis.

"Yes," replied Nike.

With Halley warmly covered, Nike turned to making supper and Canis turned to the sled of meat that was still in the middle of the floor where he had left it. He pushed it out of the way then hacked off a corner he could get free and took it over to the new mother. She sniffed at it and hummed a soft *"Thanks, but later."*

Ggrrawrr sauntered over, gave his offspring a nudge with his cold nose, then he lopped a tongue along Larrarr's whiskers before dropping to the floor a few feet away.

A week later, Canis was preparing for another hunting trip. Life with Halley was improving, but she still tended to forget herself rather often. She was finding it difficult changing a lifetime's habit. When Canis had stepped out to round up his hunting partners, Halley followed him.

"Canis," she said.

Canis stopped and turned back to her. "Yes?"

"Canis…" she started again and shifted her foot. She flexed her leg and winced.

Canis waited patiently for her to voice her concern. She was easily eight to ten years his senior and yet she looked very young just now.

"Canis…" she tried again. Then with a sigh, she blurted out the rest of her question. "Does no one ever go visiting here? I have been here for more than two weeks and aside…aside from when your father died, I have met no one here. I came here to find a mate. How can I find a mate if no one ever comes to visit?"

Canis smiled indulgently and answered her question honestly. "We all work very hard here to provide for all of us, so there is little time for visiting, but also, you came here and made a very unfavorable impression with most everyone you spoke to. You must defeat your own first impression before you will see a change in that."

"How do I do that?" she asked, dismayed.

"I have no idea," said Canis. He rested a hand on her shoulder. "You are smart. I think you can figure it out. You must remember the difference between butterflies and wasps."

"What about butterflies and wasps?" she asked bewildered.

"Butterflies are quiet and colorful; everyone likes watching them, but no one likes to be around wasps." Canis was going to leave her with that, but he took no more than a dozen steps before he turned back. Stepping past her, he grabbed her coat and helped her get it on.

Puzzled, she complied.

While they were doing this, Canis's hunting companions came into view. In answer to their inquisitive expressions, he said, "We will go tomorrow."

With raised eyebrows, they shrugged and went back to their homes.

Canis then spent the rest of the day taking Halley from house to house. He introduced her and they stayed for an hour or two, then he took her to the next house. It took all day, but she got a good chance to defeat her own first impression and make a few wary friends.

When he returned from his hunting trip, he found her making an article of clothing. It looked like it might be the beginnings of a shirt, but it was difficult to tell at this stage.

She looked up at Canis's entry and smiled. "I may have decided who I will choose as my mate," she declared happily.

Canis looked at her dubiously. "And who might that be?" he asked, dreading her answer.

"Achernar has brought me some mending. He has indicated that his children are in need of a mother and he has need of a wife as well," she answered.

Canis was surprised. "It works that way?"

Halley looked up at him. "Just because I get the final say

doesn't mean that men can't make their desires known."

"Does this mean that you have put away your wasp?"

"I think I am doing very well, thank you," she replied with a smile.

In the end, Halley did choose Achernar. Ggrrawrr, however, chose to remain at Canis's house; it is far more difficult to earn the respect of the Wulfen than it is humans.

Half-Breed

by

Anna L. Walls

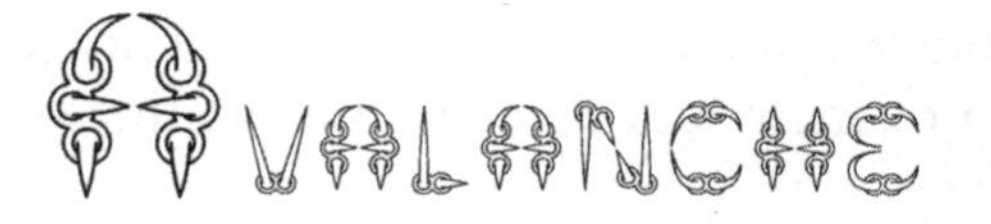

Until Canis turned sixteen, nothing more serious happened than a few new births, a few skinned knees, and a few youths being greeted into manhood. There were no illnesses, no miscarriages or even births that were more difficult than usual and no deaths in the clan.

Andromeda's oldest son, Corvus was chosen by Aquarius' oldest daughter, Carina, who later also chose Cassiopeia's oldest boy Hydra and the new woman of the clan, Halley, gave birth to a fine strong boy and was happily pregnant again.

This time of relative calm gave Canis the opportunity to settle into clan life in a much more normal manner. Canis grew tall and strong with powerful wide shoulders and strong arms, narrow hips and long legs. He no longer appeared years younger than his actual age. His human heritage gave him longer bones and heavier muscles; it also gave him his face, as he never developed the profile of a clan male.

Though all of the girls let their eyes linger on him when he passed, none of them detained him more than social interaction demanded. Unbeknownst to him, Nike had made it known from the first that she had her designs on him and Canis had made no secret of the fact that he intended to leave one day.

This time of happiness and peace couldn't go on forever. The winter of Canis's sixteenth year was a year of heavy snowfalls and avalanches. Not a week went by, but what another snowstorm brought several more feet of new snow. Hunting became almost impossible and the hunters were forced to range far in search of meat. Despite the help of their four-footed citizens, they were not always successful.

Canis and his usual hunting partners, Leo and Eridanus were no exception, though they seemed to have better luck than most. It seemed that Canis had a good instinct when it came to finding game, but even someone with good luck can have a bad day.

They were on a hunt five hard days from home, when they were caught in an avalanche. Canis had scant minutes to sound the alarm and it was almost enough. Both Leo and Eridanus were able to make it free of the crashing snow. Most of the Wulfen made it out of danger too. Canis wasn't so lucky. Though he wasn't caught in the direct flow, a flying clod of snow hit him in the head and knocked him off the trail, launching him into the ravine being filled with packed snow.

Two of the eight Wulfen that hunted with them were also lost in the crushing snow. Rrusharr, who was closest to Canis at the time he was struck, was knocked off the ledge with him, but sustained little more than a few bruises.

When Leo and Eridanus found Canis, he was piled face down at the bottom of one of the giant trees that was out of the avalanche's reach; he was also bleeding. A cursory examination revealed three puncture wounds in his back, one high in his right shoulder and one low near his right hip. The third one, deep in his left rib cage, still had the broken branch in it. He also had a nasty cut in the center of a fist-sized lump on the left side of his head and a growing black eye.

Despite their grim findings, Canis was still breathing.

"Go see if you can find a sled, Leo," said Eridanus. "We need to get him back home as fast as we can."

With Wulfen help, the eighteen-year-old youth was able to find the sleds, but the first two were broken and useless, the third was badly cracked but usable.

While Leo searched, Canis woke up and coughed, something, he discovered, he shouldn't have done; the pain it caused robbed him of the ability to breathe at all for seconds.

"Take it easy, Canis," said Eridanus. "Leo found a sled. He'll be back here in a few minutes."

Canis, still sprawled face down in the snow, clutched at it as the pain washed over him. As the tension increased, the amount of pain also increased. When he started to tremble, he finally fainted.

They loaded him on the sled and tied him in the best they could. It was impossible to make him more comfortable. They had no warm pelt to wrap him in and he was forced to ride mostly on his belly. The sleds are far from comfortable to begin with, and worse when the rider is already in pain.

Canis drifted in and out of consciousness for most of the first day of their trek, but seemed to stabilize somewhat after that. Each bump was agony and he sought the quiet of unconsciousness as often as possible, but with the tracker's instinct running strong in his blood, not even that distracted him from keeping track of where he was, especially when he had a constant feed of sights, sounds and scents from five different points.

Leo and Eridanus toiled away day and night. They took turns pulling the sled without stopping longer than it took to pass around the water skin, then fill it again with snow. There was nothing to stop for; their provisions had been lost with the sleds, and Canis needed to be taken home as soon as possible. Even though there was nothing that resembled a healer there, neither of them would have done any less. No one wanted to die out in the wilderness.

They were cutting across the terrain in search of their original trail and Canis was aware of this. He also knew that he had led them on a twisted route in search of the elusive game. "Head right," whispered Canis for the Wulfen to hear; he would do what he could to shorten their trek. It took his mind off the pain.

Leo and Eridanus learned of this change of course, and its source, through their companions, and they stopped to check on him.

"Did you tell the Wulfen to change course?" asked Leo.

With a white knuckled grip on the edge of the sled, Canis

opened what he could of his eyes. “Yeah,” he whispered then closed his eyes as he fought down the urge to cough. His lips were already lined with blood.

“Are you sure we should turn? How could you know where we are?” asked Leo.

Canis cocked half a smile. “Have I ever…led you wrong?” he whispered then struggled not to writhe as a jab of pain lanced through his body.

“No,” said Leo, “no, you never have.”

After giving Canis another sip of water, they headed out again on the new course. For the rest of their trip, Canis occasionally requested small course adjustments and in the end, he managed to cut an entire day off their trek. Unfortunately, Canis had succumbed to blood loss and cold, and he wasn’t aware of their successful return to the stockade, or how much time he had saved them.

His friends carried him into his house and deposited him on the bear hide near the hearth. Nike built up the fire and lit some lamps since it was already growing dark, then the three of them worked to remove Canis’s clothes.

His clothes were cut away and pulled free. It was fortunate that he was unconscious because his coat and shirt needed to be pealed away from his skin. Nike was relieved, and at the same time, appalled to see the condition of his coat. Appalled that so much blood had saturated the fur insulation, and relieved that it had retained at least some of its insulating ability regardless. Frostbite may have been avoided, but Canis was still dangerously cold.

With Canis settled, the men went home for some long overdue nourishment and sleep. Rrusharr, Ggrrawrr and Rrooggrr, Nike’s companion, took on the job of warming Canis’s feet and legs while Nike scooted herself under his head and shoulders trying to provide him with yet another source of body heat.

Canis draped over her lap like a dead man. Only his chest still moved, shallowly, showing that his soul still clung to his bones.

Nike knew that Canis was slowly drowning in his own blood and there was nothing to be done about it except be with him and try to make him as comfortable as she could. She pulled the bear hide over him up to the stick still protruding from his back, and chafed his shoulders with her hand.

With her vision burning with tears, she refused to shed until after he was dead, she started to run her fingers through his shiny red hair. She had always liked his hair. She would miss it. It was matted with blood on the side and she didn't try to pick it out. She didn't think he would live long enough to bother.

With her thumb, she probed the swelling on the side of his head, and in the process, her fingers brushed the stone between his eyebrows.

His hands weakly gripped the surfaces beneath them, the left one was on her leg, the right one was behind her back pulling at the bear hide. The weak grip on her leg and the wet gasp she heard caused her to lean over for a closer look, but his eyes remained closed and his hands relaxed again a few seconds later.

With a curious finger, she explored the stone again, brushing it carefully with the tip of one finger. She had grown used to its presence in his features and had almost forgotten about it, but this small reaction drew her curiosity.

With the more deliberate touch came a charge that traveled up her arm like a squirrel running up a tree. When it reached her mind, all the things of her life that lodged there came apart in innumerable pieces, then like a spring snowstorm, it all settled back down. Everything was still there, it was just slightly rearranged – a strange sensation to be sure.

Immersed in this fascinating sensation, she almost missed the fact that Canis's arm now wrapped around her hips and his head was pressed back into her belly. His other arm had been pulled back cocking his elbow up high and he was panting wetly, shallowly.

Suddenly Nike became intimately aware of the texture of his

skin. She found the damage in the shoulder under her elbow. She saw the ripped hole there in the skin and in the muscle underneath and knew that, all she had to do was move this here and that there – just put it back together – it was all so clear.

She shifted her attention to the worst wound, sliding her hand down his spine toward the area of interest. She saw the blood that filled his lung cavity, constricting the capacity of his lung, preventing his breathing. She wrapped her hand around the stick and eased it from the wound then she forced the accumulated blood out with it. Dimly she was aware of a vibration in his chest and the pulling of muscles that were trying to fold his body up.

She soothed the antagonized nerves, bringing the body relief and relaxation, then started to work on the damage. The blood had taken days to fill in between the rib cage and his lung, but she forced it out somewhat quicker. She then made the blood vessels join back together where they belonged, and she made all of the broken pieces of the ribs that had been brutally shoved aside, come back to where they too belonged.

By the time she was done, much of the damage had been undone. That much accomplished, she moved on to the other wound in his back, then lastly to the one on the side of his head. None of the wounds were completely healed and all of them would require constant attention for several days, but it was as done as it could be today. He would not die…today.

Nike came back to herself and looked down at Canis still draped across her lap. His breathing had greatly improved and already some color was returning to his pale cheeks. If that wasn't evidence enough, the appearance of the two wounds not covered by the bear hide or his hair confirmed that it had not been a dream.

She looked up at her surroundings and saw that daylight had long since come, so she eased herself out from under him and set about cleaning up the expelled blood and puss, then she spread soft leather bandages over the wounds before pulling the bear hide up to cover his shoulders.

She fixed their Wulfen something to eat, then went about her day, checking on Canis frequently. The news of what had happened to him traveled quickly around the stockade and when Nike didn't come out by midday to announce his death, Andromeda went to inquire.

When she saw what she considered to be something rather further from dead than she had been led to believe, she asked, "Nike, Leo said it looked like Canis was moments away from death and here he lies looking real bad, but far from dead. Was it just the cold?"

"No, mama. He was very bad. I thought he was going to die very soon too, but then I bumped that stone in his forehead… Mama, you remember how he healed Capricorn right after he came here? Well, I've done the same thing for him. I don't know how, but he couldn't heal himself so he made it possible for me to do it for him."

Andromeda knelt and looked closely at the stone between his brows. "How could he do that? Wouldn't he need to be awake before he could teach you?" she asked.

Nike shook her head. "I don't begin to understand it, but it's true. Look at him. It has to be."

After her mother left, Nike set about washing the blood from Canis's hair. Blood, once dried, doesn't dissolve easily, but Nike worked gently and persistently until his hair was clean. Then she proceeded to bathe the rest of him, at least as much of him as she could without moving him. The daylight was fading by the time she finished.

After stoking the fire again, she too curled up on the bear hide inches from where his right hand rested loosely. Around it, there were still signs that he had clenched at the hide in pain, but his hand was slack and straight now. She studied it. Even though its owner was only sixteen, the hand was strong. The fingers were long and graceful – talented in so many things. She studied and admired his hand until sleep washed over her exhausted mind, then that hand, and its mate, did obscure but tantalizing things in her dreams.

Canis didn't stir for two full days. Every few hours, Nike would search through his body with her new ability to heal. She kept ahead of the blood seeping into his lung and encouraged the fine tissues inside of his body to join just a little bit more each time.

At first, she touched the white stone between Canis's eyebrows in order to make use of his healing ability, but being ever curious, she tried it without touching the stone and discovered that the ability seemed to have claimed a new home.

She wondered if Canis still retained his ability to heal, or if perhaps he had given it to her. There was no way of knowing until the next time he tried to use it and he wouldn't be doing that for some time.

Canis woke on the third morning after being brought home. The sound of someone walking across the polished floor with soft feet woke him, and since he couldn't place where he was, his first thought was to defend himself and escape. Fortunately, he didn't move quickly. Pulling both his hands beneath his shoulders in preparation for pushing himself off the floor was quite enough to remind him of his current condition. It also enabled his sluggish brain to identify the bear hide beneath his cheek and feel Rrusharr's soothing presence in his mind, registering that her calm spoke of home and safety.

The whispering feet were at his side in moments and cool hands were on his arms and hands. Nike guided his hands back to their original position. "I don't think you want to move much, Canis. You're torn up inside some and it hasn't had much of a chance to heal yet," said Nike.

With grim determination, Canis fought down the urge to curl up with the pain. He remembered little of the accident, only waking in the snow in so much pain. As soon as he thought he had enough control he whispered, "How long have I been here?" He was surprised that he didn't taste blood with the words.

"This is the third day. Are you hungry or thirsty? I didn't know how to feed you with you lying on your belly."

Canis thought about it. "Starved, yes, and thirsty like a desert," he replied.

Nike hurried off to find something she could heat up. While she was gone, Canis struggled to push himself onto his side. He knew he could do that much; he'd had to ride on that side in the sled, and if he could do that, laying here among the soft folds of the bear hide should be easy by comparison.

Nike was surprised to see him on his side when she returned with his water skin. She set the bladder aside and went to retrieve a mug. When she brought the mug of water over to him she said, "I thought the water skin would be easier for you to manage on your stomach, but this is better."

Canis opened his eyes a slit and spoke with a voice strained with pain. "I thought I could do this, but perhaps not. I hurt all over."

"It's no wonder. You are more bruise than wound. I've done what I could, but bruises are difficult. Be still now." She reached out and caressed his exposed arm using the touch as a focus to go through his tense body and soothe the nerves that knotted his muscles with pain.

"What did you do?" asked Canis much relieved, and very surprised.

"I can use your healing." She reached up and gently brushed at the stone in his forehead. "You showed me how to do it."

Canis took the water and sipped at it, relishing its wetness, wondering if any of it reached his insides before being soaked up into the dry tissues of his throat. "Tell me about it, all of it."

While she fed him the warmed stew, she told him everything that had happened since her brother and Eridanus had brought him in.

He watched her nose turn slightly red as she recounted how she thought he was going to die. He watched goose bumps travel up her arm as she spoke of the sensation she felt when she had touched the stone. He watched her eyes flutter and shift as she spoke of making his flesh, bones, and blood do her bidding.

He pushed the spoon away with the bowl half finished and rested his head back against a fold of bear hide, resisting the urge to touch the stone that rested between his eyebrows. "No more now. So much for wanting to eat a whole moose, I think I will sleep for a while. Help me."

Nike set the bowl and mug aside and helped him to roll back onto his stomach. By the time he was laying flat again, he was whimpering with pain, but she soothed it away once again. As the cords of his muscles finished their trembling, she pulled a corner of the massive hide up to cover him. Then after taking care of the dishes, she moved off to do some sewing. There was a new coat to make and there was plenty of warm fur on this massive bear hide.

His pain quiet again, Canis lay with his eyes closed and thought about the things he had seen in her face as she had talked. He realized, perhaps for the first time, that Nike was in love with him. *What am I going to do? She will make someone a very good mate, but it can't be me; I will be leaving.* He decided then that he would leave as soon as he could.

As for Nike's newfound ability to heal, he knew where that came from too. The Mother had given him that ability so he could bring it here. Obviously, someone would become familiar enough with him, or be bold enough, to touch the stone, and their inclination toward petting seemed to make this a good possibility. In that way, the ability to heal would be brought to a people who needed it so badly; it was only his difference that had put it off for so long.

He didn't know how long this stockade had been here and he didn't know how many such places there were here in these mountains. The fact that Halley had come from another clan said there was more than one. Apparently the Mother thought them in need; perhaps they were.

If the clansmen had been here as long as the plainsmen had, then they were indeed in need. Only the snow kept the plainsmen out of the mountains, and aside from this winter, the snow was gradually receding and the men of the plains would follow close after. If they made it this far, the clans would be run down and slaughtered like animals or caged like his father had been, or worse.

Before he drifted off to sleep entirely, he wondered if the touch to his stone would work more than once. In a silent prayer to the Mother, he promised that he would have every woman in the clan touch it before he left the mountains, even if he had to search out every clan to do it. A warmth spread out from his heart and lulled him to sleep, telling him that he had made the right decision.

Time to Go

The next day, Canis sent for Sagittarius and his brother Taurus. Both brothers were in their early twenties, but no woman had yet chosen them, so they hunted with their fathers for the family. He also requested that their sister, Carina, come and distract Nike away from the visit. He arranged all this the only way he could, through their companions, something he hesitated to do, as it seemed so much like an invasion of privacy.

News of what appeared to be Nike's new healing ability had spread around the stockade, as all news did, and Carina was newly pregnant, so she could feign curiosity for a personal reason with very little effort.

Shortly after Nike left, Sagittarius and Taurus entered. Canis was unable to be much of a host, but he offered for them to take a seat and quickly explained why he wanted to see them. Logically, he would have chosen Capricorn for something of this nature – a return of the favor – but he had another reason for wanting these two. "I will not be able to hunt for the rest of the winter and I intend to leave here as soon as I am able. I have seen how both of you look at Nike when you think no one will notice."

Both men shifted. They might be brothers, but it was obvious that they did not share the same father. Regardless, they acted much the same; they were both somber, serious men.

Canis continued, "I want one of you, or both of you, to move in here and hunt for Nike. Since I am leaving, it is my hope that Nike will choose one of you as her husband. I have already told her that this house will be hers when I leave."

"She made it clear she will choose you as her husband," said Taurus. "I'm surprised she hasn't told you yet."

"She has hinted at it, but I have given her no encouragement," said Canis.

"We are hunting for our family," said Sagittarius.

"Yes, I know, and it is right that you do so, especially now that hunting is so hard," said Canis. "I am just asking you to accept responsibility for Nike too. There are four hunters in your family. I am the only hunter for this family." He knew his request would not be denied. No one would deny a downed hunter's request for help; they just needed a suitable incentive. "When I leave, I will take very little with me."

"Why are you leaving?" asked Taurus. "Why would you want to?"

"You are too much like your mother," commented Sagittarius, though his comment was not meant as an insult.

It was an old subject; one that almost never came up, but he owed them an answer. "I do not know that I am like my mother, but I owe a plainsman a lot of money. As a kid, I could do nothing to repay him. As a man, I can. I must leave before I have to turn Nike down, and time is short for that. I cannot be her mate and not be here to hunt for her, and I would not take her away from here. There are dangers where I go I may not be able to protect her from."

Taurus, slightly more spontaneous than his brother, stood. "I will come here and hunt for Nike," he declared.

Sagittarius stood next. "My brother eats like a bear; he will need my skill too, if there is to be enough meat for everyone. I too will come here and hunt for Nike."

Canis watched them, surprised at the exchange, but Taurus didn't seem to take offense at the jab. As he watched them leave, he wondered what kind of chaos their presence in his quiet home would cause.

As it turned out, the only chaos they caused was the

understandable chaos of moving and settling into a new environment, and the fact that there were two more people and their companions coming and going.

Nike was none too pleased to have the extra mouths to feed and the brothers *both* ate like bears, but she understood the necessity of it and didn't protest.

Like other homes with two hunters, Sagittarius and Taurus took turns hunting while the other helped with the house chores. Both men worked hard for Nike, and they worked hard *on* her. Both of them were vying for her attention and Canis encouraged them, though he found that it tore at him to do so.

Canis's strength returned slowly, and by the time the snows started to melt, he was getting around stiffly on his own. With the coming spring and his returned health, Canis began preparations for departure.

One of the things he did was to find excuses for all of the women and girls to touch the stone between his brows. Sometimes he encouraged their curiosity and other times he outright asked for it. The news of how Nike had received her gift helped. The gift was given out only one other time to Cygnus' baby daughter.

Shortly before he left, he grilled the elders of the camp for the locations of other clans and learned there were three other clans that they knew of, though they could give him directions to only the closest one, the others were much farther south, and no one had ever traveled that far.

With a sled half full of provisions, sleeping furs, cooking items and tools, Canis left by the eastern gate heading south. At the top of a ridge, he stopped to look back. The stockade had been the most home he had ever known. Perhaps, one day, he would come back.

With Rrusharr, Ggrrawrr, and another young Wulfi by the name of Rranggrr, he turned his back on the stockade. Somehow, despite his desire, he knew he would never see these people or this place again.

In his mind the scene at the house took many different forms. He hoped Nike would choose one of both of the men he'd chosen for her. He truly wanted her to be happy. He wished he could have waited to be sure, but he knew his continued presence would only put her decision off or cause her disappointment when he turned her down. Taking himself out of her choices put her on a much better path.

Canis traveled south, finding the first clan in five weeks with no trouble. A strange hunter was rare, but not unheard of; he was just so very different. News that he knew of Halley broke some of the ice and there was other news to exchange. Her mother, at least, was pleased to learn that she had found mates and was building a family. News that she seemed truly happy came as a bit of a surprise, but the news was welcome just the same. He also spotted the man who walked with a stick under his arm. During his short stay, he made him a better one with a piece across the top covered and padded with fur.

Aside from Haley's mother, Canis's welcome here was less than warm. Everyone kept staring at him – he was simply too different. Even so, after a long discussion with the elders, he was able to leave two healers here. He wondered if perhaps he should show them something of the gift, but aside from telling them that what they felt was a gift of healing from the Mother, he could tell them very little. After all, what did he really know about it? He could remember nothing about the times he had healed someone. He was confident that instinct would be sufficient. It had served Nike very well and he wasn't willing to live here long enough for some tragedy to occur; his reputation was strange enough as it was. He asked for directions to the next clan holding and moved on.

It took most of three weeks to reach the next clan stockade, and if it weren't for the scouting of the Wulfen in his company, he might not have found it then. The mountains he traveled through were laced with crevasses in the ancient ice. Cut by spring runoff deep within their depths, they forced Canis to divert his path many times before making progress south.

He finally found the clan nestled near a frozen lake and he was welcomed warmly if only out of curiosity. Though he traveled with three Wulfen, they had never before seen red hair and Canis's hair reached past his waist by now. No one in the clan had hair that reached even as far as their shoulders; it just didn't grow that long. Clan hair ranged from pale gray to black, but the closest it ever got to red was a few undertones of brown.

After staying a little over a week with this clan, he headed south once again leaving behind three healers this time, including one little boy who couldn't seem to keep his hands to himself. Canis hadn't expected the gift to be passed to males. The woman and the girl who also received the gift were both told that the gift came from the Mother and now they had the skill to heal if they would use it, but the boy was too young to understand any of this. His mother listened avidly, though, as he told them what Nike had told him of the experience.

Like all the others, they didn't know who the Mother was and Canis himself didn't know well enough to say much about it except to tell his own story about how he had been given the stone between his brows and the gift to heal, though his gift was intended to be spread among the clans.

As the giant trees that reached up above the glaciers grew farther apart, the terrain he had to cross grew rougher. It became riddled with upstart ridges of rock that made travel slow and difficult. The high altitude didn't bother him much, but it seem that the farther south he traveled the dryer the cold air became making him drink a lot of water, so he was forced to stop often to refill his water skin with snow.

Hunting grew more difficult as well, so when Canis saw an opportunity to shoot a creature he hadn't seen before, he took it. Not as big as a moose, it was nonetheless a powerful creature with an impressive many-pointed rack. Standing five feet at the shoulders, it had dark brown fur on its head and neck and creamy gray fur on its back and flanks.

Canis's shot dropped it in the snow only a few bounds from where it had been standing scraping away the snow to get at whatever was beneath it. He skinned, and deboned it as far as he could, allowing the hungry Wulfen to feast on the ribs and the meaty knuckles of what he was discarding. The rest he cut into sections and spread out on the snow to bleed out and freeze as much as it was going to this time of year.

The temperature of the air was above freezing, but not so far as to melt all of the snow on the ground. The meat would not freeze solid, but the cold would not let it go bad very fast either. He found the hide thick and soft so he kept that too and used it to wrap the meat in, protecting it even further from the warm air and sun.

It took Canis a little more than a month to reach the last clan holding, and by then the short summer was drawing to a close. It was the largest clan and perhaps the easiest to find, but if it weren't for the wide-ranging Wulfen, he might have missed this one too.

This clan's holding didn't boast a stockade. Instead, it resembled a village of the plains more than anything else. Due to the cold winds that screamed across the landscape during much of the winter, only half of the upper story of the homes extended above the ground. That combined with the average of five feet of snow that the wind packed up against any obstruction in its path made the village all, but invisible to a traveler who didn't know what to look for.

His arrival was, of course, announced through the Wulfen population well before he reached the edge of the village, so he was met by a good many of its residents before he ever saw the settlement.

His compliment of Wulfen hunters saw to it that he was greeted as warmly as at the other clan holdings. After the elders got over their first surprise of a visiting stranger, his appearance seemed to have the opposite affect as at the other holdings. They all clasped hands with him and pulled him into the crowd. They introduced him to every face that flashed past on the way into the confines of the town.

Canis was taken to the house of Capella and her husbands, Almach and Auriga. Having just married, her house had the most space, and with winter coming hard on his heels, Canis didn't have to tell them that he would need a place to stay for the winter; no one went for long trips during the winter.

Little of the meat from his kill remained to be brought into his new, if temporary, home, but what he did bring, he offered to his new hostess for their next meal; he was after all bringing four extra mouths into the house unannounced.

This was graciously accepted. Almach showed him where he could stow his sled and tools, and then took him into their home where he showed him where he could put the rest of his gear.

The house was not made out of wood like the other clans' homes had been since there were no trees around big enough or straight enough for anything other than firewood, or perhaps tools and furniture. These houses were made out of stone. Like all the clan homes, this one had two stories. The main working area was on the upper floor while sleeping, eating, and cooking were all done on the lower floor below ground level.

Since the bitter winter winds always came from the north, all the houses in the village faced south. To conserve as much heat as possible, there were no openings at all other than the door located on the south side. The roof was slanted down to the ground on the north side, thereby diminishing the chances of the bitter wind taking the roof with it in passing. This design also created a storage place for things like the sleds and other items that might be useful in making tools or furniture. The eves on the south side extended almost six feet beyond the south wall of the house. This kept the snow that drifted in on the lee side of the house from blocking the door.

Four to seven houses were arranged in five neat rows along main pathways that led down to the river that fed into the lake. The lake itself was a wonder to Canis. He had seen running water wherever he went during the summer, but if it wasn't running, it was frozen, and most calm water was frozen solid year around with any incoming water simply adding to the volume of ice in the area. This was the first body of liquid water Canis had seen since coming into the mountains. It was full of ice, but none of it was larger than a man's fist and it floated in thick brine that refused freezing in all, but the coldest weather.

Despite protests to the contrary, Canis insisted on accompanying Almach on his next hunting trip. If he was going to be dipping into their supplies, the least he could do was contribute to them. Hunting trips from this clan were different from those of the Yellowstone Clan in that the hunting parties consisted of men from every house and they hunted herds, bringing down only enough to fill all of their sleds and no more.

During this first hunt, Canis had to force his own shot by not going where he was told to go, which is *not* where the game would go. His shots were telling and the hunt was finished that much sooner.

That evening, over the campfire, Canis learned some of the reason behind his new friends' protective actions.

"You are our honored guest," said Almach. "We didn't want to put you in a position where you might be injured."

"Why? I may be young, but I am an accomplished hunter. I have been hunting as head of my house for over four years. I do not need any more protection than any other hunter," said Canis.

The men who sat across the fire from him couldn't hide their discomfort.

"You don't understand," said Almach. "You are honored."

"Honored for what? I am clan. I will hunt. I am not a child who needs to stay home until I am big enough to pull a bow. I have been using my father's bow for two years now, and I even used it once two years before that. I am no weakling." He did not tell them the story of the bear fearing they would 'honor' him even more.

The men looked even more uneasy, especially when the youngest of them, a fourteen year old by the name of Saiph, a nephew of Almach's, blurted, "The legends said she would return to us one day, but we always assumed she would be a woman."

"She? Who is this 'she'? I have never been here before?" said Canis.

The ice had been broken. "Of course you've not been here before," said Almach. "She has been dead for many, many generations. She was a small child when the first of us was set free under the stars. She taught us to build houses. She taught us to hunt and gather in preparation for the starving months. If it were not for her, we would have become little more than another wolf rolling up in a fur at night and following the hunt by day. If it were not for her, the starving months would have claimed us all long ago."

"This is all very commendable, but I do not see how you could connect any of this to me."

"You look like her. You could be her son," said Saiph.

"We will take you to see her when we return," said Almach.

"I look like her? How is this possible?" said Canis, he was definitely curious.

"We will take you to see Debhe. She's our legends keeper. She can tell you the whole story," said Almach.

True to his word, Almach took Canis to see the oldest woman in the clan, Debhe. She was a woman of only thirty some years, but like most of the people of the clan, the hard life seemed to shorten their life span. If nothing else happened to her, she would likely die of old age before her youngest daughter claimed her mates.

Debhe's house was located at the farthest end of the third street from the north. These end houses were closest to the low cliffs that followed the river and offered another buffer against the brutal winter winds.

When news that the stranger was being taken to hear the

legends reached the rest of the village, many of the others came too. The people all loved hearing the legend.

As soon as everyone had made themselves comfortable around the hearth and grew quiet, Debhe started the story. "When the first of us came into being, we were kept in separate rooms, not unlike our sleeping rooms, but we were kept...*alone*. The men who kept us did not know about our need to join with the companions who made us whole, so they were kept in another area and other than knowing of their existence, we never saw them. We were fed. We were housed and we were kept healthy, and yet we died before reaching the age of adult. We were taught many things about fighting and hunting, but the men who kept us were not happy with us. As children, we were not good enough.

"There was one man there who taught us other things. This man, called Brian, a name we must never forget, taught us compassion and tenderness. He taught us laughter and love. It pained him to see us struggle to speak to our teachers, but with him, it did not matter what we could, or could not, say. None of our problems mattered to him. He loved us all and showed us as much all the time he was with us. It is said that we learned as much or more from Brian as we did from all the other teachers put together. We all looked up to him like a father, though none of us knew what a father was then.

"One day, the sky started to fall and the ground began to shake – some among us believed that the stars we take our names from came down to punish those who imprisoned us – the great house where we were kept began to fall in upon itself. We were all so afraid. We were all going to die there in the darkness and loneliness.

"The man, Brian, he came to us. He braved the crumbling building to set us free, though the building claimed him for his efforts. We found our companions and left the clutches of the building. Some of us were suffering from the fevered death and many of us were still very small, but we brought us all out of that place and headed away from the people who had imprisoned us.

We headed into the mountains, into the darkness and away from the stars that rested on the ground.

"Our path led us to his home where we found *her*, his daughter. Because of our love for Brian, we took her with us. She was such a lovely child." Debhe paused in her story to reach out and touch Canis's hair. "She even had this," she touched the stone between Canis's eyebrows. "Though hers was not hard nor was it white."

After a pause where Debhe gazed at him with a soft expression in her eyes, she said, "Come, we will visit her. I will continue the story there."

She led them toward a thick hanging covering the eastern wall. The hanging was made out of a hide like he had brought into camp with him, but this one had been stitched and decorated extensively with colorful, shiny stones and equally shiny metals of all sorts. The effect was quite exotic and one could study it for hours and still be fascinated by its shiny patterns.

Debhe lifted the heavy hide aside to reveal a short tunnel leading off into the dark. An old man who might have been Debhe's mate picked up a lamp and led the way. The tunnel led off under the cliff that bordered the village. Several hundred yards later, it opened up into a sizable room chiseled out of the frozen rock.

Scattered around the chamber were several tables, all of which had been lovingly made and intricately carved and polished. Displayed on these tables were many different things. There were more of the shiny stones, polished bones, and bits of metal. There were small things of all sorts, carved from pieces of wood that were twisted into intricate knots to begin with.

Many of the things carefully scattered across some of the tables had to be favorite toys of childhood and favorite tools of adulthood. There were the tools she had used for cooking and other work she had done as an adult. There were things she had used for painting, dying and even for carving. Among these things were many of the items she had created. She had been quite an artist.

There were charcoal drawings of her friends, their homes, and their life. There was a striking painting of a man with silver white hair and pale blue eyes. If it weren't for the hair, Canis could have been looking into a mirror of his own future. He had a sharp nose and wide cheekbones, but he knew that the profile would be just like Orion's had been. The eyes were expressive and echoed of love for the painter and they were just as ice blue as his own. The mouth was the only other visible difference. The mouth of the man in the painting held a mischievous quirk at the corner that spoke of fun and play. Canis had never known much fun or play, and he seldom smiled.

Canis was shaken and yet mesmerized by that painting, so much so that he jumped when Debhe touched his elbow and guided him to the centerpiece of the chamber. "This is Angela," she said simply. There, in what appeared to be a massive block of ice was a woman. She was old, but there was still a good deal of copper red left in the thick braid that rested down her breast. The ice blurred her features, but Canis thought he could see a resemblance to his mother. She might have looked much like this sleeping woman if she had lived longer and had a happier life.

Canis could pick out the smiling lines around her mouth and eyes. His mother had worry lines between her brows. There, between this woman's brows, he saw the brown mark Debhe had spoken of. It almost looked like a thumbprint. Canis reached up and touched the white stone between his own brows.

Debhe brushed Canis's hair behind his ear with a gentle caress and drew his attention back to her story. "It took us a long time to find this place. Somehow, we managed to miss the falling sky that smashed everything around us. With cloths over our faces, we struggled to breathe the dirt-filled air.

"As we traveled, those of us who had been ill from the lack of joining recovered their strength and were able to help with the hunting. Some of the youngest died; we just couldn't care for them well enough. We didn't want to mingle them with the humans who had imprisoned us. We decided to send them to the beautiful stars overhead, the stars that the humans had gone to such great pains to shut us away from, so we built great piles of wood and sent their souls up into the sky.

"While we traveled, we huddled together at night for warmth around the small fire we used to cook our meat. At first, most of us were willing to follow the example of our companions and tear our meat from the bones fresh from the kill, but she insisted on a fire where she cooked her portion. Angela refused to eat the meat uncooked. Many of the younger children followed her example; hot food is good when it is cold outside. By the time we reached this place, all of us were cooking our meat; it reminded us of Brian.

"By the time we reached this lake, the stars had ceased to fall, but the air was still filled with dust, and the nights were growing colder. At first, we sheltered in the remains of their battered down buildings, but that was only until we could build a place of our own here closer to fresh water.

"It took many years to build this place. This house was the first to be built and this chamber helped to house some of our numbers until stones could be brought in and more houses could be built. It took an entire summer to build one house so it was a long time before we all had houses of our own, and by then many of those who were babies when we came here were looking to make babies of their own.

"There were no children in Angela's house, though, so she filled the emptiness with her drawings and paintings. She so loved to draw and paint, though only this much remains to show it." She indicated the handful of drawings that were displayed among the other treasures.

"When the stars stopped pounding the ground, the clouds closed them off and the days grew colder. The winter snows stayed longer, hunting became harder, and our hunters were forced to range far in search of game. We lost many hunters in those days and despite our best efforts, we also lost many mothers to the months of starvation and they took their youngest children with them. We sent them all to find the stars. We hoped that, if they could find the stars and bring them back to us, we would be able to survive. They could also look after us from their lofty place among the glittering stars and help us find our way.

"Eventually they succeeded, and the stars came back to us. During the long cold winter, our numbers were reduced, but we became better hunters and gatherers. We followed Angela's teachings and brought in enough to see us through the starving months and our numbers began to grow again.

"When the sun began to warm us again many generations later, some of us decided to divide our numbers. Hunting was very poor still and there were many mouths to feed. When this was agreed, the elders gathered together to decide which direction to go. It was decided that they would follow the brightest star in the sky for it must be her star, her soul watching over us. As you have discovered, young Canis, we have divided three different times since then and Angela has never led us wrong. Now she has brought you to us; you come away from her star. You are not Angela, but I believe you carry her soul and I know you bring us yet another gift."

Canis looked back at the ageless woman imbedded in ice. She was perfectly preserved here. "You have sent all of your dead to the stars to watch over you. Why did you not do the same with her?" asked Canis, his hand wanted to touch her cheek, but there were too many inches of ice in the way.

"She was terrified of fire, especially the big fires we used to send our dead on their journey. She made her mate promise never to send her into the fire, so he placed her in the water until it froze, then he brought her out to rest here and surrounded her with all of the things she loved in life. This place stays cold and every winter we add to the ice so it will never melt away.

History in the Blood

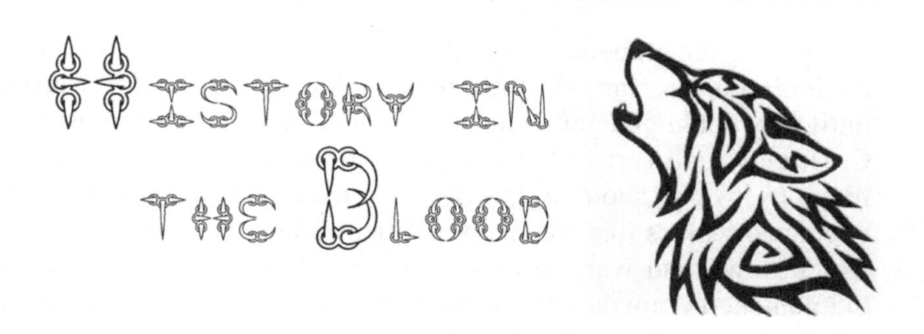

The tale was finished and the villagers dispersed, leaving Canis standing in the chamber alone. Even Debhe left him to his thoughts. She didn't notice that his hands were shaking and she didn't see him sink to his knees as memories that were not his flooded his mind. Canis relived the story he had been told and found it coming to life for him as if it were something he had only to remember.

Canis remembered the crashing explosion when the meteor crushed his home. His mother had been in there fixing supper, daddy was due home soon; he always had such fascinating stories about the children where he worked. She liked hearing his stories. She wished he could bring them home with him.

Canis remembered being cold sitting on the rock. He was watching the mountain-sized fireballs fall from the sky throwing dirt and rock amazingly high into the air; then he saw movement on what was left of the road to their house.

Canis remembered sitting on this very rock many times, waiting to spot her daddy's car as he came home from work with new stories about the children he cared for, but it was late and what he saw was not her daddy's car. Once he spotted one of the strangely moving spots, he could pick out others.

Canis remembered his deep smooth voice and his strong arms. He buried her face in his neck to hide from the falling sky. He was so terrified and fires were everywhere now. Avior's strong arms protected her from all of it. He felt so safe close to him.

Canis remembered how they moved every day until they couldn't go any farther, then they huddled together for warmth until they could go again. Game was plentiful and easy to come by. Creatures of all sorts were too panicked by the destruction around them to worry about a bunch of hungry kids or the pack of oversized wolves that roamed with them. Many creatures had been struck down and were already dead. Meat was plentiful; hunting the panicked animals wasn't necessary, and the risk of separation was high.

Canis remembered watching in horror as her new friends fell upon a dead deer directly in their path killed perhaps only moments before by stray shrapnel from a nearby impact. Canis remembered the first and last time she had been afraid of Avior. He had fallen on the carcass with the others and the wolves. In minutes there was little left of it; it hadn't been very big. He had looked up at her and his long face was covered with blood from the chunk of raw meat he was gnawing on with his suddenly very visible, very sharp teeth. Canis remembered the expression on his face when he saw that Brian's daughter had eaten nothing. Out of respect for her and her father, they never let such a display happen again.

Canis remembered that the youngest among them couldn't chew the raw meat and get enough before it was all gone so they started begging from her. Eventually all of them cooked their meat and ensured that even the youngest got a share. Brian would have expected nothing less of them.

Canis remembered when the first baby died. It had been too young to eat what food they had, and none of them could provide it with the milk it needed. As the older ones grew stronger after their illness, the littlest ones died. They carried them with them as long as they could. Canis remembered the fire they made to send their souls to the stars.

Canis remembered using shards of glass to skin the creatures they ate and using the raw hides to keep warm. The days were scarcely discernable from the nights and they were getting so cold,

daily activity, Rrusharr still rested at his side and Rranggrr still hunted mice, though she was farther away at the moment, and Ggrrawrr still stood guard over them all. Only the angle of the sun had changed; it was high overhead now.

He rose to his feet, hitching his shoulder where a lump in the rock had gouged a numb spot, then headed back down to the village. He'd been here less than a week and suddenly he felt like a grandfather. Well, no, that wasn't the right word. He was their guardian. He held them all under his protection. They were his responsibility.

When he reached Capella's house, she greeted him with the beginnings of a new coat she was making for him. "It is for the winter. I am still working on the pelt you brought in, but if you insist on hunting with Almach, you will need proper clothing."

"I am grateful," said Canis as he flexed his shoulders to see if there was enough room. He didn't tell her that the coat he already had was only a few months old, but then this one looked like it was going to be much longer.

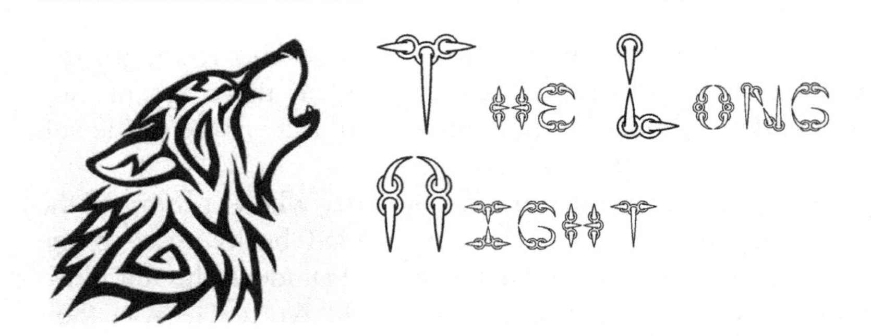

Winter came down on them with a fury. The storm howled around the village for four days. It was a time for much sleep and many other things that took place among the furs. This activity was interrupted for meals and calls of nature, but little else.

Canis busied himself with whatever he could find to do in the dim light of the lamp. The hide he had brought was mostly finished and was soft everywhere but around the edges. He worked on that until he couldn't take any more, then he put his new coat on and went outside. He leaned against the wall next to the door and watched the storm rage. He knew better than to venture out into it, even for a few feet. The blinding wind-driven snow would disorient him in seconds and he could freeze to death only feet from safety.

Auriga pulled him inside for a meal, after which the three of them disappeared behind their curtain again.

Canis went upstairs and dug out some heavy leather, then began to make himself a new pair of boots. Just standing outside for that short time, his feet became cold. He couldn't afford for that to happen out on a hunt. He worked until his fingers got too cold, then he went down for a cup of tea to warm his hands. He finished one boot before supper and the other before he went to sleep. By then the others had worn themselves out and were finally quiet. It had been a long day.

After far too long in his opinion, the storm passed and Almach and Auriga made preparations for a hunt. "With luck we'll find a herd mired in the snow and we'll make a good haul," said Almach.

"That is if the herd we find is large enough to withstand such a harvest," said Auriga. Seeing Canis's interest, he explained. "Only in the hardest years will we take more than half a herd."

Since it appeared that both of Capella's mates were intent on participating in this hunt, Canis felt obliged to remain behind. He suspected this was part of their effort to protect him from harm, but he didn't mind this time. He would take his turn on the hunt, and taking his turn also meant taking a turn at home.

When they were gone, Canis went to the river to bring back ice to fill the water barrel. Then he took his sled to the edge of the lake where he could find wood to make new snowshoes. It was difficult to find something that wasn't twisted and gnarled by the wind, but eventually he found something he could use.

With it thawing, he started to oil his bow and check his arrows. He would need more, but he didn't have any more heads. He could deal with that later. Maybe Auriga would show him where their deposits were.

By the time the hunters returned, Canis had worked his way through most of his gear and had a good estimate of what he might need before he left for the plains in the spring.

The hunt had gone well, though a wounded buck had gored one man. Capella went to offer her condolences and Canis went with her.

Adhara answered their scratch and brought them down for a cup of tea. Others came to offer their support as well, but none of them did more than express their sorrow about Turais's injury. It was not bad enough that it would kill him unless it became badly infected, but it could take him out of the hunt for a good deal of the winter. Bad luck for any family.

Canis came to do more than offer his condolences; he knelt beside Turais and started a halting conversation by asking how the accident had happened. Once the man was immersed in telling of the incident, Canis rested a hand on his leg and let the healing drown his awareness.

A few minutes later, Turais was looking at him with a mixture of fear and fascination, and the women who were still there, had stopped their conversation and gathered around to watch.

Canis pulled away the blood soaked pad to reveal a clean tear that extended from his mid thigh on his left side to split his left, buttocks. Instead of looking swollen and angry, it now looked to be half healed already with very little bleeding left, and that would make a good scab. The wound would still take him out of several hunts and he would probably have a limp for the rest of his life, but he would be back on the hunt before half of the winter had passed.

Adhara gasped to see it and muttered "A miracle" with utter awe in her voice.

"This is why I came here by way of all of the other clans," said Canis. "The Mother gifted me with the ability to heal, but mostly she gifted me with the ability to pass the gift on to others that she deems worthy of such a gift." Canis reached up and touched the stone between his brows. "This is the symbol of her touch and her gift. All it takes is for someone to touch it. I was able to leave two or three healers in each of the other holdings and I expect to do much the same here."

"You mean to say that if I touch that stone, I'll be able to heal like that?" asked Centauri.

"That is the gift. Whether the Mother chooses you to wield it remains to be seen."

"How will we know how to do that?" asked Capella with a gesture toward Turais's leg. "Who will teach us what to do?"

"Whoever receives the gift will know what to do. I do not know anything about it. Though I can do some healing in this manner, I remember nothing of the time in question. The Mother heals through me."

"You keep speaking of 'the Mother'. Are you talking about Angela?" asked Caph.

"No, Angela was a remarkable woman, but this gift came about long after her death and is sprinkled among the plainsmen. It is only right that you have your share as well. That way there will be fewer deaths among your number from accidents such as this." He waved a hand toward Turais. "It is the Mother's wish that you grow strong."

"You must teach us more about this 'Mother'," said Adhara.

"I know very little. All I know is what I have been told. That She is the mother of all things be it plant, animal or man and everything in between."

The room was silent, but Caph didn't let it stay that way very long. She pulled Canis to his feet. "Well, if we must touch the stone in your forehead to receive the gift of healing, there's no time like the present to do it. The hunt was successful. Everyone is home. Let's go."

This isn't quite what Canis had expected. In the other holdings, he had needed to talk the people into touching the stone. Actions of that nature were considered invasive unless the person was close family or one's small children. Some were willing and some were reluctant; ultimately, it took two or three days to convince people to take the chance. Each time the gift was bestowed, it sent a charge through his body. It wasn't unpleasant, but still, it was a bit of a drain in a way.

It was already near sundown when the hunters had returned from their hunt. By the time Caph led Canis from Adhara's house, it was full dark. Still, Caph led Canis to every house in the village, skipping only those that were vacant. In each house, every occupant down to the smallest baby touched Canis's stone. When the third healer was initiated, Canis was dropped to his knees by the touch. By the time they had visited the last home and bestowed the last gift on the last healer, he could scarcely stand.

Seven healers were uncovered ranging in age from a one-year-old little boy whose mother had died in childbirth, to thirty-five year old Altair, Debhe's husband.

When Caph and Altair brought Canis back to Capella's house, Capella took one look at her guest's condition and berated her mother. "Mother! How could you do this to our honored guest? He will be here all winter. You are always being so greedy."

"S-like Rayet," slurred Canis. He was having trouble focusing and was draped from Altair's shoulder like a rag doll.

Capella called to her husbands, and then turned to Canis. "What did you say?"

"Rayet…stole a bunch of Angela's pic…pichers. Hid 'em in a jar. Didn wanna share. Looks like 'im." Canis was fading by now, but Almach and Auriga were there and they carried him into the house. In the darkness of predawn, no one noticed how pale Caph went after what Canis said.

"Mother, who's Rayet?"

Caph didn't respond: she just hurried away. She didn't even thank Altair for his help in bringing Canis home or congratulate him for becoming a healer.

Capella wasn't so forgetful; she *did* thank him for bringing their guest home; no one told her that he was now a healer. She went inside with the intention of questioning Canis further, but he was already asleep.

The sun turned a full circle before Canis woke again and he still felt muzzy-headed and dull. He was slouching over the breakfast Capella had set before all of them.

"Canis," she said to get his attention. "Who is Rayet?"

Canis sat back and said, "Oh, well Rayet is…" The memory was gone. It had been right there, on the tip of his tongue. "I…I do not know. I… It was there…but I cannot remember. Why?"

"Nothing," said Capella. "It was just something you said when you came home. You said this Rayet had stolen a bunch of Angela's pictures and hidden them in a jar. You said he didn't want to share them. You said something else, but I didn't understand it, something about looks."

Canis searched his memory. It had been there, but he couldn't find it. "I am sorry. I cannot remember. The name is familiar, but I do not know why. Until you spoke it, I had never heard it before."

After breakfast, Capella went to her mother's house. She didn't return to her home until it was time for the noon meal. She was so quiet and moody that Auriga questioned her.

Canis was stunned by the story she told. A wealth of pictures had been hidden away for who knows how long and apparently, Caph had found out about it at some point but contrived to keep the secret and the pictures hidden away for herself. “Why would someone want to do such a thing?” she asked.

Then almost as if someone was smiling indulgently behind him, Canis got an idea. After lunch, he too left the house and called on Caph.

Gacrux let him in to find Caph sitting on the floor by the big jar sobbing quietly into her knees. The pictures were gone.

“Come with me,” said Canis and he pulled her to her feet. Inviting her husbands to come too, Canis led her to Debhe’s house.

When Caph, Debhe, and their husbands were all sitting around the table with a hot cup of tea in their hands, he said, “You all know by now what I have said about the Mother giving me the gift of healing. She also gave me Angela’s memories. Perhaps she wanted those pictures found, I do not know, but there is one thing I am certain of. Angela knew who took those pictures, and she knew what he did with them. She understood and she didn’t really mind. She knew they would be protected and treasured. Yes, the whole clan should share them, but I think she wouldn’t mind at all if the person who treasured them so much, continued to care for them. They need to be organized in such a way that they go along with the story. Who best to do that than the person who is most familiar with them?” He rested a hand on Caph’s shoulder. “It is a worthy task for a family who has seen them through the ages to this day.”

As he spoke, he watched Caph’s expression go from bleak desolation to fragile hopefulness. She was an elder of the clan. She could shoulder this responsibility. She would drag her honor back out of the mud. She straightened her shoulders and looked hopefully at the others around the table.

When Debhe drew her toward the hanging that covered the tunnel’s mouth, Canis raised a hand to the men and quietly slipped away.

Back at Capella's house, he went back to sleep. He was still feeling the affects of creating seven healers in one very long night.

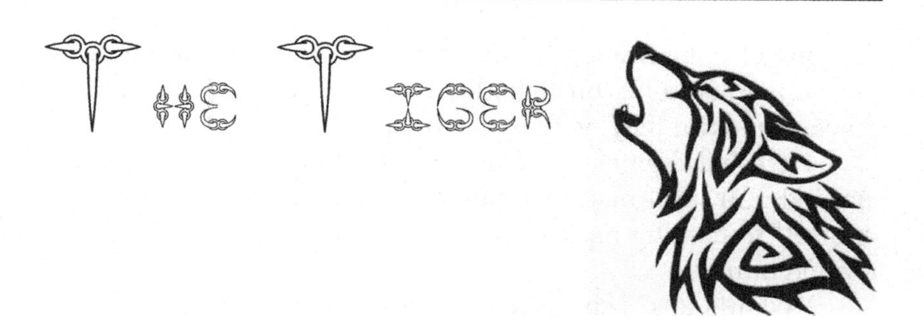

The Tiger

ALMOST a month had passed before Canis was again left home alone with Capella while her husbands both went hunting. He filled his days with whatever chores were too heavy or time consuming for Capella to handle then fell into his nest gratefully tired.

The second such night, he was wakened abruptly when Capella slid into his nest with him. “What are you doing here?” he asked in alarm. He would have jumped out of the nest, but she had him cornered.

“I was lonely,” she whispered. Her voice was sultry and fascinating. Canis found his body responding to her touch *definitely* without his volition. When her hand traveled down his chest to dive deep between his legs, his body arched as if struck by lightning.

With a growl, he forced her away from him to arms reach. “What are you doing here?” he asked again. His voice sounded husky in his ears, which felt like they were on fire.

In the darkness, he could feel her smiling. He could feel other things too. “I’m lonely. I want you.”

“No,” said his mouth. His body was saying something quite different.

“Yes,” she purred.

Unable to stand it any more and afraid he wouldn’t be able to withstand her advances any longer, Canis dumped her unceremoniously on the floor and grabbed his coat. Dressed in nothing else, he headed for the stairs. Before he went out the door, he pulled his boots on thankful that they reached well above his knees; thankful they were by the door.

He leaned against the outside of the building clutching his coat around him until his heart calmed again. He had almost resigned himself to coming back in out of the cold when Capella came out to find him.

"What's this?" she asked. "Don't you want me?"

Appalled, Canis looked at her and spoke in a tone he was surprised to hear from himself not to mention the words he uttered. "You are married to two fine men who give you all the attention you could possibly want. If you must act like a bitch in heat all the time, then I suggest you keep one of them at home *all the time*. Stay out of my nest."

She recoiled as if she had been slapped, then her eyes narrowed and she snapped back. "What are you saving yourself for, some female from the plains? Do you really think they will have you?" She stormed back into the house and slammed the door behind her.

He didn't figure he would be able to sleep if he went back into the house and he was reluctant to chance facing Capella again, so he curled up where he was and tried to calm his confused mind. Rrusharr, Ggrrawrr, and Rranggrr soon joined him. With their welcome company and body heat, sleep came…eventually.

He was startled awake in the earliest dawn by the sound of several anguished wails coming from where the loose Wulfen sheltered. He had heard it once before, though the echoes were different here. He was on his feet and running toward the sound before he remembered the occurrence during the night. Only after he was already in motion did he remember that he was dressed in only his coat and boots. That didn't stop him though. The coat reached past his knees and the boots well above; no one else would know unless he opened his coat.

He was half way to the river when he found the rest of the Wulfen and he could hear the waking village emerging with equal panic and following him.

When Canis reached the pack, a grizzled gray Wulfi turned to him. The image of a great striped cat chilled Canis's blood. He was pelting back to the village before the others had cleared the last building. "We need every arrow. A striped cat is attacking the hunters. They need help," he yelled at them and ran on, not pausing to answer questions or even to see if anyone was going to follow him.

Canis charged into the house. The constant stream of images he was now getting from the disastrous hunt was spurring him to the greatest speed he could muster as he buckled his sword belt on over his coat.

"We are coming, drop the sleds. Let him have the meat. We are coming," muttered Canis. He took no notice of Capella who huddled fearfully in the corner. He scooped up his bow and arrows, then his snowshoes, and outside he grabbed his sled with its bedroll. The carefully sorted tools and cooking equipment, he left behind in a heap.

First and fastest, he was back at the pack that still howled of the disaster. "Come," he said and turned his running feet to find the hunt.

The picture playing in Canis's head told of the run. The men were dropping the sleds laden with meat one at a time. Each drop bought them some time, but the cat was chasing them anyway, most likely because they were running, but stopping would be suicide.

The Wulfen were doing their best to keep the cat from getting too close to their hunters, but the striped cat was getting frustrated with them. Four men ran with injured or dead companions across their shoulders. Canis didn't know who and he wasn't going to distract anyone by asking now.

His lungs were burning by the time he saw the first signs of the chase. He dropped his sled and took up a position behind a snow-covered rock. "Keep them running," he whispered and watched as the tired Wulfen peal away from the fight one by one as the replacements showed up to take their place. The hunters ran past Canis without seeing him.

When the striped cat came into view, Canis stood up and took aim. Harried by Wulfen and intent on a moving target, the cat took no notice of the relatively immobile figure standing so far outside of his focus. Canis had chosen his position for that very reason and taking full advantage of it, he launched arrow after arrow as fast as he could draw the string. He aimed at every exposed spot with an occasional "Move" muttered to one Wulfi or another in order to clear a shot. He wasn't directly in line with the charge, but his first arrow ensured that the tiger's focus came away from the hunters.

The massive cat wasn't going to just lie down and die, but Canis was far enough away and not moving. That gave him the opportunity to get off three more shots before the cat spotted his new antagonist. Every arrow flew true; they had to, there was no room for error. The cat fell, coming to rest less than ten feet from where Canis stood.

The hunters had released the sleds one at a time, whenever the cat got too close for comfort, and it had attacked and ravaged each sled until it was discovered that it wasn't protesting and therefore was no longer interesting.

Canis, and the hunters who had followed him from the village, righted and repaired the sleds as they found them. The last sled, which had been the first of the tiger's catch in this long cat and mouse chase, had been smashed and ravaged beyond recovery. They divided the meat between the four sleds they had brought with them then they headed back to the village. When they passed the carcass of the striped cat, Canis noticed that someone had skinned it and retrieved his arrows. They had left the rest of the carcass; only in the most desperate of times would they take the meat of a carnivore.

It was well after dark before they made it back to the village and Canis was shivering from the cold. His coat and boots had been enough for him to huddle in the snow among his Wulfen, but after working up a sweat, running, then walking back for well over two hours, pulling a sled or not, he couldn't seem to keep warm enough.

At the village, the hunters had recovered some. They and the women came out to welcome them back. The sleds disappeared with the people into their homes where they could all find heat and food.

Almach helped Canis bring their sleds of meat in then they went downstairs to find Auriga sitting with a splinted leg propped up on a stool. "Broke it," he said curtly. His anger at himself for tripping could be heard clearly in his voice.

"Sargas has already been by and seen to it," said Capella. "It will heal cleanly, thanks to you and the gift you brought. We are all very grateful."

Canis pulled up a seat close to the hearth and accepted a cup of hot tea. He still wore his coat; he was freezing. "How are the others?"

"They too will recover," said Almach. "Caeli said he saw you shooting. He talked of nothing else all the way back here. He said you just kept shooting no matter how close it got to you."

Canis just shrugged, he was beginning to warm up so he pulled his coat open, leaving it belted.

Both Almach and Auriga looked at him questioningly when they saw he had no shirt on under his coat.

Canis saw their look and looked to see what they saw, then shrugged again. "I was in a hurry."

Capella abruptly turned away to stir the stew.

Canis went to his space in the corner and shed his coat and boots for a pair of pants and a shirt – he was warm enough now – then he went back and finished the meal set before him. He hadn't eaten all day and yet he had little appetite now. He poured himself more tea and pushed his half-finished bowl away.

He was the last to go to his nest. He had switched from tea to water. He couldn't seem to get enough to drink and he felt like he was sweating it out as fast as he was drinking it. He knew it was cold outside, but he couldn't see a reason for keeping the house this warm. It wasn't his house. He didn't try to change anything; he just went to his corner and pulled the curtains closed against the heat.

Sleep washed over him like the winter sunset, quickly and completely. He found himself dreaming of the great striped cat. He shot arrow after arrow into it until he ran out of arrows and he was forced to draw his sword. After he hit it with his sword, the tiger's claws all grew into swords that were just as long as his own, and when his attack made it past them all, the tiger shattered into ten tigers each wielding a sword twice as long as his. There was no more chance of an attack; all he could do was try to defend himself. Every time he blocked a blow, the sword he blocked grew depressingly longer.

Doomed to be defeated, Canis sought to retreat to a safe corner where they couldn't get at him all at once, but his arm was growing leaden and his chest was burning. He thrashed out to clear the crowding cats away so he could breathe, but they kept coming. He began to choke and cough. He couldn't breathe any more. He pulled at the neck of his shirt and found an iron collar there. The chain attached to the collar was dragging at him, forcing him back against a brand the size of a stove. He cried out and coughed harder. The stripes of the cat turned into the bars of a cage and giant bear paws pushed the bars closer until he couldn't move, then a hand reached past the bears, past the striped cats, past the chains and past the bars. "Gem?" Her hand had always been there when he was most terrified.

The hand touched his forehead. It was cool and comforting. The tigers let go of him. The bears became soft furs. The iron turned into a cool damp rag. He struggled to see the face in front of him and found Sargas's concerned face. Behind him were Capella and Almach. Others were there too, but they drew away before he could put names to their faces.

"He'll be okay now, I think. The fever's broken," said Sargas.

"What happened?" asked Canis. His throat was raw and it hurt to talk. His chest ached too; in fact, he hurt everywhere. He pulled an arm in front of his eyes and saw a good-sized bruise around his wrist. Puzzled, he looked back at Sargas for an answer to his question.

"You've had a very high fever. You have been delirious for three days. We were forced to hold you down several times lest you hurt yourself or someone else."

"The first we knew that you were ill, you knocked me out," said Almach. "Capella ran for help. For your information, it took six men to hold you down and it was a near thing even then."

"You have been pinning me down for three days?"

"Most of it," said Almach. "We had to, so Sargas could work on you."

"I don't understand fevers," said Sargas. "I'm sorry I couldn't give you some relief sooner."

Canis waved a hand limply; he was exhausted. He was asleep before he could find the words to tell the man that he would get better every time he tried.

Unable to struggle into his pants, Canis pulled his coat on again and wavered into the main living chamber the next time he woke. He found the family gathered around the table over a collection of empty dishes.

Almach jumped up and helped him to a chair. He felt as weak as an infant, but he made it. He looked around at the serious faces as a bowl of hot stew and a large mug of tea was set before him.

"What?" he asked, his voice rasped at the effort.

"We are trying to get that information ourselves," said Almach. "She won't tell us."

Canis struggled through a mouthful. It tasted as good as ever, Capella was a very good cook, but it hurt to swallow. He watched Capella until he had managed the food in his mouth. "If it is about my getting sick, that is no one's fault but my own. I was an idiot to run out in only my coat and boots."

"You know that's not all of it," blurted Capella. She looked at her husbands then slumped in resignation. “It’s my fault. It’s all my fault. I…I uh…I wanted to make love to him. If I had stayed out of his furs, he would never have spent the night outside in only his boots and coat.”

“He spent the night outside?” said Auriga in astonishment.

“It was not the night,” said Canis speaking with difficulty. “I was warm enough. It was the run.”

None of them were listening to him any more. Both Almach and Auriga were staring at Capella who was sitting forlornly in her chair with silent tears running down her face.

After long minutes, Almach got to his feet and picked up his and Capella’s coats. Wordlessly she accepted it and accompanied her husband out of the house.

Canis was silent for a couple more laborious bites, but then he had to ask, “Where do they go?”

Auriga still had a dark expression on his face as he glowered at the table, but he answered readily enough. “When we do something that we know is wrong, we go to Angela and confess our wrongs. We stay there until we feel forgiven.”

“But it was not her fault. I should have never tried to run so hard in this cold.”

“It’s not what she did or what you did. It’s that she feels guilty for what she did. I find it surprising that she would go to your furs, but if I cannot come to terms with this, I too will visit Angela. Ultimately, all will be well again.” He looked up at Canis. “Besides, if you had not made your ill considered run, I would likely not be here being mad about it.

Heading East

Canis spent the rest of the winter going on every hunt until their stores were stuffed, then he was going out to bring in firewood almost every day. Auriga made him a new store of arrows using cured and sharpened bone for the heads. He made even more arrowheads to take with him. Capella made the tiger's hide into a soft bedroll to go with the one he already had. Crossing the mountains would put him into a long stretch of forever snows.

Sirius was the only hunter who had gone any distance toward the morning sun and he had only gone to within sight of the tall mountains. He told Canis of what looked to be the remains of an ancient and wide trail that appeared to lead directly toward those mountains.

It sounded to Canis like the remains of a high road. They both agreed that, if he could manage to keep to that trail, it was likely he would find a pass through the mountains.

Adhara made him a necklace from the tiger claws and teeth. Now he had two of them, but the bear necklace still lay hidden with the rest of his things. He had told no one of that bear and had hidden the necklace almost immediately. He didn't know what he would do with two of them.

The last storm of the winter was like the snowstorms he was more accustomed to, though there wasn't as much accumulation. It fell soft and wet. The days were getting warmer and it was nearly time for Canis to head out. Many of the villagers came by to bid Canis a safe journey and long life. More than a few of them expressed a desire to see him again, but in truth, few of them expected it to happen. There were a few gifts too, but they were small. No one wanted to weigh him down with such a formidable journey ahead of him.

Two days after the snow stopped, Canis headed out. His sled was full of provisions; he wouldn't need to hunt for several days.

Rrusharr was pregnant, but Canis couldn't wait for her to deliver or he could be caught in the pass when winter came down on them again. Debhe sat him down and told him what to expect when she went into labor and she gave him a special jug; it was to deaden the sensations. She told him everything she could and made him promise to drug himself up as soon as it started. "It is very hard on a man to go through their companion's labor."

Canis promised to do as she said. He remembered Halley's ordeal. Privately, he hoped it didn't happen during a time when he needed to keep his senses about him.

Finally, he set out. The day was bright and the snow was white, so he tied his facemask over his eyes to protect them from the glare. The men of the Yellowstone Clan never used them since their hunting took place among the giant trees. Here on the high plateau, the sun reflecting off the white snow was doubly bright. The hunters covered their eyes with a wide strip of soft leather with slits cut for them to see through, it put their eyes in the shade and protected them from sun-blindness.

Two days from the village, Rranggrr informed him that they were being followed. Whoever it was didn't want to be found and never approached his camp, so Canis assumed it was one of the hunters following to make sure that his journey was safe.

After three more days of no contact, Canis figured that whoever it was had turned back. He was making good time and traveling fast. His supplies were growing thin so he started to cast around for game. Two days later, he shot a buck and spent the day cutting it into chunks and setting it out on the snow to freeze.

He was packing it all up the next morning when Ggrrawrr, who watched over them all, informed him that another Wulfi approached the camp.

Curious, Canis waited until the visitor came into sight. It was nearly all white with a few gray markings, but despite the coloring, it was obvious that it was a young Wulfi. Vaguely, he placed it as being an offspring of the great gray Wulfi who had first relayed him the news of the striped cat, but he couldn't remember who or even if it was companioned with anyone. She crept into camp with her head down in supplication. The fact that she was alone was enough. He didn't need the picture of her companion huddled in the snow unable to continue and unable to turn back. Leaving the camp under the watchful eye of Ggrrawrr, Canis headed back down his trail at a trot.

It was early afternoon before he found the boy staggering along the trail, barely able to manage his snowshoes. There was no sled so he hadn't brought enough supplies to make the trek.

The boy looked old enough to know better, but perhaps he snuck away from the village and had taken little or nothing with him. Canis gave him a swallow or two from his water skin, then scooped him up and headed back to his camp.

With the day wasted already, Canis saw no reason to hurry. He built his fire up again and laid a slab of meat on the wood to cook, and then he turned to the boy for an explanation. "What's your name, and why did you follow me?" he asked.

"My name's Cepheid, and I want to come with you," said the boy.

"This is no journey for a boy. Does your family know where you are?"

Cepheid hesitated, looking guilty. "No, I just left a couple hours after you did. I figured, if I waited long enough, when I caught up with you, you wouldn't send me back. I don't want to go back."

"Why? It is a good life back there," said Canis.

The boy pushed his hood back to reveal short gray hair with a brown blotch at his right temple. His youthful face had yet to lengthen into manhood. Canis wondered just how young the boy was. "I suppose it's good enough; I just want to go somewhere else. I want to see what else is out there. I can help you. No one should make a journey like this alone."

Canis considered the distance already covered. He had been climbing gradually almost ever since he left the village. For the boy to be able to make it back he'd have to take the sled and Canis couldn't afford to do without or waste the time to build another. The only weapon the boy brought with him was a belt knife, so he couldn't hunt or even protect himself. Small game was nearly nonexistent here, and the predators that hunted these expanses were large. He was surely trapped. If he took the boy back, he might as well forgo the trip entirely until next summer.

Canis growled and strode to the edge of the firelight looking into the darkness, back toward the village he'd left far behind. There was something about Cepheid he couldn't remember.

He rubbed the stone between his brows and shook his head. Bringing the boy with him wouldn't make the journey any easier, but it wouldn't make it any harder either. With his decision made, he reached out toward the village until he touched the old gray Wulfi. He delivered the message about Cepheid then turned back to the fire.

Using his belt knife, he turned the meat over on the coals then passed over the water skin. He looked over at the remains of his kill. Little was left that hadn't been shredded. He would have to make a new water skin when he killed again. He could make the kid a bow too; he could do that on the trail. He was unwilling to part with the arrowheads Auriga had made him. He looked at the kid again; he looked so young. He wouldn't be able to pull a full sized bow for some time yet. He could use fire-hardened arrows until they found a stone deposit and could make more tips.

Canis packed up again early the next morning and they were on the trail before the sun cleared the horizon. It didn't take long for Canis to discover other woeful lacks in the boy's gear. It looked as though all he had done was throw his coat on and grab a fur to use as a blanket.

"How long did you plan coming with me?" asked Canis as he gave his facemask to the kid.

"I don't know, a couple days, I guess," he replied.

"Are you sure it was that long? It looks to me like you might have planned it for about five minutes at the most."

Aside from looking guilty, the kid didn't reply.

Puppies

With food under his belt, Cepheid didn't slow Canis down too much, and he was quick to build a fire in the evenings. He did everything he knew how to do in order to justify his presence. He didn't want Canis to regret letting him stay.

It wasn't long before the two of them settled into a routine that was comfortable for both of them, and with the snow-capped peaks of the mountains finally distinguishable from the white clouds, it was important that they iron out any difficulties. Canis took to practicing with his sword again in the predawn light while Cepheid cooked their simple breakfast.

Cepheid liked to watch these sessions just as he liked to watch Canis comb through his long hair every morning. In fact, he found everything about Canis fascinating, which was the biggest reason for following, though he would never tell him such a thing.

This morning started out no different from the others already past. Cepheid was watching Canis perform a complicated spin that would end in a powerful thrust, only this time, it ended with Canis doubling over. The sword went flying and Canis piled in a tangle of arms and legs with an inarticulate cry of inexplicable pain.

Cepheid pulled the pan from the fire and ran to his side. "What is it? Did you hurt yourself?"

Canis was panting and slowly pulling himself up. "I am fine," he hissed. "Rrusharr has started to have her pups." He had never experienced such a thing before. He stumbled the few feet back toward the fire doubled over. Some of what Debhe had warned him of surfaced in his memory, but he couldn't remember what she had told him to do.

Another pain came and he curled on the snow writhing and panting. Cepheid struggled to pull him to his bedroll only a little farther away.

When the pain passed, Canis rolled over onto the fur and lay panting. The next thing he knew, Cepheid was pulling his head up and pressing something to his lips. He drank, swallowing a mouthful of the bittersweet liquid then gasping at its violent ventilation of his head.

A brief thought of stopping Rrusharr's pain passed through his mind, but the constant interruptions of Cepheid with the heady drink kept him sufficiently distracted.

Eventually the drink did its work, and Rrusharr's labor pains were muffled somewhat, allowing Canis to uncoil enough to sit up, though the strong drink did more than deaden the pain.

Cepheid put the jar in his hands then went to tend to the pup that had already been born. He took his own fur and wrapped the chubby little thing in it while its sibling was being born, then he guided them to their mother's warm belly to nurse. After a few minutes, he was able to entice Rrusharr to move onto the fur so her pups wouldn't be in the snow.

Cepheid went back to Canis to find his head drooping. He took the jar before it spilled and replaced the cork, then he lifted Canis's head to look in his eyes. They were unfocused and blank, so he pushed him down onto his furs and covered him up. They were going nowhere today.

He checked on the new family again and folded a corner of the fur over their damp backs, then he went out to retrieve Canis's sword. He emptied the rest of the contents of the jar onto the snow. It wouldn't keep much longer anyway and it had served its purpose.

The camp was suddenly quiet and Cepheid had never felt so alone before. People had always been around; even out here, there had been Canis's solid and comforting presence, but now, with

Canis drugged out of his senses, he was on his own.

Cepheid paced the camp restlessly, gazing at the horizon around their camp. A birthing out in the open like this was dangerous. The scent would carry for miles on the lightest winds and advertise their vulnerability.

Accompanied only by Nnarr, his companion, Cepheid roamed around and collected all the firewood he could find. He was going to sit up all night and keep the fire going. It was the only defense he had.

It was well after dark when Canis woke up from his stupor. He pushed himself upright and took in the scene of the camp. Still muzzy-headed, he saw blazing fire and spotted the boy pacing the edge of the light in search of glowing eyes out in the darkness.

"Cepheid," he called only loud enough to be heard.

Cepheid returned to him at once. Even in the firelight, Canis could see that Cepheid's eyes were wide and his face was drawn. "You're awake; I'm so glad. I've been so afraid."

"I am awake, though I am probably not much use. Is there anything to eat?"

Cepheid went to the edge of the fire and retrieved a pot. "I made some stew out of the leftovers from breakfast. It's not too bad."

Canis dug in. He was hungry enough to eat most anything. "How is our new family?" he asked after a few minutes of gobbling.

"Two, a boy and a girl," replied Cepheid.

Canis found her comforting presence and had to chuckle. He didn't find much regret there for what she had put him through; she was too busy being a mother. "And we know who the proud papa is too," he said as he turned his gaze to Ggrrawrr who was lying alertly near Rrusharr. Their brief tryst had been reason for another night in the snow, though he had made a conscious decision to dress accordingly that time. "You are accumulating quite a family, three females now, with no competition for your attention, and now pups, quite a pack."

Ggrrawrr's only response was to hold his head a little prouder, if that was possible.

A New Scent

They traveled slower since the pups needed to nurse several times a day. In between times, Canis carried them in pouches under his coat. When Rrusharr decided it was time to stop, they spread out a bedroll and let the pups have their way with their mommy until they were full again.

Two weeks of this and well into the forever snows, Canis caught a new scent. It took him most of a day to identify it on the harsh air, then to place its source in the temperamental winds that swirled around them almost constantly now. Suddenly the memory came back to him. He whirled on Cepheid who recoiled in surprise. "You are a girl, a woman. You are Castor's daughter. You are having your menses. Why did you not tell me?"

"I wanted to come with you," she said, her eyes wide. "If I told you, you would have sent me back, or taken me back yourself, so I let you think I was a boy."

Canis was furious. "How could you do this to me?" This explained why she looked so young. She *was* young, but she was older than she looked.

"I never slowed you down. I took care of you when the pups were born," she cried in her defense, but he was so angry.

Canis had never come so close to striking another person in anger. He'd fought them, he'd killed some, but he had never wanted to punish someone. To avoid doing so now, he whirled and strode off down the trail. His long legs carried him away from her, but she dug in and came after him tenaciously.

By evening, Canis had calmed down some, but he was still angry. He had been angry enough at being saddled with a boy, but a woman…one little more than a girl…

Canis sat and watched as she set about preparing their supper. She didn't speak to him. He watched as the occasional tear leaked past her control and her finger trembled and fumbled with their tasks.

Women never went on hunting trips and seldom went on such treks. The only time women went anywhere that didn't have something to do with their home or the food on their table was when the clan had split and one branch left to find new hunting grounds. That happened so seldom that no living member of the clan today had seen it.

He thought back on the day Rrusharr had gone into labor. She must have been so terrified. Sure, there were three Wulfen who would have protected her, and it's likely they would have done just fine. It was also likely, that if they had come under attack, he would have woken up, and most likely, he would have still been able to hit a target if he had to. But there was also the possibility that it would have worked out entirely different, and it would have been a disaster.

When she brought him his meal, Canis pulled her to sit down beside him, startling her from her thoughts. He spoke with carefully measured words, like he always did. "You are worrying; I can see it. I am not going to leave you, if that is what you are worried about. I *am* mad at you, and I will probably *be* mad for a while, but I *will* get over it. You have done all right so far. I have nothing to complain about, but I do not like being lied to. Never lie to me again." He put her uneaten supper back into her hands then went to his bedroll.

Canis was almost normal to her the next day, and the day after, it was as if nothing at all had been amiss. They made another kill and she made a second water skin. She also improved on the slings Canis used for the puppies. She used the rest of the hide as a cloth for Rrusharr so her family didn't have to be on the cold snow when they weren't being carried by Canis.

It didn't take the puppies long before they were lifting their fat tummies off the ground far enough to totter around, but they cried when they ran out of strength and had to sit down anywhere off the hide blanket.

They had been traveling for six weeks now and the wind-scrubbed rocks of the closest peaks were in sight both to the north and to the south. If they could make it to the downhill side by the time winter tried to come after them, they would be home free.

When Canis crossed these mountains before, it was dead of winter and much farther north, and it had been no joy ride. Having been utterly unequipped and ignorant, he had nearly starved to death before he found the Yellowstone Clan. He would never forget the constant need to hunt and the constant hunger. He didn't expect this crossing to be any better, but he was much stronger now and far better prepared.

He carved a bow for Cepheid and every day he had her practice with it. The things she succeeded in shooting went into the supper pot, something she was very proud of. When she missed a shot – and she missed many, he made her try to find the arrow. Most of the time this was all but impossible since the slim shaft would punch deep into the snow and be gone, but she got good at spotting where it hit and managed to recover some of the lost arrows.

As they approached the mountains, they came upon trees again, and they became taller day by day. Their height deflected much of the wind, thus making it possible to find straighter underbrush. Canis taught her where to look and how to make new arrows. He also promised to show her how to make arrowheads when they found some flint.

Strangest of all, he started to show her how to use his sword. "Should anything happen to me, you need to be able to take care of yourself," he told her one day.

“Nothing is going to happen to you,” said Cepheid.

“Well, I certainly hope not, but you never can tell. There is always the next time Rrusharr has a litter of pups.”

“What’s so important about that long knife? What good is it? Don’t get me wrong, I like to watch you do what you do with it, but other than that, I don’t see the point.”

“The point is,” he explained, “where we are going, people use these against other people. It is their primary weapon. You should know how to use it in order to defend yourself.”

“You mean to say the plainsmen fight each other?” said Cepheid.

“Yes, they do,” Canis said, “and I do not want you to be defenseless.”

As soon as she started to work with the sword, he could see that it fit her smaller hand far better than it fit his. He’d had that sword made for him when he was a child. He would have to buy another one as soon as they reached a town big enough to support a blacksmith who made swords.

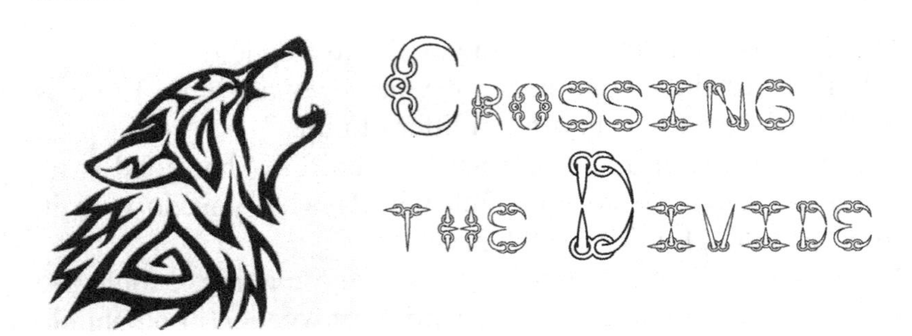

Crossing the Divide

The day came when the mountains loomed over them and they would leave the tall trees behind, Canis went through their gear one last time. They would have to hunt again before they started up the last hard grade. He was running head long into winter and he didn't want to count on hunting there if he didn't have to. He wanted to be able to travel as fast and as hard as he could. The sooner they were back down into a more habitable altitude, the better he would feel.

He checked his supplies to make more arrows. He made sure their bows and their snowshoes were in good repair. He sharpened their knives. They each had two furs to roll up in at night and even Rrusharr had one to lie on with her small family. That, cooking supplies, tools, and the meat from another kill would make for a very full sled, and from now on, they would be climbing hard.

He looked up at the heights, would they need to take firewood too? Would they need to choose between heat and food?

He took to shooting most anything that moved since it seemed they had left big game behind. If they didn't eat it all, so much the better. Their pace was slowed with the climb and Cepheid took to helping to pull the sled. She wasn't as strong as Canis by any means, but she helped.

Just as Canis feared, they ran out of firewood. If there were any trees in the area, they were either buried under hundreds of feet of snow or had been broken away, who knows, nothing was visible above the vast expanse of white except the occasional rock that had been scoured clear of snow by the wind.

They took to eating their meat much like the Wulfen did, though they let their portion bleed out on the snow and become partially frozen. It was in the stories and Cepheid was familiar with that, but she had never tried it before. She found the taste to be oddly invigorating, something she would fight over, well…perhaps. For Canis, it was merely a necessity.

Inevitably, despite his best rationing, the time came when there was nothing more to eat and still they climbed. Cepheid fell behind as the trail narrowed through a ravine. Near dark, she slipped and fell, but she climbed to her feet again quickly. She fell again a few yards later, then again shortly after that.

Canis stopped and let her catch up. "Are you all right?" he yelled over the howling wind.

She nodded and yelled back, "I can't feel my feet. I'll be fine until we stop."

Canis didn't say anything else. He unlaced her snowshoes and dropped them in the sled, then despite her protests, picked her up and carried her, looking for a place out of the cutting wind. Half a mile farther on, he found a small cleft that gave them some shelter.

He set her down and pulled one of her boots off. What he saw horrified him. "How long has it been since you could feel your feet?"

"I don't know, last night I guess. I get warm at night."

They had long since started to share their sleeping furs in order to be warmer without a fire.

Canis pulled her other boot off and threw them in the sled too. "Find us some shelter," he whispered to the Wulfen.

"*We mustn't stop here,*" said Ggrrawrr.

"I know. I just need a few hours out of this wind."

"*This may be the best we have,*" replied Ggrrawrr.

"Maybe." He pulled out the big tiger pelt and went back to Cepheid.

She was crying. "I've done it, haven't I? I've succeeded in

messing things up. If it weren't for me you'd be down on your plains by now."

"Stop crying. You are wasting water and it will freeze on your face. You have not made a mess of things. I did that. I checked everything with us except your boots. They were not made for this kind of cold. They were made for a woman who lived in a village." He wrapped her up in the hide like she was a baby and picked her up again.

Out in the wind again, she buried her face in his shoulder. He set her down for a moment while he slung the strap to the sled over his shoulders, then he picked her up again.

He stopped only when he couldn't see the trail any more. He spread out the other furs near the edge of the cliff wall and sat in the middle of them with Cepheid in his lap then he pulled the furs around both of them.

He hadn't intended to sleep. He'd intended to start moving again as soon as he could see the trail well enough not to lose it in the dark. He was wakened by Cepheid crying again.

She had been trying her best to be quiet so Canis could get some rest. He had such dark circles under his eyes.

"Why are you crying?" he asked and gave her the water skin.

She pushed it away. "I'm sorry. I didn't mean to wake you, but my feet hurt. They hurt a lot."

Canis frowned and pulled the fur open around her feet. They were angry, red, and swollen. He touched them then closed his eyes.

When he opened his eyes again, the day was bright and Cepheid was sobbing openly. He was aware of holding her tightly and he let go abruptly, almost dropping her.

She clutched at him and continued to sob, begging, "Please don't do that again. It hurt so much, please don't do that again, please."

"I am sorry," he said and covered her again and hugged her close. Her feet were still red, but they weren't swollen anymore. *I must have done a healing. I hope I saved her feet.*

He set her aside and rolled up the furs. He stowed the puppies back in their pouches hanging at his sides, slung the rope over his shoulder again, then picked Cepheid up once more.

"You can't keep carrying me," she said through her sniffs.

"You do not weigh as much as these two fat puppies. If you had been a man, we would have been stuck here. You, I can carry."

"You would have put a man in the sled," said Cepheid

"I suppose I could put you in the sled too, but then we could not have this conversation. Would you rather ride in the sled?"

She looked up at him. Tiny creases were at the corners of his mouth. A crinkle was in the corners of his eyes. "This is warmer," she said, and suddenly shy, she ducked her face back into his shoulder.

They stopped about every hour to rest and drink some water. Some stops were longer than others so the puppies could come out and attack their mother. The bitter cold didn't seem to bother them much; then again, they weren't out in it all that much.

About half way through the afternoon, the Wulfen located a small crack in the side of the cliff that almost qualified as a cave. They all fit in, and though it was tight, they were most thankful to be out of the bitter wind for a while.

Canis immediately went to work. Sacrificing their smallest hide, he started to make boots for Cepheid. They weren't real boots, all they were was another layer over the boots she already had. He wouldn't be able to make her a proper pair of boots until they probably wouldn't need them any more. It was too cold to do much more than a quick stitch, but the extra layer around her legs and feet would keep them from freezing again and not encumber her walking very much. She wouldn't be able to tell the difference wearing snowshoes.

By the time he was finished, darkness had almost fallen, so there was no point in trying to continue. One night out of the wind would be welcome.

The next day, Canis made Cepheid walk in front of him. Until her feet were completely better, she would set the pace. The cold, the wind, and the lack of food were already slowing them down, so she didn't slow them any more, and Canis was proud of her for being so brave. He caught up with her at a wide stretch in the trail. "Are you sorry you came with me?"

She looked up at him in surprise, but the look she saw in his eyes was soft and gentle. "No, though I don't think I'll want to cross these mountains again."

"We will cross them again someday, but we will do better next time." He was forced to drop back again as the trail closed in again.

Two days later, he felt a difference. They weren't climbing any more; they had made it over the top. They were also starting to feel the effects of no food for too long. They rested more often and stopped for the night sooner. During the other crossing, Canis and Rrusharr had been able to follow the hunt pretty much wherever it led as long as it was remotely west. During much of this crossing, they had been confined to this ravine with a high cliff wall on one side and a deep cleft on the other. Nothing else came here. There was nothing to come for.

Canis began to despair making it at all. Cepheid was so thin and she hadn't been very big to begin with. The Wulfen were also growing too thin, and he knew he was in no better shape. Only the puppies stayed fat, though it drained Rrusharr.

There was no choice but to continue. With his concentration set on putting one foot in front of the other and keeping Cepheid in sight, Canis missed the change in Ggrrawrr and Rranggrr as they lifted their noses, then disappeared.

By the time their doings penetrated his dull mind, they were well involved in the hunt. He struggled to string his bow while Cepheid untangled his arrows from the sled. *Fine hunters we are*, thought Canis by the time he had things ready.

Leaving Cepheid with the sled and the puppies, he sprinted ahead toward the hunt. The trail opened out of the ravine into a wide flat area and what he saw out in the middle of it brought him up short. He had never imagined such a creature in his wildest dreams. It was huge, standing at least six feet at the shoulders, and perhaps taller, depending on how much was obscured by the snow. It had course hair covering a body that looked to have been made of several massive chunks of stone, and aside from arrowheads and such, he'd never tried to shape stone. Its face was long and heavy, sporting a massive horn in the center of its snout. Its size and strength made traveling in this snow possible, but it wasn't very fast, though it might have been if it was on dry ground.

A gentle prod in his mind recalled him to his task and he took aim. He fired eight arrows into the neck and shoulder before the creature huffed to a halt. It had trampled a wide circle several feet deep in the snow. The Wulfen were out of reach and it was spraying blood from its nose with every huff. Canis took careful aim one more time, taking advantage of the fact that it stood still, amazed that it still stood at all, the arrow flew true and the creature sank ponderously to the snow with an arrow securely imbedded in its brain through its small eye.

Cepheid came into sight around the last bend pulling the sled. The puppies were in their sling, but on her, they bumped against her knees with every step. She cried out in joy and wonder at the sight of the massive kill, breaking the spell that held Canis immobile.

He went back to her and helped her to the edge of the trampled circle then they started to work on the odd creature. The hide was indeed hard and thick which told why the strange creature had been so hard to drop. The arrows had only penetrated a hand's breadth at best. With the ones in his neck doing the most damage, it would have bled to death eventually.

He was able to recover the arrows, but three of them had broken in the shoulder. Only one of those tips was reusable.

He worked hard to peal back the heavy skin and its layer of fat. As he worked, he cut away generous chunks of meat and tossed them to the hungry Wulfen. He even cut a couple chunks of fat and offered them to the puppies who wrestled over them happily, though their milk teeth were doing little damage. Then he pealed away another chunk and handed it to Cepheid.

It was still hot and bleeding, but she devoured it hungrily. With everyone chewing on a hunk of hot meat, Canis took time to feed himself. He never wanted to be this hungry again.

They spent the rest of the day and the night there next to the kill, gorging themselves in an effort to drive away the memory of hunger that had haunted them for far too many days. Even the puppies took an interest and tried to tug at a bloody leg bone that dwarfed their chubby bodies. They could scarcely get a tooth hold, but that didn't stop them from happily licking the blood from their baby faces and trying again.

By the time darkness had set in, they were all lying around with distended stomachs, and there was a sled load of meat lying out to freeze. Still there was more than half of the creature left that they couldn't possibly handle.

"It's a shame to waste it," said Cepheid.

"I agree, but we can't take any more with us and we can't stay here," said Canis. He smiled to watch the puppies play tug of war with a strip of fatty hide he had cut for them. "Eating our meat raw is fine I guess, but I hunger for cooked meat."

Cepheid didn't long for cooked meat, but she wasn't ready to reject Angela's teachings either, so she nodded and snuggled deep into Canis's warmth.

Canis lay awake, though he thought he was the only one, exempting perhaps Ggrrawrr. He didn't know how many more nights he could lie next to Cepheid without doing something more than sleep. It had been a long time since he had slept for an entire night. She seemed so young and he felt so old, yet he had never had a woman. He didn't know what to do. Well, he did, but he didn't want to be clumsy. He didn't want to do it wrong. He didn't want to hurt her and he couldn't bear to frighten her.

A full stomach and warm furs, the winds whistling far overhead all contributed to wiping Canis's cares from his mind. He dreamed of wild and crazy canine sex and dimly knew that in a few more months there would be another litter of puppies. If he hadn't been so tired and so full, Cepheid might have felt his attentions anyway, but he was already asleep.

With full bellies and a sled full of meat, they made good time once again. They were able to make their first campfire three days after killing the nameless creature and once again, they gorged themselves, though not nearly like before.

The descent out of the mountains was much steeper than the long slow climb up the western side had been, and hunting improved just as quickly. They saw two more of the strange creatures, so Canis decided to call them ‘one-horns’ for lack of a better name, pared down from ‘one-horned mountain of rock’.

With plenty of other game, they didn’t need to try for another one, and as the snow depth decreased, they gave them a wide berth. Rranggrr, ever impetuous, had approached the next one they saw and she was nearly trampled. They did indeed move quickly when they weren’t mired in deep snow.

Rranggrr came upon the humans from upwind. They were the first she’d seen since leaving Cepheid’s village. She was delighted to see people again, and broadcast this news to Canis who spotted the danger long before she did. His warnings unheeded, he dropped the sled and sprinted ahead as fast as his snowshoes would let him. He was in time to deflect at least some of the missiles the men launched at her.

He took two already launched chunks of ice on his back while Rranggrr dodged back to the others and out of sight with a yelp. Then he turned to face the men.

"Hey mister," said one of them. "That wolf belong to you? Ain't never seen one so big before."

"Yes, there are others with me as well. We mean you no harm. How far is it to the nearest town?" Canis was reminded of their teeth, which they bared simply by speaking. He had forgotten the difference. It was another reminder that they were venturing into dangerous territory.

"It's only a few hours from here. We're fixin' to leave here shortly. You can come with us if you like."

Canis studied the men gathered. There were two slave drivers and a chain gang of eight slaves. They were all burly men out here mining glacier ice. "Fine," he said and went back for the sled. When he reached Cepheid, he said, "These are big, rough men. Stay close to me and try not to let them know you are a woman."

"Why?" asked Cepheid.

"I do not trust them," was Canis's response.

This surprised Cepheid. In all of her life, trust had never been an issue of concern.

When they rejoined the men, they were already packing up in preparation for leaving. The two wagons were loaded to overrunning with snow and ice carved from the base of the glacier and the drivers had chained the slaves, four behind each wagon. One of the drivers helped Canis load his sled onto one of the wagons and they started out.

The horses and the wagons churned the snow into a knee-deep, shifting mire that made footing difficult, so since there wasn't room for both Canis and Cepheid to ride together, he declined the offer to ride the wagons and walked well off to the side of the road where the snow was relatively undisturbed.

With slaves chained behind the wagons, they couldn't travel very fast. With the exception of Rrusharr, who was glued to his side, he admonished the Wulfen to stay out of sight. They did as he requested, mostly, but not so far as to be totally unseen. A watchful eye would be able to pick out a shape moving along the edge of the trees, and if he was very watchful, he might be able to discern that there was more than one of the massive creatures.

Canis also warned them, especially Rranggrr, to stay away from the horses. They might be placid creatures, but they could still bolt if they were pressed by a large wolf. Such a happenstance could cause the deaths of the slaves chained helplessly to the wagon and could even cause other damage, all of which was trouble Canis didn't want to cause so soon after meeting the plainsmen again.

Cepheid took in this arrangement with wonder. She tugged on Canis's sleeve to get his attention. She could feel his unease at being around these men, but she had to ask, "These men must be incredibly rich to display so much metal, why are they so…so sad?" Sad wasn't the word she wanted to use, but she couldn't think of a better one.

Canis looked at her in surprise then he looked back at the display, seeing it with her eyes. There was very little metal among the clans. "They are not rich," he said. "They are slaves." He liked her mouth. Though smiles and laughter were common, if anyone of the clan were to show their teeth, there would be no doubt as to the meaning.

"What are slaves?" she asked having never heard the term before.

Canis tried to find words she would understand. He had worn chains very like the ones here, though perhaps slightly finer. "They are not free," he said simply and shuddered at the memory her questions dug into.

Cepheid looked up at his words and saw the haunted look in his eyes before he could hide it. *Not free.* She could scarcely imagine such a concept. The women of the clan led a life that was the closest to 'not free' as it ever got, but in return for their captivity, they were given the right to choose their mates and the right to say it was time to get more meat or more wood. The men did all of the heavy and dangerous work outside of the home.

She looked again at the chains and saw their ungiving strength. She saw the thick circles around the necks of the men.

She saw the heavy links of the metal that joined them, one to the next, then to the wagon. She had never seen such large men before, but she could see that even they were not strong enough to break free of those chains. Even she could now see how these large, powerful men no longer had the will to contest those chains.

With a small hiccup, she quickly looked away. Canis's words echoed in her mind. "*Do not let them know you are a woman.*" What would they do if they suspected that? Did they put their women in such chains?

Canis heard her small sound and turned to look at her. He saw the single tear leak down her cheek before she quickly dashed it away. He dropped back to walk beside her. "Do not cry," he whispered. "Not here."

She nodded and reached for the gray puppy as it was trying to climb out of his pouch.

"Do not let him down, he might run under the wagons," he said.

She nodded again and clutched the puppy close, much to his dismay. She used the distraction of handling the puppy to take her mind off her dismal train of thought.

It was after dark when they reached a good-sized town with more buildings than could be easily counted, even from a vantage point. Lanterns hanging outside of shops to light their signs also lit its main street. Surrounding cliffs of blue ice marked the very edge of the forever snows.

The drivers pulled their wagons into a large barn where other handlers came out to put the slaves and horses away. Canis noticed that the slave pens were cold and small, but there were warm blankets inside and a steaming bowl of gruel liberally laced with meat waiting for each one. They were well treated for slaves.

One of the drivers helped Canis unload his sled. "If you'll wait a few, I'll buy you and the little lady a drink at the inn."

Canis considered the offer, struggling to hide the alarm he felt at knowing this man was aware of Cepheid being a woman despite his efforts to conceal that fact. He hesitantly accepted; it would be nice to sleep inside for once, and this close to people, he felt safer behind a door. He called the Wulfen in close and admonished them not to explore on their own here. Rranggrr's greeting when she first saw these men was warning enough for Canis, and there were plenty of men here armed with more than chunks of ice.

Canis and Cepheid accompanied the driver, who introduced himself as Joe, into the small, but spotless inn closely followed by Nnarr and Rrusharr, leaving Ggrrawrr and Rranggrr to guard the sled outside.

The innkeeper greeted Joe well enough, but took one look at the fur-clad strangers and their wolves and said, "Them can't come in here," he waved a rag at the Wulfen.

"Very well, we will go elsewhere," said Canis and turned to leave. He hadn't really expected anything else, but it had been worth a try.

Joe must have said something to the man because he came outside after them a few moments later. He stopped when he saw two more wolves, but shrugged and asked. "Can you pay in something besides furs?"

Canis looked down at the portly innkeeper in his very white apron. "I can," said Canis. He had the last of his money and he doubted the currency had changed much since he had crossed the mountains less than eight years ago. "I would like a room for the night as well. Do you have one?"

"I do, but that's extra."

Canis looked at his sled. "Do you have a place where I can store my sled or do you advise that I take it to the room?"

The innkeeper looked at the sled and shook his head. "You better take it to your room. I can't guarantee your things won't get stolen during the night."

"Very well then, I have some meat that would thaw if we took it to the room. Could we interest you in that?" He threw back the hide for the innkeeper to see it clearly by the lantern hanging over his door.

The innkeeper looked at the chunks of meat. "You cut out the bones already." He picked up a chunk and looked it over closely. "Looks clean. What is it?"

"Moose," said Canis. "I shot it day before yesterday."

The innkeeper considered the meat displayed before him. With the money he could get for one private room and a meal, he wouldn't be able to buy a quarter of this amount of meat. "I'll give you one night for the lot," he said.

"I want supper for all of us, a room for the night and breakfast in the morning, for all of us," replied Canis. The meat in the sled would feed them for three more days on the trail; he wasn't going to part with it cheaply.

"All of you," said the innkeeper questioningly then he realized, "*All* of you. Now listen here, I can't have them inside."

"Then we will go elsewhere. Good evening, sir," said Canis and once again prepared to leave. A light snow began to drift down.

"Now just hold on there," said the innkeeper. He looked at the four huge wolves arrayed before him. They returned his gaze openly waiting for his decision. "Can you guarantee they won't attack anyone?"

"Yes, I can," said Canis. "That is, up until someone attacks them. If that happens…"

"That won't happen. All right, all right, I got one big room upstairs, ain't nobody staying there tonight. I'll let you have that one and two meals, but I don't want no dog mess on the floors."

"That will be fine," said Canis.

They all trooped into the inn and Canis pointed to a table in the corner, away from the other guests, where Cepheid and the Wulfen went. He helped the innkeeper carry the meat back to the kitchen where a woman and a young girl took charge of it, then the man helped him take his sled to their room. Canis spread out Rrusharr's fur on the floor and deposited the sleeping puppies in the middle of it still in their pouches, then went back downstairs to the others.

The girl was approaching their table with two plates laden

with food when Canis returned to the main floor, and he could see that she was afraid to come too close. He took the plates from her hands and thanked her with an encouraging smile then he set the plates down for Rrusharr and Ggrrawrr to eat first. The next two plates went to Nnarr and Rranggrr and by the time the last two plates arrived, Rrusharr and Ggrrawrr had disappeared upstairs.

Joe joined them from where he had been sitting with other ice miners, discussing plans for the morning as well as the unusual occurrences in Canis's corner. "What did ye offer him to let ye have them critters in here?" he asked amiably.

Canis smiled. "We came to an agreement that was beneficial to both of us," he replied.

Joe shrugged and flagged his mug at the girl who swung by and collected it on her way through the sparsely populated inn. He hung on to it for a moment to get the girl's attention. "Bring one for my friends here."

The girl nodded and made to leave.

"Make it water for us," said Canis. When both the girl and Joe looked at him in surprise, he continued. "We have no stomach for your beer, thank you."

"Ah now," protested Joe. "Bors makes a fine brew. You should try it before you turn down a free drink."

Canis merely looked at the girl again. "Water please, thank you."

"Bors'll charge me as much for the water as he would for a beer," he said sulkily.

"Well then, you will have bought us a drink just as you wished," said Canis.

Canis and Cepheid saw Joe through three more of his drinks and dodged a good deal of his questions before finishing their water, then Canis thanked him and escorted Cepheid up to their room, leaving Nnarr and Rranggrr to follow at their leisure, and leaving Joe even more confused as to where these two strangers had come from. They certainly weren't trappers, though their furs, what he saw of them, were the best he had ever seen.

Just as the innkeeper was about to protest, Nnarr and Rranggrr also went upstairs, gray and white shadows side by side that unsettled the eyes and nerves of those who still sat in the common room.

Canis waited for them at the door. “Showing them who the boss is, were you?”

The smug attitude he got in reply was enough of an answer.

He turned around to see Cepheid standing in the middle of their furs with nothing on. She had lost weight and her ribs were plain to see, but that was not what he was looking at. In fact, he wasn’t too sure what he *was* looking at. He wasn’t sure of anything except the fact that she was so far away.

He was at her side without quite knowing how he got there. His laces were being unruly, but her warm hands pushed his away and pulled the laces free before he could tear them out of his way. His coat dropped away and his shirt followed soon after. A chill rippled his flesh as she pulled at the lacings to his pants.

If his coat and shirt vanished with astonishing speed, she pushed his pants down slowly, and he melted after them, and found himself suddenly sprawling on the pile of furs that was the soft nest she had made.

She unlaced his boots and tossed them aside, then pulled the pants free of his feet with languid movements that took many detours back up his legs. With hot hands, she rubbed his feet, each of them, slowly and carefully while Canis struggled not to pant. Satisfied, she began to crawl up his frame all too slowly allowing the full length of her body to caress every inch of her path. By the time she found his mouth with hers, he was putty in her hands. He couldn’t have protested if his life had depended on it. He wasn’t even sure he knew how to breathe.

She had curves in all the right places. She was soft in such a fascinating way. She took his hardness and consumed it with her heat. She molded him to her demand. He was lost in the sensation of touch. Their climax shattered his senses.

Somewhere shortly before he fell into a sated sleep, he had a brief thought of how vulnerable they had been. If someone had tried to attack them, it was entirely possible he would have been utterly unaware until it was far too late.

"*I am here, friend,*" said Ggrrawrr. "*I watch over you as you watch over me.*"

With a sigh, Canis lost the all too brief battle to stay on the alert. It had been utterly washed away from him. He slept.

Finding Work

Canis woke early the next morning to the sound of the puppies fighting over one of his boots. He struggled to put his body back in order so he could get dressed. He had to remind himself of the proper order of dressing in order to accomplish the task. Boots did not go on before pants and his shirt needed to go on before he picked up his coat. He was thankful he didn't possess too many different articles of clothing.

Cepheid woke slowly and stretched languidly, then she sat up behind Canis and began to untangle his braid. He sat straighter at her touch then sighed. "My comb is in the sled," he said, unwilling to move.

She retrieved the pouch where he kept his personal items and sat back down. He watched her walk across the floor without a stitch on and found himself forgetting his efforts to dress in favor of thinking of his coin and buying another night here at the inn.

She dumped the pouch out between her legs to find several coins, a necklace of teeth and claws that were longer than her hand, and his comb. She admired the necklace and tied it around his neck. She shortened the tiger necklace so the tips of the tiger claws just brushed the cord of the bear necklace, then she started to comb his hair.

She felt him stiffen when she put the necklace on him, but he quickly relaxed again as she fussed with them. He relaxed even more under the comb, despite the tangles. When she was satisfied, she tried to braid it back the way it was. "I can't do it back. How did you get it like that?"

He reached back and showed her. He had been braiding his hair ever since it was too long to simply tie back. It had become second nature to him.

Dressed finally, with the wriggling puppies safely stowed, they made their way back downstairs, sled and all. The racket of their descent roused the innkeeper who groggily agreed to fix them something for breakfast as he'd promised. While he worked on the kitchen fire, Canis built up the fire in the main room then took the Wulfen outside.

While he waited for them to return, he looked up and down the street. He had missed much in the darkness of the evening before, but the early morning light did little to improve the view. Despite the new snow, the streets were muddy and rutted. The shops that he could see were unpainted and splattered with mud. The place gave him a bad feeling. He would be glad to be quit of it.

Back inside, he stood at the door to the kitchen and asked the innkeeper, "Are there any horses for sale here?"

"Horses? For riding? Eh…nay, I can't think of any. Don't use 'em here much. Might be able to scrounge you up a buggy, though, if you're interested."

"No, thank you. I have little understanding of horses anyway. We will walk."

"Where're ye headin', if ye don't mind me askin'."

"I have no real plans. I guess we will start out by heading east. There is not much of any place else to go, is there?"

"Ye got a point there, sir," said the innkeeper.

"Since you don't have many horses, I do not suppose you have a blacksmith who makes more than horseshoes and wagon wheels?" asked Canis.

"Na, he can put an edge on your sword, if that's what ye need, but other than that, he makes a solid chain and good traps."

Canis had no use for chains or traps and he kept a fine edge on his sword himself. He thanked the innkeeper and helped to carry their breakfast into the main room where the rest of his family waited for him. Cepheid waited at the table playing with the puppies who were so happy to be somewhere that wasn't covered with snow and ice that they were resisting falling asleep and riding in their pouches.

The innkeeper saw them. "I didn't know you had a couple puppies too." He set his tray down and scooped up the chubby balls of black fuzz. Canis felt Rrusharr go tense and he saw Ggrrawrr sit up and take notice. The innkeeper rolled the puppy on her back in his arm and rubbed her tummy causing her feet to kick and her tongue to loll out the side of her little mouth.

Canis stepped forward and returned the puppy to the floor close to its mother. "I know you meant no harm, but I think you forget your company."

The innkeeper started and looked at the many sharp eyes that were watching him. "Oh, yes, I'm very sorry. I always liked puppies. I had a dog when I was a kid."

"You should get yourself another dog, but let me warn you, playing with wolf puppies might not be a healthy pastime."

"Yes, yes. You're right. I wasn't thinkin'." He turned to Rrusharr. It was obvious which wolf was the mother. "I'm sorry to disturb your family."

Canis frowned at the man's back. *Could he know about the connection between the Wulfen and the people of the clan? Did he know how intelligent they were?*

The man came back in to collect their bowls. "I was thinkin', sir. I don't do much of that 'til after I'm awake for a bit, but since you're already headin' east, you might be able to get on as a guard, if you know how to use that sword of yers. Wagons will be leavin' here today, loaded with ice for the city."

Canis was thrilled at the prospect. To find work already was better than he had hoped. "Who do I need to speak with about this?"

"Just hang out here a bit longer, all the drivers come in here before they leave, to have a bite and get their marchin' orders. I'll introduce ye to the foreman when he comes in."

"Thank you," said Canis. "I will wait."

The foreman took one look at the rangy youth in all his furs and asked, "Let's see your blade."

Canis drew his sword and offered it for the man to see without offering it for him to take. He wasn't sure he would have allowed him to take the sword if he had tried, but he didn't.

The foreman seemed to scrutinize the blade as if it mattered. A man could learn a lot about a fighter by looking at his sword. He could also learn some by watching him draw it. "Sword's a bit short for ya, but you'll do. I'll pay you one silver if my wagons reach Lincoln unmolested."

Canis raised his chin with indignation. "I do not know how far Lincoln is from here, nor do I know what is so valuable about ice that requires a guard, but I would think the safety of your load might be worth more than one silver coin if you are willing to hire a guard at all."

"What; you think you know the value of my load, do you?" said the foreman.

Canis took the now sleeping puppies from Cepheid and started to step around the man heading toward the door.

"Now hold on there," said the foreman. "I'll make a deal with you. I'll pay you one gold if my load is unmolested, but it'll be a silver if it is, provided I get my wagons and horses back."

Canis waved Cepheid past him, and the Wulfen filed around the man coming much closer than he liked.

"All right, all right, a silver a day, but if the load is lost, then you don't get nothing, and if those are coming along, you better consider adding to the pot."

Canis turned back to the man with Cepheid at his shoulder and the four Wulfen arranged on either side of him. "It is a deal." He strode the rest of the way out of the inn.

The foreman muttered as he turned back to his drivers. "He didn't give me a chance to tell him where the wagons were. If he don't show up, I'll have to find him. Bloody wolves in town.

Attack

The sun was setting on the end of their second day out of Kimball when Canis was given his first opportunity to earn his keep. They were just beginning to slow down to camp as the daylight was dimming. Upward of twenty men swarmed out of the surrounding snow-covered brush. Many of them were mounted double and they headed directly for the wagons. The seconds were dropped off at the wagons where they did their best to gain control.

"Clear the wagons," said Canis sending the Wulfen up onto the wagons to protect the drivers while he moved among the rest like a whirlwind. He felt Rrusharr flow up and over the seat and driver of one wagon, and he felt her carry a screaming man to the ground. He tasted hot blood in his mouth as she turned to find another target. The mere presence of the Wulfen sent the strange horses into a panic and few of the riders retained their seat as they pitched and bolted from the area by the easiest and fastest route.

Men died when they came too close to his blade as carnage flooded his mind from four other points of destruction. Their longer blades caused their share of damage as well, but he scarcely felt any of it. Moments into the fight, he picked up one of those longer swords and consequently took less damage.

When the last of the bandits ran, many were left lying quite still in the red-stained snow, and the night's darkness was almost upon them.

Canis found Kolar helping the drivers to sooth their teams. "If you will allow, I think we should keep moving through the night.

We can stop early tomorrow."

"It's too dark to travel at night," protested Kolar, though he didn't really want to stay in this place.

Canis looked up at the star strewn sky. "You have eyes for the night."

Kolar looked at Canis closely then spoke softly, "Are you saying you can see in the dark?"

Canis didn't answer the man's question directly. "Will you allow it?" he asked.

"Yes. Let me check on the horses and tell the men. We'll need to move slowly."

While Kolar spoke to the other drivers and checked over the horses and their harnesses, Canis went to Cepheid. "Are you injured?" he asked as his hands caressed her face scarcely able to refrain from trembling. He had seen one man fall to her knife.

Cepheid looked up into his face. She could still see the effects of the fight in the tightness around his eyes and mouth. Even the way he strode up to her spoke of 'hunt' and 'kill'. "I am unhurt," she said, "but you have several wounds. We should…"

"Not now. We are moving ahead through the night. I will be fine until we stop. Take this." He handed her his sword and its belt. "You remember your lessons. If you must use it, think of those lessons. Do you understand?"

She took the belt and looked up into his glowing eyes. They were intense. They were dangerous.

"Answer me; do you understand what I am telling you?" He gave her shoulders a gentle shake.

"Yes, I understand, but what about you? How can you disarm yourself like this?"

Canis showed her the other sword he'd picked up. It too was straight and double-edged, but its length was easily twice that of the sword Cepheid now held. "I am not disarmed. Go back to your wagon. Watch over the babies." He watched to insure she started back to the wagon then began searching among the bodies looking for the sheath to the sword in his hand. He was just unbuckling its the next morning and Canis felt much better for it.

Kolar reported the attacks and their results to the local police who went out to investigate. Actually, they weren't too concerned with an investigation. The bandits had been causing trouble for everyone in the area for months. If someone had cut their numbers down, they couldn't be happier, but they did want to clear the bodies away from the road and bury them. They might even be able to identify some of them, which might give them clues to further attachments.

Becoming a Plainsman

Canis continued to ride on the wagon for the three days it took to reach the tiny farming community of Chappell, allowing Cepheid to patrol using her new mount, but he started and ended each day with exercises with his new sword. He liked the reach, but the weight felt awkward.

He also spent time with the new horses. Kolar agreed that he could keep them. Normally, he wouldn't even have bothered with the stock, but if Canis could use them, he could have them.

Canis *could* use them. He had a lot of distance to cover and doing it on foot would draw too much attention. Only the poorest traveled on foot here and few that were so poor had anywhere to go. It could also enhance his ability to take on other jobs. Judging by the attitudes of the drivers when they first started, he almost didn't get this one for lack of horses. And if he was going to have horses, it was important that they and the Wulfen became better than uneasy traveling companions.

Canis and Cepheid learned everything the drivers could teach them about the horses and their gear, and by the time they reached Chappell, the horses seemed to be quite happy with them despite the Wulfen.

The horses were shaggy and rough looking, but then much of that was their winter coat. One of them was black with a wide white slash on his nose that tapered to a point long before it reached his eyes. The only other white mark on him was his left back hoof. When it wasn't muddy, it looked like he accidentally had their new wardrobe, Canis had spent about half of the silver Kolar had handed him. They both had two pair of wool pants, four linen shirts, a heavy wool coat, and a cloak with a detachable lining so it could be worn in the summer as a dust cloak. They even bought several changes of silk under clothes to protect their skin from the itchy wool.

With the lighter clothes, it was easier to tell that Cepheid was a woman instead of a boy, but she walked with such a stride that few people would make any remarks about her choice of dress. Of course, 'Ice Eyes', who always walked at her shoulder, was another deterrent to loose comments of any sort.

The next place they stopped was the cobbler's shop where they were able to buy boots that reached almost to their knees. By the time they quit the shop, Canis was convinced that the elderly man hadn't seen that Cepheid was a woman. He was not a betting man, but he would have laid coin down that the man hadn't seen anything above their knees. The passage of another silver coin here bought them their boots and also low cut shoes that were sturdier than slippers, but they would be comfortable for walking the city streets in the summer. Cepheid was as fascinated by them as she was with the idea of walking anywhere where there was no snow. She had seen slim stretches of ground with no snow, but they weren't places where anyone walked unless they had to. Places without snow were at the bottom of very large trees, of which there were very few around her home, or right along the banks of the salt lake, and that was only a couple feet wide during the heat of summer.

Among their shopping, Cepheid spotted a shop that made and sold bows. The one she had was the one Canis made for her on the trail. It worked well enough, but there was a fine composite bow on display and pulled them inside to see more. After trying several, Canis bought her one that was tipped with shiny black horn. She liked the red color in the wood too. In actuality, it was pretty and she could draw it. Canis bought her a fist full of shafts and a quiver to hold them to go with it. The quiver she picked out was soft leather with many tassels tipped with colorful beads; it was pretty too.

When they were assembling to leave the city, Canis discovered that his horses all had new gear; even Star had a new pad that could pass for a saddle if it had to. When Canis looked at Kolar for an explanation, Kolar said, “Ah, the drivers all went together and did it for you…for what you did for us back on the trail. I can’t remember the last time we made it this far with our load and our hides still in tact. ‘Sides, you two got all them fine new clothes and those are fine animals, you ought to have fine gear to go with all the rest. That tattered array you had weren’t good enough.”

Canis liked Kolar and appreciated the gesture. “Thank you. Perhaps I can do the same for you, someday.” Then they were mounting and heading out of town. Neither he nor Kolar spent much time on pleasantries when there was work to be done.

It was four days of slow wet travel to the next town with an inn, and another three to the next one, and another four to the last town before they reached their next major stopping point. It snowed almost the entire way, but it was such a wet snow that it didn’t really pile up much more than a foot. However, underneath it all was several inches of soggy wet slush that carried the foot most any direction other than down, which turned walking into hard work. Even the horses had some trouble.

When the lead team began to tire, Canis started to rotate their marching order every couple hours. By the time the last team had passed over a point, the road was more muddy mush and slush than snow. The drivers weren’t used to changing their marching order, but even they had to admit they made better time and the horses weren’t quite so tired at the end of the day.

In the town of Kearney, Kolar picked up water barrels to fill at the crossing where they would leave the river to enter the desert plains. Canis thought they would be able to melt enough snow to use for drinking even for the horses, but Kolar had been this way many times, whereas Canis had only made a similar, though solitary and much slower, trek a hundred miles north of this whole route eight years ago. He would not presume to advise Kolar on how to take care of his stock on those memories. He was only curious as to how he planned to keep his water from freezing.

By the time they left Kearney, the snow stopped and the wind picked up. Long before the end of the day, both Canis and Cepheid had discarded their fancy town clothes in favor of their trusty furs even to include their facemasks while the drivers hunched down in their cloaks and kept the horses moving.

The puppies had long since outgrown their carrying sacks and had been doing fine keeping up with the wagons, but they were getting disoriented in this cutting ground blizzard so they rode on the horses with Cepheid and Canis. He told them to sit very still and they were happy to lean up against another warm body. They were still short enough for even Cepheid to see over as they perched in their laps.

After two days of this, Canis was forced to search out the road because the wind driven snow had obscured all contours in the landscape. While Canis wove from side to side, probing for the sides of the road, Cepheid followed, leading the lead team, keeping to the center of his weave. The four Wulfen roamed the length of the caravan and kept the wagons in line since each driver could scarcely see the wagon in front of them.

At Lexington, Canis went over all of the horses' legs checking for ice cuts and bruises, then he ordered the stable master to feed them hot mash; they had worked hard. They spent two nights here hoping the wind would let up, but when it didn't, they pushed on.

Normally, it would have taken four days to reach the river crossing, but in wind driven snow, it took them an additional two days. The crossing itself took only a few hours, but there were chunks of ice flowing in the water so when they were on the other side Canis once again went over the horses while the drivers filled the barrels.

Two days later the snows stopped, but the wind continued to blow out of the north with merciless aggression. As the clouds blew away, the temperature dropped. Visibility improved though and once again, Canis scouted around for bandits who might be interested in a lone caravan out in this windblown landscape.

Over the next four days, the depth of the snow on the ground decreased to only the few inches trapped by the tall grass that would have reached up to the horses chests if it hadn't been laid over by the wind and weighed down by the snow. Then as quickly as it had started, the wind stopped, leaving an unmarked and desolate landscape under an equally unmarked, pale blue sky.

The Hunt

They were only a few hours into their second day on the flat expanse of the plains when they found their way blocked by a herd the likes of which neither Canis nor Cepheid had ever seen or heard of. There must have been thousands of the beasts in the herd, but they were such strange beasts. The head, shoulders, and front legs were massive and powerful and covered with curly dark brown hair. The flanks and back legs looked like they should have belonged to a smaller animal; they were undersized and the short hair was slick and shiny. This back half was a lighter brown in the younger members of the herd.

"The winter must be hard if they are this far east," commented Kolar.

Canis could feel the hunting assessment going through the Wulfen.

"*Sharp horns and feet.*"

"*Hard to get a grip on the throat.*"

"*Hamstring, trip it up.*"

"*Pull it down by its nose. Tender noses.*"

Canis smiled, almost showing his teeth. "I think we are going hunting." He readied his bow and quiver. "We take only one," he said to the Wulfen.

"You be careful out there. Those buffalo are pretty agile," said Kolar.

As Canis trotted toward the herd, he spoke to his hunting companions. "They are called buffalo. They are agile. They are not mired in snow. Be careful, I cannot heal you when you hunt among the stars."

"*You are the one who must be careful,*" said Rrusharr. "*You have never ridden this horse-creature on a hunt before.*"

By the time they reached the herd, it was moving at an easy lope, but it was picking up speed. Canis picked out a young bull and zeroed in on him. Rrusharr went immediately for the nose while Nnarr picked the heels. Ggrrawrr dodged between their target and the rest of the herd and leapt for an ear. His move, like no other, caused the bull to dodge away from the rest of the herd and Canis dashed in with Ggrrawrr to push it farther from the herd. Alone, it would be brought down quickly.

Unfortunately, it couldn't be so easy. Canis had never hunted a herd of this type. With a closely-knit herd such as this one, when one member changes direction, it's likely others will follow it. First one, then other buffalo turned in the wake of the one Ggrrawrr and Canis had been able to turn aside, and Canis suddenly found himself in more trouble than he anticipated. Within seconds, Canis was immersed in the bulk of the herd and those small curved horns looked dangerous enough when bobbing so close to his legs and his horse's shoulders or ribs. He looped his reins around his saddle horn. Midnight would need no help running with the herd; its members had them trapped.

The four Wulfen were now running along side; all thoughts of taking a single young bull were gone. Canis looked across the sea of curly-haired humps to the edge of the herd. He stood up in the stirrups and drew his bow. Its length was unwieldy from horseback when the targets were this close.

He began to carve himself a path to the edge of the herd. With each buffalo that dropped, a small gap was created. He learned quickly that if he didn't take advantage of the gap, it closed up fast. As soon as one of the hulking creatures dropped, Canis leaned Midnight over into the space while he took aim at the next heavy neck.

Eight arrows later, Canis managed to carve his way to the

edge of the herd and reunite with the Wulfen. He reined away from the herd and pulled up to look back. The caravan was out of sight. Though he regretted having to kill so much more than he could use, the hunt had been exhilarating. The danger was a distant thing now that it was past.

"*We are watched*," said Ggrrawrr and Canis pulled his eyes away from the thundering herd. Standing about five hundred yards away, on top of a small rise, was a cluster of men and a few women dressed in shreds of furs and tattered material that hardly resembled clothing. Even at this distance, Canis could see that there were only a few crude bows among them. He looked back at the herd, then at the people again. *Were they herd followers? Had he just killed members of their herd?*

He dismounted and started toward the people. If he had broken one of their laws, he needed to make amends somehow. "Stay here, I will be fine," he said to the Wulfen. Rrusharr stayed close to his side. The others stayed with Midnight.

When they saw him walking toward them alone, the grandfather of their family stepped out to meet him. When they were about ten paces apart, the old man sank to his knees.

At this display, Canis froze. He didn't know what to do. This isn't what he expected.

"Never, in all my days, have I seen such a thing. I thank the Mother for letting me live long enough to witness it," said the old man. He held his gnarled hands high and was shaking to the point that Canis thought he might fall on his face.

"Please, sir, let me help you to your feet. The ground is too cold for this," said Canis as he covered the remaining distance and took an arm to pull him to his feet. His grip on the old man's arm told him what the wind had not until Canis had stepped close. This old man was about as close to starving as he had ever seen. He looked at the rest of the group and saw that they could well be as bad as the man standing before him. "Have I damaged your herd?" he asked.

"Our herd?" said the old man in surprise. "This is not *our* herd. We follow it in hopes that one or two would die of old age or perhaps the cold. Sometimes, in the spring, we find one having problems calving."

"I only intended to take one." Then something the man said floated to the surface of his memory. "The Mother must have caused me to take several more so close to where you can find them. May you find some use for her gift."

The old man threatened to fall to his knees again, but Canis retained his grip on the unsteady old man. "Bless you, bless you for this gift," gushed the old man. "With this, we will be fat and healthy by spring."

A younger bull of a man from the group on the hill saw the old man's near collapse and he couldn't stand to watch him in the grip of the tall stranger so closely shadowed by such a large wolf. He sprinted up to them intent on breaking them apart, but he wasn't quite brave enough to contest a snarling black wolf that stood as high as his waist and blocked his less than amiable approach.

"Ready everyone," said the old man. "The Mother has given us a great gift this day." The old man waved his hand over to the churned landscape left behind by the passing of the herd. "We have meat to gather before it freezes. Also, someone will need to help the Mother's hunter with his choice kill."

The younger man was shocked. He took in the dotted field and turned back to the others. While he was organizing the butchering party, Canis went back to his horse and the other Wulfen. As he collected his reins, he said, "Nnarr, head back to the caravan. Tell Cepheid we will be following soon."

The white Wulfen sprinted off already telling her companion all the news of her adventure.

Canis made his way from carcass to carcass retrieving his arrows and cutting out the arrowheads if the shaft was broken. Two men from the family caught up to him as he was straightening from the second carcass. He was already toying with the idea of leaving half the one kill he had intended to take to these people. A buffalo was very large when you had to move its dead carcass.

The younger man from before, who named himself Bill, and the other, Riley, brought him a sturdy rope tied into a crude harness. When he saw Canis's glance at the rope, he said, "You got a good strong horse there, but there's no way he'll carry all of this. We'll make camp here close by and drag the carcasses in close. We have a few horses. We usually use two per carcass, but your horse should be able to manage one alone for a short distance."

Just as Canis was about to move on, Bill bent over the buffalo and opened its throat. He pulled its nose far back and steaming blood immediately began to seep out into the grass melting the snow it touched.

Two kills later, Canis asked, "Tell me something, if you can. Why do you and your people lead this kind of life? Why do you not move into the city? There must be something you can do so you do not have to live on the edge of starvation in this way."

Bill and Riley looked at each other. "We do well enough like this," said Bill.

"Your people are freezing and starving. You should build warm shelters and learn to…"

"You're a stranger. What makes you think you can tell us how we should live?" said Bill.

Canis bent to cut his arrowhead from the next carcass and Bill slit its throat with an unusually harsh move. "I *am* a stranger, but living off the hunt is something my clan has done for generations. Find a place where these buffalo go every year. Build warm homes there. Hunt what you need to get you through to the next hunt. In the summer, gather all the grains and roots in the same manner. Learn to store it so there are no starvation months. You will hunt all the time and gather all summer. If you never let up, the rest will be easy and then you will have family and friends, people who will share your fortune."

"You make it sound so easy, but we are outlaws. We cannot settle in such a manner. We are hunted more than they are." said Bill. He waved at where the herd had vanished and his shoulders hunched with resentment.

"There are many places where you can settle and not be touched. Keep your settlements small and scattered far apart. Keep your people away from roads and towns and no one will notice you. Do not forget your crimes, though. Being outlawed does not make you outside of the law. Laws are for the protection of everyone and should not be taken lightly."

Bill flew into a rage and leapt at Canis brandishing his bloody knife. "Who do you think you are?"

Canis caught him and held his knife at arm's reach easily. "Is this your crime? Can you not control your temper? Remember what it bought you and teach that to your son." Canis released him and he deflated just as quickly as he had flared up.

"How did you know I had a son?"

"I did not, but I think most men wish for one."

They finished with the rest of the buffalo in silence. It was past midday by the time Canis, Bill, and Riley reached the first buffalo Canis had killed. All of the arrows Canis had fired were broken – he had expected nothing less – but most of the fletchings were still good so he kept them for that. All but one of the arrowheads was still good. They had been deep enough in the flesh to be protected from breaking in the fall. The broken one was accompanied by a smashed shaft. The hapless creature had likely been trampled after it fell.

Between Canis, Bill, and Riley they gutted and bled the buffalo, and tied it by its horns to Midnight's new harness. Canis handed the liver into Bill's hands. "I want the old man I spoke to, to have this. It will make him strong. Tell him it is a gift from the Mother. Tell him whatever he wants to hear, but see to it that he eats all of this within the next two or three days. Do the same for everyone. Have a grand celebration to honor the success of the hunt and make the livers the prize."

"We have always discarded the innards," said Riley, his voice was soft and quiet. He was not used to speaking.

Canis looked at the man, he was scruffy and unwashed like all the others; he didn't seem to fit among them. Something was different about him. He went to the gut pile. He pulled out the heart. “This is a little tough, but it has good flavor and makes a hearty stew that few will turn their noses up to.” He pulled out the smaller intestines and pointed to below the stomachs and above the larger intestines. “Cut and tie this off here and here, then tie knots about every hand span, so each section can be separated. Fry it in the fat you can find under the skin around the neck and inside along the spine. The taste takes some getting used to, but it is the greens you all need in order to stay healthy until you can gather your own. You will find none better this time of year.” He pointed to the stomachs. “You can clean these out and use them to carry water. If every person has one, they can fill it with snow every day and carry it under their coats to melt. Drinking enough water is always important.” He took the time to open his coat and show them the one he carried slung under his arm.

“That doesn’t leave much behind,” said Bill.

“To waste is an insult to the gift,” said Canis, then he pointed to the hooves. “Boil these and they make a sturdy glue.” He indicated the horns. “These could be cleaned out and used for drinking water. Even the bones can be useful.” He let them take a closer look at the arrowheads Auriga had made for him from bone.

“I think we could learn a lot from you. Stay with us,” said soft-spoken Riley.

“I have other obligations. Remember what I have told you and you will do well. Never be so proud that you cannot learn from a stranger, and never allow yourself to take what a stranger is unwilling to give.” Canis turned to his horse and started to lead him back to the caravan dragging the buffalo. He was unwilling to let them see how the last sentence had unsettled him. He had no idea where it came from. It didn’t fit with the rest of their conversation.

“We will remember you, and what you have taught us here,” said Riley calling after Canis as he was heading away. “We *will* remember.”

Lincoln

When they pulled into Lincoln four days later, much of the buffalo had been consumed. After the wagons had been delivered to the warehouse, Kolar handed Canis four gold coins and ten silvers.

Canis attempted to hand one of the golds back. “You have already given me eleven silvers.”

Kolar pulled Canis aside. “Listen kid, never in all of my years of driving that route – three times a year by the way – never have we been able to make the trip without some loss. Never have we pulled in here with the cargo utterly untouched, and never have we reached this point with a good deal of our supplies still intact. The horses are healthy. The drivers are also healthy and in good humor. You have saved the company much more than eleven silvers by your actions, so I know no one will protest the extra money in your pocket. The boss might even give you another gold or two if he manages to find you. I know you’re leaving us and I truly regret it. I, for one, wish you would remain.”

Canis extended his hand to shake – an action he showed few people. “There are things I have learned from you as well. Travel safe; perhaps we will meet again one day.”

Canis went to collect his sled and the rest of his belongings. He was considering them when Kolar came back inside. “That won’t be much use to you here. I’ll take it off your hands, if you’re willing.”

“You are right. It is good for pulling behind when on foot, but much too small for behind a horse. Star can carry all we need. I gift the sled to you, if you think you can find some use for it. Perhaps you can get some coin for it back in Cheyenne," said Canis.

"Just what I was thinking, but I'll pay you for it," said Kolar.

"No, I will not take more of your coin. You have given me many things both large and small on this trip, it is only right I give you a gift in return. My sled and our snowshoes are the only thing I can give without depleting what I need, and I like knowing that something I have made goes to someone I like."

Kolar raised his palms to Canis. "All right, all right, it's a gift. I've learned that arguing with you seldom does any good. Thank you; I plan to give the sled to my brother, and he'll appreciate the snowshoes too. He runs a trap line with his son and I think they could use them."

It was impossible for Canis to find lodging in the city that would accommodate six giant wolves, but it didn't stop him from visiting the different inns in search of more work that would take them to Omaha city. It would only take them six or seven days to make the trip, but if work could be found, so much the better.

Over the next two days, news of Canis's skill as a guard made the rounds too, so, as he was making his way through the market square, he was approached by a graying man in a uniform.

"Word has it you are a very skilled guard," said the man. "The wild people have been reported in the area and Lord Lincoln must send his daughter to Omaha for her wedding ceremony. The job pays fifty gold coins if Lord Lincoln chooses to hire you. If you're interested, I will escort you to the manor to meet with him."

Fifty gold, just to escort a woman, was impressive wages. "Can you tell me more about the job? It seems a little much to escort only one woman."

"The lady Enid will be traveling with an entourage that may encompass three or four wagons. Aside from the lady and her maids, there will be wedding gifts of high value."

"I see," said Canis. "I will speak with your lord."

When they started walking across the square, Cepheid and the six Wulfen joined them. As always, Rrusharr enjoyed the reaction from the man who was guiding them.

His eyes darted from wolf to wolf, four of which were almost big enough to saddle and the other two, though they might be considered a more normal size, they had feet big enough to trip over. His eyes then darted to the tall man who walked beside him and took in his white eyes as well as the stone between his brows and the long cable of red hair that hung down his back. Then he eyed Cepheid's young face topped with its short mop of course gray hair and its incongruous black blotch at her right temple. Few of the clan had hair that was a single color, and none of them had red hair, but both were highly uncommon here.

This man's attention on Cepheid also directed Canis's attention to her as he tried to see her through a plainsman's eyes. He noticed another thing too. Her scent had changed; she was pregnant. He would have to find a place for her to shelter and raise her children in safety. Her children…*his* children…he was going to have *children*. He almost missed a step when the man led them up to the gate flanked by two more men dressed in the same uniform.

At first, the house manager balked at letting even one wolf into the house let alone six, but when Canis offered to meet the lord in the courtyard, his escort would hear none of it. He overrode the manager and brought Canis and all of his companions into the main room of the manor, then he went to find Lincoln.

While he was gone, three little girls skipped into the room. With the fearlessness of small children, they went right up to the puppies and started playing with them. The puppies hadn't had much human interaction, but children were children and it wasn't but moments before they were all rolling on the floor. The girls were giggling and laughing and the puppies were bouncing and rolling around acting like big-footed clowns.

A short, but trim man with a full head of white hair entered the room. He carried himself with a haughtiness that said he was more than just the lord of the house. He was just in time to catch his youngest daughter falling into the side of the black puppy who allowed both of them to flop over sideways in a wriggling, giggling mass that had a lot to do with a long wet tongue. He looked at Canis and Cepheid; the two stood quite close to the playing young, watching over them closely. He also saw four much larger wolves lying around the room in various poses that didn't detract from their alertness. This was all obviously play, but he was embarrassed that his daughters should act in this manner in front of strangers. "Girls," he said. "Go. We have business to discuss."

The girls reluctantly disentangled themselves from the puppies and left the room less energetically than when they came. When they were gone, the lord turned to Canis. "You must be the Canis I have been hearing about. You look a bit young, but from what I've been told, you work miracles. After seeing these, I think I can understand why. Come over here and we'll go over the logistics of the trip."

As they walked over to a table at the side of the room, the black puppy went to the door where the girls had disappeared.

"No," said Canis without looking at him. "You two will remain here."

Lord Lincoln looked at Canis to see who he had spoken to and saw the black puppy return to her place among the others. "You speak to them? They must understand you very well."

Canis wasn't about to try to explain how the Wulfen could understand him, so he let the man assume what he wished.

After they were finished with the lists of people, presents, and supplies that would be going along with his daughter, they went out to look at the wagons and carriages. Three carriages would be for the women, two wagons for the presents and another for their supplies.

Lord Lincoln wanted two men on each wagon, one driver, and an armed guard. Riding along in escort were another twelve armed guards on horseback.

"Sir, I do not understand. If you are sending eighteen guards to protect your daughter, why are you sending me?"

Lincoln looked at Canis with an appraising eye. "I'm sending eighteen boys with no officer. They will be my daughter's personal guards for the rest of her life. You will be the officer they lack during this trip. That way, I will not short myself."

Canis didn't see the sense of a group of men on a mission without an officer of their own, but the decision was not his to make. "I would like to meet the men before we depart."

Lord Lincoln nodded as if he expected nothing less from him so they went to the garrison to meet the soldiers. After inspecting the chosen men, Canis pulled out three men and insisted that they be replaced. Two smelled of illness and another had an injury in his wrist and elbow that would hinder his use of a sword.

He went over the drivers the same way and discarded one of those as well. All of his discards were done solely on scent. If he was to be in command, he wanted able men, and if they smelled of illness, injury, or even alcohol, he wanted nothing to do with them.

When everything was settled, plans for departure were made for the morning after next. In the meantime, Canis asked to bunk with the horses so they could get used to the Wulfen.

Here is where Lincoln's composure cracked. "You want to stay in the stables? With the horses? I have an apartment arranged for you and your young friend. I have even ordered Hasfras to allow the wolves inside with you."

"That is generous of you, but it is important that the horses become accustomed to the wolves. We will stay in the stables."

Lincoln blustered for a moment, quite disconcerted, but then he said, "Well…well all right, but you will eat here. Someone will retrieve you when it's time to eat." The poor man was quite unused to arranging such details or even having to.

Canis and Cepheid went back into the town to complete their interrupted shopping then retrieve their horses.

With a lot more work than he expected, Canis managed to get the caravan moving almost on time. He would have liked to leave at dawn, but young women were notoriously difficult to get moving so early, especially when they were not at all anxious to be going in the first place.

They reached the edge of the city before he could organize the soldiers where he wanted them. He quickly learned that they were all headstrong trainees and none of them were too keen to follow the orders of a complete stranger. He arranged them so there was one guard on each side of each wagon. The horse that belonged to the guard sitting on each wagon was tied fifth-wheel beside each wagon team within easy access. The soldier need only leap to the saddle and cut the lead if such an emergency occurred that called him away from the wagon.

Cepheid took up tail guard with Nnarr and the puppies at her side. At least they knew what they were doing and even the puppies behaved better than these young soldier wannabes.

Long before the end of the day, Canis took to throwing clods of muddy ice at the young men whose attention wandered away from their duty all too easily. They learned to watch for him to dip down from his saddle and pick some up, but it usually did them little good. It seemed that he had eyes in the back of his head because they were caught even when he wasn't looking in their direction.

That night, after camp was set up, Canis counted the marks on each of the young men and their uniforms. He made each young soldier do five pushups in the snow for every mark then he didn't allow them to bed down until their uniforms were clean again. This was not an easy task on the trail, and it was made more difficult by the fact that it was winter. He made them all stand in formation until the last of them was finished.

The next day, the men did infinitely better. They seemed to accept that it was easier to do what Canis said. As a reward, he broke up the boredom of their trek by sending them off in different directions, to the front, to one side or the other, one at a time, each in his turn. He even allowed the guards on the wagons to take a turn, though someone was required to replace them for that time.

"Pick a spot on the horizon we cannot see past. Go there and have a look, then get back here and report. Do not allow yourself to get out of sight of the wagons. We are guarding here, not playing out there."

Rrusharr and Ggrrawrr did the real scouting while Rranggrr stayed close to the wagons. Canis noticed that she was looking a bit wide. He was reminded of Cepheid and looked back at her. She smiled back at him then looked off to the right. Canis groaned; his children had found a new way to act up. It didn't take him long to start thinking of them as children. They were no younger than he was, in fact, most of them were at least a year or two older, but they acted like children – irresponsible children.

When he stopped sending them out, they began to grumble, but they stopped when he started throwing mud again.

He knew the missing scout was waiting just on the other side of a small rise about a quarter mile back now. Ggrrawrr was watching over him, so he knew the boy wasn't in trouble. Canis wondered how long he would wait before returning to the wagons, but he wasn't about to find out. Scouting wasn't something to take lightly.

As soon as he was sure the boy could no longer see the wagons, he dismounted and handed his reins to Cepheid. When he returned to the caravan an hour later, he had the young soldier stripped of his uniform and tied across the saddle of his own horse. He tied the horse to the back of the last wagon and retrieved Midnight.

For the rest of the day, the other soldiers were very quiet. Seeing one of their number tied like so much meat across his saddle for most of a day, was daunting. He was able to move some, so everyone knew he was alive, but the way he was tied left him little room for such movement, and with only his cloak tossed over him, he wasn't very warm either. Knowing that Canis had gone after him on foot was another quieting point.

When they stopped for camp, Canis was the one who tended to the 'side of meat' and his horse. He pulled the kid from the saddle and propped him up against a tree while he unsaddled their two horses and tied them to the picket line. Then he guided the kid to the center of camp, supporting him until circulation returned to his legs and feet. In the center of camp, he halted him and left him standing there alone.

When all the other young soldiers had finished their camp duties, which included pushups for muddy marks, then cleaning said marks, they took their positions in their formation. Through it all, the one soldier stood alone shivering in nothing but his small clothes.

When everyone was assembled, Canis rounded up the women and the drivers for a semi-formal affair. Speaking for everyone to hear, Canis said, "You men have had two days to try my tolerance. We have had two days of grace, since we have not been attacked. From this moment on, if I decide that you are a danger to our mission, I will strip you and discard you. We already have one man here who is guilty of desertion. Since I am your commander only for the duration of this trip, I will leave such decisions up to a final vote of the men and women we are here to protect. If it were left up to me, after two days of putting up with your shameful behavior, the snow would have been stained with blood today, and this…would not be standing here." He tossed the man's uniform to him allowing more anger than he actually felt to show in the move.

Speaking directly to the offending young man, he said, "You will stand guard tonight, all night, and you will remain alert all day tomorrow. Do not even consider that I might not notice whether you slack in your duty." He turned back to the rest of them. "You had better hope that no one out there was watching us over the last two days."

The kid caught his uniform and succeeded in not letting it get any dirtier than it already was. "Yes sir," he said. While he was dressing, Canis set up the rest of the sentry roster, then settled down to eat his supper, glowering – again something he wanted them to *see*.

As he was eating, Enid came up to him. "I realize that my

father hired you to get us to Omaha, but do you have to be so harsh with the men? I know all of them and they are good with a sword. They all earned the right to be my guard."

"I am glad you know all of them. As I understand it, you will be their supreme commander after I have left, but being good with a sword is only one small step to take in seeing to your protection. All of these men must be alert and watchful all of the time. The more alert and watchful they are, the less likely they will miss their chance to put themselves between you and a killer."

He turned and faced her directly. "How lucky do you think you are?" he continued. "You had better hope that you are very lucky because as long as these boys continue to play at being soldiers, the sooner you will die, or the sooner you will lose all of them. I strongly suggest you start treating them as your guards rather than your friends."

Enid didn't know what she expected, speaking to this strange man with glowing eyes, but it certainly wasn't being painted as a target for a killer with only human flesh as a shield. "I didn't want this, you know. I didn't want any of it."

"Your father has seen fit to tie himself tighter to the seat of Omaha. You have a duty to your father to honor his obligation. With things this big, if you try to escape your duty, your father and all you love could be destroyed."

Enid backed away indignantly. "You don't know what you're talking about."

"Perhaps," said Canis and he turned back to his stew. She didn't have to tell him he didn't know what he was talking about. He didn't.

Enid went back to her fire and was soon in a heated, though soft-spoken conversation with one of the older women there.

Cepheid watched her for a moment, then leaned over and said softly, "I don't understand these customs. What is it that you speak of between her, her father and this Omaha we are taking her to?"

"I do not understand it either. The words are not mine," said Canis as he looked into his stew and frowned.

"How can you say it if you don't understand it?" asked Cepheid.

"It is like the healing. The words come out of my mouth as if another were speaking them. It has happened before."

"You frighten me when you do things like that. Are you a puppet?" she asked in a hiss.

"No, not a puppet exactly, more like…more like a messenger, I think."

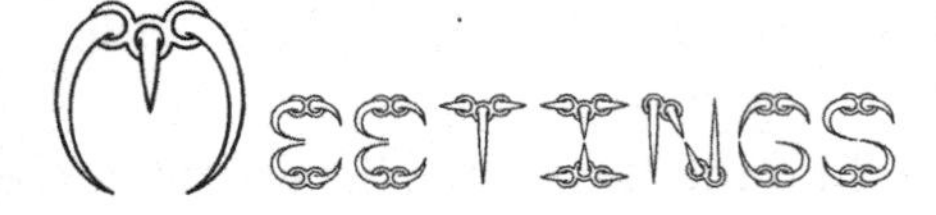

The river came in sight on the horizon early in the afternoon of the next day. Their journey was half over and there had been no further incidents that weren't simple mistakes made by inexperienced men on the march.

Shortly after sighting the river, the scouts returned from both the south and the north with an unusual urgency to report that they had seen riders. Canis tightened up their line. "How far away? Do we have time to cross the river before they reach us?"

"No sir," said one of the young soldiers. "If we ran the horses all out the rest of the way, we might reach the water before they do, but even so, we won't have time to cross. We'd barely have time to get one or two wagons in the water."

Canis let out a piercing howl that got the undivided and completely astonished attention of everyone around him. "Circle the wagons. Have the teams inside. You, wagon guards, get everyone inside the circle. You are our last line of defense. The rest of you, get in another circle around the outside of the wagons. Cepheid, you get inside with the puppies."

Another time, Cepheid would have protested, but she had another life to protect besides her own, so she went with the women. She could fight there if she had to. If their attackers made it that far, Canis would be dead and there would be nothing else to live for, but she would fight. They would pay dearly for coming within her reach.

The wagons were circled quickly and the men assembled

around them. "Keep your eyes toward your front. Never assume that just because we are attacked from one direction that we cannot be attacked from another as well. An open attack may be a diversion for a much more stealthy attack elsewhere. This is where all your training will be needed. We are not so numerous that we can afford to make mistakes, so do not make any. Friends die when friends make mistakes, and I know you are all friends." He turned to the four Wulfen who were closing on his location from their different directions. "Rranggrr, guard our backs."

She too resented being sent from the fight, but she also had other life to consider and went to find a vantage point that overlooked their back trail. This flat country that hid so many ripples was difficult to guard.

When their attackers didn't show up as expected, Canis began to get nervous. He hated being cornered in this wide-open plain. When they still didn't show up, he questioned the men who had reported seeing them. "Why are they not here? Tell me exactly what you saw."

"I saw several mounted riders, perhaps a dozen, I didn't wait to count, but they were coming fast," said one of the soldiers.

"I saw riders too, but I only saw a handful before I turned back," said the other, "and they certainly weren't walking."

Canis growled to himself. Where were they? He was tempted to send out scouts again, but that was just asking to get them picked off. The river was in sight, but it would still take them a couple hours to reach it if they hurried.

Canis knew he was being watched; he could feel it. They didn't expect him to be ready for them. He paced around the wagons again, and again admonished the men to watch the area directly in front of them and to let the men behind them worry about the area behind them. Even if a fight was brought, it was important to watch every direction.

Rranggrr's soft rumble came into his head, "*They come. Side and side. Slow and low. They have left their horse-meat behind.*"

Horse-meat? Rranggrr considered the creatures as any other

game – huntable as long as they didn't belong to her clan. He looked where she had indicated and saw nothing yet. He was thankful she had found such a good vantage point.

A few minutes later, they found themselves almost surrounded by long lines of men both to the south and to the north of the road. Circled as he was, he could move in either direction along the road, and if he decided to head back, they could very well outrun the men on foot, but it was entirely likely that the men with horses had circled around in order to block the road farther back, so Canis opted to stay were he was. If they managed to get strung out, they would be slaughtered.

The bandits stopped when they were well within sight and two men from the north side of the road continued forward at an amiable pace.

Canis watched them warily for a while then dismounted to meet them. As he handed his reins to the closest man, he said, "Watch them all."

Only Rrusharr and Ggrrawrr flanked him. Nnarr stayed close to her companion; this was no hunting trip.

As he got closer, Canis recognized Bill and Riley from the buffalo hunt. The others behind them, he did not, but then he had seen very few of them and no old man would be on such a mission as this.

Before they reached speaking distance, Canis saw the two men halt for a moment and Bill firmly set Riley aside, he was denying him something and obviously telling him to stay behind, then he came on himself.

As soon as they could speak without yelling, Bill said, "When I recognized you, I called off the attack. You have given us too much. I will not take what you are guarding."

"It is dangerous to take what another is not willing to give," said Canis. "I told you that once."

"And you are very right. For many years, we have been forced to 'take' because we were not allowed to 'earn', but you showed us a much better way. As sketchy as the teaching was, it will provide us all a much better life than what we had before. This was to be…"

There was a commotion back at the wagons. One of the women was running in their direction and hard on her heels were two men on foot and one on horse. All of them were having difficulty catching her. She was a very fast runner, and though she couldn't outrun the horse, it's very difficult to catch a person on foot from a horse, if you are unwilling to injure the runner.

She cried out as she ran and dodged, and Riley suddenly cried out and started running as well. Both Canis and Bill sprang into action, each of them trying to intercept their target before damage to the negotiations could occur.

Bill caught Riley and took him to the ground in a flying tackle while Canis caught Enid and quickly sent the men back to the wagons. Many of Bill's men had started forward as well, but they halted when the situation didn't turn into a fight, at least it wasn't a fight between the two parties. Enid was still kicking and struggling in Canis's arms and Riley was doing much the same on the ground, though the bigger and stronger man was able to hold him down.

"Stop struggling, both of you," growled Canis, "or I will feed you to the wolves." The obvious growl in his low rumble of a voice cut through their struggles and froze them all, even Bill looked at him in stunned disbelief.

Bill pulled Riley to his feet and shook him by the shoulders. "Calm yourself, you fool, or I'll feed you to the wolves myself."

He dusted himself off and turned to Canis who still held Enid off the ground. "Well, as I was saying, this was going to be our last raid. Riley didn't want to leave without trying to take his girl with him. We knew Lincoln would try this, but we didn't know when. We got the message the day after we met you and headed for this place as soon as the elders were in a comfortable camp."

"We passed no messenger," said Canis.

Bill didn't really want to give up a secret, but he felt he owed Canis, so he said, "There are four of our number who can speak into others' minds. It's not very common, most people are hung for it, if they are ever discovered, but some are able to run away first. I am one and we have another in the city."

"Put me down," said Enid. When Canis set her on the ground again – he still kept a hand on her arm – she said, "I love him. I want to go with him. I would have run away long ago, but father wouldn't let me out of his sight. He actually set a guard on me even at night, outside my window too."

"You cannot go with him. You have a more important obligation," said Canis. "We spoke of that last night."

"No," said Riley, his soft voice almost a wail. "You can't mean to make her go. She doesn't love him. She doesn't even know him."

"This is not a marriage of love," said Canis, "it is a marriage of diplomacy. It is a treaty between two great houses and it is sealed with blood, not blood *shed*, but blood *joined*. This marriage must happen."

"I don't care what happens to my father," said Enid. "He is a prig and I want nothing more to do with him."

"That may be so, and indeed you may be able to live with the fact that this whole district may become embroiled in a war if you leave. You will be far away. You will not see what might happen, but what will you tell your children when they ask after their grandfather or where you come from? Children ask questions and they are not always easy questions to answer. Will you wave the question away? Will you lie? If they ever come back here – and children tend to do that too, what will they see? What will they think when they learn that, at this moment, you decided to run away together and let it all happen? Will they think it was very romantic? Or will they think that surely their brave and intelligent parents could have thought of some other solution that would have prevented so much destruction? You *are* brave, you know, and intelligent. The fact that you are willing to start a life so very different from what you both know, shows that."

"But there is no other solution, there is no other way. Father would never allow…" Her protest was interrupted by Canis's raised hand.

He had an idea. “Bill, how good of a commander do you think Riley is or could be?”

Bill looked back at Riley standing indignantly and anxiously behind him. “Oh, I don’t know. I know he ran away from the palace garrison before he came to us. I believe he was due to be impaled. He has a solid head on his shoulders, but he’s a bit shy, and I don’t think he’s had any experience at commanding anyone.”

Canis turned to Riley. “Riley, could you stand in Enid’s shadow? Could you allow her to marry another man if you could still be close to her? Could you help her honor her obligation to her father and protect her from any harm even if it meant dying for her, all for the privilege of being close, but never touching?”

Riley looked at Enid and both Canis and Bill could feel the love that radiated from his soul. They could see it pouring from his eyes. “I could, it would be very hard to see her with another man, but if the only choices I have is ‘close’ or ‘nothing’, then I choose ‘close’.”

“Bill, if you have no objection, I will take Riley with us. He will be captain of this guard. Enid’s father need never find out.” He turned to Enid. “From what I understand, Enid, your men were to have no officer other than yourself, unless one is to be provided by your future husband, but I think this is better. Your commands should come from yourself, but you lack experience. It is my recommendation that you deny any need for foreign officers and I also recommend that you, Riley, change your name. Riley, the outlaw under sentence of impalement, should die here today so that Captain…”

“Michael,” supplied Bill and Riley nodded his approval. “After the man you spoke to before…at the hunt.”

Canis nodded. The old man who had watched his hunt of the buffalo – he remembered. “…so that Captain Michael can be born.”

The newly named captain came forward and knelt at Enid’s feet. “I will serve you with my body and my soul and obey all of your commands whatever they may be."

Canis guided Enid's trembling hand to rest on Michael's head. She hesitated saying anything, but everyone seemed to be waiting for her to speak. "I accept your pledge gladly and happily," she said tremulously. She wasn't too sure she wanted this new arrangement if it meant him kneeling at her feet.

Now that their relationship was much more formal, the new captain took his responsibilities seriously and chose to act accordingly. He stood straight and tall, trying to look important in his tattered and mismatched clothes, shaggy, unwashed hair, and scruffy beard. He turned to Bill and said, "I will take my leave now, Bill. Thank you for taking me under your wing. I will never forget you." They shook hands then Michael took custody of his new charge and escorted her back to the wagons. Enid hung on his arm as if she needed help standing, or as if she might be whispering something in his ear. Perhaps it was a little of both.

Canis looked back at Bill. "Well, I guess that pretty much concludes our business here."

"It looks that way, doesn't it?" replied Bill. He extended his hand to shake and Canis returned it closely, his off hand clasping Bill's wrist. Bill looked toward the river, then at the late afternoon sun. "I suppose you were planning to camp on the other side of the river."

"I was; it will be late for that now."

"We held you up so we'll help you across the river, then perhaps you and I can have a sit-down and share a meal. I'll supply the buffalo if you will supply the tea, and you have my word that none of my men will touch what I know you are carrying."

"I will accept your offer of help and of meat. Hunting has been poor this side of the city."

"Yeah and I bet you got a lot of opportunity to hunt with that lot," said Bill.

Canis smiled a tight smile and turned back to the caravan. Bill smiled as well and turned back to his men. By the time Canis had his wagons straightened out and the men lined up, Bill's men had joined them. True to his word, none of them went near the gift wagon or the women unless it was to keep wheels turning in the mud.

With the extra hands to help, they crossed the river quickly. Bill's men plunged right in to keep the wagons on the crossing in the water's current.

Bill had his men gathering wood for their fires as soon as the wagons they had guided across the river were on solid ground. Camp was set up in record time and Canis was glad for the fresh meat that was simmering in his stew. As soon as camp was settled and the animals wiped down, he called everyone to gather again. Almost all of Bill's men had already returned across the river and their own fires could be seen on the other side.

While everyone was gathering, he pulled the new captain aside and presented him with a new uniform – there were several extras among their stores of supplies – then he guided him to the center of camp dressed in his new splendor.

"Allow me to introduce you to your new captain. Captain Michael has already proven himself a capable and honorable man, one that Lady Enid trusts with her life, so I am making him your captain and I expect you to keep him there."

"He needs a mark," said Cepheid, "something to set him apart from the others, something other than his name and title."

Canis remembered nodding his agreement, but the next thing he remembered was removing his hand from Michael's shoulder. Left on the young man's face and neck were three small marks. Under the outer corner of his left eye was a teardrop shaped mark about the size of a large man's thumbprint. Close examination showed that it was a tiny wolf that looked like it had just leapt from the corner of his eye to run down his cheekbone. Another mark, also teardrop shaped, though smaller and bright red was just below the left corner of his mouth. The third was on the side of his neck directly over the throbbing vein there. It was in the shape of a white sword; the curve at its tip was pronounced, making it look eager to taste the blood that throbbed so close under its edge.

"May your eyes be as sharp as a wolf's eyes, may the blood of your enemies flow freely, and may you die swiftly by the sword," he said, though the words were merely an echo of someone else's, overheard from far away.

Michael could not see the marks, but he had felt them being set into his skin and he reached up and touched each one as Canis spoke of it, then he knelt before Canis. "You are indeed touched by the Mother. I will honor these marks and carry them with pride. All who come against my Lady will go down before my sword."

Canis was still trying to grasp what had happened when Michael rose and went to the men who seemed unnaturally quiet.

As Michael was setting up the duty roster for the night, Canis, Bill, and Cepheid went to their fire. Canis was glad that the command had fallen to someone else.

At the relative quiet of their fire, Canis accepted his bowl of stew and cup of tea from Cepheid and asked, "I missed some of that. What happened?"

Bill accepted his meal as well and asked, "How could you miss some of that? You did it, though I can't see how."

Cepheid took her stew and sat down beside Canis. She explained softly so that no one else in the camp could overhear. She also watched their guest closely, she had seen Canis shake his hand and she knew how seldom he surrendered his hand to anyone else's control. She said, "I suggested that you mark him somehow, so he could be seen to be different from the rest of them. I was thinking of some kind of badge or belt on his uniform, but you just reached up to touch his face with your thumb. You touched each of those spots and left behind those marks. Do you remember the words? I'm fairly certain the words weren't yours either."

Canis reached up and touched the stone between his brows. Was this something new or just something special? He shook his head. He would probably never sort it all out.

Bill interrupted his thoughts. "You have memory gaps?"

"Sometimes. It is my belief that the Mother is guiding my actions. Sometimes the guidance is a little stronger than other times. How is the tea?" Canis was reluctant to give any details of his weakness even to a man he felt was a friend.

Omaha

The next two days were uneventful for Canis. Michael blossomed under the responsibility of command, and took the unruly boys and had them running sentry duty much like before, but they returned promptly and reported fully. Michael was an intuitive leader and seemed to be able to spot trouble before it had a chance to germinate, and he did so with a smooth and even hand that earned everyone's respect. Then again, with Michael calling the shots, Canis had more time to scout around on his own, and he kept coming out of unexpected directions and appearing behind whoever was most distracted. It served to teach them the meaning of being alert.

They spotted a major jumble of stones half way through the second day, the first Canis had seen since leaving the city of Chicago. Michael told them that such places were once long ago cities, but Canis couldn't fathom it. Along with this unmarked border came an increase in the number of trees, though there was no river near that might support them.

Canis and Cepheid went to explore the ruins and found little of interest. The only reason they were labeled ruins was because of the unnatural blocky shapes and portions of obvious walls, all buried under trees, bushes, and grass. If this was where people had once lived, there was no sign left, and they weren't inclined to dismount and dig.

Michael met them when they returned. "You should be wary of ruins; they tend to harbor the more unsavory members of our society. There have also been cases of the ground around them opening up and dropping the unwary explorer to their deaths."

"I have seen things like that ever since we came out of the foothills, though none of them were this big," said Cepheid. "Why are there so many of them? Even this road seems unusually wide for the use it gets."

"It is said," said Michael, "that the land was once covered by vast cities that dwarf the settlements we now have, and I have seen some evidence that this might have been true, but I can't picture it. Surely, the mere size of such a society would crumble from its own weight. The farms would never be able to support them. And the roads, perhaps the ancient peoples used very large wagons drawn by great fire horses and what we have today has grown small, like our cities."

Canis remembered the story he had heard back at the Salt Lake Clan. There had never been any mention of cities or roads, but there had been a mention of coming out of a dark, clutching building and heading away from 'stars that rested on the ground', and he remembered the memory of one small girl very long ago. She had looked out over a vast sea of lights and fires, but it was in the darkness of the closer landscape where she had been concentrating her attention.

They didn't come across any other ruins visible from the road until they made camp that night. It was at the base of another pile of blocks, but it was a well-used campsite, so there was little fear that the ground would fall out from under them.

"Why aren't there any ruins on the other side of the mountains, or did they only have their cities on this side?" asked Cepheid after she had handed out their stew.

"I have no idea," replied Canis. "The story said that there was something at the other end of the lake. They sheltered there, remember, and they took stone from there to build the homes they have now. Perhaps there is more under the snow. Perhaps the lake has grown and consumed it."

They reached the ferry house a couple hours before sundown.

The ferryman and his crew pulled them across the river one wagon at a time and grumbled about the hour every inch of the way. By the time they were all across and the man was paid, it was well after sundown, but they had reached the edge of the city at last.

Canis stopped them at what looked like a good inn and bought them all a hot meal and a messenger. Michael had the food taken out to the guards who he insisted remain on duty while the ladies went inside by the fire to enjoy some mulled wine with their meal. The messenger was sent to Lord Omaha to announce their arrival and to bring back his wishes. The horses were watered in their harnesses. Neither Michael nor Canis expected to be staying here for the night; they would find out for sure when the messenger returned.

When he finished his supper, Canis went outside to watch over the wagons; he wasn't comfortable being responsible for something he couldn't see.

Two hours after their arrival at the inn, the messenger returned bringing an entire company of guards in the blue and green livery of the house of Omaha.

When the men arrived, the captain glanced over the wagons and their escort then dismounted to go into the inn; Canis followed him uncontested.

"A messenger arrived two days ago. He said a guard named Canis would be in charge of this caravan. Where is he?" said the captain with an imperious tone in his voice.

"He is here," said Canis in his softest voice from directly behind the man. Canis's softest voice was reminiscent of a snarl only much smoother, not unlike a hiss. It was very unsettling when used face to face, but when heard coming from your unguarded back, it was cause for alarm.

The man whirled and drew his sword in the same move, or at least, he tried to draw his sword. Canis's powerful hands had the man's arms imprisoned before he had scarcely completed his turn.

"You come in numbers enough to cause alarm. What are your intentions here?" asked Canis, his pale eyes looking close into the eyes of his quarry.

"I come to escort you and Lady Enid to Lord Omaha. Our numbers are to ensure safe passage through the city to the palace."

"Really?" Canis's voice dropped into an even deadlier hiss. "Have you no control over your own citizens? Very well, you and your men – all of your men – will lead the way. We will follow. I will hand this caravan over to Lord Omaha myself." He turned loose of the captain and stepped back.

The man offered a stiff bow after only a moment's hesitation. "As you wish. Follow me." He left the building, his cloak billowing with his stride.

Canis tossed a coin purse to Michael and said, "Pay the bill and load the women into the wagons." Then he followed the man outside. As he suspected, there were several men down from their horses and wanting to approach the wagons. Michael's men were blocking their way, but it was obvious they weren't sure if they should.

"Get back to your horses," ordered the captain. He looked again at the wagons and the carriages. He was startled to see wolves standing boldly on top of them; startled enough to take a step to the side. He'd never seen such a thing before. There had been no mention of wolves in Lincoln's message.

As the women were climbing into their wagons, Michael touched Canis's elbow. "Why did you do that?"

"I don't trust him. He puts my hackles up. There are certain looks some men have. One is the look that says 'I think I can take that', something you and Bill have perfected. Then there is the look that says 'I already own that; it is my right'. That man will try to take whatever he wants regardless of who it might belong to, and he believes he has the right. You watch him closely and never trust him – never." He saw Cepheid onto Thumper then mounted Midnight. "Take the front, Michael. I will watch from the back."

Men from the new company passed lanterns out to the drivers and some of the guards along the side of the caravan. "Light them. Part of our way is unlit," said the captain.

As soon as everyone was ready, they headed out. First went Lord Omaha's captain and his men, then came Michael and the caravan, followed and flanked by Canis and the Wulfen that moved like shadows within shadows.

An hour later, they were passing through an unlit forest, and shortly after that, they came out onto a rocky spit of land that extended over a half a mile out into a vast, frozen lake. A large castle dominated the far end of the spit, its towers overlooking the pristine landscape and the crystalline waters.

As this came onto sight, Canis sighed. They did not pass through the slave market. *It must be farther north, closer to the crossroads*. Not that he worried about running into the slave master; the timing was wrong, but he might meet someone who knew Patro, someone who might remember a certain slave boy with white eyes. He wasn't ready for such a meeting yet.

When they entered the courtyard, men came out of the side buildings. They looked to be ready to take the horses to their stables, but they found their way blocked by wolves. "Stand clear," called Canis and the men moved back from the too-big wolves gladly. "I would speak with Lord Omaha," he said next, as he dismounted and walked to the front of the caravan to stand between it and their escort. He stood alone in the pivotal spot, but somehow, though he was on foot and most everyone else was mounted, he did not look small.

A soldier ran into the castle at a wave of the captain's hand and announced their arrival, returning moments later with a barrel-chested man of early middle years. "I have been informed that there is a disagreement between my men and the men of my soon-to-be bride. Where is this man called Canis?"

"I am here," said Canis. "I was paid to escort Lady Enid, her maids, and Lord Lincoln's wedding gifts here, and to see them directly into the care of Lord Omaha. Are you that man?"

"I am," replied the man. "Did you think you could stand alone against the best of my men?"

"I am not alone," said Canis. "Can you offer me any proof that you are who you claim?" He didn't need proof. The man radiated authority, but everyone needed to know how much store he put on his responsibility.

The barrel-chested man rolled his head back and laughed. When he had recovered his breath, he dismissed his men. He approached Canis and held out his hand palm down. "I don't know what proof you require, but here is my ring with my seal. Inside there is a crown that I don't wear very often; it fits my head and very few others. Will that do?"

Canis recognized the seal on the ring and Lincoln had given him a description of the man, so he nodded. "The ring and your honesty will do, Lord Omaha. He looked behind him. "Captain. Lady."

When Michael led Enid forward, Canis introduced them, then he stood aside as they in turn introduced the rest.

Introductions complete, Omaha waved for men to come and take custody of the animals and wagons. Other men from the palace came out and carried the gifts and the remains of their supplies inside. As the wagons were unloaded, they too were taken away.

Canis, Cepheid, and the Wulfen stood back in the shadows and watched. He looked up at the large stone building. The last large stone building he had been in had almost been a trap for him, and all the ones before that had all been filled with cages designed for human occupation. He wondered what he would find in this place.

Just as he was about to believe that he could leave without being noticed, Omaha called out into the dark courtyard, "Guardsman Canis, are you coming in?"

Canis sighed and stepped forward. Cepheid slipped her small hand into his. All six Wulfen followed in their wake. As they neared the large door, Omaha's captain and eight of his men fell in behind them.

Inside, Canis found the main hall well lit and warm. A slave boy took their coats and gloves trembling with fear at the array of wolves that came in with them. The puppies lifted their tails hopefully at the sight of the boy, but were disappointed when he darted away with their coats and Canis moved on. His grim mood left no room for play.

The remains of the evening meal still lingered in the air and the scent of beer was strong. In one corner were a couple musicians. One played an instrument by blowing into its top, another strummed strings across a wide square panel. The combination was soothing, but the sight of collars around their necks soured the feeling.

Michael had taken pains to school his men for this meeting and they had paid attention. They were to guard Enid, wherever she went and whatever she did, especially this night. There was nowhere in the hall Enid could wander where there wasn't at least two guards within half a dozen steps. Nor was there a single one of Omaha's men that wasn't shadowed by another pair somewhere close. The red of their uniform made them easy to spot.

Another slave poured beer and Omaha offered it to Michael with his own hands. Enid was offered wine, then he squared himself off with her and said, "The politics of our marriage are complicated and between your father and me, but I want you to know that I'll be a good husband to you. I'll do everything in my power to make you happy."

Enid was speechless at this and she looked around for support. Fortunately, Michael did not happen to be within her range of view at that moment or Omaha might have seen what was between them. Instead, her eyes landed on Canis and she remembered his advice, *all* of his advice. "I will be a dutiful wife, my Lord. Between us, we will make our country strong and prosperous and our sons will carry on in kind after we are gone. With you as their father, they can do no other."

"Sons…sons…*our* sons. I like the sound of that," said Omaha. "As soon as you are rested from your journey, we will say our pledges before the Mother, then we can begin… Well, we'll let things develop as they may after the wedding." He took her free hand and bent over it to kiss her knuckles. “Thank you, my Lady. You have surely blessed this house.”

She managed to hold herself calm until he released her hand, but when he turned away, she gulped her wine and set the glass aside quickly to hide her hands in her skirts.

Canis watched her, and he watched Michael, who stood a few feet away behind her throughout this exchange. Though Michael had accepted the beer Omaha had given him, he had set it aside as soon as the man’s attention was elsewhere. Enid was pale, and by the time Omaha had finished his speech, her hands were visibly shaking. Michael was very still; he was holding himself with an iron grip. He too was pale, but he had taken an oath. He knew what had to happen here, and he was watching it develop as it must, but that didn’t mean he liked it. Canis could see the decision flare in his mind: if the man was good to her, he would have no choice but to stand aside, but if he tried to injure her, Omaha would die regardless of who he was.

Canis glanced around at the rest of the men he had brought here. They no longer looked so young. To some degree, they all echoed young Michael’s resolve.

Omaha came to speak to Canis next, he glanced at the wolves who had arranged themselves along the edge of the hall behind him, then he said, “You have my thanks for seeing my bride safely here. I don’t suppose I could interest you in taking on a permanent position here?”

Over Omaha’s shoulder, Canis could see his captain stiffen as he overheard these words. “You are generous, sir, but I have another obligation that I must see to, and the wages of a soldier would not fulfill it. I will be departing in the morning.”

“So it’s gold you’re after. Are you a mercenary, or will you take on a task as a killer for hire?”

“I have no inclination to fight another man’s battle or hunt another man’s target.”

“There is little else that will earn you large quantities of gold.” Omaha looked at his captain and saw the distaste in the man’s face that he wasn't quick enough to conceal. He stepped close to Canis and spoke for his ears only, "Can you use that sword of yours?"

"I have had some training," replied Canis cautiously.

"Then perhaps you can help me with a small problem. I'll make it worth your blood if you can win." Then, speaking loud enough for everyone in the room to hear, he said, "I offer a wager. Our young guard here who was bold enough to stand alone against an entire company of my private army, against the captain of that company; the best swordsman I have."

Canis stepped up to Omaha and hissed, "Why?"

"Because he is an evil brute and I cannot be rid of him any other way," whispered Omaha in return.

Omaha strode to Enid's side waving back the other occupants of the room as he went, while his captain followed in his wake to halt in the center of the room with a gleam in his eyes that said something of this nature had been done before and he enjoyed it.

Canis followed more slowly while Cepheid drew back among the Wulfen, her eyes were wide in her small face.

Canis watched the man waiting for him in the center of the now cleared hall. He wondered if he would fight with only his sword. Most men did when fighting over principles, but men fighting just to fight tended to get more creative.

He slowly drew his sword, thanking the now dead hand that had provided it for him. He thought briefly of the last time he had sparred with a man, it had been during his tests at the sword master's school against the tall dark man; the king's bodyguard. This man…this man resembled that man in many ways, but not in this: this man wanted to see his blood. He liked to see a man's blood.

Canis and the captain circled each other in the center of the room like two prowling cats or perhaps a tiger and a Wulfi, comparable in size and threat if not in breeding. The torchlight glinted off their polished blades as their owners shifted their grips and took a few more steps – circling and wary – watching for an opening – a weakness.

Omaha stepped forward. “Salute,” he called, but neither man did. They had both had teachers who taught the same thing. ‘Salute’ indicated sport and no ill will. That was definitely not the case here. This might be a duel, but it was to the death. They circled another slow round – the sharp edges of their swords thirsted for conflict.

Omaha stepped back beside Enid. He could feel the menace on the floor. He fairly quivered with anticipation. “Begin,” he called.

Canis and the captain clashed together with brutal force, the meeting of their swords echoed from the rafters, and the spectators around the room took another step back at the violence of it. As soon as the man reached his free hand toward Canis, he in turn reached out and snagged the captain’s hair at the nap of his neck using the handle to force the man’s head down onto the sharp edge of his sword. As soon as a drop of blood appeared on the man’s cheek, Canis pushed away from the grapple and they circled again.

Canis’s sword, inches longer than the captain’s, now carried blood. First blood had been drawn. They circled yet again. Now the captain knew to stay out of his grip – out of his reach. Now the fight would be a matter of skill with a sword, at least until the next time.

Their swords rang and clashed against each other, flashing in the firelight and jangling with their own echoes. Enid found herself holding her hands over her ears and Cepheid crouched low beside Nnarr with her hand on the hilt of her own sword.

The fighters’ skills appeared to be comparable, though their style was very different. All that remained was to see which could be craftier or last longer.

The captain was far too used to grappling during his fights, and out of habit, was constantly reaching into the fight to lay a hand on Canis and pull him into his blade or at least off balance. When he reached in a second time, Canis made little effort to clear his sword from between them and the captain stepped into the blade, taking the tip of Canis’s sword in his shoulder near the joint – there had been no time to pick a better target. Startled, he drew back and flexed his wounded shoulder, but they weren't fighting just to draw blood. Canis had drawn blood twice now; it was time for him to die.

Canis continued to block all of the captain's advances, and since he wasn't in the habit of expressing any emotions on his face, it appeared as though he was doing so with casual ease.

Infuriated, the captain made a third reach for the tantalizing handle hanging down Canis's back.

Canis had already deflected the captain's blade; his hand was high and his blade low, when he saw the captain's hand reach out yet again. He took half a step back and brought his blade up in a high arc and down. The hand came away easily and it spun in the air for a moment, the fingers still clawed, before dropping to the floor to be kicked out of sight when Canis stepped back.

With a cry, the captain pulled back from the fight and cradled his bleeding stump, but then the sight of his own blood, drawn yet a third time, enraged him and he roared back into the fight once more; he *had* to draw blood – he had to *kill*.

With a cry of horror, Enid turned away to hide her face in the nearest shoulder while the owner of that shoulder, Omaha, watched the fight avidly.

Her movement recalled Michael to his duty and he glanced around at the rest of the guards arrayed around the room. All of them were, to some degree, gape mouthed in surprise.

He returned his gaze back to the fight helplessly and saw Canis in a spin. The man in bloodstained blue and green had his sword flung wide after dealing out a powerful blow that missed. His bleeding stump was also flung wide as a counter balance to the move – spraying many of the spectators with blood – but no one noticed a few drops of wet with Canis in motion. He was a tight blur high in the air. A blink before he touched the floor again, he casually reached out with his blade and his momentum carried it down on the man's shoulder to stop somewhere past his spine and breastbone.

The fight was suddenly over – the vast chamber silent – the

people frozen. The captain's sword, clattering to the stone floor, echoed loudly; its unblemished length still glittered in the torchlight. For a moment, the two men stood gazing at each other then the captain sank to the floor pulling himself free of Canis's blade.

As the light went out of the captain's eyes, Canis turned his focus to the rest of the men in the room. This had been a lawful duel, called by their lord, but that didn't mean the outcome would be a favored one. No one heard what Omaha had said to him before the fight.

No one moved for a protracted moment. Not until Cepheid and the Wulfen moved to stand with him. After another moment of frozen silence, she drew him toward the door. She no longer felt welcome here.

Canis backed away with her, allowing her to guide his steps while the Wulfen surrounded them. Nnarr chased the slave boy out of his corner with their coats before allowing him to flee again.

They were about to open the door when Omaha caught up with them. "I must admit, that was unexpected, but I am a man of my word." He tossed Canis a coin purse. "I had rooms prepared for you here, but perhaps you had better find lodging in the city tonight. He had some followers who were loyal to him more than to me."

Canis caught the purse and hefted it. It was heavy. He nodded and said, "May the Mother's peace follow you and yours." Outside, Canis said, "Find the horses."

The Wulfen sprinted off toward the stables where they guarded the door while Canis found the stable master's quarters. He gave them their gear and pointed out their horses. As Canis was tightening the last cinch, a slave came with their belongings. Rrusharr herded him in to hand the packs and roles to Canis before allowing him to escape again.

Canis added his coat to the load then herded them all out of the barn and down the road in front of him. He didn't mount until they were well out of sight of the castle.

He didn't take them back to the city; in fact, he took them nowhere near people. He couldn't be seen coming from the palace covered in blood regardless of the fact that he was not followed…yet. Soon after mounting, he led them off into the woods heading west in hopes of finding the river they had crossed at dark.

It was near midnight and near impossible to see a path through the thick trees. After nearly being scraped from the saddle for the second time, Canis decided to stop and camp where they were.

Canis lay awake through the rest of the night. The sparring match had brought out things about himself he had almost forgotten. He *was* dangerous, far more dangerous than the normal man. The king's man – he didn't remember his name – had wanted to put him in a cage for it. Perhaps he had been right. Perhaps he was too dangerous to be free among men.

As soon as the encroaching daylight allowed them to see, he had them change from their warm winter furs to the woolens they had bought so long ago. It was a small change when he was branded so plainly with his long red braid and white eyes, but perhaps they would attract less notice for a time. It would take time to clean the blood from his leather clothes.

Cepheid could feel his unease and she set him down to comb through his hair, knowing how it soothed him. As she braided it, she twined the two necklaces into the plait causing its lower half to bristle with claws and teeth. The rest of the beaded cords she twined around the hair between the barbs making a weighted and deadly mace of his braid.

At the unaccustomed weight, Canis pulled her creation around to inspect it. "Why did you do this?"

"When you spun, it came alive and reached out for him. This would have laid open his face and forced him away from your back."

Canis gave her a small smile. "Good idea. I like it." He tossed the braid back and reached for his cloak.

Cepheid opened the purse Omaha had given them. "I think we

can pass up trying to find work to take us farther east."

Canis looked at what was in her hand and calculated what was already in his possession then he nodded. "Perhaps it is for the best." They mounted and headed east again.

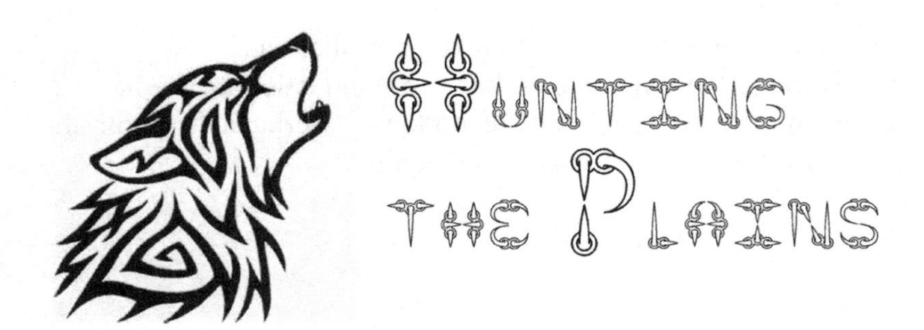

Hunting the Plains

Free of wagons, they could cover ground much quicker. They found a smaller road heading east within only a couple of hours of setting out. It was nowhere near as wide as the high road they had taken out of Cheyenne, but it was smooth, uncluttered, and covered with a short coarse grass that didn't hold much of the blown snow. It wasn't long before they discovered places where it disappeared. For the next few miles holes and ridges caught the blown snow making some of those hazards hard to spot. These stretches had to be circumvented, and then the road would pick up again. Overall, since they had no wagons to hinder them, and since the Wulfen took to scouting ahead, these stretches were no obstacle, and in many places, the road had been reconstructed around such terrain.

They stopped at the first farm along this road and asked for shelter. The old man was happy to house them in his barn and feed them for the cost of a few chores, so Canis shed his cloak to split some wood and Cepheid hauled water and grain for his stock housed in the barn for the night. When she was finished, she stacked the wood Canis split.

A cord of wood later, the man stopped them saying, "If you don't stop, you'll miss supper. You've split enough for a month. You needn't have done all that."

"You are generous with your food and shelter. It is only right that I be generous with the labor that earns it," said Canis.

During the meal, Canis asked after the road they were following. "Will the road out there take me to Chicago?"

"Well now, I wouldn't know that," replied the farmer congenially. "I do know that it goes for a long way mostly as straight as an arrow. I also know that Chicago is east of here, but I've never been there. I suppose you can't do too wrong by following that road for a while anyway, though I'd think the high road north of here would make for easier traveling."

"What is this?" asked Cepheid as she held up her half empty cup of white liquid. It was not the beer or wine that Canis never touched, nor was it water, which is all she had ever had, shy of tasting the other.

"That's goat's milk, dear," said the farmer's wife.

"Goat's milk," she said disbelievingly. She had seen goats before, from a far distance. She had even eaten goat before, but they were notoriously difficult to hunt. "Those are goats in the barn?"

"Haven't you ever seen a goat before?" asked the farmer who said his name was Treynor.

"I have, but they looked nothing like those small creatures. The goats I have seen are large white animals that live on the sides of cliffs. They are too difficult to hunt so we seldom bother them, but sometimes they fall."

"I've never seen anything like that, but then there aren't any cliffs around here. My family has raised these goats for generations. We sell the milk in the city."

"It's very good. Surely, you trade it for gold. Are you rich?" Cepheid still didn't understand the exchange of money very well, but she knew that the yellow metal was valued highly.

Mr. Treynor laughed. "No, child, but it pays the taxes and leaves a little besides. I can't ask for much more than that."

Canis watched Cepheid gulp down the rest of her mug with relish and saw her eyes glow when Mrs. Treynor refilled it for her with a smile.

"Thank you, Mrs.," said Cepheid with a smile that came close to showing her teeth.

It was watching interactions like this that Canis was reminded of how different the clan was from the plainspeople. For the clan, an open show of teeth was an open offer of hostility. For humans, the more teeth shown the friendlier the man wants you to believe he is, and most of the time the offer is genuine. It was a custom that neither of them could afford to adopt, though Canis could get away with it to a certain extent. Cepheid's front teeth were small – almost like small sharp pebbles – but her canines were long and sharp; they would be easily visible if she were to smile fully. Canis's front teeth were also small, but more like his mother's; an open smile would still reveal his long sharp canines, nature-made for tearing flesh.

Mr. Treynor came to rouse them for breakfast just as the yard was light enough to navigate, only to find them already sparring in front of the barn. "Come to breakfast while it's hot," he said.

Breakfast was potatoes with ground meat in the gravy. Cepheid came to the conclusion that she would take what opportunity offered to learn more about this kind of food and cooking – she liked it. It was much better than the trail rations offered by either of the caravans they had worked for. The potatoes were soft and sweet, not like the roots she had grown up with, which were stringy and never sweet.

They spent the next night at the farm of Mr. Corsun. Mr. Corsun was a bit more irascible than Mr. Treynor, but he wasn't above working them for their food. He and his son worked along side them, then they were sent to the barn while supper was being prepared. They were never invited into the house and Canis never saw any women; he wasn't even sure there was a woman living here.

The son brought their stew out to them, and in the morning, they were given a packet of biscuits and cheese then sent on their way.

That day, they took to hunting again. It felt good to hunt with the Wulfen. They found a herd of trim creatures with short black horns that stood straight up between their ears. They were a soft brown on their backs and sides and a perfect white on their bellies with only a little black around the face.

It was fortunate that they were given the opportunity to stalk them because the creatures were alert and quick. Canis brought one down with a chancy shot at a distance and Ggrrawrr took another one at about the same instant when the hapless creature came near to tripping over him. Canis hadn't intended to take more than one, but they were small so they could carry them, and the meat would feed them for a couple days.

That night, they were thwarted in their efforts to build a fire. They were a long way from the forests that surrounded Omaha City. There were some small scrub brushes, but they did little more than smoke or burn up too fast to cook anything.

Canis gave up on the fire and they fed on chilled, but raw meat before they rolled up in their bedroll. "You don't like your meat uncooked, do you?" said Cepheid as she pulled their furs close around them.

"Not much," commented Canis. "It does not satisfy. Perhaps it is just cold." But he knew that wasn't it either; he'd had hot meat fresh from the kill, and that had not satisfied him either. Canis's thoughts were turned away from bloody meat, Cepheid's hands were exploring. He growled and stretched and Cepheid giggled from somewhere under the furs.

Midday of the next day they passed a large crater with a row of blocky ruins along one edge. Near the end of that row was a sturdy stone farmhouse with smoke rising from the chimney, nothing else moved in the yard as they passed by.

Midmorning of the next day they came upon a crossroads that would lead them north or south. Canis knew that the high road they had been following before coming to Omaha City was still north of them, so that's the direction he chose. A few hours later, they came upon another crossroads and he chose east. He wasn't interested in using the high road; he liked this open opportunity to hunt and be away from people and their wagons.

At midday of the next day, they stopped and spoke to a farmer named Massena. He let them fill their water skins at his well and offered them much the same advice on the road as Treynor had. "If you're headin' east, you can't go too wrong with this road."

That evening they brought down a creature that resembled the elk from the other side of the mountains except that it was smaller and stockier. It had no horns and the black hair on its hide tried to be curly, though it was too short for it.

That night they found enough scrub brush to make a small fire and keep it burning. Cepheid made them a soup out of the liver and dropped some sections of the intestine in for flavor.

The meat was rich with fat, so she kept as much as they could carry sharing some of the weight out to be carried by all of the horses when she saw that there was too much for Star to carry alone.

The next night they stayed with the Greenfield family. The Greenfields were an extended family encompassing three generations. There was grandfather and grandmother Greenfield, their three sons and two daughters, three wives for the sons and one husband for the oldest daughter. The youngest daughter was about ten and not old enough to marry yet. The three young wives and the oldest daughter each had from one to four small children ranging from infant to toddler.

Each family had their own home to go to at night, but for the most part they all lived in the great house that was the heart of their little community. They welcomed Canis and Cepheid warmly; even the Wulfen were welcomed, though it was a hands-off welcome, and they were not invited into the house. At the mere mention of learning to cook, Cepheid was whisked away to the kitchen with the women while Canis went with the men to tend the animals in the barns.

There were three large barns. One was full of small white furry creatures the men called sheep. Canis learned that, in the spring, their hair would be sheered away and the resulting wool would be woven into cloth to be sold in the city.

When Canis asked if they sent their wool east to Chicago, old Mr. Greenfield said, “Sometimes we send it west to Omaha, and sometimes we send it northeast to Deemoin, but Chicago is a little beyond my reach.”

“How long before I reach this place you call Deemoin?” asked Canis.

“With your horses, you’ll likely reach it in about five days. With wagons it takes us a might longer.”

Another barn held ten oxen and Canis’s horses. The meat from their hunt the day before was stored in a far corner where it wasn’t likely to thaw out.

The third barn held their hay and grain – enough to feed their animals through the winter and still have some to sell if they needed to.

When Canis came in for supper, he noticed that Cepheid was upset, though no one else seemed to see it. She was holding the youngest baby in the house and the chubby child made her look small.

That night, in bed, he asked her, “What had happened while I was outside to so upset you?”

“I think perhaps it is a small thing. It’s just that the baby, that poor baby, is five months old and can hardly roll over. Also, it has no teeth. If such a child was born in the clan, it would be cause for the whole village to wail, and yet these people are all so delighted with him.”

“You must remember, these people are different from us. Perhaps that difference is most visible in the young.”

She cuddled close into his arms. “I hope so,” came her small voice from somewhere near his chest. “I want my children to be strong and healthy, like their father.”

Canis held her close. “They will be,” he whispered.

That night, Canis’s sleep was interrupted. “*Small cousins are stalking the barns,*” said Ggrrawrr, his tone fairly dripped with distaste at having to claim any relation to the creatures.

Canis and Cepheid had been invited to sleep in the house, so Canis ran down the stairs and outside in his small clothes. In one hand, he had Cepheid’s bared sword – the first one his hand fell on.

His hosts were light sleepers, and though Canis moved with the grace and silence of a hunter, his passage did not go unnoticed. Old Mr. Greenfield was close on his heels, though he only had an ax close at hand.

“Stay here,” said Canis. “There are hunters in the night and there are my friends as well. You might find it difficult to tell the difference in the dark.”

The night was punctuated with the howl of a coyote as she called to her pack and was answered.

“You *cannot* go out there in the dark. They’ll tear you to shreds,” said the old man.

“I am no mean hunter. Keep your sons close to their homes. I will be shooting arrows and I do not want to hit the wrong target.” He grabbed his bow and quiver by the door and disappeared into the dark. Behind him, he heard doors opening and he heard the old man call out across the dark yard, “Get back inside. Get back inside.” He hoped they did. He would be careful where he aimed, but he could spare little thought as to what might be beyond his target.

He came back to the house two hours later; his arrows were spent and it was too dark to find them. His blade was bloody and he had a long cut down his leg as well as a few scratches across his shoulders from a tumble in the brush.

All the men were gathered at the big house waiting anxiously for his return. The women were barricaded in their homes with the doors and windows barred. Their children were still asleep in their beds.

Old Mrs. Greenfield had the fire built up and Canis was thankful for the heat. While Canis submitted to the attentions of Cepheid and Mrs. Greenfield, allowing them to push him into a chair near the hearth, the men looked on expectantly.

"There is one pack of…of small cousins that will never bother this place again. I will need to gather my arrows in the morning. Their pelts are warm, would you like them or shall I destroy the carcasses?"

"We wouldn't know what to do with them," said Mrs. Greenfield. She didn't comment about what Canis had called the coyotes; she had seen his traveling companions.

"We'll load the carcasses in one of the wagons and haul them away in the morning," said one of the younger men. "I still can't believe you went out there in the dark and killed them all."

"I did not kill all of them, only a few. My friends did most of the killing. I am ill suited to fight canines in the dark."

"But you did it just the same," said the youngest man there.

"Yes, he did," said Mrs. Greenfield. "Now you boys go on back to your families. Your wives are worried and you stand around here gawking. There'll be time enough for tales tomorrow."

When they were gone, Cepheid knelt at his knee. "Heal yourself or tomorrow you will be fevered."

Both of the Greenfields were stunned by these words, but only Mrs. Greenfield's reaction was audible as she gasped.

Canis looked at her. "What?"

"Are you a licensed healer? You don't dress like one."

"The Mother heals through me. I have been asked this question before. What is this license you speak of and how should I dress?"

"Healers go to a great school where they learn their craft then when they are ready to leave, they carry a paper that says they have attended and passed the school, and they are required to wear plain brown as a badge of their profession. It is law in all the lands. There are stiff penalties for healers who practice without a license."

"Where is this school?" asked Canis.

"I don't know," replied Mrs. Greenfield. "Men come around from time to time – every couple years or so. They test everyone and if they find someone with promise, they take them away to the school."

"Healing is a gift from the Mother and should be used freely by anyone who can. Teaching may help, but it is unnecessary." Canis rested his hand on his scored leg and stepped aside for the healing to take over. When he opened his eyes again, Cepheid was wrapping a bandage around his leg and Mrs. Greenfield was draping a blanket around his shoulders.

The next morning, Canis rose late to find that his arrows had all been collected already and the coyotes were departing in the back of a wagon. "You should not have let me sleep. I could have helped."

"You helped last night," said old Mr. Greenfield.

"Sit down and eat your breakfast," said his wife. She had one of Canis's pack baskets standing open by the counter, and after she set a large bowl of boiled grain and honey in front of him, she went back to filling it.

"If you fill that, there will be enough to feed us for days," said Canis. He was silently thankful that the Wulfen had eaten the last of their meat the evening before else there would be no room for her generosity.

"That was my intention, but I'm afraid I don't know what to do for your animals. You can't carry enough grain or meat for all of them without a wagon. I don't see how you made it this far."

"We hunted," said Canis. "We are very good at it."

"I noticed a tiger hide in your bedroll," said Mr. Greenfield. "I'd like to hear that story. I never heard of anyone being able to kill a tiger before."

"It was not easy. It took a lot of luck, a quiver full of arrows and a pack of wolves. Actually two packs; he did not go down easily. I would not wish to meet another one."

"I saw one once a few years ago," said Mr. Greenfield. "I was thankful that he was heading away from me at the time. I didn't rest easy until I was home safe. I didn't stop for three days until I got here."

Canis wasn't happy to hear that. He thought he'd left them on the other side of the mountains. He hoped they didn't run in packs, or even in pairs.

They were packed and leaving the yard by noon. Canis waved to the family arrayed to see them off one last time as they turned onto the road, then his thoughts were already ahead of him. What Mrs. Greenfield had packed for them would supply them for several days, so he let the Wulfen hunt what they wanted as they moved along at a leisurely pace.

They reached a crossroads at noon of the third day after leaving the Greenfield family farm. Canis chose the north fork, which took them north then east again, past the small village of Winterset, where they filled their water skins.

The landscape had begun to wrinkle up more and now the road was starting to weave around the hills as much as cut through them. The snow-marked fields were growing substantially smaller and fenced pastures were becoming more frequent. Forks in the road became more frequent too. Canis took all of this as signs that another city was close.

They came to a river with a ferry house early in the afternoon of the third day after Winterset. The ferryman refused to come out of his house when he saw what looked like giant wolves. Canis was forced to give him two silver coins just to get him to open his door and three more for him to take them all across the river.

They found the high road a couple miles farther along their route, and they camped a few miles later at the base of a big square block with a smashed corner. By noon of the next day, they entered the city of Deemoin.

The Brown Knights

Canis didn't try to find lodging in the city; he preferred to camp with the Wulfen and they would not be welcome in any inn. That didn't stop him from looking for information and work. On the second day in Deemoin, Canis was visiting the inns and bars to see if anyone had been interested in his search for work. He was passing through the market square when a party of strangers came into the square from the east. They were bedraggled, wounded, and horseless, but constables swept them away to be cared for and Canis thought little more about them.

He was going to give his search one more day and if nothing panned out, he would head out anyway. He didn't have to work in order to pay his way across the country, but it was an opportunity to build up some of the gold he needed to pay his long overdue debts, and the pouch of gold Omaha gave him put him nearly half way to his goal.

The third morning of his stay, Canis and Cepheid had scarcely set foot in the market square when a man in his middle years stopped him. "Are you the guard who is looking for pay east?" he asked.

The most noticeable thing about the man was the fact that he was dressed in plain brown robes that reached half way to his knees and it was cinched at his waist by a wide, unadorned sword belt. His pants were a lighter brown, loose fitting and tucked into the tops of his boots. Around his neck, displayed openly, he wore a necklace, the chain of which was made of thick links of silver. The silver pendent looked like a small wand about three inches long with wings near its upper end. A snake entwined the whole thing. In his hand, he held an unusually long walking stick, though he didn't look like he needed one.

"I am heading to Chicago," said Canis. "And I would take work that will take me there."

"Good, we are heading to Port Daven. That's half way there. We've already made one attempt and we were attacked by bandits. They took everything we had. We were lucky to escape with our lives. We have decided to take on an extra sword. My name is Wayne. What are your rates?"

"What are my services worth to you?" returned Canis. He didn't have any 'rates'; he just wanted to reach Chicago. He was certain he knew how he would be able to earn his gold once he got there.

The man laughed and said, "Come, you can speak with the leader of our party. He's at the Prairie Wind Inn. The inn keeper says some interesting things about you."

"Nothing bad I hope," said Canis. *What could the innkeeper have to say about me?*

"No, nothing bad. How do you think I found you so quickly? All he can talk about is your eyes. He says he saw a wolf with eyes like yours somewhere north of here about ten years ago."

Canis was shaken by this news. His mother had died somewhere north of here about ten years ago or so, and his father's companion had died at about that same time in that same area. He didn't know if it had blue eyes or not, though.

They reached the inn and Wayne took them to a room on the second floor. An older man was lying on a bed there. "Columbus, I believe this is the young man the innkeeper was speaking about looking for work," said Wayne.

"Yes I do believe so," said Columbus as he pushed himself to sit up. Wayne went to help him.

"What are your names, boys," said Columbus when Wayne had him propped up and had stepped aside.

This man had on a white linen shirt with his light brown pants, but the dark brown robe was draped across a chair, and the heavy sword was lying on the table with another silver necklace. "My name is Canis and this is my wife, Cepheid."

"Forgive me, my dear. Dressed like that, I assumed you were perhaps a younger brother."

Cepheid nodded her forgiveness, but offered no excuses for her attire. Many people had assumed she was a boy, even Canis had at first.

"I hear you are looking for work going east. There are six of us. Accompanying us is a woman, two boys, and a girl. The children are scarcely teenagers and the woman searches for new students to take to the school."

"I am told you lost everything to bandits. Can you tell me more?"

"Are you taking the job, or are you fishing for information?" asked Columbus.

"I have decided I will head east tomorrow if I cannot find work by then. If you pay well enough, I will take you with me," replied Canis.

Columbus considered the two of them for a protracted stretch of time, taking in everything he could see. "Can you use that sword of yours?"

"I can, but I do not depend on it exclusively."

"That means you fight with whatever means that comes to mind," said Wayne with a chuckle. "Not a bad idea if you can manage it."

"I am a fair marksman with a bow, which I have left with the rest of my belongings," continued Canis.

"Where are you staying?" asked Wayne. "It's not at any of the inns in the city, I checked."

"Six other friends travel with me and they are seldom welcome at an inn, so I am camped on the edge of town."

"Really? I'll need to meet these other friends of yours before we decide to take you on," said Columbus.

Canis looked at the other two men, then back at the innkeeper. “My supplies are growing thin.”

Columbus nodded and the innkeeper bowed his way back out of the door to return with help delivering the required number of plates. When that task was completed, he asked, “What will you all be drinking?”

“Beer,” said Columbus and Wayne in turn.

“Water for the rest of us,” said Canis. “Bring bowls for my friends.”

The man nodded and departed. Two mugs of beer, two mugs of water, a stack of bowls and two large pitchers of water were delivered in short order and they all began to eat their lunch in silence.

Healers and Hunters

Canis used the delay in their departure to stock up more on some of his gear. If he was going to be guarding again, there were things he needed that he could do without otherwise, and with the news that tigers roamed the plains ahead of them, he wanted to be fully prepared. The arrows he'd brought with him had dwindled in number and size as the occasional arrowhead broke off the end of the shaft. He found a fletcher and purchased new arrow parts. Wood was precious here, but the man's shop was well stocked. He even had shafts the size and length that Canis wanted, though he didn't have any completed arrows of that size. He did have many that would fit Cepheid's bow and draw, and Canis purchased a bundle. He also had a large bin of flint and obsidian stones as well as many roughed out blanks. Canis purchased many of the man's blanks and had them wrapped in a leather wallet to protect them from each other. He also bought some of the unworked obsidian; they could be useful for many things. Those he had managed to keep from the Yellow Stone quarry had outlived much of their usefulness and he had found none since.

Next, he went to the blacksmith. There he had the shoes on their horses checked and their swords sharpened. It was here that he saw something unusual. The man's apprentice had made a pair of gloves with sharpened 'claws' attached to the back of the hand.

Canis tried one on. Protruding through leather on the back of the hand were three curved metal blades shaped like the claws of a large predator. They came out of the leather and arched forward to reach past the middle knuckles on Canis's hand. The curved outer edge as well as the point of each claw was quite sharp. They were stabilized by a wide strap of heavier leather sewn both around the palm and around the wrist, which buckled tight to keep the glove from slipping. The glove itself was sturdy, but soft and pliable and had half fingers so his grip otherwise was not obstructed.

The blacksmith saw his interest in the gloves and said, "My boy made those. He did fine work on the gloves, but I think he ruined them when he added those claws. He said he had a dream about making them."

"I like them," said Canis. "I will take them and pay you for them when I pick up the rest of my gear tomorrow." He strapped both gloves on and made a few experimental fists. They were comfortable and had a comforting weight. He figured he knew the source of the boy's dream. The Mother was looking out for him.

Cepheid was also doing some shopping. She went into a seamstress' shop and bought thread and needles. She also bought new pants and underclothes. The ones she had were getting too tight.

Then she went to a leather shop and purchased the heavier thread and needles used to sew leather; she was down to her last needle and there had been little chance to make thread.

Next, she was directed to an herbalist's shop. Rranggrr would be having her puppies soon and Canis would need something to deaden the experience. He was not so closely attached to Rranggrr as he was to Rrusharr, but that didn't mean he wouldn't experience her delivery just as hard.

Curiosity drew her into a jeweler's shop where she found that someone had some interest in wolves. In one corner of the display shelf was a small collection of pieces made of colored glass melted skillfully together that had wolves as a model for the pictures. There was a heavy ring with a wolf's head on it and a pin that almost matched, but the pose was different. Then she saw the thing she liked the most of all; affixed to a black, V-shaped leather strap was a brooch that looked almost exactly like the tear-shaped tattoo Canis had left on Michael's face. It was designed to rest snuggly in the hollow of the throat. It was only right that Canis should wear such a thing, so she paid a full silver coin for it. For herself she bought a small necklace of polished stones. None of the stones was bigger than her smallest fingertip, and none of them looked like any other on the strand. It only cost a couple copper pennies, and since she had already bought the brooch, the jeweler let her have the necklace for nothing.

That evening they exchanged their purchases for each other. Canis handed Cepheid the bundle of new arrows, and she handed him the brooch. The brooch reminded Canis that of all the opportunities they'd had to shop, he never bought her anything that wasn't practical. He promised himself he would find something nice for her before they left the city.

The next day, his quest proved to be far more difficult than he imagined. She had already bought herself a pretty necklace and when the jeweler saw the brooch, he commented that it couldn't be sitting in a better place. After searching for a good portion of the day, he ended up buying a looking glass, comb, and brush set in a small decorative case. It was still a practical item, but it was pretty. The backs of the comb and brush as well as the case were inlaid with colorful chips of wood and stone and lacquered to a high polish and the case sported a tiny silver clasp. He also bought a new comb for himself; his had lasted several years and was starting to fall apart. When he watched Cepheid fuss over her new box, he knew he had chosen well.

The next morning, shortly before dawn, Canis and Cepheid met Columbus and the rest of his party in front of their inn. They walked up on a small commotion that no one had anticipated; the girl, who was only about ten, was refusing to get on her horse. After what had happened before, she was terrified of the horse and of the road ahead; she was refusing to go any farther.

"No, I won't go; nothing could make me take that journey. I just want to go home," she was saying with tears in every word.

"You could be a great healer," said the woman with them. "You have to go to the school or else you will be nothing more than a farmer's wife."

"I don't care." The girl continued her protests until Canis dismounted and approached the two. The boys were already mounted, but they didn't look too pleased about the journey ahead either, though their young male egos weren't letting them say so.

Columbus and Wayne watched Canis approach. It wasn't their custom to interfere with the healers except to protect them, but it looked as though Canis had every intention of doing so. They were curious to see what he would do.

Canis didn't interrupt with anything but his too-close presence. Eventually, the woman broke off her argument with the girl to look at him in askance.

Canis turned to the girl and said, "Will you walk with me for a moment?"

The girl was surprised that this tall stranger with the glowing eyes was speaking to her. "Who are you?" she asked.

"My name is Canis. We have joined your party in order to help ensure your protection. May we speak privately?"

The girl looked at the other men and received a slight nod from Columbus, so she stepped away to follow him.

During his search for a gift for Cepheid the day before, he had discovered a modest shrine to the Mother, so he headed there now. As they walked, he said, "Will you tell me what has happened to change your mind about going to the school?"

She hesitated; he was a stranger and he was so different. "We were attacked by bandits two days from here. My horse threw me. When one of the bandits tried to catch my horse, it dodged almost on top of me. I have never been so frightened in my life. I thought I could go, but I can't. I never want anything to do with them again, and if I have to cross a bandit-ridden countryside to reach the school, then I don't want to go. Nothing is important enough for that."

They reached their destination and Canis turned to her. "Being a healer is very important. No one can take that away from you, but being licensed is the law in this country, and you cannot become licensed unless you go to the school. Come, lets ask the Mother for guidance and strength." He opened the door and went inside where he went around and lit the candles standing in each corner of the room.

When he was finished, he turned to see the girl standing just inside the door, watching him. He offered his hand to her, and after a moment's hesitation, she took it. He led her up to the modest statue and they knelt on the rug at its base.

Canis closed his eyes and said, "You have set hard tasks before our feet, and we have tried to do your will. Lend us strength that we might continue to follow the path you have laid out before us."

A breath of cold air brushed Canis's face and he opened his eyes. He was standing on the peak of a tall mountain surrounded by many other white-capped mountains. In front of him was the Mother in her flowing blue and white robes that draped from her head all the way to her feet in many delicate folds ruffling softly in the wind. She reached up a fine boned hand and touched the brooch at his throat, then plucked at the black material of his cloak. "You've done well; I'm proud of you." She reached up and touched the stone between his brows. "You already have my blessing and you will have all the strength you need to face what you must, but ultimately this will have another resting place before you stand in your final place." She cupped his cheek. "Lead on my fine young wolf-warrior."

Canis opened his eyes again. He was still kneeling by the side of the girl. He saw that once again she had tears running down her cheeks. She too opened her eyes, then with a sigh, she brushed her tears away and rose to her feet. Without a word, they went back to the others.

She quailed when it came time for her to mount her horse, but she did it anyway with Canis's helping hand, though she gripped the saddle with white knuckles.

Moments after they were in motion, the woman rode up beside Canis. "What did you say to her?"

Canis turned his luminous eyes on her; it was still dark enough to make it seem like they glowed from beneath the shadows of his brows. "I said very little to her, Healer. We had a small discussion with the Mother."

"Very well," she said, "but in the future, you would do well not to interfere."

"I will interfere wherever I see fit, Healer, and you will not waste my time questioning it," said Canis.

The woman's reaction was just short of a huff as she pulled back to rejoin the younger people of their party.

It was full light by the time they cleared the outer edge of the city where the Wulfen joined them. The horses noticed them first and began to dance and snort their unease before Canis could warn the Wulfen off. "Stay clear of these horses; they do not know you. We will make your introductions in camp tonight," said Canis.

Wayne, the only person close enough to hear him, looked around to see who Canis was speaking to. "Who are you talking to?" he asked, but then he knew the answer to his question almost before it was out of his mouth. He saw first one, then another of the giant wolves fade from his range of view. He never did see all of them; he counted.

Columbus's party had twelve packhorses and each of the men and boys were forced to lead a train of four of them. The bulk of their load was water, which said much to Canis about the country they were about to enter. Snow still covered the countryside, but it was little more than a white shadow among the grass and covered the grass only where the wind could not scour it out of some depression in the ground. Though it was still midwinter, it had not snowed for more than a month.

Columbus, with his four packhorses, led the way and Wayne brought up the rear with four more. Cepheid rode with the women, leading Star. Canis ranged wide, with the Wulfen ranging even wider.

That night Canis had the horses tied to a long picket line with his three spread out among them, then he called the Wulfen in. They were used to this ritual, they worked their way slowly toward each horse and didn't move on until the creature had gotten a good nose full and had settled. Canis and Wayne helped keep the animals quiet for this, and Canis's horses helped by being unconcerned. When they were finished, they sauntered into camp and won a few exclamations from the rest of their party who had been unaware of these members; they'd paid no attention to the happenings by the horses.

Rrusharr especially liked the squeal she won from the woman. As far as she was concerned, anyone who tried to dominate her companion deserved a little more *personal* attention. A good deal of Rrusharr's evening was spent staring at her. It served to make her very uncomfortable, but she couldn't complain since Rrusharr did nothing but stare, though she went out of her way to ensure that she was laying wherever she needed to be in order to keep the healer in good view.

The puppies, a little better than half the bulk of their elders now, hit it off with the boys right away and were soon playing either tug-of-war or keep-away with most anything that won a laugh. The girl wasn't quite so sure and hung back from the rough play.

Cepheid came up to her with Nnarr at her side. Dainty white Nnarr was smaller than the rest of the adult Wulfen, she was still young, but she was also much finer boned, therefore, she wasn't quite as intimidating as the larger, heavier gray or black Wulfen. "Hello, what's your name? My name is Cepheid. This is Nnarr; she is my companion. We have been companions ever since I can remember."

The girl studied Cepheid while she talked, then tentatively reached a hand out to explore Nnarr's face. "My name is Shania. I've never seen a…she's not a coyote; what is she?"

"Nnarr is…a wolf; you've never seen a wolf before?" said Cepheid.

"I've seen coyotes before, but not close. They're so frightening; I wouldn't want to see one up close. These are all so much bigger than a coyote, I'm glad they're not mean. They're *not* mean, are they?"

"No," said Cepheid, "they're not mean, but that doesn't mean they're not dangerous. They perform a very important part in seeing to our safety." She guided Shania's hand to a spot under Nnarr's chin. "She really likes to be scratched right in here." She showed her and Shania giggled as Nnarr moaned her pleasure and stretched out for more of the same.

With the ice broken, Shania helped Cepheid fix supper and quickly discovered that she was a much better campfire cook than the others had been. Canis joined them for supper and greeted Shania. When he had finished eating, he rose and disappeared into the dark.

"Where is he going?" asked Shania.

"He guards us," Cepheid said. "It's what he does best."

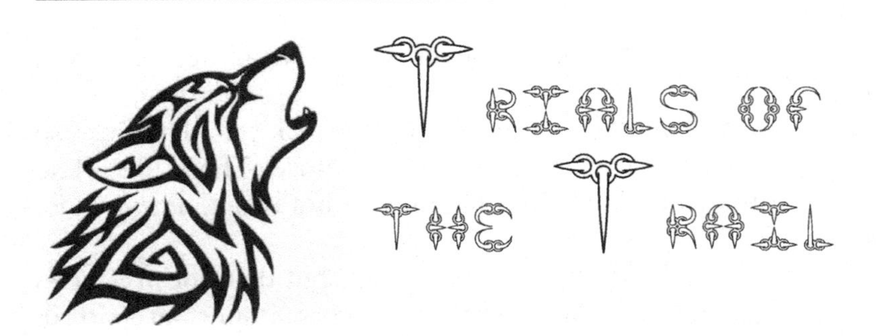

Grrawrr discovered the bandits just as they were settling in for their third night out on the Empty Plains. Too close to be there for any other reason, he alerted Canis and then watched as they dismounted and started crawling toward their new fire under cover of the rapidly waning light. Canis and the others began to converge on his position, but daylight was gone before they met.

With a warning from Nnarr, Cepheid was able to alert Columbus and Wayne, and the three of them stood together, sheltering the others between them and the picket line, their campfire in front of them. Very wide Rranggrr also remained behind; she watched for the sneaky approach that might come from another direction.

As the sounds of the clash reached their ears, the men started to go help. “Stay here,” said Cepheid. She too had her sword drawn and her bow was close at hand. It occurred to her then that the walking sticks the men always kept close must be more than simple walking sticks. Both Columbus and Wayne seemed intent on using them.

“We can’t leave him out there alone,” said Wayne.

“He is not alone, and just now, everyone he meets is an enemy,” said Cepheid. “In this dark, it is best to keep it that way. It can be the same for us here if we stay together.”

Wayne grumbled. The screams of panicked horses and those of the panicked and dying men were not easy to listen to, out there in the black of the night, beyond the light of the fire.

A short time later Cepheid gave a soft gasp, and by the light of their campfire, Wayne could see her chin tremble. "You are the one who said we should wait here," he said, thinking she was going to start crying because of what they were hearing – because of who was out there all alone. "Be strong," he added.

She didn't say anything; she only spared him a brief glance. How could he know that Nnarr had been wounded in her shoulder and was now handicapped? How could he know that Nnarr still chose to fight, even though she couldn't put any weight on her injured leg?

Moments later, she was relieved to hear, "*I return. I cannot help here.*" The white Wulfi hobbled slowly into the firelight and lay down between them and the fight. She would still fight if their attackers ventured this close.

By the light of the fire, Neola, the healer, could easily see the blood on the white wolf's shoulder and stepped forward.

"Not yet," said Cepheid. "We will tend our wounded when the fight is over."

Neola hesitated, but when Cepheid glared at her, then Columbus waved her back, she returned to the others who were clustered near the picket line. The children were clutching each other in fear.

Twenty eternal minutes later, both Nnarr and Cepheid relaxed then a moment after that, Canis called out, "We're coming in." He managed about three more steps into the firelight before he stopped swaying.

Wayne caught him in time to prevent him from falling all the way to the frozen ground.

"I think…I need…a thicker hide," he said as he closed his eyes and allowed Wayne to lay him out flat.

Cepheid was there with their bedroll so he would not be lying on the frozen ground.

He had no less than four deep slices along his left rib cage and two on his left shoulder that went to the bone, but in his defense, his blade was bloody to the hilt as was the clawed glove on that hand. Even the claws and teeth that decorated his braid were bloodied, though they didn't discover that until the next morning.

Nnarr received a deep cut to her left shoulder and Ggrrawrr sported a not-so-deep cut along his right rib cage. All of the rest of them were plenty covered with blood, but none of it was their own.

As Cepheid helped Canis eat some stew, she had to ask, "Why do you go out there alone? I saw you, back in Omaha's castle; that man couldn't touch you. Twice now, you disappear into the dark to fight alone and you come back near dead. You know there are many men out there. I don't understand."

"I go alone because there is…there is carnage and death flooding my mind and I must kill. I am dangerous, Cepheid, dangerous to everyone and everything around me when I am like that. I don't know how else to say it. Our people are very good hunters; I am more than just a hunter – I am a killer."

Puzzled she tried to offer him another bite, but he shook his head. I cannot eat more. You must watch tonight." He closed his eyes, frowning.

Cepheid too frowned, but did as she was told.

The next morning, Columbus and Wayne explored the killing field. It was uncomfortably close, only a few hundred yards from camp. All the horses had scattered, their tracks fanning out in as many directions as there were horses, deserting in their panic. They counted about thirty dead men all looking like so many broken and bloody dolls. No less than eight of them had died by the sword and some of those looked like they might have met with a cat. The claw marks they could attribute to Canis's unique gloves, but the teeth marks didn't look like they fit any animal. The rest had obviously met a Wulfi in the dark, and though their mouths gaped in surprise, they would never be able to tell of what had transpired in the darkness. Most of them had their throats ripped away. Some had their sword arm or shoulder savaged and torn.

"I'm sure glad they're on our side," said Wayne. "Do you suppose these are the same men that attacked us last time?"

"It's likely," replied Columbus. "Let's get back to camp. There's nothing we can do here."

When they reached the camp, they found Canis up and around, though he was not moving too quickly. Cepheid was helping him into a clean shirt.

"You made this area much safer for a few years," said Wayne. "I've seen worse, but not when I know that it was only one man and a handful of wolves that did the damage."

"Are none of them left alive?" asked Neola.

"Only the horses and they are long gone," replied Columbus.

"Do you want to look for their camp?" asked Canis. You might recover some of what you lost in the last attack.

"No," said Columbus. "The only thing of value that might be left would be the horses and they are probably still running. It'll be days before they settled down enough to think of some place they might consider home, and they might not even choose their camp to go to. It would be a waste of our time to look for them."

Canis thought he could have those horses rounded up in a day, two at the most, but they weren't his horses and he certainly didn't need any more than what he already had.

Cepheid helped Canis put on the fur coat he had worn over the mountains – his injured arm rested in a sling and she laced his coat closed over it – then she and Wayne helped him into his saddle when they were packed and ready to leave.

That night, shortly after Neola had performed another healing on him, Columbus came up to Canis and Cepheid. "Since you seem to like getting close to the business end of a sword, I have something that might keep your hide more in one piece." He held up what looked like a shirt except that it was made entirely of small black rings.

"What is this?" asked Canis as he felt its unique texture.

"It's steel. It might even stop an arrow unless it's one of those clubs you shoot. It *will* stop a sword slice, though perhaps not a stab. At any rate, it's my way of saying thanks for last night. We wouldn't have stood a chance against that many men without you and those wolves of yours. I wish I could give them something too, but I wouldn't know what."

"Thank you," said Canis. He spread the unusual shirt out on his lap to put it on right then.

"You have my thanks as well," said Cepheid. "I prefer that his hide be thicker too."

Columbus smiled and helped Cepheid get Canis into the shirt. The metal rings extended to just short of his wrists where it buckled there as well as above the elbow. The rest of it extended down long enough to where he could sit on it – but only just. Columbus buckled Canis's sword belt around his waist for him. "There, it fits you better than it fit me."

Canis shrugged the metal shirt into place and winced as the move pulled at his scarcely mended wounds. "It's comfortable and not all that heavy."

Six days after the bandit attack, Canis called them to a halt early. "We camp here," he said and walked away with their oilcloth under his arm. Only Cepheid suspected what was wrong. Rranggrr was panting heavily.

Cepheid didn't help much with setting up their camp. After the fire was going, she turned the job of cooking over to Shania then went to find Canis. He was some distance away out of sight of the camp, sitting on a rock, watching over Rranggrr who now occupied the oilcloth.

"Are you all right?" asked Cepheid.

Canis looked up at her with hollow eyes and a pale face. "I am not made for this. Go back to the others and keep watch. Do not let on about this. They would not understand."

"I knew this was going to happen soon so I got this for you." She handed him something that looked like a blood cake. "It's not the same thing we use at home, but the lady back at the city said that it worked really good against the sickening headaches. It might help you through this. Eat it."

Canis took the cake and ate it mechanically. Blood cake was something made as a treat. It was made from blood and honey and stiffened with meal then fried. He didn't care for it much, but it didn't taste bad. He didn't taste this at all, though he did notice that the flavor wasn't the same. He groaned and hung his head.

Cepheid knelt beside him and wrapped her arms around him. "Someone needs to watch over you at times like this."

"We cannot both be away from camp at night. They will worry. Go on back. I will be fine."

Cepheid stood and looked over at Rrusharr who lay a short distance away. "Watch over him. He will be helpless tonight." She looked back at Canis. His shoulders hunched with another contraction and the metal shirt he wore glittered in the setting sun. She watched for a moment longer then did as he said.

When she reached the fire, Shania handed her a steaming bowl. "Why are we stopping so early? Is Canis's arm bothering him?

"No, Canis is fine. His wounds are healed enough. We stopped early because we are soon to increase our number," explained Cepheid with a smile she hoped would hide her worry.

Columbus overheard her words. "What do you mean, 'we are about to increase our number'. He's not trying to catch something out there is he," he said, as he gazed of into the darkening landscape.

"No," said Cepheid. "Rranggrr is in labor now. Canis watches over her."

"Out there? Shouldn't she be here with the rest of us? Wouldn't she be safer here?" asked Wayne.

"It is better this way," said Cepheid. "The…wolves always seek out an alone place to deliver. There are fewer distractions."

That night, Wayne suspected that the delivery of wolf puppies was somehow more important than Cepheid was allowing it to seem. She and the white wolf, her almost constant shadow, paced just beyond the edge of the firelight until he changed his shift with Columbus, and when he woke again, before dawn, she was still pacing until she met Canis returning to camp with two tiny puppies in one arm and the folded oilcloth in the other. Even in the predawn poor lighting, he could see how pale Canis looked. Surely it wasn't the birthing of a couple puppies that so disturbed him.

The sun was just beginning to touch the western horizon the next evening when disaster nearly found them. Coming at them from the south at a distance far enough away as to seem rash, a tiger charged directly at Cepheid who was riding near the middle of their long line of horses. Thumper threw herself sideways leaving the unprepared Cepheid in a heap on the ground. Star, who had been tied to her saddle, reared and screamed in alarm, breaking her lead and bolting away.

Canis, who had been ranging to the north, got the alert from Rrusharr who was ranging to the south. Rrusharr remembered the scent, but the tiger had come across their scent from the east and had begun its stalk between her and the road. Both of them were too far away to interfere with the attack. When Canis reached the road seconds later, the horses were in a panic as were the people who were struggling to maintain control of them. Rranggrr stood over Cepheid, as did Nnarr. The tiger, for the moment, stood at bay screaming its anger and frustration.

Canis drew his bow. "Stop," he called and Rrusharr and Ggrrawrr both slid to a halt mid-charge so as to not interfere with his shot.

The tiger whirled to face this new threat and took Canis's arrow high in the shoulder. Canis leapt from his plunging horse and took aim again as the tiger charged toward this new source of pain and threat.

Wayne watched in horror as Canis stood his ground and fired another arrow and then disappeared beneath the massive creature.

The whole scene was unnaturally still now that the tiger had stopped moving. Wayne was relieved to see that Canis was alive enough to start pushing the beast off himself. He grabbed a heavy paw and helped, then he pulled Canis to his feet. With the tiger laid out before them, he saw the last arrow buried almost its entire length under the beast's jaw. "Are you injured?" he asked.

"No more than a few bruises, I think," said Canis, then he saw Cepheid still lying on the ground where she had fallen. He ran to her. "Cepheid," he gasped. He saw that blood stained the black patch at her temple. "Cepheid," he called again and looked to Nnarr.

Cepheid was curled up around a now wriggling mass wrapped in her cloak and Rranggrr was nosing it anxiously.

Canis closed his eyes and rested a shaking hand on Cepheid's head.

Wayne, who knelt at his shoulder, recognized what he did and looked into his face in surprise. "How is it you are a healer?" he hissed, but Canis was beyond hearing the question.

Cepheid unwound from her coil and opened her eyes before Canis was finished. She saw the alarm in Wayne's eyes and knew what Canis must have done – must still be doing as she felt what could only be his touch explore through her body in search of further injury.

She reached up a hand and cupped Canis face. "Canis," she said softly. When he didn't answer, she glanced at Wayne. "He has no control over this and never remembers it. All he knows is that he can and so he does. Everything else is a blank. You cannot fault him for something he cannot control."

Canis opened his eyes then and clasped Cepheid's hand to his cheek with a sigh. "You are well then?" he said.

"I am now," she sat up and unwound the cloak freeing the babies inside to the attention of their anxious mother. Since she had curled around them in her fall, they were uninjured, but now that they were awake, they were hungry, and Rranggrr was happy to oblige.

Canis looked around at what remained of their train. Columbus was nowhere to be seen, neither were the women, but the boys had managed to retain control of their packhorses at least, though the effort had pulled them from their mounts. They were several hundred yards away and making their way back to the road.

Canis stood and said, “Round up the rest of the horses. Find Columbus and the women; they cannot be far.”

“Who are you talking to?” asked Wayne as he looked between Canis and Cepheid.

Canis only took Wayne’s shoulder and guided him back toward his horses. “We will not camp here.”

“But you just said to round up the horses,” said Wayne bewildered.

“I was not talking to you. Come.” When Wayne hesitated, he said, “I will not willingly explain. Be easy, and know that it works.”

Within the hour, Nnarr had found the women who had managed to stay on top of their panicked mounts. Columbus came back into view with all of his horses, and Rrusharr and Ggrrawrr rounded up the rest. Their damage assessment revealed only a few bruises, broken harness leads, and Thumper, who was still quite jumpy, had a small scratch on her rump. Neola went over all of them and found that Canis had suffered two cracked ribs from taking the dead weight of a tiger full on him. She also learned that Canis could heal and she questioned him extensively.

“Well,” she said, “perhaps it is just as well that we are going to the school. You can be tested there and receive your license. You could not be expected to have one if you come from so far away.”

“I do not want your license. The healing is a gift given to me only to carry and I will not carry it much longer. After that, your license will have no meaning.”

Neola was appalled. “The gift of healing is not a package to be set aside when you are tired of carrying it. The Mother drips the gift into our blood at birth and people such as me search the country for it so that people like those children can be brought to the school for proper training.”

“Neola, you and I can argue about this until the day we both die of old age. As far as I know, I am unique in this. My people had no healers among them until I carried this gift to them. Soon I will return to where I started and the Mother will decide who my burden will pass to. At that time, I will no longer be able to heal any better than Wayne can with a bandage or a needle. Keep your piece of paper, I will not need it." Canis stood up and strode off into the dark leaving Neola gape-mouthed at the fire.

The next afternoon, they came upon broken ground cut by flash floods and their path became twisted as they were forced to wind their way through such ravines. By evening, they came down into a small valley that had once been the site of a small town, but now it was nothing more than ancient smashed ruins on the banks of a river.

The next day was spent first by swimming the horses across the river, then by winding their way through the river valley. By the time they found the high road again, they had only covered perhaps five miles all day long.

Five days later, they spotted more ruins, and by noon of the next day, they had reached Port Daven on yet another river.

The Testing

They were ferried across to an island in the middle of one of the wider rivers Canis had ever contended with so far. He had crossed it before far south of here with Patro's caravan, and north of here too, when he was heading west; hearing the word 'Missip' confirmed it.

The only island Canis had ever seen, not counting assorted gravel bars seen only when the water was low, looked to be at least two and a half miles long, and courtyards and gardens dominated its entire surface. Looming over it all was a massive stone structure – the healer's school.

Parts of the building were four stories tall and other parts were only a single story; taken all together, it looked like a jumble of toy blocks.

The docks were full of barges unloading supplies, and today at least, there was a constant stream of wagons heading into the heart of the complex.

Neola and Columbus led them through the ordered chaos to a grand entrance where they left the horses in the care of men who came to take them. Inside, the new students were whisked away, and soon after, Wayne also left to take care of some private business elsewhere in the complex, that left Canis, Cepheid, and the Wulfen to follow Neola and Columbus deep into the maze of buildings.

Eventually they reached a central meeting chamber. The room was obviously used for much larger meetings, but at the moment, they were the only ones present.

"Please wait here," said Neola and she left them.

Cepheid helped the puppies find the important part of their mother then she sat down on the floor near them to wait.

Canis explored the perimeter of the room studying the portraits of men and women hanging on the walls.

Columbus found a chair and sank into it.

A couple hours later, Neola returned with three other people: two men and a woman. They all looked to be the oldest people Canis had ever seen, though they didn't carry themselves like they were old. They took seats behind a large desk and Neola went on into the room to stand in front of them. Columbus joined her and waved at Canis to stand with them.

As soon as Canis and Cepheid had joined the other two, Columbus made the introductions. "Masters and Mistress, may I introduce Canis and Cepheid who helped us cross the Empty Plains from Deemoin. Canis and Cepheid, these are Master Healer Gordon, Master Healer Rochester and Mistress Healer Madison. They are the council of our school and our society here on the island."

Canis nodded as each of the elders were introduced, scrutinizing them for any sign that they might regret making them wait for so long – there was none. Columbus continued, "Masters, Mistress, I was forced to promise wages to Canis when we reached our destination because shortly before we met, our party was attacked by bandits and everything that was not on our persons was stolen. We had enough to restock for another trip, but not enough to pay Canis for his time and effort. And I must say, if it weren't for Canis and his friends, our second foray would have failed just as miserably as the first."

Reminded that he held the man's necklace in lieu of said payment, Canis drew the necklace out from under his shirt and returned it to Columbus who accepted it and returned it to its former resting place.

"What kind of wages did you promise, Columbus?" asked

Gordon. "Was it the wages of a mercenary or the wages of a guard?

"Numbers were not discussed," said Columbus. "It was decided that the pay would be…fair."

"Fair wages," said Gordon. "What does that mean? Fair wages could be anything depending on who you ask."

"That's enough, Gordon," said Madison. "We'll hear the story. I'm sure we can come up with something agreeable to all of us. What troubles me is that Neola says he's an unlicensed healer. That's not so bad since apparently he traveled almost directly here from his home, but she tells me he refuses a license. This troubles me very much."

So that's why they took so long. "As I tried to explain to Neola…" started Canis.

"You will answer our questions when we ask them. Please be silent until then," said Rochester. He had a surprisingly small voice.

Canis's hackles rose immediately. *I do not need this*. All the Wulfen moved at once, and it was obvious that none of the elders had noticed any of them until then. Cepheid scooped up the puppies, and they all turned for the door.

Columbus caught Canis's arm as he turned and Canis said, "Surely you know that it would not be wise to try and stop us. Keep your gold. I am glad we were able to get you here safely." He followed the rest out of the room. Behind him, he could hear Columbus speaking, and it seemed that the volume of his words increased as the distance between them stretched.

Ggrrawrr led them out of the massive complex unerringly then he found their horses.

They were leading their horses across the courtyard toward the main gate when Columbus caught up with them. "Don't go yet. They're not used to being denied about such things, but I think they may listen to reason."

"I do not see how they can listen to reason if they do not allow reason to be spoken," said Canis. "We are headed east. We will find a campsite for tonight then we will be gone in the morning."

"There *is* no road east of here," said Columbus. "If you're heading east, you need to take a boat north to Paul City or south to Louis City. From either of those two cities, you can head east again."

"Are you telling me it is impossible to travel east from here?" asked Canis.

"Well, I don't suppose anything would be impossible for you, but the route goes through an arm of the desert. Few people who venture there are ever heard from again."

"Perhaps it is merely a crossing they decide not to make again," suggested Canis.

"Mr. Canis," called Madison from across the courtyard. When she reached them, she said, "Mr. Canis, we have come to a decision about you. If you will allow us to test you and if you pass that test, we will give you a pass as a healer. As a stranger to our laws, you cannot be held to them while you are here, but since you have come to this place, by accident or design, we can offer you a pass that will be good until you return to your home. Will this be acceptable to you? At least, with a pass, no one will trouble you about healing while you are here."

"What is this test?" asked Canis guardedly.

"I must confess, the test we have for you is somewhat stiffer than usual, but Neola says you claim that the Mother heals through you. Surely, what we have will not be too difficult for the Mother," said Madison. Canis did *not* like the tone in the woman's voice.

"And if the Mother decides that your test subject does not deserve to be healed, what then?" asked Canis.

"Then we will purge the healing gift from you," said Madison matter-of-factly.

"Who are you to decide whether a gift from the Mother can be taken from someone the Mother has chosen? I cannot comprehend the audacity that you believe you have the right to decide who can be a healer and who cannot. Perhaps you should visit one of her shrines. It has obviously been a long time since you have been properly thankful for the gift you have been given." He turned to Ggrrawrr. "Stay here and guard my wife with your life. Rrusharr, with me." He turned back to Madison. "Take me to this person in need of healing, but understand that if you try to take what has been entrusted to me, you may find yourself to be the one in need of healing." Canis was very angry.

Canis was fully aware of exactly how dangerous he was, and normally, anger wasn't necessary. But when such danger was blatantly ignored, then there was no recourse *but* anger, especially when such ignorance put a friend in danger. He knew that if he were pushed to a fight, he would be fighting a man he had come to like, simply because it was his sworn duty to defend the healers. To be forced to kill Columbus would be such a waste.

Oblivious, Madison led them back into the building and into the eastern wing. Echoing down the long hall were various cries of pain or sorrow and hurrying up and down the hall were several men and women dressed in somber brown. She led them past all of the hushed noise and subdued bustle to a room with the shades drawn. In the darkened room, lay a man on a bed. The man was quiet, but the odor in the room spoke more of death than life.

Canis frowned. "What is this?"

Madison said, "I'm sorry, but we don't know. This man came to us from the south. We don't know how far south, but we believe very far south. We get people like him once in a while and we can do nothing for them except try to make them comfortable."

Canis turned on the woman and glowered at her, his fierce icy eyes slitted in anger only inches from her blue ones. "You do not want me to pass your test, do you? Or is it that if I pass this test, you will take what I carry for yourself, and if I fail you will take it so that no one else will get it. Is that your plan?"

Madison backed up, gaping and working her mouth, trying in vane to come up with a proper response to such accusations.

Canis strode to the side of the bed. "Open the shades, Columbus. Please." In the light from the window, he saw that the man who lay in the bed looked to be in the advanced stages of decomposition. The only sign of life was the fact that his chest still rose and fell, and breath still wheezed in and out. He had never seen such a thing. He wondered if even the Mother could cure this. He tried anyway.

When he opened his eyes, he found Rrusharr standing over him and Columbus holding Madison back while blocking three other people from crowding too close. The fact that he was looking at a generous amount of Rrusharr's belly finally sank in, and he realized he was sprawled on the floor.

"Canis, you're alive," said Columbus. "That wolf of yours won't let anyone near."

"That is why I brought her," he said as he slowly climbed to his feet and leaned on the edge of the bed for a moment.

The occupant of the bed reached over and touched his hand. "Thank you," he whispered, then closed his eyes again.

Canis looked at him and was fully as stunned as anyone else in the room. The man's skin was whole again and his breathing was no longer rasping. Though he remained very weak, he was healed – completely.

As soon as Canis had regained some of his strength, he turned to the now silent audience clustered near the door. "Nnarr, tell Cepheid I am well. Well, Mistress Madison…" He swiftly stepped forward and grasped the woman's wrist, and before Columbus could react, he placed the woman's hand on his forehead. The rush nearly dropped him to his knees again, but he grasped Columbus's shoulder for support, as well as to stay his interference. "Perhaps you will believe me now," he said as he dropped her hand and swam his way out of the room using each shoulder he passed for support.

By the time he had covered half the length of the hall, he was walking under his own power, and before he stepped out into the sun, his knees were only slightly wobbly.

Madison and Columbus caught up to him shortly after he stepped out into the chill air of the courtyard. "What was that?" asked Madison as she snagged his arm.

Canis allowed her to turn him to face her. "As I tried to explain to Neola, I am merely a carrier. I carry the gift so that I may give it to those the Mother deems worthy. In my opinion, you should consider yourself lucky that she still considers you worthy to feel her touch, after what you have done here. I would not have agreed, but the decision is never mine."

"No, please wait. I need to understand," said Madison as Canis started to turn again.

"I can teach you nothing. There is nothing for you to understand. I am leaving now. I expect you to use the Mother's gift well."

"Where are you headed?" she asked.

Canis sized her up. He didn't like her, and she had done little to earn his trust. "I am heading east."

She tried to look chagrined, but it was not something she was accustomed to. "We owe you much. We will pay your passage on whatever ship you wish, and if you will wait a while, I will get the gold we already owe you. But the reason I ask after your destination is that there is someone here who desires to go east as well. Would you consider taking him with you?"

Canis thought for a long time about this. All the while, he stared at the woman. When he came to his decision, it was not one she wanted to hear. "No," he said and turned away to rejoin Cepheid. He didn't see the quiet exchange between Madison and Columbus.

He took his reins from Cepheid and started toward the path leading to the docks. He was drained and tired.

Columbus caught up with them once again and said, "Canis, you're still determined to go directly east?"

Canis paused to look at him. "Before I came here, I knew nothing of horses, but I learned, we both learned. But boats – what I know of boats is limited to the ferries I have needed to use to cross some of these larger rivers. Perhaps the boats you speak of are better, but from what I know, I do not think I want to learn more. Water is made for drinking or for washing, but not for walking on. I think I will stick to what I know." He extended his hand toward Columbus who took it. "Fare well, my friend, and travel safe."

"The same to you, but if you still plan to go east, you'll want to cross to the south side of the river and you might as well do it here. Come with me, I'll show you."

He took them to the south side of the island were there was another sprawling dock.

Before they descended to the water, Canis paused to look across the river at the darker spread of civilization that fringed the southern bank.

Columbus followed his eye and said, "Those people are river rats and the families of river rats. They're a rough lot. You be careful over there."

"I am always careful," said Canis as he headed down the slope.

"Yes, I suppose you are at that," he said to his retreating back before following.

After they found a ferryman who would take Canis's entire party across, Columbus vouched for their fare from the school and saw them loaded. He stood there and watched them until they were safely on the other bank and disappearing between the buildings. Mistress Madison would be furious with him, but he could bring himself to do no less. He could see no point in delaying him any longer

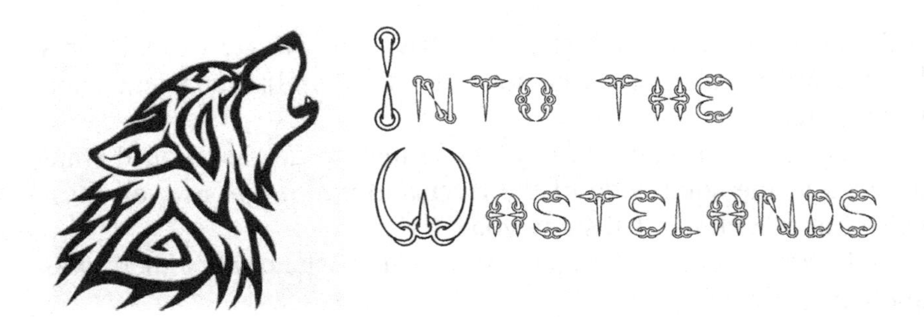

Gorrawrr found them a campsite a couple miles south and east of the fringe of humanity hugging the south side of the river. They stayed there for most of a week while Canis and Cepheid prepared for crossing the desert that Canis was sure lay to the east of them. If it was the desert, it was the northern most reaches of it. He couldn't compare this crossing with the others he had made with Patro's slave train, but he wasn't a fool to discard his experiences there, even if they were the experiences of a child dependent on the care of others at the time.

Using the things he had learned from all the men he had traveled with, he went to the docks every day where he bought supplies. He bought meat, which Cepheid dried over their small fire. He bought wheat and oat grain. He also bought a wide stretch of sailcloth when he overheard men speaking of the winds in the wastes. He was very familiar with the winds that swept across the miles they had already crossed and such winds would carry desert sands at a scouring force. With that in mind, he then went to a blacksmith and ordered heavy stakes; he ended up buying an old hammer from him as well. Before he left, Canis bought a pair of water bladders that would fit down in his panniers. He didn't think they would have much trouble finding water, but there was no sense in being foolish about it.

When everything was as prepared as he could make it, the end result looked puny. He had no idea what was ahead of him. He had no idea how far he had to go. He didn't even know if the city he was searching for was north or south of his chosen direction. The only thing he was sure of was that he would run into someone someday who would be able to tell him where Chicago was before he was too far off track.

Even with all the people he had had around him, he felt more lost and adrift than he had the day he set out from the Yellowstone Clan in the company of only three Wulfen close to two years ago.

As if she could read his mind, Cepheid wrapped her arms around him. "We'll be fine. We'll find what you're looking for and everything will be fine."

He held her close, pulling her inside his coat mostly because of his desire to feel her as close as possible and wishing that it could be so much closer. Last night he had slept with his hand cupping the slight bulge of her tummy. *Can I keep them safe? Can I provide her with the home she needs?* "Perhaps you should have chosen another mate. No proper mate would drag his pregnant wife off into such an uncertain future."

"There have been uncertain futures in the lives of the clans ever since long before we found our way out under the stars. I am happy with the husband I have chosen. Just as our ancestors have done, we will make our future. I love you and I would change none of my choices, nor would I try to steer you to a different path."

With a long deep sigh and a long rub up her back, he set her away from him then helped her into her saddle.

He led them down onto a frozen flat stretch of ground that he suspected might be swampy in the summer and headed roughly east. They soon came across another small river where he swam them across. Perhaps there was a better crossing somewhere, but he saw little point in searching for it. As it turned out, the horses hadn't needed to swim, and he only got wet to his knees and none of the wet got through to his skin. Cepheid was able to pull her legs up high and didn't get wet at all.

On the other side of the river, they came across a stretch of a high road, and Canis set them to an easy lope in order to warm up and dry off. It felt so good to stretch out for a while.

They took to traveling this way almost every day. With many stops for the puppies, the pace was not difficult. Even Star, who carried the bulk of the weight, seemed to delight in the change of pace.

The road lasted for three days before it was lost completely, so Canis opted to stay with the edge of the scrub grass poking its way above the dry snow. As soon as they left the road, they discovered that someone had passed this way before them.

With a wary eye to these tracks, Canis made no attempt to catch up with them, but they were moving much slower than he was, and unless he wanted to range far around them, he would catch up to them anyway.

He came across the remains of their campfire and knew why they must be moving so slowly. Their party had brought at least twenty horses, but if they were prepared like Columbus had been equipped, there was likely only four or five men among them. The extra horses would be laden with water, and obviously wood, or there wouldn't have been a fire.

Two days later, Canis caught sight of a sparkle on the dark horizon as he was topping one last ridge in search of a lower spot to make their camp. After seeing Cepheid secure under their staked down shelter of sailcloth, he said, "Stay here until I return. I'm going to see who our trail companions are."

"Will we be traveling with them?" she asked.

Canis shrugged. "We'll see." He discarded his furs for his black cloak, pants and jacket and dug out his facemask. With Rrusharr and Ggrrawrr, he disappeared into the night.

When he reached the camp, he spotted two sentries, one on either side of the camp. They were in a decent location, but they could have chosen better. He slipped up behind one man and pulled him into his chest with a hard hand across his mouth. When the man lunged for his knife, he trapped his hand there and used the lever to lift him off the ground then he whispered into his ear,

Half-Breed

by

Anna L. Walls

"Do you like to breathe?"

After a moment's hesitation, the man nodded; the very long, sharp steel claws that were so very close to his face helped him make his decision. Canis set him back on the ground. Without letting up on the pressure across his mouth, Canis tossed his hand away from his knife hilt and relieved him of his sword belt. "You will remain silent," he whispered and stepped away giving the man a prod toward the campfire.

The man took about three steps, then turned to say, "Where did…" The rest of what he would have said was lost, as a blow laid him out senseless.

Canis knelt over him. He hadn't intended to break the man's nose, but the blow couldn't be taken back. He still lived, so Canis straightened his smashed nose then heaved him over his shoulder. After depositing him by the fire, he bound him with his own sword belt, and after gagging him with a wad of cloth he found in a pocket, he went after the other sentry.

The sun was almost clear of the horizon before anyone stirred inside the tent. "James should have woke us up hours ago. If he's dozed off, I'll…" The speaker froze when he saw the black shadow sitting on the other side of the blackened fire pit. Nearby lay the bound and gagged forms of two men, and only a couple feet from them, rested two huge wolves. The two wolves and the strange man, all three, looked quite relaxed; that is, if a loaded and drawn catapult at rest could look relaxed.

The man sat on the ground, his cloak was ruffled in the wind, he was so still, he could have been carved from wood, if there was any trees around large enough; and then there was the steel claws he openly displayed. They were about the only thing about the man that wasn't shadowed.

Another man and what looked like a half grown boy pushed their way out of the tent to take in the deadly scene as well, then the boy noticed the unusual eyes staring out of the black mask.

"Columbus said you'd headed east."

Canis slowly unfolded from the ground, but he said nothing.

"After Madison recovered from her little tantrum, she gave me something. She said I was to give it to you as soon as I found you. Columbus said it was more likely you'd find us instead, and he made it sound like he wasn't too sure you'd bother. He indicated that Madison managed to piss you off, and you might not want anything to do with us."

Canis continued to study the young man who was speaking. Something about him was ticking at a distant memory, but he couldn't place it.

The young man continued once again after a short pause. "My name is Dagon. My father sent for me. I wanted to return to Chicago by the shortest route."

After another moment of silence Canis said, "I knew a man named Dagon once."

"So you *can* talk. I was beginning to wonder. Did you kill them? Since they're tied up, I don't suppose so. Their names are Tory and James. They are knights provided by the school. These are Folco and Earl. They're my bodyguards."

"Who chose your guards for you?" asked Canis.

"Apparently not you. Uh, are we hostage or something; what are you going to do with us?" asked Dagon.

Canis studied the young man. "How old are you?"

Dagon pulled himself to his fullest height, which was only a few inches taller than Cepheid, and replied, "I'll turn sixteen in a few days."

Canis looked the three men over, taking in their tent and their picket line in the process. "Pack up and be ready to move. I'll be back in an hour." He strode off past their horses. *Twenty-five horses. Insane.*

Cepheid had their camp already packed up and she handed him his coat. After she put his cloak away, she handed him a handful of jerky and a cup of water. "So, are we going with them?" she asked.

"After a fashion," replied Canis.

They must have worked like a team of slaves to have all of those horses saddled and loaded by the time Canis returned with Cepheid. He only had to wait long enough for them to mount up.

As soon as he was mounted, young Dagon rode up beside Canis and tossed him a small pouch. “There’s four gold coins in there and what Madison called a ‘pass’. From what I understand, you’re quite a healer. Everyone at the school will be talking about you for years.”

Folco handed Dagon the lead to his train of horses and he turned away to tend them.

Canis set a leisurely pace for them. At least it was leisurely for his party. For the men leading five packhorses each, the pace was grueling.

“Show yourselves a little,” said Canis. The leader of the train, Tory, looked at him strangely, though the expression could have been the result of the spectacular set of black eyes that were rapidly turning blacker as a result of his broken nose. “Let the horses see you just enough to wake them up a little.”

“What did you say?” asked Tory, but he couldn’t spare much attention to any answer because he just caught sight of the black wolf that had rested so close to him that morning in the camp. The horses saw her too, and others, and had definitely perked up at the sight.

The Wulfen had all been around horses long enough to know how much they could push before panic set in, and that is the limit they set for the entire day. Canis was with them sometimes and not sometimes. Unknown to them, he rode ahead or aside somewhat and let the puppies have their way with their mother then he scouted around for game or water. Both were scarce, but not gone altogether, and invariably, he either brought back meat or led them all to some small spring.

Canis had little to do with their camp and typically vanished off into the dark after they stopped. After three nights of this unusual distancing, Cepheid said, “What is it about them that bothers you? They seem nice enough.”

Canis shrugged. “I am not sure, but the boy might be the son of a man I am not ready to face yet. He was nice enough too, at first.”

“Is that the man you owe money to?”

“No, that is another man. I do not expect to see him until spring.” He reached for the warmth of her body and further conversation was swept away by the wind that howled over their shelter.

Canis was following an indistinct line between grass and sand, but his chosen route began to bend too far south so he led them across the sand, through a dry creek bed and up onto another stretch of grass. That night, they made their camp down in another dry creek bed and relished in being out of the wind for a while.

Two days later, they found a small spring and spent the day filling their water stores. The spring was small enough that it took that long to gather that much water plus water all the animals.

He took the time to hunt as well and brought in two of the grazers like he had shot before spending the night with the Greenfields on the other side of Deemoin. These were mostly red with a white face, belly and legs rather than black. They were strange creatures, but the meat was good.

He butchered the creatures a short distance from camp and Cepheid insisted the meat be shared between all of them. She also insisted they accept Dagon’s invitation to eat at their campfire.

The hot meal of juicy steaks and potatoes was good and the heat from their small fire was nice. Canis had thought about fire along the way, but suspected he would have to haul the wood for it. That’s why he’d had Cepheid dry their meat. Such trail rations weren’t quite as satisfying as a good hot meal such as this, but it would do for a while. One look at the number of horses these men had seen fit to bring only confirmed his decision. Ten horses hauled nothing but wood for their fires. The other ten all carried a partial load of water as well as food and their camping supplies.

During the meal, the five men were poking fun at each other

and going out of their way to try to make Cepheid laugh, even Canis started to smile at some of their antics and jokes. All of their jokes were about healers and Canis didn't understand them very well, but watching the men laughing was funny enough to win a smile out of him. Cepheid was doing much the same thing. She was laughing at the men, not necessarily at their jokes. Most of the time they were making fun of the way Tory talked since he was the one telling most of the jokes and his words were coming out all stumpy since his nose was so swollen. All in all, they had a good time.

After the meal, Canis spoke to Tory, "I can fix your nose, if you like. I did not mean to break it."

Tory chuckled. "I got what I deserved, I suppose. I just hope it ends up straight. I never was much to look at, but a crooked nose sure won't help any."

"It should be fairly straight; I took the time to straighten it as soon as I checked to make sure I had not killed you."

"Did you now; I guess I aught to thank you for that then," he said, and took Canis's plate.

"You aught to let him fix your nose, Tory," said Dagon. "You'll scare my aunt to death if she sees you like that."

"Oh that's right, you did say she was quite a looker," said Tory. He turned back to Canis. "If you don't mind then. I wouldn't want to frighten the lady away."

Canis smiled and said, "You better sit down."

Tory handed the plates to James and sat back down on his saddle.

Canis knelt down in front of him and rested both his thumbs on his face on either side of his swollen nose. He used the rest of his hands to grip Tory's head so he couldn't jerk back inadvertently.

When he opened his eyes again, there were tears streaming down Tory's face, but much of the bruising had been washed away and most of the swelling was gone.

Tory sniffed and said, "That hurt. Are you done?"

"I guess so. You look a lot better," said Canis.

"What do you mean, 'you guess so', you're the healer," said Tory as he touched his tender face.

"It is more than I am willing to explain. It is something your Madison and I were at odds over. Perhaps tomorrow I can make more of the bruising go away."

Over the next four days, Canis's relationship with Dagon and his men relaxed a good deal. The horses grew accustomed to the Wulfen as well. They took to sharing the same camp, though he refused to dip into their supplies unless he was adding his share to it.

The next day they headed out onto the sand again. "Conserve your water," said Canis after he tested the dry air unnoticed. "It may be a while before we come across another spring."

"What makes you say that?" asked Dagon.

"Just a feeling mostly, this sand is not here because there is plenty of water around and I cannot see the other side from here."

They spent two days in the sands of the desert before finding another strip of land with grass for the horses. They camped early to let them eat their fill.

The narrow spit of grassy land lasted them for another three days, then they came upon what Canis thought might be some ruins. They were eating their supper when Canis suddenly jumped up and drew his sword. "Stay here," he said. He was gone into the dark with all but two of the Wulfen running in his wake.

Cepheid stood and drew her sword. When Tory and James started to go after him, she said, "No, stay here. He said for you all to stay. It's definitely safer for you here. Bring the horses in close. We should guard them at least until he comes back."

"What's he doing out there? What happened?" asked Dagon.

"I'm not sure," said Cepheid, "but it would be very dangerous to go after him."

The first scream echoing from the dark galvanized the men. Before she could stop them, Dagon, followed closely by Folco and

Earl charged off into the dark. “No!” she yelled after them. She turned to the white Wulfi at her side. “Tell him to watch for them.”

“What are you saying?” asked Tory. “Did you say something to that wolf?”

She whirled on him and snarled. “Pay attention to what we must protect here and hope that they don’t find him, because if they do, he might kill them before he knows who they are.”

“What are you saying?” he asked again and turned to face the dark again as another scream sliced through the night.

“He hunts in the dark. With all of us here, every person he meets out there is a person who threatens us. He may not be able to tell who they are before he strikes, and if he takes the time to identify every person he finds, it could cost him his life. Believe me, if they all survive this, I know three men who will have to answer to me.”

Over the next two hours, the sounds of fighting and death echoed in the dark then it was quiet.

A few minutes later, Canis called out, “We’re coming in.” All four men were blooded, as were all four of the Wulfen who had gone with Canis at first. Close examination revealed that none of the men got away unscathed, but none of the injuries were very bad.

After splashing snow on his face and touching a small scratch there, Canis went to each of them and healed their wounds then he sat down and poured himself a cup of water.

Cepheid saw his jaw muscles clenching as he gave an inordinate amount of attention to his drink. Choosing Folco, the tallest of the three, she strode up to him and hit him hard on the jaw. Then before he had hit the ground, she whirled on Earl and did the same. She would have meted out the same to Dagon, but Canis caught her hand. She snarled and jerked her hand from his grip and hit him as well, though he was slightly more prepared for it and wasn’t knocked down, then even Dagon felt her fury.

No one moved against her; no one moved at all. She stood in their midst and turned back and forth in a furious sway that constantly shifted her view from one to the other of the men around her. “If you *ever* do anything like that again, I’ll kill you.” Then she stormed off to where their furs had been placed.

Canis was calmer, or at least he looked calmer, but his voice was smooth and low. “She means it,” he said, then started toward their furs after her. He paused and looked back over his shoulder at them. “And I’ll let her.”

The next morning was understandably strained. All four of Cepheid’s targets of the night before sported a glorious fist-sized bruise somewhere on their face and none of them asked to have them healed.

By noon, they came across a tiny half-frozen creek and the horses drank thirstily; they also finally ran out of wind. It was a welcome relief. That night they were definitely among the ruins of a city, though Canis had no way of knowing which city it was.

Two days later, he knew exactly where they were; he had hunted these ruins and swamps for almost a year. At the north end of the Grand Market Street, Canis stopped them and said, “I’ll take my leave of you now.”

Dagon asked, “Why? Why don’t you come with us the rest of the way? It’s not far. I think my father would like to meet you.”

“Perhaps another time; I must tend to business of my own in another direction.” Canis retreated, back the way he had come, and Dagon watched them until they disappeared. As soon as Dagon and his party were out of sight, Canis turned north and went deeper into the ruins.

He found them a corner where there was a tiny trickle of water running among the stones and made them a camp for the night. That night, he said to Cepheid, “Now it is your turn to lead. I want you to look around until you find a spot you like. That is where I will build you a home; one that will last us a while at least.”

“A home? Really? Oh, this is so exciting,” she said and snuggled close, smiling.

Chicago

Canis and Cepheid spent nearly two weeks happily roaming and hunting the ruins around the city of Chicago until Cepheid found a place she liked. It was less than two miles from the northern end of the Grand Market Street and close to good grazing and water for the horses. The place she selected had a wide sloping hole for an entrance that led deep under the massive jumble of stone. Even in daylight, the way was quickly lost in dark, so Canis made them a crude torch to continue exploring.

The wide entrance quickly choked off to a narrow hallway before opening up again into a large, pillared chamber. Off to the left was a doorway that gave onto a good-sized room with another smaller room after. Being underground, there were no windows for light, and if there had been doors at one time, there were none now.

"Here," said Cepheid. "We can stay here. We can have our sleeping furs there and our living room here. Even the smoke from the torch seeps away somewhere here. I think this place will be fine."

Canis examined the walls and the ceiling closely. There were a few cracks, but nothing seemed to be inclined to sag. He found a place in the corner where his torch smoke seeped out through a slightly wider crack. "I will put the fireplace here. We can house the horses in the outer chamber if we have to, but it would be better if we found them someplace outside; they would not like this dark." He turned to face her. "How would you like to go shopping?"

Over the next month, their little den evolved into a cozy home. While Cepheid washed, cleaned, and arranged their belongings around their two rooms, Canis bought mortar and built a fireplace. He went to the clearing and brought in firewood and stacked it just outside the door. He also went to the market street to buy whatever Cepheid wanted to complete their space: a barrel for water, blankets for their nest, baskets and boxes for their supplies and milled lumber for a table and a counter and many other things.

Shopping was not the only thing Canis did when he went to the market street. He also fished for information, taking great care about who saw him. He never approached or left the street from the same direction or location and he avoided shopping at the same store more than once if he could manage it. With a market street stretching four miles, this wasn't much of a problem.

Most of the Wulfen followed him when he went out, and when he was out on the market street; they roamed the alleys nearby, always staying close should he need them. He was sure the constables who roamed the market thought it rather odd how those alleys became devoid of the seedier members of society.

One day he caught a scent he recognized, it belonged to a young woman who was about thirteen or fourteen years old. She had curly brown hair that brushed the hood of her cloak and Canis suspected that she had large dark eyes, but he never let himself come within her range of view. Curious, Canis followed her as she did her shopping. She smiled and chatted with the shop owners, but didn't linger long anywhere. Canis continued to follow her to her home, which confirmed who she was, and he smiled. So, she had managed to stay safe from her father. He wondered what it would be like to kneel at that shrine again. He reached up and touched the stone between his brows, then turned away. Behind him, each Wulfi dropped their nose to her path.

When he finished buying the things they needed, he settled down to building their furniture. He added stout legs to the table and fixed a counter to a wall near the fireplace. He made them chairs and blocked up several shelves along another wall. He hung their largest hide over the door to hold in the heat.

Through all of this, Cepheid's tummy grew rapidly, or at least it seemed to. Now that they had stopped traveling, she was no longer wearing her bulky furs. One of the things Canis bought for her was a warm woolen robe. She sometimes wore his clothes, but she looked so like a child in them with the sleeves and legs rolled up. He had to laugh the first time she did it, then he had to hold her and comfort her when she started to cry. He loved her so much.

The day finally came when their home was complete. Warmly lit by several candles and lamps as well as the firelight, the empty square chambers had become cozy and comforting. Rranggrr and her growing family dozed in a corner near the hearth and the others cluttered the floor wherever they dropped.

One morning, when they lingered in their nest, Cepheid said, "Spring is not so far away now; I smell it on the wind. Go and earn your gold so you can be free of your burden. Then we can be a proper family." She rubbed her rounded belly.

Canis rubbed her belly too and felt a tiny arm or leg slide beneath his hand. "Yes," he said. "With all do speed. I will be glad to be rid of it." He left the building with a determined stride, Rrusharr, Ggrrawrr, and the still nameless half-grown pups in his wake.

Over the next two months, Canis went out in the evening and returned some time before dawn. Every time, he brought with him two to four gold coins or the equivalent in silver.

Since he occasionally came home with blood splatters on his clothes, Cepheid knew that he fought battles for his gold, but she didn't comment about it. She knew he did it only because he needed to earn the gold quickly. She knew he would stop as soon as his debt was paid. She looked forward to that day.

During the day, Canis did whatever chores needed to be done to ensure Cepheid's comfort and he showed her the joys of spring that were starting to show up as the snow melted. He brought her to tiny plants that poked through the snow to open small feathery blue flowers, or yellow, cup shaped flowers that showed up later. She had never seen flowers before and whenever he showed her a new discovery, she added it to her round of visits. Every day, she visited these colorful wonders and watched them grow, bloom and die back to be replaced by other wonders large and small as the snow receded farther than she had ever experienced.

They were as new to him as they were to her, though he had seen them before. Canis loved to watch her discover them, and through her, he enjoyed them as if he was seeing them for the first time too, but these little joys were shadowed by his concerns for their future. He had been getting paid well enough guarding caravans as they crossed the country from city to city, but Cepheid couldn't travel any longer. She needed a home. His family needed shelter and security and none of that would happen if he were away with some caravan for large chunks of time.

Long ago, he had planned to fight for the gold he needed and doing so now allowed him to be here every day, but there were dangers that hadn't mattered before Cepheid came into his life. There was always the danger that there was a fighter out there who would get lucky and he wouldn't be able to come home.

He saw little choice, so every night he went to the fight club north of the market street on the banks of a small creek. Every night he took on any challenger who stepped forward, and so far, every night, he won. Crowds of people started to gather in growing numbers to see him fight and the odds were becoming stiffer every time he stepped into the ring. He wondered when his notoriety would force him to quit. He wondered if he would know when the wrong person learned of his existence.

The man who ran the fight club was always very careful, but his resources were becoming strained, and yet he refused to ask Canis to stop. He liked the generous tumble of gold that was falling into his pockets. He liked to watch Canis fight. He liked to see blood spilled.

The day finally came when Canis thought he could stop. One or two more fights and he would have enough to pay Patro back for what he had cost him. He stepped into the roped off ring and the ringmaster started to call for takers naming odds and bets as they occurred and touting Canis undefeated record.

After several tense minutes, a tall man stepped into the ring and the betting was furious. Canis didn't hear any of it. The man was powerfully built, though he had a generous amount of gray on the sides of his head, and the rest of his black hair was dulled by it. A familiar scar ran from his right eye to the corner of his mouth that pulled his face into an indecipherable mask. The day had come. The wrong person had learned of his presence. He was surprised to see the shiny steel collar around his corded neck. He wondered if Dagon had sold him into slavery after capturing him. He wondered who owned that collar now. He wondered who else was out there.

The first clash was fast and furious, and the crowd's roar was deafening. The second clash went so completely wrong.

"*Double-crossing fatherless scat-eaters,*" snarled Rrusharr, and Canis felt her launch herself to avoid arrows aimed at her and the others.

Time slowed as many things happened all in the span of a few heartbeats.

Thump-ump

Canis whirled to face the danger behind him.

Stanton grabbed his braid and jerked him back off balance.

Rrusharr's shriek said she'd been unable to dodge to safety.

Ggrrawrr and his black-furred son tasted blood.

Thump-ump

Rrusharr's light went out as she, bows, bowmen, and Canis all hit the ground and stayed where they lay.

Thump-ump

People screamed and scattered.

Stanton sliced Canis's studded braid off at its base and pulled the barbs from his hand.

Canis watched in horror as the black chasm that was Rrusharr's death engulfed him like a tidal wave.

Thump-ump

Just before it pulled him under, he whispered. "Keep her safe. Take her home." And then he knew no more.

When Ggrrawrr returned to Cepheid, he brought with him the only thing he could. He found Cepheid curled up in her nest. She smelled of grief and fear. He dropped Canis's severed braid on the edge of the blankets. Without sacrificing the rest of them, he could do no more. The odds were too great and he had Canis's last wishes to consider.

"*We go home now*," said Nnarr softly.

"No," said Cepheid as she gripped the braid and picked at the blood on its barbs. "No, I cannot go anywhere. This is home. Is he alive?" When she got no answer, she asked again, louder, "*Is* he *alive*?" She did not miss the one other glaring absence here.

After a protracted moment Nnarr answered, "*He walks in shadow*."

"No!" wailed Cepheid and her wail trailed on into a howl of despair as she curled up around her bulging belly.

Canis hung from bound wrists that were stretched over his head far enough to lift his feet from the cold stone floor. Shackles, separated by a short bar, kept his feet apart and another chain attached to the floor would keep him from curling up or kicking out. His head hung on his chest and his red hair obscured his face. He didn't flinch when the cell door opened with a screech though he heard it. Nor could he decipher the words spoken there.

"He hasn't moved other than a few twitches," said one voice. "He doesn't make a sound or nothing. I think he's sick. He's running a fever."

"What do you mean, 'he's running a fever'? He wasn't even wounded, was he?" said another voice.

"No, my lord, he took no injury," said the first.

The lord strode into the room and gripped a fist full of Canis's hair to lift his head and reveal his face. He got no response. "Have you struck him?"

"I did, a couple times, when I thought he might be faking it, but I don't think he felt anything. He never moved."

The lord swiveled Canis around to look at his back. The fading red stripes revealed the truth of the turnkey's words. He touched his skin in several locations, feeling the damp slick of sweat and the heat. "Take him down and get him a healer. Get him a *real* healer, mind you, not one of those surgeons you keep. He is not to be damaged."

"Yes, my lord," said the turnkey, as he stepped aside to allow the man to leave the room.

With her shock less intense, Cepheid's mind turned to trying to find some way to help. This was a very big city and Canis knew it well, but just because it was a city, didn't mean it was safe. Cepheid was more concerned with making her chosen place a home, but she didn't miss the fact that Canis never let her go anywhere by herself. That had been fine with her; he was always going to be there…only now he wasn't.

She needed to find him and help him, but she didn't know where to look. She needed help, but she knew no one. The only person she could think of was the boy, Dagon. He had been coming to this city. He lived here. His father was here. Surely, he and his friends would still be here. Tory had liked Canis. Dagon had leapt into battle for him. Surely, they would help him now when he needed help so badly.

She stood up and grabbed her sword belt. It would no longer fit around her waist so she buckled it on its last hole and slung it over her shoulder, then she draped her cloak over it. "Come. We must find Dagon or Tory. Help me find them."

Canis was tied to the bed hand and foot, but he had yet to move. His breath rasped and his hair was wet with sweat.

A knock came at the door and the healer opened it. "Lord Corbin, I expected to see you yesterday."

"I was detained," he said as he strode over to the cot. He touched Canis's cheek. "He's still fevered. Why?"

"I can find nothing wrong with him. There is no sickness or injury in his body that would cause such a fever. I'm at a loss."

Corbin turned on the woman. "Are you telling me he's dying?"

"I don't know. He could, if the fever doesn't let up soon," she replied as she clutched at her breast in fear.

"You listen to me, Healer. That man is potentially the most valuable man ever born. You get that fever down. If he dies, it is entirely possible that every person that has a single drop of your blood running in their veins could find their necks encircled by either a rope or steel depending on my mood at the time. Do I make myself clear? I'll be back tomorrow to see your progress."

The woman gasped and paled. "Yes, my lord," she whispered and watched as the man stalked from the room.

The healer reverted to old tactics to reduce Canis's fever. She packed his body with ice, and when her use of so much ice began to draw too much attention, she used well water and kept him draped with cold towels. Her efforts eventually began to show some signs of success. Canis began to move and occasionally moan. It wasn't much, but it was an improvement.

He opened his eyes for the first time almost a week after coming into her care, so she sent a message to Lord Corbin with the news and he renewed his daily visits.

CANIS swam in darkness for an eternity.

He became aware of light once, but before he found it, he forgot what he had been looking for.

He opened his eyes to colors and shapes that drifted across his mind with no rhyme or meaning.

He was shaking. He knew that it had to mean something, but…

Sound beat at his oblivion; he opened his eyes to the confusion of color and light. It meant nothing to him.

Pain and sound stabbed at him. He wanted to flinch away, but he couldn't remember how.

His oblivion was punctuated in this manner until he tried to understand why. With that wind-tossed feather of a thought came another feather. *Who am I?*

"Wake up," echoed a voice from beyond his chasm of blackness and a sharp sting sent lightning through his dark.

Slowly, after a fashion, he became aware of the passage of time. Slowly he began to remember that different events of awareness had occurred – not necessarily *what* had happened, but that *something* had happened.

Eventually, he was able to keep his eyes open long enough to study his surroundings. Now all he had to do was figure out what he was seeing.

A man came into his range of view whenever he had his eyes open. This happened several times before he realized that it was a man's face he was seeing. He held something in his view. He made sounds. Over and over, he showed him the same thing and made the same sounds. Eventually it made sense, but it was still confusing. He was seeing the face of another man and the sounds formed into, "You will kill him."

His awareness formed into days and nights, though he could find no string to it. The man came with his ? ? ? with his picture and he would say his words. Canis couldn't understand.

A woman was there too…sometimes. She moved his body. She…cut…she cut his hair. Beyond her was the ceiling…that's what it was called. *It didn't have any cracks in it. It should have. Why was it supposed to have cracks? What were cracks?*

The man who kept showing him the picture, and the woman who had cut his hair talked, but he couldn't follow their words. He couldn't think.

Cold touched his awareness and he wanted to pull away. He opened his eyes to bright light and the woman…the woman who cut his hair was laying a cold towel around his ribs. "The fever's back," she said. The man who looked over her shoulder shook his head. He too said something.

The woman who had cut his hair pulled him to sit up, but he couldn't remember how to stay there. That thought bothered him. *Up. Up. I need to get up. What is up?*

He rolled over and pulled his legs up. His feet fell off the bed. He pushed himself up…yeah…up.

He reached…that was a chair…there was a crash and a sharp pain in his knees…and his hand…?…and his head.

The man rushed into the room with the woman behind him. Between them, they lifted him to the chair. *What had been wrong with 'up'? Something wasn't right. What did I forget?*

Half-Breed

by

Anna L. Walls

Cepheid paced the city following the Wulfen who searched for one or another elusive scent. She had been searching for days now and she was having to stop to rest more and more often. Every time she stopped, she found herself starting to cry, so she would push on.

She pushed off from the wall one time too often and she doubled over with a cry of pain.

The Wulfen all knew the scent. "*Puppy*," said Nnarr.

Home was too far away. Cepheid knew fear. Her child would be born in some dark alley and they would all die because she couldn't find his father, because she had been foolish enough to believe that she could do something.

Ggrrawrr pushed up beside her and he was big enough for her to lean on. His black-furred son led the way.

They came to a door where Nnarr scratched and scratched until someone came to investigate.

The woman who opened the door stepped back in alarm, but the black wolf sparked a memory and the girl among the giant wolves was obviously in serious trouble.

"Help me," said Cepheid. "Canis is in trouble." *Why did I say that? I am such an idiot; these people couldn't possibly know who Canis was.* But apparently, they did.

"Canis?" said the woman, and the memory fell the rest of the way into place. "Come in here." She took up the arm of the very pregnant girl and led them all into the house.

A girl came to investigate the odd sounds and she gasped and pointed to the black wolf. "Isn't that…his?"

"Yes, Dora," said the woman. "But this girl's in labor. Help me get her upstairs."

"I have to find Canis," cried Cepheid. "He's in trouble. Help me find him."

"We'll help you find him if we can, but right now, you are the one who needs help," said the woman.

As soon as Cepheid was settled in a soft bed, the woman

patted her hand and tried to calm her. "My name is Loren. Canis helped us several years ago. I'm glad you came to us for help."

Cepheid was still crying, but she was heartened. "You know him? Can you help him?"

Dora brought in a glass of water and Cepheid sipped at it. She was thirsty, but she didn't have the stomach for anything right now. She handed the glass back and grit her teeth with the next contraction. No one noticed that two of the wolves had left the house before Dora had been able to close the door.

Canis was awake for about half of every circuit of the sun. He understood most of what went on around him now, but he felt lethargic and slow.

The healer, fed him his meals at a table now, but she had to coax his every bite, otherwise he would stare at his plate or some other point, and drift for hours. She had to coax him in almost everything he needed to do, but sometimes he would do things on his own. Sometimes she would find him staring out into the night.

Something was pulling at him, something urgent, but he couldn't remember what it was. There were huge gaps in his awareness. Memories were over there on the other side of the chasm of darkness. They floated there just out of reach like indistinct ghosts he couldn't focus on.

He felt a soft touch and flinched away from it. He remembered pain attached with a touch like that. He remembered pain and loss, but he couldn't remember what he had lost. He felt a tear trail down his face. He felt pain again.

The healer touched his neck with a cold towel. "Your fever is rising again," she said as she tried to drape the towel around his shoulders.

He turned before she got it in place and he took the bundle and buried his face in it. He sponged his hair back then wiped the sweat from his throat and chest before handing the cold thing back to her.

The man, Corbin, still came every day with his picture and his mantra, but now Canis recognized who was in the picture. He had always thought that Corbin was the king's most trusted bodyguard. Why would he want the king dead? He couldn't puzzle it out. He couldn't think.

One day, Corbin showed Canis the picture and said, "You will kill him."

That day, he was rewarded when Canis said, "Kill?"

Unknown to Corbin, the single word was Canis's attempt to ask why. He didn't remember about Canis's inability to speak. He didn't know that Canis had not been so handicapped for years. The only difference was that Canis could manage words now, it was just very difficult, and he was only just remembering how.

Patro came with Corbin that night. Canis remembered him. He remembered who and what he was, though a few definitions were lacking in the memory. He remembered that he had wanted to see him, but it was far from a friendly desire. He couldn't remember why.

Patro was delighted to see him. He didn't seem to notice that Canis backed up as he approached. When he had him backed up to a wall, he reached up and gripped Canis's chin tipping his head back and forth, then he prodded the white stone between his brows. "Where did you get that?" he asked.

Canis didn't answer. He didn't know. He didn't remember. Patro's touch had awakened the feeling of revulsion, and the feeling descended quickly into hate.

The healer woman entered the room with her cold towel. Canis's fever was up again that morning. He took it from her and tried to scrub Patro's touch away.

"Still hostile as ever, I see," said Patro. "Why isn't he in chains?"

"You can put him in your chains after tomorrow," said Corbin. "Until then I have him under control."

"You should remember," said Patro, "he has always been far more dangerous than he looks."

"Not right now, he isn't," said Corbin. He didn't want to tell Patro how weak and sick his prize slave had been…still was. Patro might blow the whole plan if he thought Canis was damaged.

The two of them watched as Canis went to the black window and stared out. The healer watched too. Sympathy pulled at her. He always seemed drawn to the window at night. He never seemed interested in it during the day.

Patro and Corbin went into another room to talk. They didn't see the single tear that trailed down Canis's cheek. The healer woman handed him the towel again.

Early the next morning Canis was awakened by an inner feather touch that carried elation with it. He flinched away and sat up. Further thought of trying to puzzle out the meaning of what had wakened him vanished as the healer came in with two young men.

"You're already awake, good. Today's a big day for you." She turned to the men. "Get him dressed and make sure you do it properly or you will answer to Lord Corbin."

The men bowed low to her then turned to Canis while she flung the shades wide to let in the morning light. They washed and dressed him in tight red hose and pulled a white tunic over his head. One of them combed his hair while the other closed a red enameled band around his neck.

Canis touched the cold band. Something else was supposed to rest there, but he couldn't remember what. He looked down at his red-sheathed legs; he didn't like red.

The two men – Canis realized they were slaves. They were dressed like he was – they placed white slippers on his feet and pulled him to stand. One of them tied a red sash around his waist and adjusted the knot just so.

The healer scrutinized their work, then she produced a small knife and hid it under his sash. "Remember Corbin's words," she said, then she turned to the others. "Take him. You know what to do."

The two slaves propelled him out of the room and down the hall. They descended some stairs then went down another hall. They did this again before the hall they walked became decorated with paintings and tapestries. The next hall sported tapestries that covered entire sections of wall space, and the carpet on the floor was plush.

Canis recognized the carpet; he remembered the smell of the place he just couldn't remember where that place was or why he would remember such a thing in the first place.

The two slaves stopped him just short of rounding another corner. One of them presented him with a scroll. "You hold this in both hands, like this." He placed the scroll in Canis's two hands and adjusted them to the proper height. "Give this directly to the king." He looked directly into Canis's eyes as if looking for understanding there. "Remember Lord Corbin's words." He gave him a gentle push to get him moving again.

No less than twenty paces down this hall, Canis felt the inner touch again only it was much more than a touch. The flood caused him to stagger and reach for the nearby wall for support.

He struggled to silence his cries of joy as the flood brought back his missing memories and connected his fractured thoughts. He struggled to retain his feet as the creature that was Canis filled the chasm that had so darkened his mind. He struggled to contain the agony as his memories told him of what Rrusharr's death had done to him, and the worry about Cepheid came back to him. How long had it been? Where was she now? He reached out for Nnarr and was relieved to find that Cepheid was safe.

"Do not tell her that I live," he whispered. "That is not certain yet."

Nnarr gazed at her companion who slept with her two new pups in her arms, then rested her head back down on her paws. This strange nest was too tall and too long, but then that meant that there was room for her at Cepheid's feet.

Ggrrawrr sank down to the carpet beside the bed, his elbows made a dull thunk on the rug. Canis could learn the status of his family later when he was safe.

Canis pulled himself together and straightened his tunic. He looked around for the source of his glorious filling. A black Wulfi stepped out of a dark corner a little ways ahead of him, and to his surprise, a pale gray Wulfi also stepped into view. *How had the two half-grown puppies found their way into the palace past the lacework of guards and slaves without being noticed?*

He stepped forward and was pleased when Terrorr and Danggerr took up positions under his hands. A brief brush of a memory that involved swinging warm and safe in a sack at his side, told him that they had learned this place during their earliest memories.

He rounded the last corner and entered the vast chamber that was the king's throne room. As before, there was a crowd of men and women all dressed in fine, colorful clothes full of lace, shimmers and rustles. Slaves dressed like the two who had brought him here, moved among the throng with trays of different foods and drinks. At the other end of the room, on an overlarge, ornately carved chair that was elevated on a raised platform, sat a gray haired, very thin man wearing a red silk jacket. On his head rested an ornate crown that, despite its scrollwork, was little more than a wide band of gold. Corbin stood at his shoulder. Young Dagon and the four young men who had traveled with him were speaking to the older Dagon a couple steps away. A slave with a red sash was leaving the dais with an empty tray.

As Canis moved into the room, the people closest to him gasped and moved aside, which drew the attention of those who stood closest to them, who then gasped and drew aside in their turn.

As this wave made its way through the crowd in front of Canis, Corbin looked up to see the expected red head move into the room, but he couldn't understand why the people were moving so far aside from him. Dressed as a trusted slave, he should have been able to move virtually unnoticed. He didn't see the wolves until Canis had come considerably closer to the throne, and by now, the king had also noticed the unusual movement through the crowd.

As the last of the people moved aside, Canis saw Patro turn to see what had attracted the attention of the king. His mouth gaped and he started to move aside with the crowd, only to freeze when the gray Wulfi mirrored his move, then cut him from the herd as the rest of the spectators were allowed to draw away, but he was kept standing out conspicuously.

Trying to hang onto what looked like the shredding of his plans, Corbin moved to stand closer to the king, but with a lightning move, the small dagger that had been hidden in Canis's sash appeared imbedded and quivering in the floor at his feet.

Canis stepped up onto the dais and the king rose to meet him with his hand reaching for a sword he was not wearing. Young Dagon move closer to Santos's other side. With him, stood Folco, Earl, and Santos's brother, Dagon, a short distance away was Tory and James. All of them were armed and poised, but they were uncertain what they were poised to do. Canis returned his attention to the king.

With a casual hand, he held out the scroll. "I was told to give you this so I could get close to you. Corbin..." he looked toward the man, "...and Patro..." he glanced at him as well, "...wanted me to kill you." Santos took the scroll and unrolled the blank parchment.

Corbin might still have been able to prove Canis's words a lie, but Santos had turned to him for an explanation, and he'd seen the look on Corbin's face; he also spotted the mistake Corbin had made. Tiny though it was; on Corbin's hand, plainly visible as it gripped his dagger hilt, was the royal signet ring. He had forgotten to remove it this time – this time it was supposed to be his. He felt it the instant the king's eyes rested on it. He drew his dagger and lunged at Santos.

Canis covered the last two steps and grabbed Santos before anyone else on the dais could react. He pulled himself the remaining distance necessary to put himself between Corbin and the king.

Half-Breed

by

Anna L. Walls

Corbin's dagger tore through the material of Canis's white tunic and penetrated deep between his ribs. Red stained the white and Canis gasped and clenched at the king's shoulders for support. Dagon, Earl, and Tory, cut between Canis and Corbin, but they weren't in time to save Canis's life. Nor were they in time to be first to kill Corbin for his crime. Terrorr got there first and his black jaws came away stained with blood.

Patro tried to run, but gray Danggerr bore him to the ground with vicious fury. His head struck the edge of the dais and his neck broke. He too had paid for his crime before he could suffer the humiliation of a trial.

Canis sagged to his knees and reached futilely for the hilt that protruded from his back. Still gripping Santos's sleeve, he closed his eyes and healed himself. It was either that, or die here with these betrayers.

When the knife had fallen free from the closed wound, Canis touched the white stone between his brows and felt it come away in his hand. He opened his eyes and blinked at it. He had never been able to see it very well. He wasn't in the habit of looking in a mirror.

He rolled the robin's egg-sized stone between his fingers. He marveled at the sparkling star that twinkled in its core. He looked up at Santos and saw his scrutiny. His gaze focused on Santos's crown, and there, in the center, was a spot of the perfect size. It was as if the long-ago maker of that crown had planned for this day.

He climbed slowly to his feet and looked at the king who watched him closely still. He set the stone into that spot and the spark that welded it into place caused a wave of gasps and murmurs to wash across the room.

"My people are constantly in search of the stars. I think…I think the Mother thinks that you will be a very important star," said Canis. He considered the stone for a moment longer. "Either that or She considers you a healer. I think she has a great healing in mind for you and yours.

Canis looked around at what surrounded him, the bodies and blood, the silent crowd, the men surrounding the king. He reached up to the metal circlet that enclosed his neck. It came away in his hand and he held it up. “Slavery is an insult to the Mother.” He dropped the circlet on Patro’s chest. “Too many people are enslaved for simply being vulnerable.”

He stepped down from the dais with the Wulfen again at his side, and headed toward the door. He passed a very pale woman dressed in a shiny red silk dress that fit her figure closely until it flowed out and down to brush the floor. At her throat, resting on a new silk ribbon was a wolf brooch. He reached out to lift it from her skin, ignoring her recoil. As he scrutinized the brooch, then her increasingly pale face, several clues fell into place. He gripped the brooch in a hard fist and drew her close. “Where is he?”

“I…I’m sure I don’t know what you mean,” she replied in a quavering whisper that, nonetheless, carried across the silent chamber.

Santos had seen his pause and had noticed who he was interested in. He stepped down from the dais, followed by his son, his brother, and the others, but he had also heard the question.

“You wear this as a trophy. He won it for you at the fight club. His scent is all over you. It was you and your men who captured me.”

“Christina? Canis? What is going on here?” asked Santos.

Canis answered without looking away from the woman. “I am speaking about a man I knew as Stanton. You remember him, Dagon? But he is a slave, so perhaps he has another name now. Are you so bold that you keep him here, or do you keep him at the arena?”

Canis’s words were making some connections for Master Dagon. “That would explain why we never found him. I never thought to look in the arena.”

“Christina?” Santos tone asked for explanations just as his hand sent guards in different directions. Both her quarters and the arena would be searched.

"I saw him last at the fight club," said Canis and more guards left on the run. Everyone knew of the fight club; careful attention would be given to any bodies found around there.

The lady in fine, shimmering red looked old now. Her black hair and careful makeup no longer hid her age, and tears slid down her cheeks. "I know nothing," she insisted, but the hint of desperation was clear. "I did nothing wrong. You can't prove anything." The last sentence was uttered in a whisper that hovered on the brink of being a whimper. "Santos, you wouldn't do this to me, would you?" She sought to throw herself at Santos's feet, but Canis still clutched the brooch and the silk wouldn't part.

"Sister, your manipulations are over. If this man Stanton, or even his body, is found…"

Canis looked hard at Santos when the word 'sister' left his mouth. "She is your sister?" Using his grip on the brooch, he thrust her into Santos's arms roughly and drew the man's belt knife. As she shrank back into Santos's grasp, Canis cut the silk. "This…is mine." He handed the knife back and spun away to stride off across the hall. No one had moved into the path he had created with his entrance.

"Are you coming back?" asked Santos.

Canis turned back to face him.

"I seem to be short a bodyguard," continued Santos.

Canis glanced at young Dagon. "You are *his* son?" he asked.

Dagon nodded with a tentative smile; he still had the look of shock in his eyes.

"I will be back," he said. He stepped into the crowd and relieved a man of his cloak, which he threw over his white tunic.

Epilogue

Canis found Cepheid and admired his tiny son and daughter. Both of them were only slightly bigger than his two hands, but according to Cepheid, they were strong and healthy like their father. Unlike the one other baby he had seen, they had tiny nubs of teeth on both the top and bottom, as well as sharp canines, though there was room for little else in their tiny mouths. His son already had a healthy shock of fine red hair and his daughter had her mother's black blotch. They were the most amazing things he had ever beheld.

As soon as Cepheid was strong enough, they moved into the palace. Santos allowed her to pick whatever apartment she wanted and watched in amazement as she turned it into a foreign nest of the clan, using much of the things brought from the den they had so recently lived in.

The Yellowstone Clan

Men	Women	Children
Cancer & Aries	Andromeda	4) Corvus 16, Leo 14, Nike 12, girl 10
Capricorn	Lyra	3) boy, girl, boy
Cepheus & Achernar	Halley	2) boy, girl / 2 boy, girl / boy
Cetus	Cygnus	1) boy
Crux & Draco	Aquarius	5) Sagittarius 18, Taurus 16, Carina 14, girl 12, boy 10
Gemini & Eridanus	Libra	4) boy, girl, boy, girl
Gemini	Pisces	2) boy, girl
Herculis	Virgo	1) boy
Hydra & Corvus	Carina	soon
Orion	Stephanie	1) Canis 13
Pegasus	Pisces	2) boy, boy
Scorpius	--------	2) boy, girl
Ursa & Algol	Cassiopeia	6) Hydra 16, boy 14, girl 12, boy 10, girl 8, girl 6

Red ink = Deceased

The Salt Lake Clan

Men	Women	Children
Caeli & Turais	Adhara	5) boy 11, boy 9, boy 7, girl 1, girl 1
Achernar & Suhail	Alhena	4) boy 7, boy 5, boy 3, girl 1
Acrux & Sirius	Centauri	5) Wezen 12, boy 10, boy 8, girl 6
Al Nair & Schedar	--------	2) boy 4, boy 2
Aldebaran & Sargas	Atria	2) Alkaid 15, boy 11
Algieba & Velorum	Bellatrix	2) Pollux 18, boy 11
Alioth & El Nath	Hydri	1) Nunki 13
-------- & Eltanin	Betelgeuse	1) Rasalhague 14
Almach & Auriga	Capella	0) +
Alnilam & Gacrux	Caph	4) Schedar 16, Capella 15, Alphekka 12, Procyon 10
Alnitak & Hadar	--------	1) boy 1
Alphard & --------	Denebola	1) Deneb 10
Alpheratz & Harnal	Diphda	4) boy 4, boy 4, boy 2, boy 2
Altair & --------	Debhe	6) Regulus 16, boy 14, girl 12, boy 10, boy 8, girl 6
Arcturus & Kocab	Mira	4) Menkent 16, Saiph 9, girl 5, girl 5
Avoir & Menkalinan	--------	1) boy 3
Cruces & Mirfak	Mirach	4) Formalhaut 17, boy 10, boy 6, boy 6
Gruis &Miaplacidus	Shaula	3) boy 9, boy 7, boy 7
Canopus & Mizar	Spica	2) Murzim 19, 8
Castor & --------	Vega	5) Rigel 18, Cepheid 16, Mintaka 14, girl 12, boy 10
Cetus & Naos	Lyrae	1) boy 3

Red ink = Deceased

I am a self-published author and I live in the wilderness of Alaska. My connection to the outside world is restricted to a post office that is nearly thirty river miles upriver from where I live (Skwentna Alaska is on the map), a fixed wireless telephone, and recently, an internet satellite dish. We don't own a car since there are no roads out here. The end of the closest road is at least sixty river miles downriver from here. From there, it's another sixty-mile taxi ride to the next town of any size (Wasilla Alaska is on the map too). Needless to say, I don't go to town very often.

Browse through my website - http://annalwalls.weebly.com/ - and see what else I've published and what might be waiting in line.

Made in United States
North Haven, CT
21 September 2022